the ROOT

the ROOT

A NOVEL OF THE WRATH & ATHENAEUM

NA'AMEN GOBERT TILAHUN

Night Shade Books
New York

Night Shade books may be purchased in bulk at special discounts for sales promotion, corporate gifts, fund-raising, or educational purposes. Special editions can also be created to specifications.

For details, contact the Special Sales Department, Night Shade Books, 307 West 36th Street, 11th Floor, New York, NY 10018 or info@skyhorsepublishing.com.

Night Shade Books® is a registered trademark of Skyhorse Publishing, Inc.®, a Delaware corporation.

Visit our website at www.nightshadebooks.com.

10 9 8 7 6 5 4 3 2 1

Library of Congress Cataloging-in-Publication Data

Names: Tilahun, Na'amen Gobert, author.
Title: The root : a novel of the wrath & athenaeum / Na'amen Gobert Tilahun.
Description: New York : Night Shade Books, 2016.
Identifiers: LCCN 2016003935 | ISBN 9781597808637 (paperback)
Subjects: LCSH: Fantasy fiction. | BISAC: FICTION / Fantasy / Urban Life. | FICTION / Fantasy / General. | FICTION / Fantasy / Contemporary.
Classification: LCC PS3620.I496 R66 2016 | DDC 813/.6--dc23
LC record available at http://lccn.loc.gov/2016003935

Cover illustration by Charlie Bowater
Cover design by Claudia Noble

Printed in the United States of America

To:
Sarah Griffin—For your words, your viewpoint, and your encouragement, my writing buddy no matter how far apart we are.
&
Beyoncé—For your music that got me through my dark night of the writer's soul and fourteen-hour days of editing.

SAN FRANCISCO

ERIK

The door had barely opened into the lemon-yellow infirmary before Nurse Dan was hurrying over to help him onto a cot, resignation clear on his round, pink face, the skunk of weed thick as always.

He reached for Erik's arm but pulled back at the appearance of the two men that followed him. The school's flashlight-wielding security looked decidedly unhappy bracketing the young man who was covered in scrapes, sporting both a black eye and bruised knuckles. Despite his appearance, Erik was not moving as if he were in pain—nothing like the bent over, cradling vivid yellow-green-purple bruises under his clothes posture that he usually appeared here with.

Erik took all this in through a haze of euphoric sensation, and made no noise as the school nurse shook himself and moved to help him sit. The security escort stayed at the door. Dan hurried over to his supplies and brought them along with a chair to sit across from Erik, seated on one of the three cots. His pupils were blown wide, head moving lazily around.

"Bastion and Melisande?"

Erik nodded at Nurse Dan's words, smile stretching his aching lips. He felt the vibration of the man's voice in his hands where he was cleaning up split knuckles, felt the shockwaves of the man's breath against his face. He giggled. Partly because it tickled and partly because he could never call those two assholes Bastion and Melisande without laughing.

Two of the stupidest stage names he'd ever heard. What kind of private arts school let teenagers pick their own stage names for fuck's sake? It was why there were students running around calling themselves Morgana and Amaranth and Tam Lin!

At least the two idiots weren't here with him.

He hissed in surprise as the alcohol bubbled on his knuckles, but the sensation wasn't bad, merely as if the chill and fizzing of the liquid had entered his blood.

"Where are they?"

"Hospital."

Dan froze for a moment then hummed and broke a small cold patch between his fingers, to activate it, before placing it over Erik's black eye.

Every school from pre- to graduate and every level in between had its psychopathic bullies. Not the ones who were misguided or had bad home lives, or were suppressing their feelings or were in danger themselves.

No.

The ones who were just junkyard-dog mean all the time, every day, with little or no cause. The ones who liked to hurt those weaker than themselves just to hear them scream and went further and further each time just because they could. All schools had at least one, most more than one. Sometimes they were kept in check by strict rules, watchful parents, or a bully just a touch more sadistic.

And sometimes two of them found each other and joined forces.

Bastion and Melisande were the latter, an unholy duo, bullies with no redeeming qualities who played the "poor misunderstood me" act to the hilt whenever they were reported. Somehow they never got in trouble.

Erik was sure it had nothing to do with the money their parents continued to donate to the school.

They were careful in their choice of victim. Picked the ones no one would believe, the ones who were always in fights anyway, or the ones who'd never tell.

The ones no one liked.

They picked their prey and they played. They'd been playing with him since he transferred in last year but had stepped it up at the beginning of spring semester. Today had been different though; something had risen up inside Erik, something hungry and red and uncaring. It had unfurled from his core and cocooned him in this soft new world.

It had also allowed him to whoop their smug asses.

For almost two years now he'd been searching for something—a direction, a hobby, love, something to be proud of, and now he thought . . . no, he felt—deep in his gut—he'd found it.

NA'AMEN GOBERT TILAHUN

He clenched his fists and the knuckles of his right hand split open again, leaked more red sluggishly onto the yellowed-white and grayed-black linoleum floor. One of the rent-a-billy-club folks—calling them guards gave them way too much credit—met his eyes before their gaze darted away. Ignoring them he turned back to Dan, who was clucking his tongue and working on the knuckles again.

"Sorry."

"What happened this time?"

Erik sighed, and the sound felt like it hissed out of him forever. He knew if he changed the subject Nurse Dan would go with it, would pontificate on whatever liberal crusade he was on this month and allow Erik to remain silent, but for once he didn't mind talking.

"They cornered me in one of the courtyards, like usual."

"Mm-hmm."

"Started talking the same bullshit as always." A flare of hurt pierced his comfortable haze as he remembered their words: "has-been," "arrogant," "full of himself": phrases that repeated in his own brain every night, yanked him from sleep. "Then I just . . . I gave in."

That was the only way to describe it, the tide that rose up inside of him, swamped and coddled his mind even now. He started to hack at something lodged in the back of his throat and Dan held up a large stainless steel bowl. Erik leaned over it, hrokking up the blood and mucus slicking its way down his throat. The mix of black, red, and yellow stained the sides of the bowl as it slid down to the bottom.

"It was beautiful," he whispered and smiled.

"I'm sure it was and they deserved it." Dan said as he put the bowl to the side, then paused. "You didn't do any permanent damage, did you?"

"No. I just roughed them up a little." The memory was actually fairly hazy; he remembered the satisfying snap of bone, the grace of his body moving under their childish swings and kicks. He remembered them lying on the floor, but he assumed if he'd hurt them too badly it wouldn't be the faux-lice here, but the police. He shuddered, trying to remember the fight more clearly, and crossed his legs, hoping Nurse Dan wouldn't notice the hard-on he was now sporting.

"Take these."

Erik swallowed the pain pills down without complaint.

"And lie down, nothing else you really need."

"Cool."

Erik lay back on the cot and waited. His parents would be on their way already. His mom's art kept her schedule flexible and he couldn't remember the last time Robert had actually done anything. Mom would be worried. Robert would be furious. He was running for city council and to have his already "failed" son draw even more attention wouldn't sit well. Robert had a love/hate relationship with Erik's life. Robert knew it was the only reason he was known at all but he resented the way it had ended and how it "tainted" the family.

He could see the argument now, the two of them toe to toe. The extra two inches he'd gained since his eighteenth birthday meant he was only five foot seven, but it still allowed him to loom over Robert. He could imagine their mouths open, voices screaming, hands flying through the air like so many times before. Robert might even try to hit him.

He shivered at the idea of Robert throwing a punch, his own body moving like it had only a few minutes ago to intercept the hit, turn it into a hold. He imagined snapping the elbow like a twig, the scream of pain and the way it would soothe his anger. He made a sound of satisfaction at the back of his throat and relaxed.

The next half hour was spent in relative dreaming peace, interrupted only when Erik occasionally coughed up another wad of disgustingness to add to the bowl. The intensity of emotion did not fade from Erik but neither did pain come. He still only felt the sharp shock of sensation, as if his whole body was covered in new skin exposed to air for the first time.

He had drifted into a light doze, lulled by the puttering of Nurse Dan and the steady breathing of the two rent-a-billy-clubs when the door banged open, hitting one of them. Erik sat up, smiling at the man's grunt of pain, and opened his arms to his mom. She blanketed him in her hug and pressed her lips to the top of his head. She had three inches on him so her hugs always felt engulfing.

"You're fine. Good," she said pulling back, in control as always.

She smelled of turpentine and he felt the tackiness of nearly dry paint smear from her hands onto his bruised jaw as she studied his face. She must have been worried at the call; she had seen some of the bruises on his back and chest though he'd refused to talk about it.

He'd learned his lessons about trusting and talking too much very well and repeatedly.

She'd probably assumed he was in much worse shape if she was actually getting a call from the school. The first time he'd reported it, he'd been the one suspended. He'd since learned to just take his lumps.

NA'AMEN GOBERT TILAHUN

No matter money or (former) fame, he still had dark skin and it carried costs and assumptions. He gazed over his mom's shoulder. Robert was two feet away, watching them, a blank look on his face.

His mom physically moved his head until he met her gaze.

"Oh baby." She sighed and pulled him against her again. "It'll be okay."

Erik closed his eyes and wrapped his arms around her. She cradled him and from where his head was pushed into the curve of her throat he imagined he could see her bones, the cement-strong links that held them together. He smiled.

"We already spoke to the principal, let's just get you out of here."

Erik nodded and when her grip loosened he raised his head to stare at Robert. Again it was like he could see beneath the skin down to muscle and bone, but instead of strength he saw weakness, fragility, and how easy Robert would be to break. Perhaps Robert read those things in Erik's face, because he spent his time quietly talking to Nurse Dan while his mom fussed over him. He reveled in being the center of her attention. He didn't doubt his mom loved him but she was often too wrapped up in her art to express it. It was a mostly-absentee love.

He basked in his mom's focus as they moved through the campus toward the parking lot, until the car doors shut and Robert began to yell. Erik stared out of the window and half-listened to the tirade as they pulled out and made their way home.

He was entranced by the things he felt as they sped down Geary Boulevard. Though the windows were up, he could feel the speed of the wind, the pressure of gravity, the heft of the metal frame of the car; all these things affected their ride and Erik could feel it all over his body.

"What the hell were you thinking!?" They were halfway home by the time Robert actually paused and waited for an answer.

Erik shrugged and told the truth. "Nothing."

"Nothing?!" Robert's voice broke on the second syllable and he turned his attention from the back to the passenger seat. "Do you hear your son? He was thinking of nothing!"

Erik rolled his eyes and caught the reflection of his mom doing the same in the rearview mirror. It made his own smile wider. Robert's eyes flicked back and forth between them but he chose to ignore it, though his face twisted in on itself even further.

The yelling directed into the back seat again. "Well maybe you could think of me, you know this doesn't look good!"

Erik snorted. "Whatever. How much lower can you go than last in the polls? Is there a sub-basement of opinion I'm unaware of?"

Robert froze at the wheel and Erik smiled. He felt invincible. He'd never been a shrinking violet but he'd always gone with the flow. Until Daniel—since then he'd been working on speaking up for himself and for some reason now he felt fine saying things he'd only thought before. The light tan skin of Robert's face grew flushed and dark.

"What the fuck would you know?" Robert roared while Erik kept his gaze on the reflection he could see in his window.

He didn't think Robert realized they were building speed; lost in his anger, he pushed the car faster and faster. Erik smiled and leaned his forehead against the chilled glass. They cut through an intersection, the light turning red as they crossed the first of the double line. The cars around them stopped, the cars going perpendicular to them started and stopped rapidly. Their actions and reactions pushed against the surface of the car, tickled the surface of his skin. Erik threw his head back and laughed.

"Oh you think this is funny!?"

He felt Robert's anger rough and jagged against his body but he was too entranced by the speed of the car to truly care. Still, he answered Robert's question. "I think you're funny. What are you planning on doing when someone asks you a question about me? If anyone ever cares enough about you to ask questions? Duck your head? Apologize for me? Maybe have me come out and say sorry for something I'm not really sorry about?"

"Aren't you?" Suddenly the force of Robert's anger shrank and instead something slick and slimy rose from his skin, made Erik shudder. Robert smirked. "What about Daniel? Regret that consequence at all?"

And the smile dropped from Erik's face, the small sound of his mom's inhale signaled her intent to intervene but it was already too late.

Something shifted.

Erik's own anger filled the air, lifted from his body like some creature of thorns and spikes and filled the whole cab of the car, thick and hot, turning the air to soup.

His mom turned around to face him, trying to communicate with the height of her eyebrows. She took deep breaths, drawing in huge gulps of sour air.

"Do you regret that I'm already more wealthy and successful at eighteen than you are at forty? That it's thanks to Mama and I that

NA'AMEN GOBERT TILAHUN

you have anything at all? That you're the most useless member of our family?"

The silence in the car was as sudden as a gunshot.

They flew across the intersection, wheels losing contact with the asphalt as they catapulted down into the tunnel. The light was fully red and other vehicles tore around their speeding bullet of a car trying to avoid it, trying to stop.

A high-pitched scream filled the car.

Robert.

And again Erik laughed, the swift pressure of the cars that almost hit them, Robert's fear, the terror he could hear from those in the other cars. Erik saw Robert's hands loosen on the steering wheel, too afraid to keep control. Mom reached over and took the wheel in hand. She guided them through the intersection, twitching by small centimeters to the left and the right, moving the car just enough to avoid collision.

Three times he felt them scrape against other vehicles and knew there would be patches of black paint missing from the Mercedes when they reached home. Once they'd shot to safety and reached the other side of the road, his mom's right hand struck, yanking up the hand brake as her left guided the car to the side of the road.

For a few minutes the only sound in the car was heavy breathing. Robert was done screaming and was now hunched over, face in his hands. Finally he straightened and got out of the car without a word, leaning against the hood. Mom also exited and leaned toward Robert, whispering. Erik stayed in the back seat, still giggling, the anxiety bubbling like champagne in his blood.

Mom took over driving and got them home with no further delays. The remainder of the short drive was silent.

As soon as they stepped inside the house, Robert opened the liquor cabinet and poured himself a tumbler of scotch. Dayida followed suit, then tilted the bottle to Erik in offer. He nodded and took the tumbler she poured him from her hand and walked upstairs. He had no interest in waiting for Robert to recover his wits.

What few he had.

He had no interest in hearing another speech about manliness spew from Robert's mouth. He also had no confidence he could control his anger or that Robert would survive it.

He ignored the footsteps following him until his mom shut his bedroom door behind herself. Only then did he turn and face her. Her expression held none of the fear Robert's did, her dark brown skin held no traces of gray pallor; instead it was flushed and alive. Her smile was wide and Erik was surprised by the life shining from her eyes. She usually only looked that vibrant when painting. Slowly the joy and happiness faded, replaced by worry.

She took a step forward, held out her arms and he again folded into her embrace. She wrapped him in thick arms and he felt shielded. He shuddered as the comforting numbness that had lain over his mind slipped away, leaving him exhausted. He took his first breath since the fight that didn't seem to crackle with energy; his body wasn't tense and ready to snap any longer. But he could still feel it, the readiness, the anger, right under the surface of his skin.

"My poor baby. You're still riding high off your awakening. It's intoxicating but better not to give into it. For so long I worried about what would waken in you. At least it suits you." Her smile was sad but proud.

He didn't understand a word.

"Mama, I—"

"Shh." She put her finger against his lips and helped him lie down in the bed, above the covers, his clothes still on. He was suddenly exhausted even though it was barely two in the afternoon. "Go to sleep, use the exercises I taught you. Everything will be better in the morning. I've called Matthias."

She stroked his shaved head as she used to stroke his hair when he was small and would crawl into her lap. She was gone before he could ask who Matthias was. He lay there and remembered the exercises his mom taught him as a child for clearing his mind and freeing his thoughts. He was too tired for the physical aspect, but just imaging the moves in his mind relaxed his body.

When his eyes shot open, the sky outside his window was purple-black and dotted with a few stars, the others invisible among the light pollution. His thoughts felt sluggish and slow, so he lay there repeating the exercises his mom had taught him until he was more fully awake.

He stood and approached the window, looking out onto the empty streets. The room felt too close all of a sudden, the house too small. He wanted to be out there, he could feel it in his chest, and lower, a burning need to move, to breathe the night air.

NA'AMEN GOBERT TILAHUN

He opened his bedroom door and listened. The only sound he could detect was the deep bass of music from his mom's studio that meant she was working. Robert was likely already passed out from drinking Macallan 18 like it was Ancient Age.

Pulling on a coat and scarf, he made no attempt to conceal his leaving as he passed Robert's snoring body on the couch.

The street was quiet and empty until he turned on to Geary itself. It was hard to find an empty main thoroughfare in San Francisco, no matter what time of day or night. Erik moved past closed coffee shops and sad bars with regulars lined up on stools they'd claimed so long ago they were practically rooted to the spot. He kept his head down, trying to ignore the memories Robert had stirred up.

He only got a couple of slanted glances of recognition from the younger people he passed, but that made it that much harder to forget. Only two years ago he would have been thrilled at being recognized; he'd lived off the adoration and approval of the public. He'd been living his dream, or the dream he'd been told was his.

The public was fickle as fuck though, and he should have remembered Clay Aiken or Frances Farmer or any Disney teen ever. He should have been more cautious but he'd been too invested in Daniel, too involved in it to see the danger right ahead of them. The fall was long and the looks he got from those who had been fans were completely different now—flashes of pity and/or disgust. It was easier to go out at night.

Erik was trying to focus on what had happened to him today rather than two years ago when he heard it.

Except that wasn't exactly right.

It wasn't something he was hearing, it was something beating inside him. It felt like sound, like a yell for help right on the edge of his senses, but no one else on the street was reacting. He turned toward the sound, moving away from the comparatively busy street back into the more subdued suburb-like residential avenues. He followed the noise for two blocks until the sound was a constant scream in his ears and holding his hands over them did nothing. It was a sound no human could make, no matter the pain they were in.

As he passed a small recessed driveway, he saw shadows move and fell into a crouch in the shade of the hedges lining the driveway. He didn't know what he had seen, but all his instincts were telling him this was where he needed to be. The same feeling as earlier rose in his chest, beating under his skin, yearning to be free. He held it back desperately, waiting to see what was going on.

What emerged from the shadows might have been human if it weren't entirely too tall and thin, as if someone had taken a basketball player and stretched him on the rack. Its skin was a sickly yellow-green, its head too thin and pointed. Erik struggled to locate anything that looked like eyes or a mouth on the smooth surface of its face. All the limbs had extra joints, an additional curl to the fingers that felt like both disturbing invitation and warning. Curled up in one of those giant hands was a small child. Erik assumed the child was sleeping until the creature turned and he saw the wide-open eyes, the terrified stillness with which she held herself.

The thing turned onto the street and Erik realized he only had seconds before it saw him. He let go of his resistance and the tide swamped his mind, pulling him along. All thoughts of Daniel, the past, Robert, were muted. He only saw the thing coming toward him, his senses were hyper-focused and his fists clenched so hard he felt his knuckle bones groan and creak.

In the moment before it saw him he moved, charging the thing. It let out a fast angry stream of some language, similar to the scream that still sounded in his head. Instead of dropping the child, the thing lifted her high into the air, out of his reach. Its arm looked like it should have snapped under the girl's weight, yet it was firm and steady while the other hand came whipping toward his face.

Erik's own arm raised in response and their forearms met. There was a sharp crack from the thing's arm and a smaller echo that Erik could feel through his body. The sensation, not quite pain, focused him further. He used his momentum to sweep the broken limb out of his way and climb up the thing's body, slamming the toe of his boots into its legs and then torso for footholds. He pushed off of the thing's chest as it fell beneath his feet, launching himself up and reaching both arms for the child. He grasped both the child and the hand still holding her aloft, then twisted his body to the side and allowed himself to fall. The limb broke under his weight and they slammed into the ground.

He used his body to shield the child, ignoring the shockwave of his back slamming into the concrete, all the air forced from his lungs. His body did not listen to the lungs screaming for air or the throbbing through his arm and back; he rolled to his feet and sprinted back up the

NA'AMEN GOBERT TILAHUN

drive. Dampness leaked through the front of his shirt and the foul smell of ammonia assaulted his senses.

This was what he got for rescuing children.

As he set her on her feet, he realized the smell had nothing to do with her. It came from the liquid that ran down his chest in thin white rivulets from the disconnected arm he now held along with the child. He quickly broke the cage of its fingers.

"Go, now."

The little girl looked at him for a second before nodding and running back into the shadows under the house, to whatever door was nestled there. As she ran to safety, the high-pitched whine that had drawn him here faded and he noticed another voice screaming behind him.

His breath returned and though he knew his arm and back were injured in some way, he felt no pain, simply a throb that was easy to ignore. The thing was rising back to its feet, its now-shorter limb held to its chest. Erik felt the rage and pain in the air, alien but still recognizable as it flared across his skin. It ran toward him, the lope of its too-long legs making it seem as if it bounced above the ground, as if gravity had a lesser hold on it. Erik smiled as he rushed to meet it.

MATTHIAS

He watched the young man fight the Angelic. He wasn't bad, not at all. Completely undisciplined and untrained, yes, but not unskilled. Most of the hits he took were ones he could not avoid, and the blows he returned were calculated to cause maximum damage. He didn't know how to protect himself though; everything was focused on ripping his opponent to shreds.

Whatever bloodline he was, it was not to be taken lightly. A fighter bloodline, not a warrior one. Warriors weighed attacks, fought to win with the least expenditure of energy. Warriors planned long term; fighters inflicted pain and focused on winning the current conflict, no matter the cost.

The Angelic ran for him, diving low at the last second to try and catch him unawares, but the man's reflexes were too good. He launched himself up at the last second, coming down with his knees bent and smashing the Angelic's other arm.

It wasn't a fair fight; the Angelic was Al-Kutbay and they were a knowledge bloodline, not a physical one. He'd seen a lot of unbalanced fights in his twenty-three years but this was definitely one of the worst.

Only as the Angelic tried to escape with two broken limbs and the new Blooded wouldn't let it did Matthias understand Yida's worried phone call. He'd been angry, forced to cash in a favor from an Ereshkigal-Blooded businesswoman in Hong Kong for quicker transport through the realm of the dead. Now he understood her urgency.

Her son wasn't a fighter. He was a berserker.

"Fuck me," he cursed softly but quickly sealed his lips against the string of expletives that sprang to mind. If the Organization or, ancestors forbid, the Agency had found him? It would have been a disaster. The Org wouldn't hesitate to use him up, the same way they had Luz, the last berserker to join them. Two months to burn-out.

And the less thought given to what the Agency Suits would do to him the better.

Below him Yida's son was still beating the shit out of the Angelic, with prejudice. He'd broken one of the thing's legs and was in the process of digging his fingers into its chest. They were fast approaching the point of no return.

The Suits were probably already on their way. There was no time to observe more.

Matthias swung himself over the edge of the roof, running silently down the metal stairs of the fire escape. The power of Artemis-Agrotera surrounded him and he smiled wide as he jumped the three stories down to the ground and landed in a perfect crouch.

The young man growled low in his throat and Angelic blood spotted his body in white. Neither combatant noticed him, blood of the huntress making him little more than a shadow. Matthias reached into his pocket for his extendable baton. Yida's son turned just as Matthias's swing caught him on the chin, knocking him out.

That the berserker had noticed him at all spoke to his eventual power. Matthias bent, flinging his unconscious charge over his shoulder, staggering at the unexpected weight. As soon as Erik was in contact with Matthias, he was shrouded by the huntress as well.

And none too soon. Two Suits turned into the driveway seconds later. They froze at the groaning Angelic bleeding out on the ground.

"Holy shit!" the young blond woman with short slicked-back hair called as she knelt beside it. She reached for its chest, laying her hands palm down on either side. Her partner, an older Latina woman with a shaved head, leaned over to see.

"What the fuck happened?"

"Who knows! Both hearts are still functioning at least. Call it in."

The other woman was already on the phone. Meanwhile Matthias moved slowly back toward the fire escape. After muttering into the receiver, she turned it away and spoke to her partner.

"At least it's still alive! Can you imagine the Court's response to one of their own dying on a sanctioned retrieval mission?"

She pulled the phone close again.

"We need emergency services for a dimensional visitor. Currently alive but missing three limbs." The woman paused. "Four-limbed humanoid, two hearts. To be honest it looks like it was beat all the way to hell." She glanced around, her gaze sweeping over Matthias and his passenger with no recognition. "No, no sign of any others. But— I-I understand. Roger that." She hung up and joined her partner in applying makeshift tourniquets to the stumps in an attempt to stem the bleeding a bit.

"We're to stay here until help arrives. Then we complete the acquisition."

The blond's face lost all expression.

Matthias had heard enough; his plans changed. Simply getting his new charge out of here would not be enough. He couldn't take on two Suits while worrying about the unconscious young man, not to mention whoever they were trying to kidnap.

He growled.

No matter how much he hated the Organization, at least if the girl was Blooded they would offer her a choice; at least members could leave. The Agency would claim the child in the interest of national security and once they had her, getting her out would be next to impossible. There would be no going back, so he could not let her be taken. He climbed the fire escape quickly and laid the young man on the gravel roof. Pulling the b'caster he never used from his boot, he held the small triangle of metal up to the side of his head. Five lurid pink cables emerged with a wet slurping sound. He shuddered as one snaked into his ear canal, two created a loop over his right eye, and the final two traced the shape of his lips, leaving them feeling heavy and sore.

The necessity of the private network to hide from the Agency made sense, but he still hated the feel of the b'casters. The image of a young woman sputtered to life; he closed his left eye to bring her more in focus. She was pale and the hair sprouting from her head was pure white. She wore a graphic geometric t-shirt and the same repetitive triangle design shaved into the sides of her head. She looked down at something the b'caster did not deign to show him. Her head came up suddenly and her eyes widened in shock before a professional mask slipped into place.

"Independent Matthias. Ca—can we help you with something?"

"Yes. I'm standing outside of 642 17th Avenue, Inner Richmond, San Francisco, California. Two Suits are outside with a very injured Angelic. They are planning 'an acquisition' of someone within."

There was silence as the young woman again looked down at something he could not see. He controlled the urge to scream. He knew the movement of her hands meant she was doing something, probably connected mentally to several other people. He was irrational when it came to the Organization, he recognized that, but it was no reason to heap abuse on those as fooled as he'd once been.

Finally she looked up and spoke. "We have two Blooded just a couple miles away, they should be there in a few minutes. Can you watch over the situation in case anything changes before they arrive?"

Matthias looked down at his friend's son lying still behind him on the gravel rooftop. He didn't seem to be waking up.

"Yeah, I can stay for a few minutes."

"Excellent. I'll leave the line open; please alert me if anything changes."

"Fine," Matthias grumbled. He closed the eye the b'caster was broadcasting to and looked over the scene below. The two Suits scurried around the writhing Angelic as an ambulance skidded around the corner, lights dark and sirens silent. A man and woman jumped out of the back, dressed in plain dark gray jumpsuits.

Once they were taking care of the Angelic, the two women first on the scene turned toward the house. Matthias did the same, reaching for the monocle he wore around his neck and holding it up to his eye, a gift from a spell-twister of Orunmila's line. It extended physical sight into the infrared and ultraviolet spectrums, as well as a few spectrums science had yet to discover.

The night became clear as day to him and the house looked the same. He frowned and blinked quickly twice, the lens shifting to show the flow of godspower in the area. The house was wrapped in a web of violet light, no true pattern to the fibers that enclosed the house, no art but plenty of power. So much so it was leaking out, silencing the whole neighborhood. It looked like a spool of loose threads slowly spinning, threads falling loose.

As he stared he saw movement through one of the upper story windows.

Probably the girl trying to wake her parents. If the girl was strong enough, untrained, to fight off the binding that had felled her entire neighborhood, well . . . he would have loved to take her on. But he had other priorities. The body behind him started to groan as he came to and Matthias cursed and looked up and down the street.

Matthias reopened his right eye and spoke to the image of the young woman that flared to life.

"The Suits are approaching the house. ETA on the Blooded?"

"They've encountered some kind of difficulty and are taking care of it right now. ETA—three minutes."

"We don't have three minutes."

The silence that greeted him sounded like agreement. Really good Suits could complete an acquisition in less than a minute, be gone in two.

The body behind him groaned again. Matthias couldn't afford to directly involve himself, he had other responsibilities, but a trained hunter always had other options.

"I cannot directly involve myself but will attempt to wake the neighborhood."

"Understood."

He reached into another of numerous pockets sewn onto his pants and top. Everything important was on his body at all times. He'd been in Athens just two hours ago when Yida's message had finally reached him.

He pulled out a rock. Through the monocle it glowed with sparkling pink light. It bubbled like champagne and he almost expected it to tickle his fingers, but it simply cascaded down his arm before disappearing. Matthias let the monocle fall back around his neck. He took aim, but it was a simple shot, really. He threw the rock, and though he could see nothing without the monocle the effect was immediate, the backlash of the broken power swept over him, set dogs to barking and bats to flying, cats to yowling and raccoons into hiding. He felt all the animals, all of nature around him react.

Anyone with the least bit of sensitivity would feel it, like icy fingers had plunged into their sides, past skin and muscle, down until they grasped bone. A soft whimper sounded behind him and it was all Matthias could do not to follow suit. It had been messy, but the dampening spell had been lousy with power that burned as it dissipated.

Why so much effort over one person? She had to be a powerful Blooded.

The houses around them came awake. Lights flashed on so quickly Matthias was left blinking in the ambient light. The ambulance and the Suits who had come along with it had already hurried away with their charge. The two original Suits froze, lit up like Christmas trees, before continuing on to the front door, now aware of being watched by at least one nosy neighbor.

Matthias leaned back from the roof and breathed a sigh. There would be enough time for the Blooded to get here now. Matthias's teeth clenched at the idea of turning over anyone to the Organization, but his hands would be full with Yida's son. He turned to look back at his charge.

And was knocked ass over by something large and angry. Before he could catch his bearing, his breath was cut off and he was being lifted into the air by a band of iron around his throat. His vision was already growing gray at the edges when his eyes landed on an Angelic unlike any he'd ever seen.

He was barely off the ground because it was so short, only four-and-a-half-feet tall if that. Its whole body was a deep midnight black with a sickly yellow sheen to it. The coloring reminded him of some of Yaga's bloodline but they were mystics, wisewomen—Angelic or Blooded—they were not fighters.

Its face was the most disturbing, a double-hinge jaw flung open far wider than looked natural or pleasant. It had four sets of fangs on the top and bottom and the gums between the fangs looked serrated and sharp as stone. Its nose was flat and easy to miss; only the wide slits of its nostrils and the bright yellow membrane within gave them away. What he assumed was its eye was a faceted streak of black that took up the top half of its face.

Matthias kicked out and his right foot smashed something between its legs and he did mean smashed, he heard the shatter, felt the crack under his steel-toe boots, but the thing only shook him and roared in his face. The hand around his neck tightened and Matthias felt its claws puncture his neck on either side.

Then he was flying through the air, slamming into the roof, something in his leg snapping, and his whole body on fire with pain. He blacked out just as he saw two shadows tumble over the edge of the roof.

ERIK

Erik was having a surreal dream.

Then jerked awake at a growl. And saw something that just looked wrong, dark black and chitinous, inhuman, and hungry.

Correction. He was having the most surreal day.

He chose to ignore the answering growl building in his chest. He remembered the thing he'd been fighting before but not how it had ended. The memories of the fight were there but stretched oddly in his mind, recollection jerking from one scene to another lightning fast or lingering over some details entirely too long. The memories skittered and changed the harder he tried to hold on to them, to twist them into some recognizable shape.

Rushing forward to attack seemed natural and he felt his mind slip back into that place, suddenly processing a million different facts at the speed of thought. He could feel the people in the houses all around them but was focused on the two figures in front of him.

Erik hit the creature in the knees, knew exactly what angle would launch the thing's victim to safety on the other side of the roof. He winced, knowing it would also cost the man a broken leg and a couple of cracked ribs, but better than any alternative. As he slammed into the creature the odd slickness of its skin became clear, as did a miscalculation.

His intention had been to angle the thing so when it fell, its neck would land on the small upraised edge of the roof, the force causing it to break. Erik didn't know exactly what the thing was, but he refused to believe that most things wouldn't die if their necks were broken.

However, the slickness of the thing's skin meant that instead of falling back, it slid, then fell back. The angle changed enough that instead of hitting the edge of the roof, it fell over the edge and took Erik along with it.

He struggled with the thing as they fell, its claws sinking into the soft skin of his chest. Erik wrapped his own arms around the thing's chest and tried to crush it. More importantly he kicked out at the wall as they fell, using that momentum to turn the thrashing body toward the ground so it would cushion his fall.

There was a sharp shattering sound as they hit. Erik's body flared with a vibrant, all-over, pins-and-needles feeling. Every sense lit up and he could see nothing but white, hear nothing but his gasping breath, smell nothing but his own fear-sweat thick in the air.

As his senses returned he realized he was alive, flat on his back in the street and unable to stop gasping, but alive. Even as he realized this, the details from the fight dimmed; he remembered what he had done but all those little reasons that had factored into his decision-making were slipping away. He turned his head to the side, trying to catch sight of something besides the streetlight above him. Had he breath, he would have screamed at the monstrous face that greeted him, mouth open, prepared to take a chunk out of him.

Erik scrambled and slithered back, groaning. He had managed to struggle a couple feet back before he noticed the large crack down the center of its face. He glanced around and realized he was lying among the cracked remnants of his opponent. Jagged pieces of black surrounded him, some of them leaking a thin pink liquid. Even as he watched the pieces shrank and began to disappear. As soon as the realization of his winning penetrated, the pain hit twice as hard and he whimpered as he fell back to the ground.

People were moving around him; he could hear the soft murmur of voices but was too wrapped up in the pain that permeated every fiber of his body. His pained moan turned into a shout as a pair of hands grabbed his shoulders and pulled him into a sitting position.

"Kid, can you walk?"

Erik opened his eyes and focused on the smoky blur in front of them until the woman crouched in front of him came into focus. Her skin was a warm golden tan and her thick dark hair was shaved to stubble on the sides but stood tall and thick in the center. She snapped two large fingers in front of his face.

"Hey, you in there?"

There was a huff of laughter from his right and Erik tilted his head. A young Asian man stood next to her, his hand on her shoulder. His paler skin was dripping sweat, drops threatening to extinguish the cigarette clenched between his lips. Erik took stock of his body, and yes, everything hurt as he tensed and released his muscles, but there was no sharp pain.

The woman pulled his face closer and rubbed her finger across his lips. Erik jerked back.

She turned to her companion. "Doesn't look like he swallowed any of the blood, thank god. This is going to be hard enough with him being high on Angelic blood."

He stared at the woman. She turned back to him.

"Can you walk?"

"I think I can walk." He didn't know who they were but he didn't feel in a position to turn down help from anyone right now.

"Good, cause we got to get out of here before Elliot's power fails or more Suits show up."

She helped him to his feet and he stumbled into her shoulder, leaning against the solid strength of her form. She was maneuvering him down the street when a memory shook loose and he stopped.

"Wait. What about that other guy?"

Both of them stopped to look at him.

"What guy?"

"The one that monster was trying to kill, the guy on the roof."

The woman's head snapped around to the man.

"We have time, right, Elliot?"

"Yeah, Patrah's still getting the girl, but we need to move out of the street. Shielding all three of us from this much attention is draining me quick."

His voice was strained, cigarette long since fallen away.

The woman pointed at the fire escape on the side of the building Erik had fallen from and Elliot nodded in reply, chuckling.

"Probably an easier way down next time, man."

Erik frowned at the man but the words didn't seem to hold any actual malice, just good humor.

"You might be right," he acknowledged with a small smile as he reached the foot of the fire escape with the woman's help. Over the last year he'd forgotten what it was like to be teased by someone who wasn't actively trying to hurt him.

The man climbed the ladder to the first stairway easily but Erik struggled to climb in tandem with the woman. He slipped, taking them both back to the ground twice, when the woman finally swore in frustration. Erik yelped as his world spun and she flung him over her shoulder in a fireman's carry. He thought about complaining but she was climbing the ladder quickly and smoothly, plus the position was easing some of his pain. She was steady as she scaled the three stories of neutral-painted metal and Erik barely felt a thing, until his world was spinning again and he was set down on the roof with a thump.

Erik sank down to his haunches immediately next to the silent form already lying on the roof. He was exhausted and wanted a closer look at the man.

The body was still breathing, which was good. His dark hair was a full curly mass, held back by a simple metal band. His face was young in unconsciousness; he was in his early twenties at the latest, maybe twenty-two. His skin had a dark Mediterranean cast. Before Erik could observe more, he was interrupted by the woman and Elliot cursing almost in unison.

She broke the silence that followed. "Matthias." Her tone was odd, it shook, but Erik could not tell what she was feeling. "Of course."

"So, what do we do?" Elliot's voice held the same odd quality as the woman's. As if they were happy to see him and also scared by the fact. "No way I can carry one of them and maintain the shield, and no way you can carry both, even in full-blood, Daya. Not without hurting one or both of them worse."

The woman, Daya, glared at Erik and Matthias. Erik did not flinch, fairly sure she was frustrated at the situation, not him. Daya did not seem the type who liked to be told she could not do something. She also didn't seem the type to strike out in frustration, but impressions were deceiving, so he stayed on guard.

Finally she turned to face Elliot again. "You're right. We'll wait for Patrah to retrieve the girl and call for an extra vehicle."

"Up here?"

"Yeah. Can you hold the street-wide shield while I go check on Patrah?"

"On just you two? Yeah, sure." He bit his lip. "Hurry."

Daya nodded and took off for the fire escape briskly. Erik took the chance to rest and lay down on the gravel roof, still keeping his gaze on the man he'd just met. Rocks dug into his back, but the relief on his aching muscles was worth it. He looked up at Elliot.

"So what is all this?"

Elliot looked at him, hesitated. "How much do you know?"

Erik considered lying but only for a second. He didn't know what these people could do. The strength coiled in Daya, the speed with which she moved, could be natural, could be the result of training and conditioning, but considering what he had seen? Considering all this talk about shielding directed at Elliot? They could do things, things like what he apparently could now do. Maybe they could tell when someone lied.

Maybe he could. That thought stopped him cold.

Best to tell the truth. Only enough to get by though.

"I went for a walk, and suddenly I'm living in a Joss Whedon series. Monsters but no cute bumbling sidekick to make it worth my while." Erik caught Elliot's eyes and allowed his lips to turn up into a smirk. "At least not yet."

It was a risk, flirting with the strange man; he might be straight, but Erik got the reading that even if he was he wouldn't react with the typical dude-bro fear.

Erik's intuition was right. Elliot chuckled at the comment and a slight blush lit up his sweaty cheeks.

"So you don't really know anything?"

Damn.

Erik was sort of hoping he wouldn't focus on that. His frustration built and his tongue slipped the leash he was keeping it on.

"That's what I said. Is this one of those shows where you're cute so you're not that smart?" Elliot wasn't really Erik's type but it wasn't the first time he'd flirted with someone he wasn't actually interested in to get something. He'd been raised in the Hollywood machine, for god's sake—using your body as currency was lesson one.

Anyway, Elliot wasn't unattractive. He was a little shorter than Erik and had that stocky without being a muscle-head thing going on. His nose crooked definitively to one side and his practically nonexistent top lip looked anemic next to its Cupid's bow bottom partner. It gave his face good character.

Erik's ambivalence had more to do with the fact that he read something weak in Elliot's posture—in his obvious reliance on someone else.

Elliot flushed at the compliment. Or the insult. "So how do you know Matthias?"

Erik rolled his eyes at the evasion and shrugged. It hurt but not the sharp pain he'd experienced on the ground below. Instead it felt like the ache of sore muscles, a couple-days-after-hard-workout ache.

"Woke up and he was being slammed into the roof. Took a wild guess that it wasn't a good thing. Didn't even know his name until the two of you said it." All true. No need to mention his fight earlier today or that his mom had mentioned a Matthias before he'd fallen asleep this afternoon.

"So you attacked and killed an Angelic to save someone you didn't know?" The suspicion was thick in Elliot's voice.

"An Angelic? Didn't remind me of any angel I've ever heard of."

Elliot snorted at his answer. "Not a fan of the Bible, I take it?"

"I know all the dirty bits." He did; they were the best parts.

"Well, next time you get the chance, look up the actual descriptions of angels in Ye Olde Testamentito. The whole pretty blond, white people thing is fairly new. The last thing people who actually saw them would call biblical angels is pretty. Awe-inspiring, yeah, but pretty? No. We're talking burning wheels of flame covered in eyes, four-headed beings with goat feet, things that had to hide their true appearance because a glimpse would drive humans mad."

The descriptions sent a shiver down Erik's spine. The two things . . . Angelics . . . he'd seen tonight had been weird looking but more like human forms stretched out of shape, made into mockeries of humans. From what Elliot was saying, though, they were far from the worst ones.

"Well, fuck." Erik cursed as another wave of relaxation ran through his frame, the same one as earlier in his room, and he again sank into unconsciousness.

ZEBUB

LIL

"Form the word slowly. Take your time. There is no rush."

Lil frowned at the admonishment but nodded. First she thought of the word "light" in the common language of Zebub, then she built the idea around it, the soft glow, the gentle warmth, then she held her tongue ready and began.

Mayer's hands were a physical anchor on her shoulders as she brought the word—bent into a new strange shape—into the forefront of her mind, ignoring the way it struggled, the way in which it did not want to be spoken, did not want to be brought into this world. She tamed it on the flat of her tongue.

The first syllable snapped too fast, she could not slow it down, but she forced it into the correct shape at least. The second syllable dragged its proverbial feet. It refused to come quietly, it dug hooks into the softness of her tongue and the ridges of the roof of her mouth, it screeched and fought, yet still she drew it forth. She flung it after its brethren and as the first and second syllables met each other in the air, fire flashed before her eyes.

The fire passed through the leaves of the white plant bulb but did not set it on fire. Instead the bulb began to glow. She turned to her mentor with a large smile. The answering smile he wore was small and lopsided but there.

"Good job. It is very easy to set things afire with that word, harder to bend it to your will and whim."

Her tongue throbbed in her mouth and she knew that when she finally got to a mirror it would look red and have a blister or two upon its surface. Still, Lil smiled as she replied.

"Thank you, Holder."

"That is enough practice for today. You have shelving to do before the doors must be opened."

"Yes, Holder." She said it with such force that one of the blisters on her tongue burst, spilling sour sweetness into her mouth.

She hurried from the room. As soon as the door closed behind her, she turned her head to the side and spat the foulness into the corner. A clump of shadows formed a fist and caught the glob of spit before it could hit the floor or wall.

"Thank you."

The shadow bent at the wrist, as if replying, before it disappeared. She had no idea which of the Athenaeum Nif it had been but she would leave out a choice book for them as reward.

She turned another corner and opened the door to the office. All three of the shelving carts hurried forward, eager to be of use. They squeaked and squirmed and tried to get more and more pats from her. However, only one was loaded. She calmed the other two down, promising them both that they would be of use soon and led the ecstatic one out of the office.

Only the top shelf was filled, so Lil quickly rearranged the books by location. She only had a few minutes to sunset. She was sorry she had to rush; Lil actually liked her shelving duties, though she was aware most others would find it boring. She loved handling the books, familiarizing herself with their covers, the dents and stains, everything that made up their history.

The shelving cart squeaked in excitement as it followed her and she reached back, caressing the rough wood of its skin as she picked up a book. She glanced at the pages as she placed it on the shelf; she'd read it before. A collection of letters between sisters, women raised together and ripped apart by politics. Four of them disappeared in the Under Hive and were of course never seen again; the other two left Zebub immediately after.

She passed one of the high windows and noted the bronze cast to the sky that turned the normal pink to the color of old blood. She was almost late.

She hurried, ignoring the playful growls of the cart behind her as it matched her pace. The rest of the shelving was done quickly and then she made her way to the front doors. It was rather a new duty of hers. Only in the few moons since crossing her eighteenth threshold had she been trusted with opening the doors. Technically they were always unlocked for visitors to enter, but the doors were kept wide open during the darkest times at night, when the smallest delay could lead to death.

As she turned a corner, a Nif broke away from the other shadows, in their general star-shaped form. It ran alongside her, whistling and chattering. She smiled as a couple others joined it.

When she'd first been given to the Athenaeum, after crossing into six, everything about the place had scared her—the dark corners, the books that leapt out, eager to be read and held, the shelving carts that chased her about wanting a pat, the room of scrolls and bones, but the Nif most of all. The little creatures of shadow that served most public buildings terrified her. She had been a poor 'dant. What had she known of living shadow?

Now they were her constant companions, moving on a spectrum somewhere between friend and pet. Sometimes she thought they were smarter than her and other times they acted as if they were even younger than her sibs. She looked over to see one of the Nif taunting the empty cart that still followed her. Finally the cart lost its patience and shot toward the Nif. Lil watched them take off around a corner and shook her head. The two other uninvolved Nif exploded into their whistling laughter.

She wasn't worried. Nif couldn't really be hurt and they wouldn't harm Athenaeum property. She came to the main foyer and hurried down the stone steps. Bookshelves extended like wings from the bottom of the stairs and circled most of the room. The center space was filled with glass cases holding the fragile books that had not yet been recopied, or that they were forbidden to recopy at all.

Giant doors loomed at the other side of the room. Twelve feet high, made of steel and glass, layered and twisted around each other. She could feel the Babel carved into the steel bones of them as she got closer, a shiver along her spine, an electric spark over her skin. The doors were not flat but twisted into peaks and valleys; ridges and divots caught the light of Yanwan, the setting sun, held it, shattered it, and made the door look alive.

They weren't formed to look like anything specific that she could discover, because every angle showed something different. Sometimes it was an Ante, or the skyline of Zebub, sometimes a mating run of crike or a map of all Corpiliu, sometimes a wing of dragons coming to carry her away.

And rarely, very rarely, she would catch glimpse of an odd shape, one that twisted in on itself, trying to break free. She took it to be the written form of Babel, the living language. She could almost recognize them from the way the shapes had burned her throat and she studied these the hardest, trying to keep perfectly still so the vision would linger. The written form of the language had been lost since before the Athenaeum Wars, and examples were few and far between.

Tonight as she came closer the door looked to her like Zebub, the streets laid out before her in metal and glass, except that something was different. As the buildings began to fade with her movement she finally figured it out: everything looked ready to buckle and crumble. As if the whole city was in the process of breaking down.

Then it was gone, the angle of the light changing in her headlong rush to the door.

Even as she struggled to shake the image from her mind another feeling filled her, shivered across her raw and sensitive tongue. Anxiety. The closer she got to the door, the more sure she was that someone was waiting on the other side. There were only two reasons someone would be waiting outside the door instead of announcing themselves.

A 'dant who was being pursued might not want the bells that rang through the city to announce his request for sanctuary. Lil finally reached the doors and pulled them open. That was probably all it was, someone looking for protection. It was always bad when the Athenaeum was under siege but simple enough for Holder Mayer to smuggle them out to another city where he had contacts.

As she placed her hands on the door, heat flared in her body; her mouth began to salivate heavily, and she swallowed. The door slid open smoothly even as she heard the footsteps behind her and realized that Holder Mayer was on his way.

Still, she hoped her prediction was accurate.

Only as she opened the door to reveal the three Antes did she face the truth of it.

The one in the center was tall, even taller than it appeared, since it was crouched down on a dozen stick-thin legs that ended in sharp points, moving and clacking on the stone. Its torso flared up and out from the point all the legs met, like a flat triangle, into two pointed shoulders. From each of the pointed shoulders, mouths opened and closed as if they longed to speak, and just below each shoulder three upper limbs sprouted, all of them ending differently—hands, pincers, and something like proto-wings. Its head sprouted from between the shoulders from a single point to a triangle, a miniature version of its torso from which two golden eyes looked out, its mouth an almost unidentifiable vertical slash. Small but sharp spines covered the top of its head and the back, almost like hair.

Its skin was a deep, dark red that pulsed and shifted in her sight.

She turned her attention to its two companions, standing on either side. They looked more like 'dants—like her—but so pale she could see the tracery of purple and black veins below their skin.

Belatedly she realized she was standing in the door staring at them, Holder Mayer coming up behind her.

"Fair Night!" she blurted as she backed into Mayer and dipped into a bow.

Holder Mayer did the same, except without the edge of panic to his voice or movements.

"Fair night to you all."

A chorus of voices answered. "Foul may it fall on your enemies."

She rose from her bow and moved to the side with Mayer to allow them entrance. She averted her eyes from the Ante in the lead, turning to the 'dant-looking retainers, who were easier to handle. Still, Lil had not missed the sash of office it wore.

The two could have been twins, their features even and the same. Too smooth though, as if their faces were not done, a carving only half-complete. They had the same twisted braids of blue and purple sprouting from their heads. They wore only pants, their torsos and feet bare. Aside from the skin color, the odd wrinkle that adorned their foreheads, and the circular markings that ran down their torsos, they could be any of those who lived in the same building as her parents.

They entered and arrayed themselves behind the other Ante.

Bodyguards?

Mayer's voice was smooth and his hand on her back calmed her even further.

"How may we be of service to a Queen of the Ruling Courts?"

Lil nodded, again looking at the sash wound around its torso that proclaimed Chayyliel not only the newest Queen of the Ruling Courts but also Head of the House of the Long Arm. The symbol for a Queen, the circle pierced by the eleven spikes, each representing a Court, done in bright silver rather than the usual rainbow, was in ascendance over the symbol of its House—an impossibly long arm knotted around itself in stylized black. Chayyliel spoke for its Court right now.

"We would speak with you, Holder." The mouths on Chayyliel's shoulders whispered echoes along with its voice. Lil looked at the other Antes and saw their pants carried the Ruling Courts circle design in its normal rainbow, the circle itself black and the silver spike pointed upward, twice as large as the rest to show their allegiance. Members of Chayyliel's Court.

They both watched her back, eyes like nothing she had ever seen, a continuous spiral of color, slowly darkening from yellow to gold to black and back again. She slid closer to Holder Mayer. This was what she had been trained for, for twelve long cycles she had studied.

Why did she feel so ill-prepared?

"Very well. Come into my office. My Apprentice will bring tea."

None of them looked at her as they turned away, and she took a calming breath. She hurried back upstairs to the office to prepare the tray. The Nif who had disappeared as the doors opened reappeared at her feet, following, leaping about, piping in their soft unintelligible voices.

"Yeah, you all were very helpful."

The pitch of the piping changed to one she decided was apology.

"I know. I know. You guys don't like Antes but I have to deal with them. It's my job and I have to do better."

The piping became comforting as they entered the office.

"Thanks, but that doesn't change how I froze."

They whistled and clustered around her feet as she set up the tray. Speaking to the Nif had become habit at this point. She was always careful to let no one catch her. Like speaking to the mizzene at her parent's apartment, it tended to make people uncomfortable. They were a comfort—Holder Mayer did not speak much except during lessons so Lil often conversed with the Nif, learning her own mind by what came out.

"Do you guys remember the first time I did this?" She had no idea if these were the same Nif as twelve cycles ago, knew nothing about their life span. No one did, and all attempts to research it had led nowhere at all. Still she treated them as if they remembered and took their long high-pitched group whistle as agreement. The small teapot they used already sat in the heat bowl.

She opened the lid, adding the water and leaves. The bowl immediately reacted and began to heat and steep the beverage.

NA'AMEN GOBERT TILAHUN

The set was yellowed with age. Mayer said it had been pure white in his great-great-grandfather's time, when aspaks roamed the outskirts of cities freely. Before they were pushed farther into the wastes. Small bumps that had once been vestigial teeth now lined the cups and were purported to purify any poison they came into contact with. Using it would show good faith, that they had no intention of violence.

She turned to the back of the office. The serving table she wanted was in the corner, growling to itself. She whistled to it, a tune of coaxing, no Babel this time but one of the lesser magics, just a hint of calm. The table was the fancier sort and not often used, so it had gone a bit feral in the meantime.

It came forward cautiously but relaxed once it saw the tray in her hands. The faded yellow of the tray looked lovely and stark against the warm gold and crystal of the serving table. The table growled a little as she placed her hand on the front handle, but it let her lead it from the room. They hurried to the meeting room, the Nif around her melting away the closer she got.

The Queen, the two companions, and Holder Mayer were all staring at her as she entered. Her nerves returned but she sucked in a deep breath.

"Tea." She guided the table forward to the center and took the empty seat next to Holder Mayer as her own. She met his expressionless face with a placid mask and accepted the small nod of approval.

Chayyliel broke the silence in that same odd echoing voice. "So it has been decided."

Holder Mayer's head snapped around. "Nothing has been decided as of yet."

The Holder sounded firm and strong in a way Lil had never heard before, even at his most angry. Even that time she'd knocked over that shelf of older texts and one had broken into tiny fragments and dust.

Chayyliel and Holder Mayer locked their gazes. Lil faintly felt the very building still and pay closer attention as the Holder called on it. Lil only had a small echo of the Holder's connection with Kandake, so she could not communicate with the Athenaeum yet. It felt warm like honey, but fleeting, not yet hers, she was only vaguely aware of when Mayer called on it.

Chayyliel's two drones watched her and she met their gaze with blankness, no longer shocked or off-center. Looking closer, she saw the blue and purple that exploded from their heads was not hair but something artificial screwed into their skulls. Chayyliel's blended voice broke the staring contest.

"The invitation has already been sent. The terms agreed to."

"Without my consent." The building pulsed around them and the two drones looked nervous. As well they should be. To challenge a Holder in their Athenaeum was close to suicide even for an Ante. Being Head and Queen meant almost nothing in these walls.

"I have acknowledged the debt." Chayyliel's echoing voice came together on that, firm and unyielding.

Holder Mayer nodded but Lil could see the reluctance in it.

"And if you choose to have her stay you will lose face with your compatriots."

The nod this time was quick and angry. "Yes, how neatly you've manipulated this."

Chayyliel said nothing, simply waiting.

"Lil, you will be going home for the night."

She blinked but otherwise did not allow the surprise to show. "It is my duty to be beside you. To learn."

"All true. However, this evening is not one you will witness. I shall tell you everything when you return in the morning."

Lil was the one to nod reluctantly now. She rarely returned to her parents' apartment to sleep, instead staying in one of the sleeping rooms in the lower levels of the Athenaeum. She went once a six-day to spend some—supervised—time with her sibs and have an awkward and boring dinner with her family. Watching her parents' gratefulness war with the fear and hate was not her idea of a fun evening at home.

"There are many things afoot. Thiot shall carry you home and bring you back in the morning."

She stood and bowed to the Queen. Holder Mayer stood as well and for the first time she noticed she was now taller than him; it was only by a hair but it made something in her stomach churn. She had no idea why, though, the Holder placed his hand on her upper arm. The silent reminder was unnecessary; she would not question him further in front of company. To question was part of being a Holder, but not at the cost of showing weakness.

One of her first lessons—never show weakness to others whether they be allies, enemies, or something in between, because those categories shift on whims and winds.

NA'AMEN GOBERT TILAHUN

"Go to the side entrance, Thiot shall be waiting for you—"

"No." The multitoned voice of Chayyliel spoke from behind Holder Mayer. "Arel and Jagi will accompany her home. They will make sure she gets there safely on my personal crike."

Holder Mayer turned back to the Queen. "I would not like them to miss any of the discussion."

"They will not miss a thing."

There was no elaboration on this and Holder Mayer drew in a breath.

"Swear on your House or Court that they will safely conduct her home and leave her there."

"I swear on the House of the Long Arm."

Some of the tension left the Holder but not all of it. He held Chayyliel's gaze, searching, before turning back to her.

"Go with them. I will tell you all in the morning."

The two pale ones rose and moved to either side of her. She nodded at the Holder and walked with them back to the large front doors, now open to the night breeze. Small packs of Nif scattered at their approach. They emerged onto one of the larger 'dant market-circles, bursting with last frantic activity before everyone went home for the night.

At no signal that Lil could hear or see from her companions, one of the sleekest crikes she'd ever seen scuttled up to them. Its carapace was a slick red that reflected the dying sun's light beautifully; its six legs were a matte black other than the thick bristly white hairs which spiraled up and down them.

Its eyeless face twisted their way and it extended its front leg into a slope for them to climb. Lil paused but the Antes—she had to remember they were Antes, despite their 'dant-like appearance—were clearly waiting for her. She stepped into the bend of its claw and grabbed the first hair. She was used to such travel aboard Thiot, though he was much smaller and not as geneered, so she climbed upward and swung through the neck opening into the first section of the crike's thorax. She settled on one of the bones shaped like reclining seats, the Antes settling across from her.

"Where do you live?"

Lil did not catch which of them had spoken.

"At the Athenaeum." She considered simply stopping there, but she wanted to continue this conversation. A Holder learned whenever they could from whoever they could. "My family lives in the Court of Sorrow and Riches district."

They nodded, not quite in unison, and the crike began to move.

"What are your names?"

The one on her right smiled. "You may call us Arel and Jagi."

"And your bloodline?" She treaded on rudeness to ask so bluntly, but there was no time for subtlety; the crike was moving through the city at too fast a clip.

"Many names." The one on the right again, his smile growing broader, revealing even, stone gray teeth.

Lil refrained from rolling her eyes. Of course, the first Ante she had the chance to question would be a radical. She cared not for controversial theories of divergent bloodlines; she wanted to know what she was dealing with.

"Bloodline Tlazolteotl was the name we were born to," the one on the left answered.

Lil nodded in thanks.

Tlazolteotl, the eater of filth, corrupter and purifier both. She wondered how their blood expressed but it would be beyond rude into dangerous territory to ask. So she changed the subject and tried to question why they'd come to the Athenaeum, but they talked in circles.

Whenever one spoke of Chayyliel or their Court, revealing nothing she did not already know, she would look to the other for any nonverbal clues, but their opposite was always staring off into space. She wondered if they might share one mind? Some other bloodlines had group minds but it would seem to make them inconvenient bodyguards if only one could function at a time.

Were they listening to something else?

Were they reading her mind?

Telepathic abilities were rare in Tlazolteotl but not unheard of.

Or were they listening to their Queen?

She glanced out of the hole in the crike's carapace, down, down, down at its long spindly legs deftly moving without spearing any of the 'dants or small personal crikes scurrying about. It minced delicately between buildings and through alleys. They were discussing the welcoming parade in a couple months for the delegation from Ghinai when they passed Hypatia Athenaeum, the burns on the walls evidence of a war that they refused to erase.

"They have been most resistant." Lil's head turned when she realized it had been two voices for the first time since the ride began. She met their gazes and saw that not only were both her companions present, but they had moved from their seats while she was distracted. They now bracketed her, all of them looking out at Hypatia as they passed.

What did it mean? Both watched her, waiting for a response of some sort. She settled on, "To what?" wondering if the conversation at the Athenaeum was over, if they were finally going to tell her something worthwhile.

"The Holders of Zebub and their Apprentices are being called to the Ruling Courts."

Her mind went blank with surprise, every bit of her training keeping her face a still mask. She concentrated on the part that made sense, Hypatia being resistant. She lived not far from the Athenaeum and knew very little about the inside. That was enough to judge. Unlike Kandake, which encouraged 'dants to visit and learn, to read and stay, Hypatia did not allow many to enter. They treated knowledge as something to be hoarded and doled out to a select few.

Still, they would have little choice no matter how they resisted; they had been ordered to the Ruling Courts. None of them could refuse. One of the two oaths every Holder and Holder-Apprentice took was to offer the Ruling Courts help when requested.

She needed to respond to the revelation but had no idea what to say. What did one say when the impossible happened so quickly? Had they read anything from her expression . . . or her mind? Her blood being untainted meant she could work in the Athenaeum and could learn Babel with less danger. It also meant she had no way to tell when bloodline gifts were used.

She could not lie in case they read the truth from her, but if they did not possess that ability, it would be folly to give too much away.

"Interesting but not surprising." She smiled at her response, truthful but vague. Mayer said a Holder should appear wise no matter what and the best way to do so was to be vague in your replies. Allow your listeners to read what they want into it.

"Where do we go now?"

The crike was stopped in the street; the screeches and cries of other blocked crike reached her ears. She directed them to turn down the next street, trying to push the worry to the back of her mind.

She remembered her history lessons. Mayer, despite his long tenure as Holder, had never been called to the Courts; neither had the Holder before him, Dereda, and before her Kalyn, and before her Jinju, and too many of those before him. Occasionally a representative would come to Kandake to consult but even that was rare, and the last time she could recall it happening was right after she had been given to Holder Mayer.

No Holder had been invited to the Ruling Courts since the Athenaeum Wars, millennia ago.

The crike stopped next to the squat, pink, pulsating mound that was her parents' apartment building. She did not ask how they had known the specific building or, if they had known, why they had asked her for directions. They were Antes; even if they answered, it would not be the whole truth. She nodded politely to both of them and without waiting for the crike to bend down stepped lightly over the edge using the crike's own exposed ropy flesh to inch her way to the front right leg, which settled in front of her front door. Gripping the limb lightly between her knees and arms, she slid/climbed to the ground.

As soon as she was balanced on the ground, the crike began to move off.

MIN

M in didn't understand why people were so weird around her big sister. Her memories were spotty due to the fact that Lil had been given to the Athenaeum before she was born, but Lil had still come around regularly until she was five. That was when they moved and everything changed. The neighbors treated Lil badly, either staring or ignoring her completely. Still she had visited often, at first. Then the visits slowed, until now they only saw her every six-day for an awkward dinner. Davi didn't know any differently. He had been born here, into this. He didn't remember Lil telling stories, or Lil comforting her when the crikes outside grew too loud and scared her. He loved Lil because Min loved Lil, not because he knew her.

They had already had their awkward family dinner this six-day so when the door cracked, a small hole in the pink at first then a fluttering wave of opening to allow her sister entrance, she was surprised.

Min rushed over for a hug. Lil smiled down at her and squeezed back.

"How are you, my Minnie?"

Min frowned and pulled back. "Don't call me that." She would have continued, but a weight slammed into her own leg and she saw their brother Davi holding them both, smiling up with gap-teeth.

"Lil." Mom's voice was quiet. "We weren't expecting you."

Lil dropped her arms and turned to face their mother in the kitchen. A large hand settled on Min's shoulder and pulled her back against the mountain bulk of her Pop.

"Yes. Holder Mayer had a meeting. So I came home for the night."

"With Antes?" Pop's voice was low and his hand tightened painfully on Min, so she wiggled until she escaped his hold.

"Yes." Lil hesitated. "A Queen and its attendants came to see him."

"I see." This was from Mom before she disappeared back into the kitchen.

"What did they look like?" Davi's voice whistled a little because of his missing teeth.

"Davi!"

"What? I want to know!" He stamped his foot and Lil laughed.

She moved to the living room and gestured for Davi to follow her. Min hurried behind them before Pop could stop her and so he followed as well. They all settled into one of the half dozen seats scattered around the room. Min sighed as the bottom and back contoured to her form.

Until her mother called them for supper, Lil described the Antes that had come to visit, and if Pop stayed silent and unapproving in the corner Min hoped that her and Davi's enthusiasm made up for it. She wasn't faking; she'd never seen an Ante before, that's what a better district meant in Zebub, a place one could live and see an Ante rarely or never.

Dinner was quiet. While one unapproving stare could be overcome, having both of her parents glaring was harder to ignore.

After dinner they were quickly ushered off to their rooms despite the complaints that it wasn't near time for resting yet.

Min lay awake in her bed, waiting for the noise outside to die off so she could try to sneak into Lil's room to speak with her. She'd never been inside Lil's room before, none of them had. The door would not open when she was gone and she never stayed long enough to use it anymore. Min wondered what exactly it looked like in there, but more than that she wanted to talk to her sister again without feeling like she was doing something wrong.

She jerked awake to the sound of muffled screaming. She leapt from the bed toward her door, which was already sliding open. The screams were louder but still deadened, traveling through walls to reach her ears. It reminded her of the time she had seen a small crike break its leg against the side of a building and the sounds it had made as two larger ones of its kind ripped it apart and devoured it.

Her pop was in the hallway, Davi in his arms.

"Minnie! C'mon girl." He reached for her but Lil moved around him quickly and grabbed her hand. Min was still in her sleeveless sleep gown, but Lil was already dressed in her official white tunic and pants. Min pressed herself against her sister. Pop would have picked her up like a child. She was past ten cycles despite her shortness. She was not a child like Davi.

"We need to get outside. I summoned Thiot. He will take us to Kandake for shelter."

"No!" "No!" Pop and Mom both shouted at the same time.

Lil's hand tightened around Min's almost painfully.

"Do you have a better plan? A better shelter in mind? From the screams out there, whatever is happening is not stopping and the longer we fight about what to do, the more chance we are caught."

There was silence and Lil stalked forward, Min following closely behind, and pulled open their front door. They exited their apartment and were engulfed in a river of neighbors all trying to move toward the stairs and out.

"Stay together. Hold hands," Lil yelled back.

Min reached back, grasping her mom's hand in her own; her mother reached back to grab Pop, who still held Davi. Her brother looked half asleep and terrified, turning his face into Pop's shoulder. They moved with the panicked mass, fleeing from something they still hadn't seen. The screams still happening were enough for Min. Then all movement stopped. Min slammed into her sister and Mom into her back. There was a loud scream from in front of them and Min looked through the gaps in the group before her, catching her first glimpse of what they were running from—what had found them and cut off their escape.

It was nothing.

A darkness that was not shadows, not the fleeting glimpses Min had seen of Nif, not the sweet, quiet, comet-and-moon-filled dark of night. This was something devouring, something alive and hungry and full of invisible teeth that she could nonetheless feel. It was coming for her and everyone and everything and there would be nothing left—no life, no light, not even cool, calm darkness—but an endless nothing, no hope, nothingness for all time.

Min began to weep. She was not the only one.

Lil growled something out under her breath and Min felt herself moving, being yanked around. At first it was a struggle, but it slowly became easier and easier not to look. The effect spread out from them, as they moved through the frozen crowd, the front ranks continuing to scream as they were devoured.

Did that mean they were no longer paralyzed?

Did the nothingness unlock them only to eat them as soon as they were free?

She shuddered as she recognized a voice. Wasilav. The new crack in his voice was unmistakable. He was a neighbor, one of the few who would play with Davi and her. He'd liked to play Crikes & Antes. He had been her first kiss. And now he was dead.

No, worse than dead. That thing did not kill, it erased.

Then they were back in their apartment and Lil ordered the door to seal and reopen for no one through a flurry of coughs. Min saw small specks of blood dot the pink surface of the door in red with each cough.

"Follow me."

She led them to her room.

"Why did you seal the door?" It was the first thing Mom had said since her earlier protest.

"Touch nothing," Lil warned as she opened her door and let them in. Mom pulled Min to her and positioned them in the center of the room. Min could not help goggling. The walls were not the warm, living pink flesh of the rest of the apartment. Instead they were a dark, burnished wood. Most of the walls were covered with bookcases layered with bound books and scrolls and spiral notepads and every configuration of paper Min had ever seen and many she never had. There was a chill wind that moved through the room without disturbing anything. The night outside the window was the same as outside Min's room, but somehow the light was dim and duller through Lil's window.

"They'll try to come in here. The neighbors, they saw that I wrenched free of that thing, they will think I can fight it or help them escape."

"Can't you?" Pop asked, his voice shaking.

Lil's laugh was bitter and empty. It made Min shiver. "No. It was all I could do to pull our attention away from it. The effect on the others was . . . unexpected. This must be what the Ruling Courts want to see us about."

Min was pretty sure that last part was meant to be to herself but everyone in the room reacted to it. Lil continued talking before anyone could speak, shoving some of the materials on her shelves into a hip-bag that took them all but did not grow fat.

"As for helping them escape." She paused. "Maybe I could, but my priority is getting you all to safety. They may follow if they wish, but if they panic you all may be hurt. Also, I do not want to be near them when they start to blame me. Those who are different are always blamed and shunned. I've . . . seen it many times before." Her tone was very even on the last words and Min felt Mom tense. "Ah, here it is." She pulled a bundle of sticks and rope from the back of a shelf behind a row of books. They heard the sickening sound of the front door being forced open, the schlurp and screech of the fiber being torn and shredded.

Lil turned to her window and dropped her bundle. A ladder.

"Min, you go down first."

"No."

"Mother—"

"No, Lil. We don't know what's down there, someone has to go down that can watch out for them. You go first. Then Min and Davi, we'll come last in case they get through."

"Mother—"

"No, we have done you wrong . . . for many years. It was us who gave you to the Athenaeum and we blamed you for our choice." Mom looked away from Lil and Min wanted to run up, to hug her, but she knew it wasn't her place. This was not her story. Pop placed one hand on Mom's shoulder, the other on Lil's and nodded in agreement.

"Your mom is right. Hurry and we will join you."

Someone was pounding on the door, trying to force it the way they had the front door. Lil must have changed this along with the walls because though it bulged it did not break.

"It will hold them for a while."

More voices joined the ones already outside the door, all of them raised in anger. Lil nodded and Min saw her eyes widen in shock as Pop pulled her into an embrace, Davi still sandwiched between them. Mom did the same and Lil's mouth opened and closed before she simply hurried out the window.

Min ran forward and embraced both her parents as well. She was scared, more scared than she'd ever been, because she knew that she had to do this. She followed Lil out the window. Halfway down the ladder it jerked as Davi started down, and as she waited for the movement to settle she realized the ladder was not sticks and rope. The white rungs she clung to were bone and the brown dried muscle, like jerky.

She peered more closely and noticed the healthy pink of the building wall was turning to a sickly sepia, as if rotting away.

"C'mon, Minnie. Just a little farther."

Min took a deep breath and continued her descent. She reached the ground and fell into Lil's waiting arms. They both turned to watch Davi continue down; he was tall and lanky for his age, the opposite of Min, but he had still only crossed into six. Their mom followed and Davi reached the ground just as she was halfway down.

Then the ladder jerked. They all looked up to see Pop trying to climb out the window while more and more arms pulled at both him and the ladder. He yelled down for Mom to hurry, more and more bodies trying to force themselves out alongside him. Mom doubled her speed of descent and called up to Pop for him to hurry as well. It jerked again and Min heard the snap. She would never forget.

A hand covered her eyes and her head was yanked around until she was pressed into Lil's side. There was another snapping sound and then a scream and a crack of a body hitting the ground, the sound of a life ending. Min struggled against her sister's hold but it was strong as iron. Sobs built in her chest, tumbled into the air around her, joining the wails of her brother Davi. Lil jerked to the other side and she figured Lil was also holding Davi against her body, shielding his sight as well. That was good. He was a child but Min was not. She deserved to see, to know.

She heard the unmistakable steps of a crike coming closer.

"What are you doing here?"

"Holder Mayer sent us to assist in any way you may need." The voices that answered were a hairsbreadth from unison.

"How did he know what was happening?"

"He did not; he simply assumed for you to summon Thiot so late into the night that all was not well."

There was silence and then Lil ordered.

"Come. Take them."

Min was lifted into the air; all she could see was pale flesh, too pale. Whoever held her smelled of that sharp scent of new rot mixed with lightning. It had to be an Ante.

Min went still.

"Take them to Kandake. When you arrive, send Thiot back for me. I am going back in to try and get my pare— my father."

Min began to struggle again. She thought Pop had fallen as well. If there was a chance, but—

"Lil, no!" Her mom was dead, her pop likely dead. She could not lose Lil as well.

"I will be fine, Min. I will meet you there. I promise."

Min was carried, her struggles nothing to the steel bands that held her. She rose into the air and then they were moving swiftly through the air and she looked down. Just in time to see her home disappearing behind them.

SAN FRANCISCO

ERIK

He woke up naked, in a clean white bed. His first thought was that this passing out bullshit had to end, his second was that the whole place smelled too clean. It was not a hospital chemical clean but rather the air right after a lightning strike. The bright, burning scent of ozone. He sat up; his clothes were folded on the lone chair. Other than the chair, the only other furniture was a bed and a wash basin.

The walls, all the furniture, everything in the room with the exception of his clothing and the sheets was the same plain industrial gray. He touched the wall and jerked back from the cold cinder block. At least the room was warm enough.

"Well this doesn't . . . quite look like a prison."

He stood, washed quickly before pulling on his clothes, trying the door, and finding it open. He peeked out but no one was stationed in the long monochrome hallway. He stepped outside and when no alarms sounded, he relaxed a little and looked down the identical stretches of dull gray to his left and right. Doors lined the walls on either side and both dead-ended in little cul-de-sacs. He was smack dab in the middle. Erik shrugged, pirouetted until he was dizzy, and took off in a random direction.

If he was being too cavalier about the whole waking up in a strange place thing, he figured he'd been unconscious for Beyoncé knew how long. If they'd wanted him dead, he would be. If they'd wanted him imprisoned, he would be. Instead he was rested, healed, and given free rein of the facilities. He didn't trust whoever had him but he doubted they would shoot him on sight.

Unless they wanted to hurt him. The thought wrecked his calm a bit before he pushed it aside. He could defend himself. He remembered what he had done, what he could do, and the worry and anxiety that always bubbled just under the surface of his skin quieted.

Thinking of the little brown girl he'd saved and the Angelic he had memories of ripping apart. He was nowhere near defenseless.

He smiled. The faked confidence he'd displayed for the past two years finally felt real, like the fire in his chest had been rekindled. He'd felt this before during the fight at school, or with the two . . . Angelics. But unlike then it didn't threaten to overtake him. The power simply sat there, warm and pulsing.

As he continued on he gave all the doorknobs a cursory twist. Most were locked, and the ones that opened led to empty single rooms exactly like the one he'd left but without the furniture. The right hall-way ended in a single door, painted red. The first bit of color he'd seen in this monochrome shithole since he woke up.

The knob turned easily under his hand and he found himself look-ing into a large white room. The floor curved downward and the ceil-ing arched up so the whole room was a endless white parabola; it was disorienting even from the doorway. After a few seconds his eyes began to water and the room warped even more in his sight. He closed the door and leaned his forehead against the cool wall next to it until the dizziness passed.

Once he could stand without swaying, he headed away from the unlocked door in the other direction. The other end opened into a round atrium, three large trees holding leaves of silver and dangling heavy ver-milion fruit up to the starlight that streamed from the opening in the ceiling. Three doors lined the wall; the two on either end were closed but the middle one sat open and loud voices emerged. He did what any smart person in a weird situation would do and crept closer to listen in.

"He's much too dangerous to train with the others!" The voice was a tenor, made deeper with age.

"And what would you have us do? Turn him over to be trained by Matthias alone, at a time like this?" That voice he recognized. The woman he had met on the roof—Daya.

"We will train him in secret with no involvement from Matthias," the unknown voice spoke again.

"How do you propose to do that? Matthias is the one with a connection with his family. He's the one entrusted with the training, not us. Also, the young man is at least eighteen, so he should really be here involved in the discussion himself." That was Elliot. Now that he wasn't under a strain, Erik found him soft-spoken but sure and smiled at his words. At least someone thought he should make his own decisions. "Where is Matthias?"

Erik was wondering the same thing. Nothing about this felt right.

"And you would endanger—"

"There will be no danger. We will both be here training an aspirant as well. This is our only chance to influence this Erik so he doesn't completely adopt Matthias's hatred of the Organization." Daya's voice hardened. "His very valid critiques of how it is run. And you still haven't answered Elliot's questions as to his whereabouts."

"Well, as you said he is . . . critical of the Organization. Before he could be allowed free range of one of our safe houses, he had to be questioned."

Erik really did not like the sound of the person speaking. He hurried off, back down the hallway, pressing his ear tightly to each locked door he passed until he heard the murmuring of voices. He studied the door; it was fairly weak-looking wood. He could try to kick some of it out of the jamb, but that felt like it would be too loud. He didn't know how much longer the meeting about him would be going on, and didn't that piss him the fuck off, that they would dare to talk about him while he was supposed to be passed out.

The fire in his chest flared and he felt the muscles in his arms go tight and hot. The need to fight, to punch something, rose in him but he controlled it. He grabbed the doorknob and turned until the lock stopped him, then turned some more. There was a sharp crack as the lock was forced and broke. Erik paused, waiting to see if he would hear footsteps pounding toward him. There was nothing, so he prepared to push the door open.

There was no way those on the other side of the door had missed the sound. He quickly pushed the door open and, relying on his new instincts, ducked into a ball and rolled into the room. He passed through something that chilled his body.

He popped to his feet and was met by two pairs of wide blinking eyes. The young man he'd been looking for, Matthias, was watching him from the bed, naked except for black boxer-briefs and the stiff wraps around his arm and leg. His mahogany hair with auburn accents hung wild into his dark eyes. He was eating soup from a tray on his lap and staring at Erik. Erik's gaze snapped to the other person in the room.

She looked almost exactly like Elliot. Her face was softer and rounder and her longer hair was curled and pulled back. She wore a long, flowing gown of sapphire that brought out the cool blue tones in her skin. This was all trumped by the fact that she was floating a foot off the ground and was mostly see-through, though.

She spoke with a hint of a smile. "Well, he's certainly as rash as you. It's either a match made in heaven or you'll burn the city down around our ears. Either way it'll be interesting."

"What exactly is going on?" Matthias asked.

Erik rubbed the back of his neck uncomfortably.

"Well, I . . . overheard that you were being held. So I came to rescue you." As Erik looked the man over, he could see that the bed was equipped with straps to hold a person down—they were just currently undone.

Matthias snorted. "Didn't Yida ever teach you that eavesdropping is a great way to hear bad things about yourself?"

Erik smirked and answered. "Yes, but she also said you need to know when people are talking shit about you. So you can confront them later."

Matthias smiled. "That sounds like her, all right."

Erik narrowed his eyes. "So you do know my mother. And I am who they were talking about." He figured, but it was nice to have confirmation.

"Well, I'll leave you two to figure things out and let the Maestres know that everything is okay."

"Thanks, Elana," Matthias called as she floated out.

"What is she?" Erik asked, staring at the wall she had passed through, ignoring the open door.

"A ghost."

He turned back to Matthias.

"Ghosts are real?" Erik had always been vaguely atheist. Robert broke from the Greek Orthodox church years before Erik was born and his mom had done the same with the Southern Baptists. They both were indifferent to matters of the soul or God but now Erik wondered if that was just an act with his mom.

Whatever his parents' reasons, Erik had simply become atheist without making a conscious decision. He trusted his own eyes and senses

NA'AMEN GOBERT TILAHUN

more than anything written in books or passed through word of mouth. This was right in front of his eyes, though.

"Yeah, not as plentiful as some people think though. I've only met three and I've been around. Elana's good people despite her allegiance. Her brother and Daya too."

"So Elana and Elliot are related?"

"Yeah. Twins."

Erik nodded, frowning. Then he cocked his head to the side and waited.

"I'm guessing you'd like some answers now, yes?" Matthias questioned, sitting up farther.

"Well, that would be good but I'm not sure the explanation won't send me screaming into the night. I've seen some fucked up things over the last twenty-four hours—Shit!" Erik stopped cold.

"What?"

"How long have I been out? Mama is probably freaking the fuck out right now."

"It's Saturday morning and don't worry about it, I talked to Yida. Everything's cool. And you're strong enough to take this talk. Have a seat."

Erik sat in the single chair, turning it to face the bed. He took a deep breath and braced himself. He knew that tone of "talk"—it implied a revelation, a shift in his world. He'd been given many talks in the past—from agents and producers, from Robert and his mom, from lawyers and judges and pundits and people on the street. He'd survived all of them and would this one as well.

"In the beginning, there was the Creatrix. Call it God, call it the Universe, call it whatever you want, it made this world. It crafted the sky and the earth, it crafted the animals of the sea and humans and plants. Then the Creatrix birthed—rather than crafted—its children, the Nephilim. Some cultures viewed them as angels, some as nature spirits, and still others as gods. The Nephilim were all this and more, gifted with shapes and forms and powers far beyond those of even the mightiest of the Blooded—that's what you are, by the way."

Erik tried to interrupt. "What—"

Matthias held up his hand. "Please hold all questions until the end. The Nephilim made a garden of the world and shielded those weaker crafted life forms that did not have the Creatrix's power burning in them. Finally they had children themselves. They tried to create a paradise, but a portion of their children rose up in anger and jealousy. Still others rose in defense of their forebears, and though the aggressors were banished, they still managed to kill all the Nephilim. The Blooded are the descendants of those who remained loyal. Angelics are the children of the betrayers."

Erik narrowed his eyes but didn't interrupt.

"Or in the beginning there was God. From where the Nephilim came no one knows, but they spread across this earth that God created and God was pleased. The Nephilim began to breed and multiply, they bred with each other and with all the pieces of creation—trees, rocks, starstuff, waves, flame—and from these matings was everything alive born. And God saw this and thought it good.

"The world now teemed with life and, as life is wont to do, it attacked and devoured itself, which was also good. Which was nature. Then the Nephilim came to wonder, 'Why should our descendants not worship us? Are we not the well from which they all sprung? Are we not the beginning of life?' And so they enslaved their descendants and all the life they had brought forth and God saw this and was not happy. It sent a devouring wind to scour clean the face of the earth, sending warning to their descendants but not the Nephilim themselves. Even with this warning many creatures and people died along with their forebears. The Blooded are those of their blood who survived and the Angelics are the Nephilim that managed to hide in the dark corners of creation."

Erik tilted his head. "But—"

Matthias interrupted him.

"Or there is no singular God. People came about through evolution, millions of years and thousands of evolutionary dead ends to get to this. The gods and goddesses came later, sprung from the minds of people, sprung from communities, sprung from abstract notions and ideas. They fed on their parents—humanity—as some children do, sucking the invention and ingenuity that was produced. They also blessed warriors, protected cities, and taught humanity machining processes that would take them centuries to master otherwise. These abstracts made flesh bred with humans, spreading their abilities far and wide. Too late they discovered their own power had limits and was shared with their descendants; the more of their line that existed the less power they themselves had to use or even sustain themselves. Eventually most simply faded away. Those who survived killed the children they could find and hide even now because of the rumor, not too far-fetched, that their descendants did this deliberately. Some descendants even learned how to draw more power from their forebears, turning themselves less human and more abstract, the Angelics who even now search for a new power source before they all die. We are the descendants of those they blessed, their priestesses and priests."

Erik rolled his eyes.

"All of these stories are true and none of them are. The truth is buried under the many former worlds that were Earth, not to mention millennia of lies and misdirection and mistranslated truth on top of that. Plenty of Blooded have spent their whole lives trying to find out the 'true' tale and all we have to show for it is a multitude of revisions and arguing."

"What do you mean, former worlds?"

"This is not the first world. Depending on who you believe, it is the beginning of anywhere from the third to the thirteenth—both numbers of power. Every culture has stories about the end of the world; this is carried from those who survive the destruction of the previous world and pass into the next, but all that is for philosophers to debate."

"It all sounds like philosophical bullshit. I mean, that's not an explanation. How do you explain something by saying there's no true explanation? Bullshit."

The smile dropped from Matthias's mouth. "It's a real-world explanation. The real world is messy. What some people view as truth isn't necessarily true at all and sometimes there's no objective truth at all. From what your mother said, you know all about that?" Matthias raised one eyebrow and the smile returned but it was darker now, a little more mocking.

Erik tightened his lips and thought of Daniel. No one had cared about the truth then. He nodded and gestured for the man to go on.

"The basic gist is that in the old days giants walked the earth, whether they were angels or gods or abstract ideas they could interact with the world, change it with their power, and breed with the humans and other matter. They were responsible for miracles of magic and engineering, feats of daring and wonder, things the world has never completely forgotten, even if what it remembers is distorted and less than it actually was," Matthias summarized.

"And they made the pyramids and the Nazca lines and all that. Listen, I've heard this old people/gods bullshit before but mostly when people just can't believe that people of color in some part of the world were ever more advanced than Europe." Erik had once had a weakness for the History Channel before it was all Hitler and aliens.

"No, by the time those things were built we were mostly on our own . . . excepting the Reborn. I'm talking older things like the Tower of Babel and Passageways into Past and Future Worlds. Things not completely of this world. Besides, I have something to prove my theory that all those other people didn't have." Matthias smirked wider.

"What?" Erik could feel himself returning the expression despite the dark thoughts of truths and Daniel that swirled behind it.

"You saw some fucked up shit last night."

Erik couldn't help but nod and laugh out loud.

"What you did? That can be explained by you being one of the Blooded." Here Matthias paused and watched Erik's face as if expecting surprise or horror. Except that Erik had worked some of this out. What he did last night wasn't normal, even if he could explain some of it with adrenaline. The fall from the roof wasn't normal no matter how he twisted physics. Not to mention that he could barely feel the aftermath today.

"Your mother knew this might happen. She never really expressed the bloodline that flows in you . . . and to be completely honest, neither have you."

This time Erik did blink in surprise. "What do you mean?"

"Your mother is descended from Mami Wata's line—that's healing, divination, water. Powers can vary within a bloodline because most of the old ones were patrons of many things. However, you're a fighter, not even just a fighter but a berserker—you gain strength and power in a fight. A fighter in Mami Wata's line would be rare but explainable, but a berserker? No, the only answer is that your father is Blooded too."

"Yeah, I don't think so." If Robert had mythic gods in his background, Erik didn't doubt he would have thrown that detail in Erik's face along with all his other reasons Erik was a failure.

"He probably doesn't know. Many of the bloodlines that survived the transition to the new world were then lost through war, colonialism, some were even deliberately hunted down. Some keep themselves apart from the rest of us, some don't know their history and believe themselves to be something else. Also, Blooded have one-night stands, leave their families, keep secrets, same as anyone. What's your dad's background?"

"Greek mostly, a little English and French mixed in."

"Okay. We'll do some research."

"So it's about ethnicity?"

"Sort of. The old ones traveled the world for eons, all of its people and hidden places, they knew them all but they showed different faces to different people. So St. Raphael is Isis is Aesculapius, but which aspect is the source of your line gives us a clue to how you'll express. The Organization could probably find out in a couple of hours, but I don't want anyone else having the knowledge before we do and using it against you."

"Against me?" Erik felt a chill run across his back.

Matthias looked at him. "Every line has different strengths, different attitudes, and special weaknesses. It's always better to know your weakness before anyone else does."

Probably sensing Erik's discomfort, Matthias changed the subject.

"Anyway, to finish up the lesson. Eventually the giants of myth disappeared. Some of their descendants left this world, or were chased out, and found another one to live in. They still come here, mostly to steal people."

"What for?" Erik felt tense.

"We don't know." Matthias's face looked as grim as Erik felt.

"So that's what was happening last night?"

Matthias nodded.

Another disturbing thought occurred to Erik.

"So I'm . . . related to those things from last night?" He felt a little nausea churn his belly.

Matthias laughed. " Well, depending on the story but even then, no. I mean that's like saying you're related to every Black- or Greek-American. There were hundreds, more likely thousands of bloodlines."

"So what does it mean exactly?"

"You're descended from at least one thing that wasn't human. Angelics come into this world, they have some sort of deal with the government. We don't know all the details but basically our government pays for things, technologies, knowledge, things we'd call magic, with its citizens."

"Our government is selling us?" This was getting more and more surreal and Erik wanted off. "So that little girl last night?"

"A newly awakened Blooded like yourself, set up by our government as trade for gods-know-what. The Angelics . . . they don't view us as relatives; to them we're second-class citizens. At best. They come from a world where they rule, where there is nothing to stop them. They are the law. The only reason they deal with our government at all is the danger widespread knowledge of them could cause."

Erik mulled this over. "So who stops them?"

"All of us. Some team up with the Organization like Elliot and Elana and Daya, and some work on our own."

He nodded, taking all the new information in. "Is the girl safe?"

"Yeah. Daya and Elliot retrieved her. You'll see her later and train alongside her."

"So you took her instead of them?" The accusation clear in his voice.

"Well, the Organization did. With the full knowledge and permission of her parents. She will train every weekend here alongside you until her powers are under control. Then she will return to her parents with a Counselor to monitor her and watch out for her until adulthood."

"That is better, I guess," Erik grumbled. Although what wasn't better than being sold out by the government that was supposed to protect you? Then again, the girl had brown skin, and Erik knew from experience you didn't last long as a brown person in America believing the government actually cared for you.

Matthias snorted. "Well, if you don't consider the fact that most of those they 'save' end up joining the Organization when they turn eighteen. They're constantly reminded that they were rescued, never allowed to forget it, and then they think they owe everything to the Organization." His voice steadily rose as he talked until he was almost but not quite yelling.

A soft voice interrupted him.

"I wouldn't put it quite like that."

They both turned to watch Elliot enter the room followed by three new people. An Asian man with graying hair and creased tan skin wearing a simple but stylish charcoal gray suit moved into the doorway and no farther, watching Erik with suspicion. The two women—a tall Latina woman whose white-streaked dark hair bun did not match the flawless smooth youth of her golden skin wearing a gorgeous white wrap dress, and a shorter Black woman with a large Afro, red on the edges, wearing a red suit jacket over a black button-down and blue jeans—were forced to go around him. Well, the taller woman went around, the shorter woman stuck out her hip, and deliberately knocked the man into the

54   NA'AMEN GOBERT TILAHUN

door jam as she passed. The two women were also looking at Erik with blank expressions, though after a moment the Black woman smiled at him and he returned it.

"Erik, these are Maestro Hu, Maestra Luka, and Blooded Patrah. They will be staying here on the weekends with the rest of us." Elliot introduced, nodded at each in turn.

The Maestro was busy splitting his glare between Matthias, Patrah, and Erik himself. The Maestra was more composed, no emotion crossing her features. Meanwhile Patrah's smile had slowly grown and she was now looking between Erik and Matthias with undisguised glee.

Erik narrowed his eyes at all three of them. Considering what he'd overheard only a few minutes ago, he was fairly sure they were there to watch him.

"And who will they be training?" Matthias's voice was sharp enough to cut flesh from bone. Erik didn't know the reasons for the tension in the air but he liked that someone was on his side. Or at least against the Organization, which, given the wariness he was feeling, amounted to the same thing.

The Maestro and Maestra were now both looking at Matthias but it was Elliot who answered.

"Patrah will be training Melinda and Daya and I will be training Tae. The Maestro and Maestra are just here to observe."

"And if Erik and myself have no wish to be observed like a museum exhibition?" Matthias's voice went even deeper, rougher, more dangerous. His voice echoed around the room, though Erik felt sure the tiny room was not large enough for that.

Elliot was at a loss for words though the Maestra was certainly not.

"Enough of this, we know that mistakes were made with—"

"You don't—" The booming of Matthias's voice filled the room, the air pressure shifting until the room felt like it was filled with molasses.

Erik suppressed the urge to giggle as the pressure tickled against his skin, even under his clothes. All the smaller sounds in the room were muted and Matthias stretched in Erik's vision, becoming something large and made almost entirely of shadow. The other people in the room did not look amused at all. Except for Elliot, who was sporting a wide, mad grin.

The Maestres looked scared and nervous and Patrah simply stared at Matthias, frustration radiating off her. Then as quickly as it had started it was over, the feeling sucked from the room as if someone had pulled a drain. Erik could hear again and Matthias panted loudly and swallowed hard on the bed. When he spoke again, his voice was quieter and lower but no less dark or angry.

"You do not have the right to say their names. Do you understand me?"

The Maestres simply nodded before turning to leave the room in unison. They paused as they noticed their shared movement and then frowning, moved again, turning away from one another as completely as possible. Though Erik had seen something like guilt in their eyes as they stared at Matthias, they said nothing as they left the room.

Elliot was grinning again, so many of his teeth visible Erik worried his lips would crack open. He sauntered over to the bed and plopped down next to Matthias. Patrah took a few steps closer herself and cocked her head to the side.

"I feel refreshed." Elliot was bouncing in place and when Erik looked closer, he could see his whole body was vibrating slightly. His dark eyes were wide, spinning pools of shadow. And it was hard to pick out among the sickly fluorescent lights, but his skin seemed to also be glowing slightly.

"Of course you do. I'm exhausted, as I'm sure Matty here is." Patrah responded.

"Hey, Patty." He panted between every word but reached out to dap her.

She leaned against the frame of the bed and Erik narrowed his eyes at her and Elliot before turning back to Matthias.

"If you hate the Organization so much, why do you have so many friends in it?"

Matthias winced. "Most Blooded end up training with the Organization unless they have another older Blooded willing to take them on, which is happening less and less. I'm from the Bay originally. Elliot, Elena, and Daya were all training at the same time as me and Patrah was a specialist brought in to work with us on meditation and focus."

Erik looked at them all again. Elliot and Matthias both looked like they were only a few years older than him but Patrah looked beyond that, in her early thirties at least.

"And my mama?"

"Well, I was bounced around a lot of Counselors for a while. Your Grandma Hettie trained me for a while. I met your mother through her."

"You're not that much older than me though; how come I never met you?"

56   NA'AMEN GOBERT TILAHUN

"You were Los Angeles with your father, just starting to act, and Yida was going back and forth, remember?"

Erik nodded distractedly, deciding to ask his mom for any further details. Instead he asked another question that had been bothering him. "So . . . why is Elliot glowing?"

Patrah snorted, "'Cause your Counselor here was stupid and let his power free—raw and undirected." Her voice switched to a smoother cadence, one Erik associated with teachers. "Most Blooded only use it when they have no other choice because, one, it lets your enemies know exactly how strong you are, and two, it drains you as much as everyone else. We're tired because our bodies expended power to stop him overwhelming our senses completely. It's an automatic reaction." She gestured toward Elliot with a curled lip. "And the reason he's high right now is that he and Matthias have enough crossover that he just absorbed what he could. Now he has way too much power under his skin and he's enjoying the rush."

"You're high right now?" Erik directed his incredulity at Elliot who simply shrugged his shoulders and giggled. Erik could understand the need for a little chemical refreshment from time to time, but getting high off the power under your skin was new to him.

He sort of wanted to try it.

"So why aren't I exhausted or high?"

All movement stopped and Erik realized he'd said something odd.

"You felt nothing?" This from Matthias who if he wasn't quite panting anymore was definitely still breathing deep. His skin, which Erik had noted was a deep golden-fawn more than tan, had a pronounced gray cast to it, but his dark eyes were still bright and curious.

"I felt something . . . thick against my skin but it sort of tickled. It didn't feel like it was fighting to get in or anything."

"Interesting." Patrah sounded curious but Erik didn't know her well enough to guess what she was really thinking.

"Yes." Matthias just studied him. Erik was looking for a way to change the subject when Matthias slumped back in bed, strength and energy gone.

"Here, I can help out with that." Elliot giggled and climbed cross-legged onto the bed near Matthias's head. He laid his palm against Matthias's cheek. Some of the light and the giddiness, the too-bright smile drained out of Elliot, though he still sparkled. The effect on Matthias was more dramatic: a wash of color filled his cheeks, his breathing was easier, and he sat up straighter.

"So how long is this training going to be? And will I be able to do things like that at the end of it?" Erik asked. He was still unsure about the Organization and these Angelics, but he didn't feel at all ambiguous about the feeling that had raced through his body while he fought. He had felt right, not because he was fighting but because of the power flowing through him, the connection he'd felt to this body, to the world while it had moved through him.

He wanted that all the time.

Patrah answered. "As for what you can do—all Blooded are more durable and can release their powers in a burst as Matthias did. Other than that, everything will depend on your bloodline and what you can do with it. The length of training depends. The goal is to get you enough control that you don't accidentally kill someone or expose us. This can vary because of the nature of the power, the strength, and the Blooded's ability to concentrate. For some it only takes a day, some weeks, some months. Normally you would be isolated until then, but you have a very specific set of problems."

He nodded. They knew his history. He didn't know how much but it saved him an explanation and no one was treating him differently, so he called it a win.

"So we'll have you here on the weekends. If anyone asks, you're in a special tutoring program."

"What about school?"

Patrah spared him a look. "We've managed to keep Bastion and Melisande, or Harry and Melissa—"

"Ha! I knew their real names were some basic-ass shit!" Erik smiled.

Patrah returned it before dropping back into stern teacher mode.

"Well, we've stopped the families from pressing charges."

"They started it." Erik shrugged. "As mama says—don't let your fist write a check that your ass can't cash."

"But we were unable to convince the school to not expel you."

Erik tried to find it in himself to care, but this past semester and a half had been miserable. He'd made no friends except for Nurse Dan, and he obviously didn't need what they were teaching. One thing did worry him, though.

"How exactly did you 'fix' the problem?"

NA'AMEN GOBERT TILAHUN

Patrah shrugged. "Don't know, the Organization took care of it."

"Well, that's fucking ominous. I mean, I don't give a shit about Harry and Melissa, don't get me wrong, but I don't like when things are done in my name without any explanation."

Patrah frowned and looked at Matthias, who simply spread his hands and shrugged. "Sounds valid to me."

Patrah made a noise of frustration. "I don't know exactly what they did. The Organization has a lot of options. Sometimes it's money, sometimes favors . . . sometimes powers."

"Powers . . . like telepathy?" Erik tensed. The idea of someone controlling or reading his mind made him nervous and angry; the power flared under his skin and he felt the urge to beat the shit out of something. He broke out in a cold sweat as he pushed it back.

"No, not exactly." Patrah grimaced at Matthias like this was all his fault, but he simply smiled and said, "You're the one who started this conversation."

"Asshole. We don't have telepaths but there are charmers—people it's easy to trust, easy to listen to—but they aren't able to change your thoughts, just influence them. From what we've figured out, most of the telepath lines were deliberately hunted down." She sounded sad as she said that.

Erik could understand that, genocide was never okay, but the idea of telepathy just hit all his buttons for some reason. "Okay, well. Sorry, not sorry." Erik had another thought. "What exactly do you do with the Blooded who can't learn control?"

Patrah answered him in the same level voice but the pause let him know the question had taken her by surprise. "It depends on the problem. Often it's a matter of more training so the person has better control."

"Often? And the other times?"

Now Patrah was silent and even Elliot refused to meet Erik's eyes. Matthias leaned his head back and closed his eyes. It took Erik a few seconds before he realized that none of them had any intention of answering.

"They're put down?" He clenched his fists until his nails bit into his palms and blood dripped. It was better than punching the shit out of Patrah and Elliot. Even if he thought it might feel good, he was in their space and it would be rude.

"No!" Elliot's denial was fast and hard but lacked conviction.

Erik calmed and looked back and forth between them. "You don't know, do you?"

"No, they don't. Sometimes they reappear, but they're never the same. The Organization does something to them." Matthias said this without raising either his voice or his head. It was simply a statement of fact.

"They all voluntarily go." Patrah's voice was quiet.

Matthias's head snapped up, his face weary, the pain and hurt etched into it, aging him from his twenties to his forties and then onto the verge of death.

"What is volunteering when you are told by people you trust that any other decision you might make would be wrong? Is it volunteering when you are promised help and a return and get neither? You know better." He looked set to say more but all at once his face simply fell, all animation leaving it. "I think I'd like you all to leave my room."

Erik was immediately on his feet but Matthias reached out and touched his arm, gesturing for him to sit. He nodded. He barely knew this man but he was blunt and honest. He could trust that more that any of these other people.

With nods of goodbye Elliot and Patrah left, closing the door behind them.

"What exactly have I gotten in the middle of?" Erik's voice was quiet.

"A war, an escalating war."

"Huh." Erik was glad he was sitting, because his knees seemed to have gone liquid.

"We've never known what the Angelics want, why they take our people—non-Blooded and Blooded alike. Maybe they think of this world as a playground, maybe they want us for breeding, maybe they have reasons we can't fathom. However, it's gotten more frequent lately. The Organization has had several Blooded go missing on sensitive missions recently. They've even had whole safe houses go dark. They haven't shared this with the independents or their newer members yet but they'll have to soon. I only know because of my connections." Matthias paused and looked at the door Patrah and Elliot had exited through. "People have already noticed the larger numbers of non-Blooded disappearing. Some are returned but they're . . . different. Not in a way that we can easily define; they move smoother, think faster, are just a little bit less human. Every test we give them says

NA'AMEN GOBERT TILAHUN

they're the same person but they aren't. Those who were close with them always notice."

"Okay . . . okay." Erik groped for something else to say but his mind was still processing the fact that he'd somehow become a foot soldier in a war he hadn't known about twenty-four hours ago. "But . . . you're not part of the Organization right? And neither am I?"

"True. But everyone is a target. They used to mostly take non-Blooded, but more and more Blooded, both from the Organization and independents, have been going missing as well."

"What the fuck kinda name is the Organization anyway?"

Matthias laughed. "It's shorthand for the Organization of Drum and Fire."

Erik nodded and quietly asked, "What are you doing about the missing people?"

"Nothing to do but to figure out why it escalated and try and shut it down once and for all. I'm tired." Matthias let out a sigh and laid back on the bed, maneuvering so that half of it was free in a clear invitation. Erik had just woken up and wasn't tired, but he did have a lot to think about, and better to do it in here with the one person he had a little trust for than out there among people who owed allegiance to this seriously funky group. As soon as he lay down the lights in the room dimmed.

"I have more questions, you know." Erik said into the quiet dark.

A hand flopped onto this face and patted his lips. "Questions later, now it's shush time."

Erik couldn't help but smile even if it faded quickly as he stared up into the darkness, turning over everything he still didn't know in his mind.

Why hadn't his mom ever mentioned any of this to him? What would his life be like now? The constant worry of being snatched, of someone close to him being taken? Always wondering when his next fight would be?

More and more questions appeared but none were accompanied by any answers.

PATRAH

atrah glanced back for a last glimpse of Matthias and his aspirant as the door closed behind her. She turned to Elliot, who still
looked lit, pupils blown and his lips turned up in a wide smile.
At least he wasn't glowing anymore and had stopped fidgeting
his fingers into odd cat's cradle positions.

"Where do I know him from?"

Elliot giggled and held his hand up to his mouth in apology.
"*With Love*, that super popular Disney show a couple of years
back. Two Black single parents with kids get married. His father
was a diner chef and married a woman who was a state senator.
Wacky hijinks ensue!"

Patrah scratched at her scalp. She didn't own a television and
only occasionally watched shows online, but her last aspirant
had been obsessed with celebrity gossip. Her eyes widened as
the details came back, slowly swimming into focus.

"Wasn't there a scandal and a trial? Something about Erik
and the boy who played his stepbrother?"

Elliot nodded.

"Yeah, Erik's father brought charges against his boyfriend
for child abuse right after the kid turned eighteen. Erik stood
up at the trial and said they'd been dating for a year, since he was
sixteen and the older boy was seventeen and his father knew and
everything was cool.

"Until he started encouraging Erik to break away from his
dad as manager. There was a lot of back and forth. I think the
older kid got a couple years in a minimum security facility and

had to register as a sex offender. The Mouse canceled the show and Erik announced that he was quitting acting. Even deleted all his social media. Hasn't spoken in public since. Occasionally he'll show up in a paparazzi shot or an article but he's mostly settled into some sort of performing arts school in San Francisco." He panted as he finished the long spiel.

"And you know all this how?"

He stood straighter and tried for a dignified air. "*With Love* was a great show and dealt with race and class issues really well for the Mouse."

"Mm-hmm." She smirked. "I'll have to check it out on Netflix sometime."

"You can't. The two seasons aren't available online or on DVD or anything. It's basically like they tried to purge it from the collective memory of the world, which is pretty fucked up. Sometimes episodes appear on YouTube before they get yanked down, and there are some bootleg DVDs floating around but they're all missing a few episodes."

Patrah shook her head. It all seemed pretty messed up. No wonder Matthias and Erik had bonded so quickly, even if they didn't know it yet. They'd both lost people they cared about because of others sticking their noses where they didn't belong. They were nursing the same hurts. The same rough edges.

"What are we gonna do about the Maestres?" Elliot didn't look like he was paying attention as he juggled three balls of nothing he'd wrapped in his power. It was hard enough for Patrah to force her eyes to believe there was anything there at all, let alone try to figure out what they were.

"First of all, stop that! It's giving me a migraine."

Elliot smirked at her and suddenly held two plums and a tangerine in his splayed hands.

"Thank you."

Elliot's smile dimmed a bit. "But seriously. You know Hu and Luka are more likely to trigger an episode in the berserker than help counteract one."

"Yeah." Patrah had done her best to convince the Maestres that she could handle this on her own, but they had insisted. Since she was five years from the rank of Maestra herself, she didn't have much recourse. Berserkers generally reacted really badly to condescension and Maestres were made of 45 percent condescension, 25 percent patronization, 20 percent smugness, and a dash of humanity thrown in for fun.

Patrah might be being too hard on them. They weren't all terrible. Maestres had to look at the Organization as a whole and the war effort as a whole. It was a hard job. Even though they had no control over independents such as Matthias, they had to devote resources to tracking and understanding their motives and seeing where they fit into the pattern. They sacrificed a lot of their people skills to focus on other things. "We're just gonna have to run interference. You, me, and Daya. Where is she, by the way?"

"Ghost girl came for a visit."

Patrah sighed and gave Elliot the side-eye.

"You shouldn't call her that, you know?"

Elliot sighed himself and some of the unrepentant joy of highness seeped from his body. "I know. I'm glad Elana's back, really I am. I missed her." He smiled, genuine enough but laced with hurt.

Patrah leaned forward and put her hand on Elliot's. "I know." And she did. She had known Elliot and his twin for over five years now. Daya she'd heard about from the beginning but hadn't met until two years ago at Elana's funeral. It had been clear as soon as Daya's name left their lips that both twins were in love with her, but Elana had won her heart.

Patrah knew that in the darkest pit of his soul, even as he'd mourned Elana terribly, Elliot had hoped he had a chance with Daya. Then a couple weeks later Elana's ghost showed up for semi-happy reunions and that idea was shot to shit.

He smiled at her and they stood in a comfortable silence for a few minutes until Elliot shifted, pulling away from her.

"I'm gonna go to the training room. Try to burn off some of this excess energy."

Patrah kissed his cheek as they parted at the door and she went to look in on her charge.

The girl, Melinda, had been an assignment she was not expecting. They hadn't even met yet. She cautiously knocked on the door and a small voice invited her in. The room was set up in the same way that all the others were except with more color in deference to her age. The cinder-block walls were painted a bright, cheerful sea green and the bed covered in a blue and silver bedspread that the girl held up to her chin, watching Patrah warily.

"Who are you?"

"I'm Patrah." She was careful not to get much closer; the girl had every right to be wary and she wanted the girl to learn to follow her instincts. Now she simply had to get those instincts to tell the girl she was trustworthy. Melinda looked much closer to six or seven then the eleven Patrah knew her to be, curled up into a small huddle under the covers.

"I'm Melinda."

"I know."

Slowly Melinda lowered her hands and the blanket gripped in them.

"Where's the boy who saved me?"

Patrah could have slapped herself. Of course, the girl would view Erik as safe. She should have brought him with her, no matter how raw he was.

"He's busy right now but you can see him a little later if you want." Melinda tilted her head to the side just a bit as if deciding whether she wanted to or not or perhaps whether she believed Patrah at all. Finally she nodded and relaxed.

"Did your parents explain why you had to come here for a little while?"

The little girl nodded again, "Because of the dreams I have."

"That's right." Patrah took another step into the room, approaching without coming too close. "I have dreams too, that's why they sent me to help you. Sometimes I dream things that haven't happened yet or things that happened a long time ago or things that are happening right now but somewhere else. Is it the same for you?"

Melinda nodded hesitantly. Then she stopped and looked at Patrah, really looked, the way children look at adults when judging their worth. Patrah stayed still and silent. She had no kids of her own, but both of her aspirants had come into her care young. She knew she was balanced on a precipice and one wrong move would plunge them into a morass of mistrust that might take years to overcome.

Then it was over and Melinda smiled.

"And sometimes the things I see follow me out of the dreams."

Patrah masked her shock. That was a skill she did not possess nor did any of the dreamers alive now. To bring dream reality over the barrier into the waking world took extraordinary strength or an unusual skill.

"Are they things you want to bring with you or do they just show up?"

"Mostly they just show up, then fade away."

Patrah hid her relief. If it had nothing to do with want, it was more likely an unusual quirk of her power and bloodline rather than an excessive amount of strength. Still worrisome, but not nearly as dangerous.

"Okay, well, I'm gonna help you control your dreams."

"You can get rid of them?" The girl's voice held a wild combination of fear and hope.

"No, no one can do that. *But* I can help you make sure that nothing follows you from your dreams, if you don't want it to. And you can block the dreams when you want to rest or call them when you want to know something specific."

Melinda's eyes got wider and wider with every point and Patrah came close to the bed, knowing that she had earned the child's trust for now. A child's trust was ephemeral; you had to keep proving that you were worth it or the child would withdraw it and never offer it again. She sat on the edge of the bed and reached out a hand for Melinda to grasp.

"I promise I will protect you and train you and everything will be all right."

Patrah felt a shiver go down her spine, as if her own subconscious were trying to warn her of the false words she'd just uttered. But seeing the way the young girl's eyes lit up ensured she couldn't regret them for a second.

ERIK

Eventually Erik fell into a light doze, but was too revved up to truly sleep. So he rose and left Matthias to return to the room he'd woken up in. It had felt nice to share a bed again. He hadn't since those first nights after Daniel, when he'd crawled into his mom's bed.

He was hoping his cell phone would be somewhere in the room. Despite Matthias's assurances, he wanted to talk to his mom himself. He was distracted by a new door in his room. When he'd left the door to the hall was the only one but now another one rested on the opposite wall. It was the same white as the other but with silver embossed letters in a subtle arc near the top that read WATER ROOM.

He assumed it was a fancy way of saying bathroom, and his bladder plus the ripe scent wafting from his body were making themselves known. He'd tried to block out the idea of using the wash basin to clean himself, so he now felt more hope for the weekend. He opened the door and stepped through.

And was falling immediately and before he could scream was submerged in steaming hot liquid. He tried to yell and it rushed into his nose and throat, choking him. He flailed and kicked his legs, flying to the surface like a cork. Once he broke the surface, he reached out until his hand hit something rough he could cling to, coughing and retching until his lungs and nose were clear, though they still burned something terrible.

"Probably the best entrance I've ever seen, wouldn't you say, Daya?"

Erik whirled at the voice and then almost went down again as he let go of what was a rough stone wall.

He was in a large underground pool of water, bubbling and warm on his aching muscles. The edges of it were rock and went all the way up; there didn't seem to be a way out of it, though he was a little distracted by the three naked women sitting against the opposite edge.

"Yes, definitely 8.5 for the entry and the splash. The coughing hurt your overall score, though," Daya responded.

Elana sat between them, giggling with a hand over her mouth. "You guys are horrible; be nice." Her voice was sympathetic but a small laugh ran through it. "Are you okay?"

He laughed a little. "Yeah, I'm fine; just a little surprised. I was expecting a bathroom and got a lake. What is this place?"

Daya answered. "It's a hot spring located under Marin, inaccessible from anywhere except one of our safe houses."

"We're in Marin?" Erik was somewhat horrified. He'd been there a few times, very fancy and aware of it. One of the places the rich white folks ran to in the Bay Area to escape the idea of a brown person living nearby.

"No, we're in Brisbane."

"Ugh, that's worse." Brisbane was an industrial wart on the ass of San Francisco. "So how did we get here?"

"Portals. One of the previous Blooded found this in his explorations and built a bunch of portals from our safe houses. They appear when needed. I wanna say he was Spider's line."

"Okay." Erik got the gist but the details of portals and who exactly Spider was were lost on him. "And how does one get out?"

Daya gestured to a side wall. It just looked like more rock, but as he swam closer he could discern steep stairs cut into wall. The cutting and camouflage were done well. Even knowing they were there, when he looked away briefly it took him a long minute to locate them again.

Before he started to climb the steps, Patrah's voice called out, "I have a favor to ask of you, Erik."

Erik looked back and nodded at Patrah to continue.

"I want you to meet with Melinda, the girl you rescued last night. She's scared to be in a new place and your face is one she connects with safety."

"Okay." Erik was slow to agree, not because he didn't want to see the girl again but because something in the request sat wrong with him. He had been around enough sets and child actors to see the thin thread of manipulation that ran through favors about children. The easiest way to control a child was to use someone they loved and trusted as the carrot. Maybe that wasn't what Patrah wanted, maybe she genuinely cared for Melinda's well-being and happiness, but Erik hadn't trusted adults to speak truthfully to children since he was nine years old. "I'll do that."

He moved toward the stairs; he'd had enough awkwardness for one morning, plus he still needed to pee. When he reached the ledge he grabbed up one of the towels whose color blended into the sepia of the stone and dried his head and hands off as quickly as possible. The rest of him was a lost cause, still covered in damp clothes. He followed the narrow path in the rock, taking the stairs two at a time until he reached a small recess in the stone . . .

. . . and found himself standing in his room, the only door the one that led to the hallway outside, and Matthias sitting on his bed waiting for him.

"I see you found the hot springs, or they found you?" The humor in his voice was made clearer by the lack of exhaustion straining it. Erik watched as Matthias rose to his feet easily, without the stiffness he'd had only hours ago. The roll of his shoulders and hips was fluid, absent of pain.

"I need a bathroom and some dry clothes." He'd skip the shower since he'd basically been parboiled.

Matthias nodded toward the dresser. "There should be some clothes in there your size," before saying, "Get dressed and meet me in the hall."

Erik wasted no time in stripping and drying with the towel still in his hands. He threw on jeans and a T-shirt—not his, but close enough in size and styles. Had they been in his house? Or been watching him for some time?

He moved out into the hall and faced Matthias. He plucked at the shirt, a deep blue-green shade—a color he had several pieces of clothing in at home.

"How'd you guys know what I like?"

Matthias glanced at his clothes and waved the importance of the question away. "Your mother."

"Oh." Erik found he missed his mom; even in her emotional absence she had been the only person he could ever rely on to listen to him. He hadn't actually taken advantage of it in the last year, but knowing it was there if he needed it was comfort enough. The clothes reminded him that she was still out there, thinking of him.

He still needed to call.

Matthias led him down the hall, back to the atrium, and pointed to the door on the right.

"Thank you!" Erik rushed inside and did his business. When he came out, Matthias was moving around the room in a set of complicated maneuvers that looked familiar, like the meditation exercises his mom had taught him. However, these movements were obviously attacks.

"Well, looks like you inherited some of your mother's line after all. The healing bit at least." Matthias rolled his shoulders and bounced up and down a bit.

"Really?"

"Oh yeah. I shouldn't be all healed today. Most Blooded heal fast but not this fast. It should have been at least a week until I could move normally and then another week before I was completely pain-free. Yet here I am the next day and everything feels in top shape. I didn't wake up better, so I gotta assume it's the two-hour nap with you close that did it."

"So what's this mean?"

"Nothing's really changed; it's possible you're an anomaly of Mami Wata's line or you inherited a little of it and most from your father . . . or your mother has another bloodline her mother never mentioned. Which, considering your grandmother, isn't that far-fetched."

"Yeah, Grandma Hettie is awesome. I should give her a call soon too." Erik smiled at the thought of his grandmother. It had been a couple of years since she'd been in the States, but her postcards from around the world still came like clockwork.

Matthias sighed. "We could do a lot of research or we could just ask the Maestres. They probably already have a couple of theories."

Erik was shocked and didn't bother hiding it. His mouth fell open and he simply stared at Matthias before pulling himself together. "I'm sorry, but didn't you say you didn't want to owe them anything?"

"I don't want to." The tone was light and jovial but had sharpness underneath. "But we could waste this weekend doing all this research and still be no closer to being able to train you. Or we could rely on their records. They're like the Mormons, creepy but with great records."

"Could something be wrong with me? Like seriously wrong?"

"Why, because of a possible mixed bloodline? Naw, Blooded cross lines all the time. This ain't like Ghostbusters. It'll just save us a lot of time to know what we're dealing with from the jump."

"What would the cost be?" Erik wasn't stupid enough to think the Organization would do this for free.

"Depends. Most likely a mission."

"Hmm." Erik didn't like the idea of owing a shadowy group anything, but he liked the idea of trying to have a long discussion about family with Robert less. Besides, Robert wasn't that close with his family; the idea that he had anything useful to tell Erik was laughable. "Can we negotiate so that the favor has something to do with the stealing of people?"

It was one of the things that had been running around in his head. He'd gone from fear of it happening to him to anger that it had almost happened to that young girl to wanting to have it stopped. The idea of people being sold nauseated him and reminded him of the stories Grandma Hettie used to tell him about her grandmother, who'd been born a slave. He thought he wouldn't mind working for the Organization as much if he was doing something like ripping a slaver to death.

Matthias studied him. "Yeah, in fact I know exactly what to trade them." With that, he knocked on the door of the room Erik had eavesdropped outside of yesterday and two voices, trying to fight each other in volume, called for them to enter. Before he did so Matthias hunched in on himself, let his arms hang limp, and moved slowly as if still hurt. Maestres Hu and Luka were seated at separate tables eating, determinedly not looking at one another. Matthias walked forward until he stood equidistant between them so they could look at him without looking at each other.

"What have you found out about my aspirant's bloodline?"

Hu and Luka shared a gaze, and though they said nothing when they looked back to Matthias, it was obvious something had been decided. Luka was the one that spoke, her voice smooth with the smallest hint of a southern accent.

"What are you willing to provide in return for the information?"

"One mission on your behalf. The next way-station you find we'll go in." Every word sounded like it cost Matthias something and both their faces reflected shock at the offer.

"Three undecided missions. Full debrief afterward," Hu tried to interject.

Matthias and Luka shot him looks and Erik couldn't decide whose was more murderous. It was Matthias who responded, though.

"This is not a negotiation. I have told you what I am willing to provide for you. That is as far as I will go."

"And we are happy to agree." The way Maestra Luka said it while staring hard at Hu implied it was best he agree as well. He nodded, reluctance in every motion.

"Then we have a deal."

"Yes."

Matthias nodded and pulled two chairs over to Luka's table, gesturing Erik into one and taking the other himself, his back to Hu.

"Dayida Jayl has one main bloodline running through her veins, Mami Wata, but she also has a drop of a second bloodline, one that none in her family has actually manifested—Ogun. His fighting nature might come from that, but Ogun's warrior children are just that, warriors, not berserkers. Robert Allan we are finding harder to trace. There's no recorded Blooded in his family, which could mean it's a bloodline we thought destroyed."

"That hardly seems worth what we offered," Erik said. He was hoping for answers, not more questions.

Hu answered from behind them, "We'll continue researching and let you know when we find more."

"See that you do." Neither of them turned to look at him.

"We believe he's manifested his father's bloodline—that is where his berserker nature probably comes from. The one thing that bothered us from the initial report was the falling off the roof. Even using the Angelic as a landing pad, he should have suffered more injuries than what he had when we found him. Even those were gone by morning. We think he inherited the healing from Mami Wata, but it's not under his conscious control and may never be."

"Which makes him all the more precious for you to control?" Matthias snarled. Erik now saw that he was tense and vibrating.

"I don't understand," Erik asked when it seemed like they were just going to silently glare at one another.

Both turned to face him, but it was Matthias who spoke to him.

"Berserkers are unusual but not rare. The problem is that so many of them burn out their bodies. They don't plan their attacks because they rage and often either end up dying in a fight or from their injuries after they win. They're powerful but with a short lifespan." Now he turned to stare at Luka again. "However, if you include the healing abilities, they won't have to worry about that. You're essentially a weapon that won't break and they can use over and over."

Every word made Erik more and more grim; he could feel the anger rising up inside of him. He snapped his gaze over to Luka, waiting for her response.

Luka took a deep breath and glared at Matthias before turning to Erik. "I would not put it that way, but your usefulness cannot be taken for granted. The Angelics have been more and more active of late and we have no idea why. Most of our people cannot go toe to toe with an Angelic without losing, and badly. You can."

Erik did not like a lot of things and he did not like a lot of people, but one of his biggest pet peeves was people talking as if he had no say in his future. Robert had done it for years and he knew where that ended. He stood up.

"Well, Erik doesn't plan to be anyone's weapon and Erik has a mind of his own and Erik thinks you can kiss his Black-Greek ass." With that he turned and walked out of the room, but not before he caught the proud look on Matthias's face. He paced the hallway, unsure of what to do but needing to keep his body moving as the wash of power filled him as his anger simmered and rose. His knuckles creaked as he clenched his hands into fists.

There were footsteps behind him and a hand on his arm. The only reason he did not react was the warm smell of Matthias.

"What do you want? You want to breathe through it or do you want to go somewhere where you can break a lot of stuff without hurting anyone?"

Erik stopped walking and thought about the question. What did he want? As much as smashing something to dust sent a glow of satisfaction through his body, it also made him more than a little afraid. He liked this power but he didn't like being out of control.

"I want this to pass."

"Okay."

Matthias guided him down the hall and knocked on one of the identical doors. A quiet voice called for them to enter. Matthias opened the door and shoved him inside and Erik found himself face to face with the young girl he had rescued last night. Except looking much better, her dark umber skin was free of the tint of fear, her braids weren't in disarray. Her face lit up upon seeing him and she rushed forward to take his hand. As soon as she touched him, his anger begin to wane.

"I'm Melinda. They told me your name is Eric. Thank you for saving me."

He succumbed to her yanking arms and sat down on the bed beside her. "It's actually Erik." And he wanted to smack himself; most people couldn't even hear the difference. He was just nervous; it had been a couple years since he'd been near kids and then it had always been a huge group with a barrier of security between them. This time it was one on one.

Melinda simply looked at him before smiling and saying, "Erik." She smiled wider, showing a missing front tooth. "I hate it when people call me Mellie or Linda."

Erik smiled back at her. "Well, I'll remember to always call you Melinda then."

They spent the next half hour talking, becoming friends. It didn't matter that she was almost a decade younger than him; it was good to have someone else who understood as little as he did. She was in the same book, born to a parent who hadn't manifested so no one told her anything because no one had expected her to manifest either. They were interrupted by a knock on the door.

Elliot poked his head in before anyone could say anything. Daya was right behind him and a young Asian kid slipped in behind her. Elliot spoke.

"Hey, since the three of you are going to be training together, we thought you guys might want to get to know Tae-Hee."

The kid nodded to Melinda and Erik, the huge fall of black hair moving back and forth at the motion. Tae-Hee took another step forward, propelled by Daya's hand on his back. He looked around Erik's age, maybe a bit younger; his long hair hid one of his chestnut eyes. He was also a bit taller than Erik. Daya and Elliot left, and the three of them stared at each other blankly before Tae-Hee broke the silence with a gruff chuckle.

"Well, that was the most awkward thing to happen to me that didn't involve my parents."

Erik and Melinda both giggled and the young girl gestured for Tae-Hee to take a seat on her bed with them. He stepped over Erik's legs and folded himself into a seated position at the foot of the bed opposite Melinda with Erik in the middle.

"So Tae-Hee, are you like us, had no idea until your powers woke up?"

Tae-Hee shook his head. "No, both my mother and my father are Blooded and awakened, so every year it was just wondering when I was gonna wake up. And please call me Tae." The smile he gave looked strained, like perhaps the constant wondering and questioning had not been anticipatory as much as annoying.

"Do your parents both work for the Organization?"

"My father does, mother doesn't."

Erik must have shown his confusion because Tae-Hee laughed.

"It's not that unusual, probably about 65 percent of the Blooded in the US work for the Organization. The other 35 percent either have powers not suited to it or are independent, so there's actually a bit of cross-pollination. My parents are from the same bloodline."

Erik looked at the other boy "And that's important?"

"To some." But the way he said it and squirmed Erik figured it was pretty damn important to some. "They worry that we'll die out, that our blood is getting too diluted so we should marry within our own bloodline. Which isn't as bad as it sounds, most of the bloodlines are so widespread the couples have no close relatives." Now Tae sounded like he was making excuses. Still, it was useful to know. These were the things the Maestres would hem and haw about.

"So what is your parents' bloodline?" Tae was painting a dark picture. He would question the boy again and more deeply on another date, but he did not want to do so in front of Melinda. Yet.

"Ophde."

"Yeah, you'll have to explain what that means to us."

"Well, Ophde was the many-eyed wheel of fire angel, he had many descendants, the Ophanim, and their sight was their gift."

Tae sounded like he was reciting it from some book. As he spoke his eyes took on a glow.

"Cool," Melinda whispered and leaned forward to see better.

Erik did the same. He had always heard the description of someone with fire in their eyes and thought it was stupid, imagining flames in someone's sockets. This was more the eyes remained the same but it was if they were lit from behind, some great glow that sparked inside of Tae's body. If they turned off the lights in here, he was sure that Tae's eyes would glow like some predator in a dark forest.

"Some really powerful members of the bloodline like my mother can see through things, not just material things but also lies, hope, the human psyche; they can see right to the core."

Erik leaned back a little bit. It sounded too much like mind-reading for his comfort.

"So how about you? How powerful are you?" If there was a shrill note to his voice, he hoped they chalked it up to surprise and not fear.

Tae ducked his head and didn't answer.

"I mean, it doesn't look like you need any training on your powers like the two of us, so why are you here?"

Perhaps he'd been a little aggressive in his asking since Tae gave him a long look before answering.

"I want to join the Organization and . . ." Tae finally looked up. "I don't have that much power, my eyes only work on the physical plane, like my dad. I can't see lies or someone's psyche the way my mother can. So I need to learn how to fight." Tae met Erik's glance as if daring him to say something, to call him out about his lack of ability.

Erik knew that look, he knew the pain of disappointing a parent, even if there was nothing you could do, even if you were born that way. Instead he tried to make a joke.

"Well, fighting is the last thing I need to learn so we probably won't be in that many classes together."

Tae laughed louder than the joke merited, which told him two things: Tae had already known about him being a berserker and he was grateful for the subject change.

They spent the next hour talking about everything and anything, shows they all watched, music they listened to, it was the first time Erik had felt like he was among friends in years, or at least people who could become friends.

ZEBUB

LIL

She had no idea what she was doing. She just knew she had to try.

She approached the wall, doing her best to not look at the pile of broken flesh that used to be her mother, but she could not block the scent of flowers that still wafted from her. Her mother had always smelled of flowers, as had—did her father. Ever since they'd started work in the main Zebub gardens.

Yelling, sounds of dismay and struggle still came from the window above. She focused on them. The ladder was no longer an option.

Placing her hand against the wall, she jerked it back when her fingers sank into the usually firm pink flesh. She picked at the dents that her fingers had made and saw the dark brown rot that was eating the building from within. She'd never seen or heard of anything like it. The only cause she could think of was that the building was dying, the creeping dark was killing it from within. Then she looked up at the window. With a deep breath she reared her foot back and kicked a foothold into the wall. She reached up, ignoring the feeling of slime that surrounded her fingers as they sank in. In this way she began to climb, glancing up only occasionally to make sure she had not gone off course.

She was only two floors below when the silence came, the sound of all fighting cut off, and Lil tried to move her body faster. If her father was near the window she could still make it in time, pull him from the silence. It did not matter that her throat burned from the Babel she had used to break them free earlier.

Then the screaming began.

Still she climbed, anxious to reach the window. Only when a hand-hold collapsed under her did she notice the way the wall was turning darker and darker, and then it was too late and she was falling. She scrabbled at the wall and though the pieces disintegrated under her clawing fingers and flailing feet, they slowed her enough that when she hit the ground, it was only the breath that was knocked from her body.

Until she looked up.

The same scream of pain—the night's theme—grew, larger than one person's voice, larger than a hundred, a thousand. So loud that she covered her ears and yet still the shriek ran through her skull, causing her eyes to water. Through the damp of her tears, she saw the building itself begin to throb and move, as if it tried to run away. It was the building screaming as it began to disappear.

She placed a hand back to steady herself and felt her fingers slip through the remains of her mother. She stood as quickly as possible, rubbing her fingers across her white tunic, staining it further.

There was no sign of Thiot, but she could not stay here. She looked at the building slowly sinking on itself, struggling and screaming the whole time. She did not look at her mother but could not help but think of her; memories froze her to the sidewalk. There was a new ache in her chest, a new absence.

The last words she had spoken to her parents had been in anger. She'd yelled at them and all she could remember was the shock on their faces, and the rush of good feeling that had come with finally speaking over their fear. The loss of her parents pained her, but it was the fact that she would never be able to speak so harshly with them again that truly hurt. She would not be able to finally bridge the icy crevasse of silence that had sprung up between them. Even when they had apologized, she had not been able to bring herself to accept.

The first fault was not hers, but could she have healed the divide had she only spoken up sooner? She would never know.

Mayer said over and over a Holder-Apprentice had to learn when to question and when to listen, when to whisper and when to roar. This had been her family and would never have the chance to be her family again.

She did not mourn her parents as they were; she mourned what they had been when she was a child. She mourned the connection that could have been, had they gotten over their fear, had she been more forceful, had any of a number of things happened that now never would. She was

NA'AMEN GOBERT TILAHUN

shaken from the frozen-statue grief that held her when the last corner of the building crumbled and gave way. The pieces broke apart as they fell, showering her with pink dust and brown liquid.

Lil backed across the street, staring at the place where her building had been. There was now a whirlpool of darkness, bubbling. She could see chunks of building and pieces of people swirling inside of it, slowly melting. The boundaries of the darkness spread, but slowly, as if it had satiated some of its hunger. It waited.

She did not want to see more death. She turned and looked out across the city skyline, lighting the dim night in blues and pinks and greens.

She needed to get to Kandake, and had no time to wait for Thiot.

She needed to be with Minnie and Davi, to make sure they were okay. Fear made her shiver and her throat ached with every swallow, but none of it mattered.

She turned toward Gotha Lane. That was the way Thiot would have gone, the place where she might cross his path on his return.

Where she might find his remains if something had happened—

She ruthlessly cut off the thought and began her journey.

For ten blocks she walked in silence, keeping to the shadows and alleys that dotted the streets. As she approached the turn onto Gotha Lane, she heard the sounds of screams and sobbing, saw a broken, wavering light.

She slowed.

She could backtrack and take Orao Street, but Gotha was the route Thiot would have taken. She took a deep breath and stuck her head around the corner.

Another building was being swallowed, decaying and dissolving before her eyes from the bottom up. The sounds came from the broken and dying bodies of 'dants littering the ground and from those hanging to the top floor. Some leapt for the ground, others waved to the too-few neighbors using personal dragons to try and ferry 'dants to the ground. The light came from the lanterns they carried, shining down through the dragon's translucent wings. Other than those few, the neighbors were staying inside, keeping their distance. Considering the way the building shuddered and shook as the base slowly dissolved, she could not blame them.

Movement among the fallen caught her sight.

Two boys, perhaps a bit younger than herself, the hunger showing clearly in their faces and forms, skittered about the street. They had a system: roll over the dead and dying, strip them of anything valuable; if the form fought back, a crude knife flashed in the dragon-light and they were still. They obviously knew the area well, ducking around pillars and avoiding large cracks in the pavement without looking.

The larger one—by an inch at most—had pink-rashed pale skin almost completely hidden by streaks of filth that shone in the flashes of light. The other boy was shorter, his skin a dark brown covered in less dirt, and the hair cut closely and crookedly was a rich black. She could most likely avoid them fairly easily; they were very focused on their prey.

But there was another option, perhaps they could help each other? She dug into her hip bag and smiled as her hand closed around something cold and sharp.

She was about to call to them when both froze and their heads snapped in her direction. They started for the corner she was sheltered behind. Rather than wait for them to have the advantage, she stepped out into the street. They stopped ten feet away from her and tilted their heads in unison.

"Fair night. There are bigger rewards this evening than the baubles you steal."

The boys smiled, not nice ones by any means. She saw the larger one's hand tighten on the crude bone knife in his fist. She could see the edge glistening with something. Slowly she lifted her hand, filled and spilling over with silver and red. She held it to her throat and shivered at the chill as it encircled her neck.

The boys were not moving forward, but neither were they smiling any longer.

"See me safely to Kandake Athenaeum and you shall be rewarded."

There was no mistaking the torc that glistened and settled around her neck, strings of pearled silver and fresh-blood red that encircled her throat and marked her. She shivered as the edges dug into her skin, settling into a collar that was a mark of ownership and prestige.

The boys glanced at each other, the smaller one stepping forward to whisper in his companion's ear. He nodded and turned to her.

"What exactly is in it for us?"

He did not question her, despite the imitations that abounded among some of the more affluent 'dant families. None but the Athenaeums could work the living metal and jewels that flowed around her neck.

"Sanctuary." An offer of sanctuary was one of the Athenaeums' sources of power; any 'dant could request it. They weren't obliged to

NA'AMEN GOBERT TILAHUN

grant it, but refusals were few and far between. If necessary the Athenaeum's walls could even hold off the Ruling Courts. Though if they got to that, there were far, far worse things to worry over. They would likely be overwhelmed with sanctuary requests in the morning.

"We're fine."

"Are you?" She took a step forward, folding her hands in the loose fabric of her tunic to hide their shaking. Exhaustion and fear felt like it had replaced her blood, filling her body in a tide she was constantly fighting against. She gestured to the building to their right with a nod of her head.

They glanced over and the boy nodded, taking her meaning.

"Still, we don't want to be inside for the rest of our lives. Having to listen to you and your Holder. That is no more freedom than living under the Courts." He spit a large wad of brown-colored saliva to the side.

"My Holder can settle you in another city." Now she was promising more than she was allowed, not simply toeing the line as she had with the offer of sanctuary but leaping completely over it.

The boys looked at one another again and finally the darker one nodded.

"I'm Wade. This is my brother Antny. This way." They turned and began to trot down Gotha, Lil losing some of her fear in the adrenaline and the dash to keep up with them. She did not know if what she offered them was a huge reward. Another city would have its own Antes and its own Courts, but she did not insult their intelligence by pointing this out. Perhaps they had some other history they wished to flee from.

They knelt in an alley, Lil behind the brothers, watching them. Wade started forward when Antny grabbed his arm and pulled him back into the sheltering dark of the alley.

Wade simply crouched down again, this time with the patience of someone waiting. Only seconds later she heard it. A rumble of noise coming from the direction of the Ruling Courts, half heard through the ears and half felt through the vibrations slamming up through the soles of her feet. Antny leaned over his brother, also looking down the street, and Lil moved carefully behind them on tiptoe to lean over both of them and see.

They came over the hill like a parade.

Like a hunt.

A wave of Antes. Some moved under their own power, feet and spines and wings and wheels and tentacles moving them forward.

Others rode on crikes that skittered along in the confusion. None of the larger varieties of crikes were present, only small, quick, personal breeds that seated one or two forms. Those Antes who looked more like 'dants and had the limbs for it rode bicycles and scooters, weaving in and out of the mass. Above them were the Antes that flew on wings and air on leather and fins, along with dragons of every color and shade. They flew in all directions, some carrying passengers on their back or carefully in the cages of their legs. They shone dragon-light down, filtering through their multiple wings, reflecting off their segmented carapaces.

The group was at least one hundred Ante strong, more than any 'dant in Zebub had probably seen outside of a hunt. Zebub was not like the suburban all-'dant-colonies the city owned. Lil saw Antes fairly often but almost always from afar. So much Ante business and ruling over their districts happened through 'dant families who served them.

She stared. A few had the basic body shape of herself and other 'dants, but far more looked odd—the easiest to describe was a large ball of transparent flesh covered with eyes. There were those who flipped through the air, thin as pieces of paper, mouths opening to pull in air and then spewing it downward to keep themselves aloft, cyclones of black storm clouds that spun, occasional eyes appearing in their depths. She even mistook some of the figures for riderless crikes until they rose onto their hind legs and she saw the control in the way they moved and that they had eyes.

It was the most beautiful and dangerous thing Lil had ever seen.

The boys in front of her seemed to stop breathing as they crouched back and the group passed them in a riot of blacks and blood-reds, ivories and pinks, violets and blues. Every color imaginable passed as she watched and the three of them huddled together in the small alley.

She stayed silent until the horde had passed. Long after they could no longer hear them, the boys refused to move.

"Do you know what's happening?" Antny's quiet voice surprised her.

She considered lying but doubted she could create a lie that would explain all that had happened tonight.

"No," Lil said, the word dropping into the silence, causing both of the boys' shoulders to fall, their bodies to droop. "But I am certain we will receive answers at the Athenaeum."

The words had the desired effect and they began moving again. As the adrenaline faded from her Lil struggled to keep up, not to stumble. Though they at times encountered noises and shapes that appeared backlit by fires of the three moons.

All three sisters rode high tonight—Shelgig, the red bleeding mother; Rona, the white regretful killer; and Rythi, the blue carefree daughter casting a number of conflicting shadows. It always turned out to be fellow refugees. Most did not look like they knew where they were going, simply moving forward, their eyes shocked and dead. Some were headed for Kandake. There was no sign of Thiot in those final few blocks. A sign to be sure, both good and bad. They had not been killed on the way to Kandake, but neither had Thiot been sent back for her.

She pushed her heavy feet faster and finally Kandake Athenaeum was in their sight.

It was blazing with light, a sight that made Lil pause. She could see shadows moving in every window, 'dants speaking to one another, holding one another, crying on each other. She had never seen the Athenaeum so full.

As they got closer, Lil could see that Thiot's pen near the front sat empty. She broke into a run, now only thirty feet from the doors, anxious to make sure her sibs were all right. The pounding footsteps of Wade and Antny followed her. She spared them a thought, worried they thought she was going to renege on her promise. She brushed the worry away; she had no intention of doing so and Minnie and Davi were all that mattered now. The last remnants of her family.

The nothingness came out of the shadows as if it had been there the whole time. She knew right away this was no shapeshifter Ante. Most had one form, maybe two, but this thing cycled through several forms in seconds. Mouths and eyes appeared and dissolved; wings and legs and things she had no names for formed and reached for her before melting away. A tentacle lashed in her direction and a piece of it broke off, glittered in the air, flew toward her.

She skidded to the side, her mind already racing through any Babel that might help. The projectile stopped in midair, turned and raced for her. The Babel clawed its way from her mouth like a living thing, scratching at her sore throat until all she could taste was blood. It flew from her mouth, meaning: shatter and dissolve and banish all at once. The nothingness screeched as the shard broke apart before her face; her momentum carried her through and she felt pinpricks of cold all over her skin.

She opened her mouth, spit blood to the side, and felt the chill numbness landing on her tongue. She could hear the sounds of people in front of her and the pounding of her two companions behind her. She heard a yell but did not stop; she had no idea now if Kandake would offer any sanctuary but she had no other choice. She could think of nothing else to do. She heard screams behind her and still she ran, wishing she could cover her ears.

Only a few feet from the door, she saw someone behind the frosted glass.

"Down!" It was muffled but Lil understood and fell flat to the ground. The sound of breaking glass echoed and she felt something gently falling on her. When she looked to the side, tiny black granules littered the ground, none of them giving off the same coldness as the piece she had shattered.

The girl on the other side of the door smiled at her and reached to pull it open.

Lil did not delay as tears slipped down her face. She could not look behind her where the screaming continued unabated, where she had led two boys to a painful death.

RAZEL

The Kandake Holder-Apprentice, Liliana, was not what she expected. She had done research on her two fellow Holder-Apprentices in Zebub. Haydn was nothing but a thug with an unusual talent, but Liliana had been a surprise. Apprenticed to the most powerful 'dant in Zebub, which arguably made Liliana the second most powerful 'dant, yet quiet as a mouse as far as Razel could discover. The few accounts from those who interacted with her outside the Athenaeum, even Holder Riana's most trusted informants, yielded nothing scandalous.

Liliana liked to read, never threw her weight around, and never accompanied Holder Mayer on his trips to the Ruling Courts, where they sometimes crossed paths as they each performed their own grotesque favors. It made her shiver just thinking of that room under the Hive of Sorrow and Riches. She and Riana were both puzzled as to why this weak young woman had been chosen.

Razel looked down at the young woman in question, back pressed to the glass of the door, fists clenched, breathing heavily through her mouth.

Perhaps she was simply jealous of the power Liliana could wield if she so chose? After all, she had no evidence that Liliana was weak. She just had no evidence the woman was particularly strong. Still, the girl she had researched personally would not have braved the night streets, especially when Zebub was under attack. So what had happened to change it?

Liliana finally opened her eyes. She met Razel's gaze.

"Where are my sibs?"

"You mean the boys outside? They died." Razel saw no point in sugarcoating the truth. Truth was truth, no matter how long delayed or how flowery. And she wanted to see Liliana's reaction.

Liliana's face broke, so shattered Razel expected it to fall in pieces to the ground. Then she closed her eyes, took a deep breath, and the blank mask was back in place.

Interesting. This woman was a puzzle and Holder Riana had trained Razel to never give up on a puzzle, human or mechanical.

"No. I do not mean the two who came with me. I sent my sibs on Thiot."

"I do not know Thiot but I have been here since near Yanwan set and have seen no children."

Liliana's eyes snapped to catch her own and she saw the shock swirling within, the pain that threatened to engulf her. Razel took a step forward and frowned as she stepped in something sticky. Looking down, she saw the small pool of blood spreading from the woman's feet.

"Take me to Holder Mayer. Now."

Razel straightened. "It would behoove you to be more respectful. You are injured and weak, and I am a stranger."

Without breaking their gaze, Liliana leveraged herself up. Standing ramrod straight, they were the same height.

"I know who you are." Here her gaze shot to Razel's right arm, then back to her face with a smirk. "You are in my place, you stay here on my sufferance. Now take me to Holder Mayer."

Razel nodded, not because she felt threatened—the girl was technically correct but in no condition to enforce her rights. Instead she was impressed. Liliana had just become even more interesting.

She led the way through the foyer and up the main staircase, not looking back or acknowledging the injured woman she led. Instead she looked at the rainbow explosion of books that lined every surface; the elaborate wall hangings in languages like nothing she'd ever seen; the curving wood railings and light vines crawling across the ceiling, illuminating the whole place with a soft glow.

Perhaps she did envy Kandake its opulence.

Hypatia sacrificed beauty for utility. Most travel through the archives was done via plain metal box elevators, the shelves were plain metal, and there were no great hanging tapestries or beautifully bound books. The words they kept at Hypatia were all electric, miles and miles of black type on white screens.

Razel led her to the meeting room her Holder and the rest were currently gathered in. She could hear raised voices as they approached. She had left the room when the argument started and had been wandering Kandake on her own. Everyone had been so involved in yelling at one another that only Holder Riana had taken note of her leaving. She knew that Kandake was larger than her own Athenaeum, but she had not realized how much so. While Hypatia concentrated on electronics and mechanics and Enheduanna focused on art, philosophy, and their bastard child alchemy, Kandake stored knowledge and learning across a breadth of disciplines.

She touched books of fiction and sculpture; classic Poetic Eddas shared shelf space with folktales of Corpiliu and firsthand accounts of skirmishes with other cities. There were authors called Darwin and Adichie, Herto of Ghe'ean, Butler, Yu, Asara of Zebub, Gladstone, Rankine and more. Texts she longed to read, but Holder Riana would never approve of her spending so much time at another Athenaeum.

The space was so large that it was only luck that had placed her near the front door when Liliana had arrived.

She moved inside, feeling the faltering presence of the girl at her back.

Holder Mayer, Holder Krezida, and Holder-Apprentice Haydn were still yelling at one another, though the Holders were focused on each other, ignoring the young man. Chayyliel had joined in with both the mouth on the face and the two openings on its shoulders. Holder Riana was leaning back and watching.

Riana noticed them first, of course, followed by Chayyliel. Both went silent.

Liliana pushed past her, stumbling clumsily to the table they were gathered around. As she fell into the table, leaning her weight against it, Razel noticed the dark spots under her feet and tensed. She relaxed as she realized they were not the nothingness; these pulsed with life. She saw the gaps and realized that the Nif were working together, cushioning the girl's raw and ragged feet.

Mayer spoke first.

"Lil, what happened? Didn't Thiot get there in time?" He moved around the table, holding out his hands to his Apprentice. Her hand shook as she held it up to stop him.

"Where are my sibs?" She did not look at Mayer but at Chayyliel as she voiced the question.

"How am I to know?" The mouths on its shoulders stayed silent but frowning.

"I sent them off to safety with members of your House and Court. Now they are gone, as is Thiot. Where are my sibs?"

Razel took a step back. It was a question but not truly. Her tone demanded answers and she doubted that Chayyliel would take it well. The Ante stared at Liliana for a time and was silent. Razel held her breath. He could kill her right now, and she could offer little resistance. It would depend if Mayer was willing to defend her.

Instead of the swift death that Razel expected to witness, Chayyliel's unnatural stillness broke and it turned to face the two Antes guarding the door they'd entered through. Liliana started as if she had not seen them when she passed. Razel was not surprised; the young woman was running on shock and adrenaline, she could see it in the way the girl's hands shook, the way her eyes were unfocused and glazed, the slowness of her reactions.

The Ante who came forward was tiny, half the size of herself. Short enough to only come up to her waist and unnaturally slim. His skin was a pale pink with bright red undertones, in places the color striated so much it looked like exposed muscle. The only feature on its face was the small black pinhole for a mouth.

A Turms.

Chayyliel leaned down and whispered to the other Ante and the little one tilted its head to the side, listening, before tilting its head back and whistling out an odd tune. Chayyliel nodded and looked up.

"Your sibs are safe at the Ruling Courts."

What little color had been there drained from Liliana's face and Razel had to hold herself back from moving forward and offering her sympathies. The idea of safety for a 'dant in the Ruling Courts was laughable and terrifying.

Liliana said nothing and Mayer finally looked to Razel.

"What happened?"

Razel pointedly looked at Riana and waited until the woman nodded before she spoke. She was not Mayer's and it would be best if he remembered that. The sour twist of his mouth said he did.

"She came down Gotha with two other children. Street kids by the look of them. They were almost to the door when the creeping dark appeared and attacked. The two others were devoured. She made it and some of it shattered against the Athenaeum doors."

No one said anything, simply looked at one another. Silence swallowed the room.

LIL

Lil felt her cheeks grow wet as the other young woman called Wade and Antny street kids; such a way to brush off two lives. They had been brothers and they might have become her friends and they were dead because of her.

There was silence, and Lil slipped just a little bit further into the muffled tunnel that made everything easier to deal with.

Suddenly someone was pulling her. She went limp and would not move.

"Lil, you must rest."

"Yes, child."

"In the morning—" She recognized the first voice as Mayer's but the rest simply slid away as unrecognizable.

"I will not rest until I have Min and Davi with me." Her voice shook and she could still taste blood when she spoke, her whole body ached, her throat from the Babel she had used, her muscles from the desperate shoeless flight through the city.

Through the long divide with her parents she'd always imagined it to be temporary, that at some point in the not-too-distant future they would be family again. She had clung through the sick feeling of hurt that rose in her stomach when her father flinched from her or her mother rescued Davi from holding onto her knee.

These would now forever be the memories she had of her parents.

The voices had started again, but she'd retreated too far down the tunnel and could only hear them as mumbling echoes. Occasionally someone tried halfheartedly to get her to move but she would not. The care of her sibs was the last thing her parents had trusted her with.

Chayyliel's voice broke through to her, layered with all its voices.

"We intended to move all Holders and their Holder-Apprentices to the Ruling Courts in the morning. I see no harm in doing so a couple hours early. Already Yanwan begins to rise and the creeping dark retreats."

Voices rose up in argument and Lil let herself fade away again. It did not seem they had known of what was happening. She had and she understood the danger.

She did not care.

She glanced around, barely seeing anyone until her eyes lit on the woman who had guided her through the Athenaeum, Holder-Apprentice Razel. Even with the traditional Apprentice tunic and pants turned into a jumpsuit, Lil recognized her. She looked at Razel's right arm. The lower half of her arm ended six inches below the elbow. Where the dark brown skin ended, an arm and hand of silver and red was attached.

Her torc of office, altered and repurposed.

She met the woman's black eyes and Razel nodded at her.

Lil was drowning inside, knew that if she lost it completely she would pass out, and she could not allow that to happen. She focused on Razel, took in the girl's dark eyes that were staring into her own, looked at the hair, curlier and thicker but much shorter than hers. Razel's warm, dark mahogany skin glowed against the white of her outfit and showed off the small scars that littered her exposed skin, a small burn on one finger, a line down the side of her face, another disappearing into the collar. She was covered in scars and Lil wanted to touch them, feel the rough smoothness beneath her fingers, the new pink ones and the ones so faded they were almost invisible. She was the same height as Lil but wider, with muscles and curves that pressed against the fabric of her clothing as opposed to Lil's straight up-and-down frame.

She met Lil's gaze with no hesitation or fear but instead with a confidence that seared through Lil's body. She looked like a 'dant who got things done, one who was never afraid, who faced challenges but did not let them stop her in the least. She looked like the kind of girl Lil wanted to be, one who did not care if her parents feared her, did not care about what others thought or said.

Lil looked away as there was another tug on her. She resisted before Mayer's voice came to her. "Come along, Lil. We are all going to the Ruling Courts." She heard the reluctance and strained anger in his voice and knew that he spoke the truth. Assured that she would see her sibs soon, she gave in and let the grayness enfold her.

MAYER

Mayer did not often allow himself the luxury of anger; it was sloppy and led to mistakes. However, tonight the anger was at himself and no matter how he tried to ignore it, it still reared up in him. He had known of the danger and still sent Lil home. The oracles had been screaming for weeks that Zebub would be the next to be attacked. He should have spoken to her about the darkness that was attacking other cities. She had read many of the books in the library more recently than himself and made interesting leaps of logic at times. His current theory was an attack from another dimension; there were rumors of smaller universes that stronger Antes had spun off from this one. Many of the books were from these other dimensions, traded for with the Ruling Courts.

He looked at his Apprentice's limp form and sighed.

The meeting was meant to be Holders only, but he should have never trusted Riana and Krezida to leave their Apprentices at the Athenaeums on their own. Still, he looked over at his Apprentice, her head leaning against the warm wall of the crike's body, her form swaying with the movement, eyes open and staring straight ahead.

Something had changed in the girl this evening. Even in her shock he could feel it. He had taken her for her early proficiency in Babel. Her own excelling in the language had pushed him harder and faster to stay ahead of her, to stay in control. He was sharper than he had been in centuries and she was the best Apprentice he could hope for—studious and meek. He liked her; she would never challenge him.

The other Holder-Apprentices watched her, the Hypatia girl openly and the Enheduanna boy with a sad attempt at stealth. Riana and Krezida were silent and reading, the former from an electronic device, the later from a book that looked worse than even the oldest book at Kandake.

"What do you look at?"

The girl simply turned to meet his eyes while the pale boy jumped in his seat and too late tried to turn his eyes to his lap.

"She is interesting. Unexpected."

The girl turned her eyes back to his Apprentice, having said all she intended to, apparently. The boy was still looking down at his lap, eyes hidden by his fall of brown, limp hair. Mayer did not believe the act for a second; he'd heard the rumors about the boy. He narrowed his eyes until the boy nervously rose and crossed to sit closer to his Holder.

"Apprentice Liliana." He snapped it.

". . . Yes, Holder."

The response was slow and loose but appropriate. He was glad.

"What happened this evening?"

From forward in the crike, Chayyliel's head turned 180 degrees to stare at them. Lil sighed and her body became straighter.

"Something came, something hungry and dark and it froze us. I freed us with Babel and then we tried to get away. My parents did not make it."

There was more, details she wasn't sharing. Some that might be important, but he was wary of pushing her too far this evening and breaking her apart. He would be tested in the coming days not just by the creeping dark, but also by his fellow Holders and by the Ruling Courts, and a broken Apprentice would do him no good.

He watched as she slumped into her vacant stare again.

The trip from the Athenaeum to the Ruling Courts was swift. Kandake was the closest Athenaeum to the city center. In the distance he saw some small plumes of flame. People trying to put the creeping dark to the torch? Fire would do no good.

His breath caught in his chest as it always did when he entered the shadows of the Hives. There were eleven arranged in an uneven circle, all of them towering masses that spread into the lightening sky. That was all they had in common, though; one looked carved out of a single black stone, outcroppings that frowned and moved and crawled along its surface. Another Hive, one of the oldest, belonging to the Court of Sorrow and Riches, sprouted pink and fleshed from the land as if growing, several tendrils of it flowing from the ground and rising twinning and branching and pulsing into the sky. Some were beautiful, as the one that resembled a forest of blue foliage grown into a spiral that rose ever-thinner and higher into the sky. Some were simply puzzling to his mind, such as the shaft of light that throbbed in a beat along its bulbous sections and levels.

They were all deadly. Some even showed it on the outside, like the Hive composed of a humping mass of knives shifting and piercing each other regularly.

This was far from his first time here, but he had never brought Lil before. He looked over to gauge her reaction but it was if her eyes saw none of it.

He turned back as the crike passed under the huge arch of metal and jewels that represented the current Courts. There were other more dangerous gaps to enter the circle through, places where Hives had once stood before being burned down or cut off, gaps where allied Courts had built their Hives nearer to one another in the circle. A stupid fancy. No alliances lasted in the Courts.

There was a touch on his arm and he started, yanking away from Riana's hand. Foolish of him to get distracted—what if it had been Krezida who touched him?

Riana simply nodded out the other side of the crike and he followed her gaze to the two sites of new construction. Two new Hives going up. He wondered which factions had made enough of a play to be elevated and who would be leading them. If they survived the building, there would be thirteen Courts before long.

An auspicious number.

Though anyone's guess how long it would last.

He roused Lil as the crike came to a halt and lowered itself to the ground. She followed, her eyes finally bright with awareness, scanning the busy space inside the circle of the towers. Yanwan rose bright above them, setting some of the Hives alight with brilliant halos.

Suddenly there was a scream, barely recognizable as Lil's name, and two tiny streaks came barreling out of the shadow to the right. Mayer was turning, ready to speak, Riana had a weapon of some kind in her hand, while Krezida was secreting something back into her jacket.

It was two 'dant children. The girl was darker than Lil, her skin a walnut rather than the topaz brown of Lil's face, thick black curls rather than the dark brown of Lil. The youngest's skin was somewhere between the two of them, a sepia that set off the red tones in his tight mahogany curls. Their faces were the same, same chin and nose, same sense of loss haunting their eyes. Lil crouched down and they wrapped themselves around her, the girl babbling a mile a minute, the boy simply burying his face in Lil's neck. She held them and rocked them, and her strength seemed to leave her all at once. Two figures emerged from the same darkness that the children had.

Mayer recognized Arel and Jagi as they caught Lil before she could crumble to the ground. He only hoped she would be recovered by morning; they had much work to do and no time for distractions. He frowned at the two children still clinging to his Apprentice.

San Jose Public Library

Seven Trees Branch
3590 Cas Drive
(408) 808-3056 or (408) 808-2000
sjpl.org

Checked Out Items 12/9/2017 13:56
XXXXXXXXX0605

Item Title	Due Date
The root : a novel of the wrath & athenaeum / Na'amen Gobert Tilahun. 31197007604065	1/3/2018

Total Items: 1

24 Hour Renewal
(408) 808-2665

Excellence in School
Begins with your SJ Library!
sjpl.org/StudentHelp

Facebook.com/sanjoselibrary
Twitter.com/sanjoselibrary

SAN FRANCISCO

TAE

Erik was not what he had expected. He was a mix of wariness
and desperation for friendship. His betrayals hung in the air for
everyone to see. His mission would just be seen as another one,
as would Tae's lies. He did need more training in the physical
side of combat but his prodigious Ophde abilities were more than
enough to compensate. He felt bad for lying to Erik and Melinda,
but he had enough friends and some of them were in trouble. If
Maestra Luka said this would help them, he would do it.

Erik was not cooperating, though. He was smarter than Tae
had expected. The research he had done had told him that berserkers were often not . . . intellectually gifted. The focus of their
power usually turned them away from academic pursuits and
made them easy to befriend and easy to fool. However, the way
Erik watched him, even now, closely, not missing an expression
on his face, spoke of someone who didn't trust easily. He was
happy to treat Tae as a friend but he never really relaxed.

After a few more minutes of talking, Tae yawned widely and
told them he was off to take a nap. He stepped out into the hall
and ran into Maestra Luka. She gestured for him to follow and
he entered her bedroom, glancing both ways to make sure they
were not seen. While the other bedrooms in the place were identical, Maestra Luka's was twice the size and covered in elaborate
decorations. The walls were a bright, cheery yellow and the four-
poster bed had bedding and drapes in a lighter shade. Hangings
were placed at regular intervals around the room. In one corner,
an old oak bookshelf sat filled to overflowing.

"What do you think?"

"I think that harming him would be a huge mistake and nearly impossible."

"A mistake. Why?"

Tae sat on the chair facing the bed. She watched him from the mattress and crossed her legs.

"As I said, I have very little confidence a strike will succeed, and if it did it would be taking out one of our potentially most effective weapons against the Angelics. It would also turn Matthias and the rest of the independents more firmly against the Organization. Even if you were able to keep any stink of it being an Organization job quiet, Matthias would always suspect and would be more likely to work against us."

Maestra Luka sighed, but it was not a sigh of disappointment; more of confirmation, as if Tae was only telling her things she already knew.

"Some of the other Maestres wanted this option explored. I was not one of them."

"Why would they want this?" Tae asked. He wasn't naive enough to think the Maestres wouldn't get rid of someone who made themself a problem, but as far as he knew Erik had done nothing.

Luka was silent for a time, staring at one of the tapestries hanging from the wall. Tae turned. It was a depiction of the Sundering, the war that had killed Ophde and the other old ones, their forebears. The slaughtering of them by some of their children. The hunting of the bloodlines who would not turn and the curse and exile of the Angelics from this plane.

"Things are moving. The oracles have seen darkness on the horizon, but every time they try to focus and get specific, they slip into unconsciousness. The Angelics have been coming through and harassing us more and more often, taking more Blooded. Erik is a powerful new piece on the board. Many are unsure how he will affect everything."

"To get rid of someone simply because they *might* act against your interests seems most wasteful." He did not say what he wanted to, which was that it sounded like something an Angelic would decide to do. He could not keep the disgust from his eyes completely, though he dared not voice it. There was no way to know from which Maestre the idea had started. Even perhaps his own father.

"I agree. For now, continue to observe, and if you find a way to make him more sympathetic to the Organization, do so."

Tae nodded and rose to leave. He let out a long breath as he stepped into the hallway. He would do as she asked . . . until a better option presented itself. Sometimes the crosses and double-crosses and triple-crosses—all for the greater good—made his head spin, but what good was seeing possible futures if you didn't try to guide everything to the best option? But it was hard. Especially as the details got fuzzier and fuzzier farther out. Something big was coming. Something with the Angelics, as Luka said, but Tae knew more than that.

In all of his visions, there were four people who would be crucial to the fight. Their faces had been shrouded, always invisible to him. Except for today. He had recognized Erik as one of them.

The child Melinda as another.

He would continue to work all the sides he could until more information became clear. For now, Tae retired to his own plain room to sleep off the migraine that filled his whole world.

ERIK

Erik choked back nausea as they were led into the odd white room by their Counselors. Melinda and Tae were not doing any better. The Counselors had gone pale though they still walked with a steady gait.

"This is the training room." It was Elana who spoke, the only one who looked completely unaffected by the room. "You will notice that gravity is decreased here. The gravitational pulls also have a tendency to change direction and strength on a whim. You will train until you can handle this. One of the Angelics' favorite tricks is to change the angle of attack so that from your perspective you're now fighting upside down or from left to right. They've shown this ability across bloodlines, so we think it's something artificial.

"This will help you get used to the sensation so it doesn't take you out immediately. Demonstration." She clapped her hands, though there was no actual sound. Matthias and Daya stepped forward. Before their eyes Matthias blurred and faded into the wall. Daya's own olive-tinted skin became darker and grayer, more like concrete. Her face became less human and more of an abstract statue, with her features more hints than anything solid or distinct.

Erik shivered but remembered that Matthias was her target. Daya's head swung left to right, trying to locate Matthias. The audience followed her lead, trying to find him as well. They only noticed him on her back when Daya jerked around, trying to reach him. She almost caught him but he dropped from her back and Erik lost sight of him again. Daya leapt into the air, hit the ceiling, and stayed there. Erik was suddenly aware of how nauseated he was, as if he were hanging upside down. Melinda gasped and staggered into Erik, who steadied her with a hand on the shoulder.

Something dropped up? down? to Daya, only visible in the seconds before it faded again. It was enough for Daya to lunge forward. She grunted as something connected with her back. She swung around and her arms jarred as if they hit something.

"Okay, enough." Elana clapped again and again there was no sound.

The world around them shifted again. They were back on the ground now and Erik's stomach finally started to settle down. Daya and Matthias dropped down in front of them and let their powers fade away.

Elana turned to face the kids.

"You must learn to do that, to think on your feet, to analyze a battle to discover if it is better to fight or run. Most of the time running is better. Surviving is better. Tae, you'll be working with Daya and Elliot. Patrah will be working with Melinda. Matthias and I will be working with Erik."

They all separated and Erik noticed Luka and Hu entering. They stood near the door, arms crossed, watching.

Erik, Matthias, and Elana were nearest to them.

"Erik, the thing I think we should work on is getting you to drop in and out of your power on command. You have to find a visualization that works for you," Elana said. Matthias nodded.

"How do you feel when you're using your power?" Matthias asked.

Erik thought about it. "Confident, powerful, like I can take on anyone."

"Is there a physical feeling that goes along with that?"

"Yeah, like a fire in my chest that spreads out all over me, under my skin."

"Okay, well, let's have you try to visualize that right now," Elana asked.

Erik pondered the question. He closed his eyes and felt inside for the heat that burned in his chest. He found it easily; it was small right now, more a spark.

"Do you have it?"

"Maybe?"

He remembered with his whole body, the shaking of his fists, the flush of heat filling his face. It came slowly, filling him with joy. His eyes snapped open and Matthias and Elana already seemed to know. They were both smiling at him, not that their approval mattered at all. When he was like this nothing anyone said mattered; he was the only validation he needed.

Then he looked over at Melinda. She was sitting with Patrah. Luka and Hu were walking over to them. He narrowed his eyes at the two Maestres. Then Hu smiled and crouched down to put his hands on Melinda's shoulders and something about the way he touched her, the ownership in that clench of fingers.

Erik was convinced Hu was a threat and he acted.

MAESTRA LUKA

Most Blooded suffered from some physical change when invoking the power in their bones and going full-blood. For some it was as small as a change of eye color, for others, like Daya, their whole countenance changed. So it took Luka longer than normal to realize that Erik's power was live and boiling off of him as he approached, eyes trained on Hu. The young man looked exactly as he had since she had met him. The same short and stocky build. The same shaved head and same deep brown skin with heavy bags under his eyes.

Those eyes were wide, nearly all pupil, as if high on Angelic blood. His lips were curled into a smile. The corners seemed wider than any mouth should be, more along the lines of a toad rather than human. It was the absolute joy radiating from his smile and eyes that worried her the most. She had no doubt he would enjoy perpetuating whatever violence he was thinking of.

The thinking was what scared Luka the most. In her time on this earth she had observed nine berserkers in controlled and uncontrolled circumstances, and always they had been bodies moving on instinct. They relied on whatever their last thought was before acting and did not stop until that goal was completed. Erik was looking at them with awareness—in fact, he had stopped approaching and was now watching them both.

Planning.

All other activity in the room had stopped and they all watched him, except for Hu, Melinda, and Patrah, who were speaking and had not noticed his approach or the silence.

"Did you ask her if she wanted to be touched?" His voice was nearly the same; lower and rougher.

Hu finally looked up and Luka noticed the discomfort on Melinda's face, the way she tried to shrug Hu's hands off her shoulders.

"Mellie is a child."

This only made Erik angrier and he came closer.

"That doesn't mean you have the right to touch her. In fact, that makes it even more important that she decides whether she wants to be touched or not." Luka studied his words. There was some trauma lurking inside of them. This wasn't just about Melinda; this was about his past.

Hu stood and made the mistake of taking a step into Erik's personal space. The Counselors stepped before their charges, but Erik was not even acknowledging that there were people in the room other than Hu. Elana and Matthias were close behind Erik, ready to intervene but anxious to see him in action. They trusted the Maestro to protect himself.

Erik was an unknown, though, and more than one Maestre had been taken out by underestimating an opponent based on similarities. Luka knew it would fall to her to save Hu from his own stupidity if necessary. Luka started to call her power up from her core, smiling with the odd lightness and burst of joy that accompanied it. Light built up under her skin, making her translucent. The particles of light in the room tickled her, rushing closer and closer as they tried to combine with the light coruscating from her body. Hu was mid transformation, rising up on his back legs, turning into an almost a ten-foot-tall polar bear.

With an uncomfortably human-looking face.

Erik stopped, tracking both of their forms now. The gold light she was radiating made odd shadows circle around the room. Erik crouched, hands loose on his knees. Faster than Luka could track, he was flying through the air. She ducked to the side and sent a blinding flash of light into the space where she had been.

But he had anticipated her movement and crashed into her.

It was like being hit by a freight train. She grunted at the impact and Erik screamed, his skin burning on contact with hers. He scrambled away and Luka pushed herself along the floor. The skin where they had touched on his body was black and flaking. He hissed at her and then rose to his feet again. Hu tried to swipe at him but Erik was too fast and did something that made Hu roar in pain before he backed out of the bear's range. Hu's form was less than useful in this fight and she saw him begin to shift again.

Even as she saw this, Erik's eyes were shooting back and forth between them in a way that made her nervous. Matthias simply watched, arms crossed, smile threatening to break out on his face, while Elana hovered uncertainly. Hu was shrinking when Erik moved again, ripping his shirt from his body.

Now Luka could see the form change to his body; across his torso, strips of skin were no longer their natural healthy brown but looked inflamed and red. They pulsed with something underneath. Before she could discern why he would show them this, he was moving again. Luka spun illusions of herself across the room, all of them identical, but Erik didn't pause, blowing right through one and springing from the wall directly toward her. Only as she saw his outstretched hands were covered in wrapped fabric did she realize the danger and his plan.

"Hu!—"

The rest of her warning was smothered by the large palm covered in sweat-funky fabric that came down over her face. His other hand grabbed her torso and she was flying through the air. There was a loud scream as she landed but it was not her, too stunned by the impact to even speak. Her vision was suddenly filled with Elana, standing between her and the approaching Erik.

She was speaking quickly and soothingly but Luka could make out no words, the ringing in her ears too much. Then Matthias was between Elana and his aspirant and Erik stopped immediately. He observed Matthias and then glanced behind him to Hu and Luka.

As feeling came back to her body, she saw the marks on Erik's torso fade to their usual chestnut hue and his stance change. The smile slipped from his face, becoming a somber mask he used to observe the scene before him.

"Did you see enough?" He directed this to Matthias and Elana.

"You . . ." Luka paused to cough as her light faded and Patrah and Daya helped her to her feet. Melinda took it as an opportunity to run to Erik and grab his hand. He leaned down and she could not hear the quick, whispered conversation over her own body clearing itself of its recent trauma. "You remember what happened?"

Erik looked up at her and his back became straighter.

"Of course I do. It's not like I go completely blank. It used to feel weird and jerky, as if time was skipping, but that fades more and more each time. Now it's more that the urges come and they feel like the perfect choices." Everyone was silent and Erik finally looked around. "Is that odd?"

"Only in that it's different from what every other berserker has reported." Elliot noted with a smirk.

"Doesn't actually mean it's unique," Matthias spoke up. "Not every one tells the Organization everything. And vice-versa."

"How did you see through my illusions?" Luka asked. Her illusions were reality quality; they could even fool the smell and touch of most non-Blooded.

"They felt wrong, like the energy there wasn't wrapped around anything real."

"The energy?"

"Yeah, it was like I could feel what they were made of and you were the one that was different."

"Interesting."

"Not that I'm not enjoying the third degree," Erik said, "but shouldn't one of you be worried about and/or checking on that guy?" He jerked his chin behind Luka and she realized the ringing in her head was not damage but a constant high-pitched whine. Hu was on the ground, convulsing, caught mid transformation into some sort of big cat. Some pieces looked human but others were twisted limbs somewhere in between. His neck was shortened and a ragged ruff of fur sprouted around his head. He smelled horrible, patches of skin and fur burnt where she had touched him. Even as she watched, though, parts of him were slowly becoming more human.

"Yes, let's get him to his room."

Patrah, Elliot, and Daya stepped forward, lifting the burnt man/cat/thing that was Hu. He whimpered with each jostle as they carried him from the room, and she was left alone with everyone else, her strength slowly returning.

"Why did you use me as a weapon against Hu?" she asked.

Erik answered easily. "'Cause you burned when I touched you that first time." At the reminder he looked down at his previously blackened skin to find patches of paler brown new skin peeking out from where it had flaked away.

"That's why you wrapped your hands with your shirt?"

Now he looked at her as if she were stupid. "Yeah." The "dumbass" was implied.

Luka simply hummed in response and the rest of them looked at her before beginning to speak among themselves.

She had learned much of Erik in the past few minutes and it made her more nervous. The fact that he could reason in the midst of fighting, it meant that he wasn't simply the mindless tank they had thought him to be in this continuing war. Not something they could point at an enemy and let loose. He had also stopped when confronted with Matthias. Did that mean he already felt enough loyalty to the man that he would not attack? Even in a rage? Or was it simply a sign of this better control he displayed? More control than anyone could expect.

His bloodline suddenly became a priority. She had to know what Old One he sprung from, how strong he might be, and especially his weaknesses.

She had only been hurt as a consequence of being used against Hu. Something in that man, his actions toward Melinda, had made Erik hate him. She knew why Erik disliked them both; very few young adults did well with patronizing older people telling them what to do. Despite the extraordinary control and ability to reason, he was still deeply driven by instincts while berserking and something in or about Hu had triggered an all-out attack from the young man.

She would have to watch them both in the future.

MAESTRO HU

The pain was so intense he could not even catch enough breath to scream, only gasp. It felt as if every part of him was being pulled apart molecule by molecule and then reassembled. Randomly. His right leg was whole, human and aching, but his left was still twisted into a back haunch and the muscles burned. Worst of all was his head, which felt like a hangover to shatter the world, his thoughts pulled between animal and human. He whimpered as he was lifted into the air and then jostled as he was carried.

He could hear voices over him and he concentrated on them to distract himself.

". . . would work?"

". . . no idea . . . Matthias already . . ."

". . . not the only one with a hold . . ."

He couldn't follow the conversation. He suspected his ears were not completely human and so were too easily distracted by sounds in the walls and the earth, small mammals moving that his animal ears were more interested in tracking. The sides of his head felt hollow and empty but he was slowly filling in, fading back to human, even if each piece burned like fire upon its return.

When he came to himself he was laid on his bed. He groaned and moved his legs around.

The pain was not as bad as it had been and he could think about what he had learned. This Errikos Allan was going to be a problem. His presence could change everything; the balance was already changing as the Angelics pressed them; any more issues could lead to chaos. He had no ties to the Organization and thus would have no problem disrupting their plans for the young dream-walker. But what to do about it?

He would have to talk to his friends, the other Maestres who agreed with him. They would be interested in this development. Together they would come up with a plan to deal with Erik. Perhaps they could also deal with Matthias. He was a loose end that needed tying up.

ERIK

Erik spent the rest of the afternoon in meditation, bringing on the rage at will and letting it fade away. By the end of the day he was exhausted but confident in his ability to bring on his rages whenever he wanted. Calming it was harder, and his nerves jangled from pulling his power up so often with no physical outlet.

"Good job. Tomorrow we'll focus on this in the morning and then forms and fighting styles in the afternoon. Dinner will be in an hour, so why don't you take some free time till then."

Erik smiled and rose immediately. He needed to move, to burn off some of this energy that flowed through him. The most torturous part of the practice had been sitting still. He moved past Tae, who was sparring with Daya, and Melinda, who was sitting with Patrah, both looking deep in sleep. He exited the training room and immediately his eyes began to water. So much unrelenting white for so long; his eyes were over-stimulated by the gray of the hallway.

He leaned against the door and blinked his eyes a few times to clear them before heading to his room. After a quick search, he found his cell phone in the drawer of the nightstand and dialed his mom's number. As it rang he paced the floor.

"You've reached the voice mail of artist Dayida Jayl. If this is about a commission, please contact me via my website www.djayl.com. If not, please leave a detailed message and I'll return your call at my convenience."

Beep.

"Hey Mama, it's me. I just wanted to let you know I'm okay. I'm training with Matthias this weekend so I'll be back on Monday. I hope Robert isn't acting too much . . . like himself. I have a lot of questions. Love you. Bye."

It wasn't unusual for his mom to not hear the phone when she was working on a painting. After he disconnected, he took a deep breath and dialed another number by heart.

It was a bad choice. He knew that, no use pretending otherwise, but just the chance of talking to Daniel calmed him down. The phone rang repeatedly before it also went to voice mail.

"This is Daniel. If you have this number you know I might not be able to get back to you for a while. Leave a message, I'll do what I can. Don't text me."

It always went to voice mail.

"Hey Daniel, it's Erik again. Um . . . I hope you're doing okay. I know it must be horrible but I want you to know I'm still here. Even if you just want to be friends. Or if you don't want me to call you anymore. . . just call and let me know. I'd just. . . like to hear your voice."

He took a deep breath.

"I'm sorry."

Then he hung up and threw the phone at the wall. The crack was both immensely satisfying and caused a large swell of disappointment in his gut. If he'd broken it, he'd just destroyed his one means of independent communication for the rest of the weekend. He didn't have it in him to check right now, so instead he curled up on the bed and allowed himself to fall into a restless, intermittent sleep.

He was woken by a knocking at his door. He stood and took a moment to remember where he was and everything that had happened. When he was no longer thinking through a film of confusion and sleep, he opened the door. Patrah stood on the other side.

"Dinner is being served in the cafeteria. If you don't want to eat with us, you can come fix a plate."

Erik was far from sure that he wanted to eat with a large group right now, but he nodded anyway. They had given him an out and he would take it if necessary. He thought of changing his clothes for a second, since he'd wrinkled and wrecked these through exercise and sleep, but he couldn't bring himself to care.

He followed the shorter, plump woman down the hall. She moved like a cat, silent even with the heavy boots she wore. The cafeteria had changed. Instead of the smattering of smaller and larger tables that had littered it before, there was one large oval table with the surface a mosaic of different shades of white. Everyone else was seated around it: Hu and Luka side by side, an empty seat next to Luka, then Melinda, followed by Daya, Elana, Elliot, Tae, another empty seat, then Matthias and Hu. The room was silent, as if they were all waiting for him and Patrah.

No one was dressed up but the way they sat screamed formal. He was suddenly very uncomfortable. He didn't do well with formality. He was too blunt, unable to navigate false humility and smugness at these kinds of things. Back in Hollywood, Daniel had always been able to calm him down and make sure he had fun instead of being uncomfortable all night. Even though they'd been forced to attend as "friends" and nothing more.

Thinking of Daniel was not helping Erik relax, and he wanted nothing more now than to go back in time and refuse dinner. He had assumed when Patrah invited him that it would be a much more casual affair, but everyone with the exception of himself and Melinda looked solemn. As he carefully sat between Elliot and Matthias, Erik caught Melinda's eyes, tight and nervous. She could feel the tension in the air as well as anyone. He smiled at her.

As soon as Patrah circled the table and sat, the lights dimmed, not enough to make visibility difficult, but it still made Erik jumpy.

"We gather in secret—" Hu began.

"—where once we danced in the light," Luka continued.

"We protect the world in silence—"

"—where once we sang openly."

"We stand against the dark alone—"

"—abandoned by those we once called sibling."

"We shall not be stopped—"

"—though faced with odds innumerable."

"We are the children of the sky—"

"—and the earth,"

"—the day—"

"—and the night—"

"—the love—"

"—and the indifference."

"We stand as—"

"—the light, the hope, the everything. We are the Blooded and we shall not falter."

Everyone around the table aside from Erik and Melinda had their heads bowed. They were so still that he was unsure they were still breathing. Then it ended; they all inhaled in unison and looked up. Melinda looked at him with crossed eyes but there was no true worry in her face.

Erik was wary of organized religion of any kind, and had been his whole life. It was worse during the trial when every talking head with some vague connection to religion had commented on him, or worse, tried to contact him so they could save his soul.

It was the uniformity of their prayer that unnerved him the most.

Prayer . . . poem . . . whatever. The fact that Matthias, who agreed on nothing with these people, would join in was extremely disconcerting.

Dishes floated out through a portal that appeared in the wall and landed in front of them. The covers disappeared and Erik was confronted with his favorite meal. Roast duck with farfalle and asparagus. He was tentative with the first bite. It didn't taste off at all. In fact, the duck was perfectly crisp on the outside and moist on the inside. Around him everyone else was digging into the different foods that had appeared before them. As he cleaned his plate, another one floated from the portal and landed in front of him, revealing the same meal again.

Conversations started around the table and Tae turned to him, talking over Elliot, who was sharing a joke with his translucent sister.

"How are you feeling, Errikos?"

Erik started a bit. Only his mom used his full first name and he was sure he hadn't mentioned it. It was a shock to hear someone else wrap their voice around it.

"Call me Erik." Tae smiled like it was a gesture of friendship and Erik didn't have the energy to correct him. "I'm fine, I was just tired. A nap took care of it."

Tae nodded and looked at him expectantly and Erik finally took the hint.

"And yourself?"

"I'm finding the third form of Rav-Selet to be very difficult. Especially when training with people who've been doing it for years. Would you be up for sparring? After dinner perhaps?" Tae answered, looking down and taking a bite of what looked like some sort of seafood pasta.

"Why me? I don't even know the forms."

Matthias had stopped stuffing his face with what looked like shepherd's pie and sat still. The others who had heard the exchange, Hu and Elliot, had also stopped to listen.

"But you do."

"Huh?" He looked at Matthias in confusion.

Matthias sighed and faced him. "While in your power you were using bits and pieces of the different levels of Rav-Selet."

"Advanced forms."

Matthias shot a look at the young man. "Yes, thank you, Tae."

Tae seemed immune to the censure in his gaze. Erik was beginning to think that the dislike and animosity between the Organization and independents was more than he was lead to believe. The friendship between Daya, Elliot, Elana, Patrah, and Matthias might be the exception rather than the rule.

"We all assumed your mother had been training you in the forms?" Tae continued.

Hu and Elliot nodded. Did that mean that they had been thinking the same thing or were they saying that they had all spoken about him when he was absent?

"Was that not the case?" Hu asked.

Erik began to shake his head and then nodded and finally just paused. He realized she had in fact been teaching him, all of the meditation exercises, the forms she had made him move his body into. All of it had been for this. Yeah, he had a lot of questions for his mom and he didn't want to give away anything until he had a chance to talk to her. Erik settled on shrugging his shoulders and directed his gaze down into his dinner plate, shoveling mouthfuls of duck between his lips. From the corner of his eye he could see Matthias begin to eat again as well. They were going to have to have a talk about secrets in the near future.

Tae broke the silence. "In any case, sparring after dinner? It would help our food digest."

Erik turned to look at the boy. There was something in his eyes, some spark of mischief. Was he deliberately baiting Erik or was it something else? Either way, Erik shook his head.

"Not this weekend, perhaps next when I am more settled."

"Of course." Tae's smile was a bit disappointed but he simply went back to his food and did not try to press his point, which Erik appreciated.

The rest of dinner was mostly quiet. Hu and Luka occasionally brought up details about the Organization and current missions.

NA'AMEN GOBERT TILAHUN

Matthias mostly chimed in with a sarcastic comment here and there, most of which were ignored. Erik listened. A lot of the details went over his head and he wasn't able to learn anything he hadn't already been able to infer.

Erik's exhaustion crept up on him again and he excused himself to go to bed. If his early departure offended anyone, either they didn't show it or he was just too tired to parse it. He wandered back to his room and fell asleep above the covers, clothes still on.

That night he dreamed.

He was fighting something he could not see. In fact, he could see nothing at all but he could feel it, the pervasive nagging shoulder itch of being watched, the grief of knowing that he could not win, the choking fear that someone he loved was dead. He brushed up against other fighting forms in the darkness and smelled the fresh, salty sea scent of Matthias, the crisp metal of Tae, the combination of smoky incense and child that made up Melinda's scent. Then others; people he didn't know. The scent of fresh blood and the smell of icy wind; a smell that reminded him of corruption and rotting compost heaps.

Slowly the scents were taken away until he was all alone. He was bloody and tired but he was alone now and he could not stop fighting. To stop fighting was to let everything and everyone die.

He had to keep fighting.

For the world.

ZEBUB

LIL

il woke up in a strange place. The room didn't smell of life and of sweat and blood like her family's building did; neither did it carry Kandake's scent of old wood and sandstone. Her eyes snapped open and she took in the dark black stone of the roof. The only thing that stopped her from jerking upright was the two smaller bodies curled up against her. She could smell the still almost-baby scent of Davi and the musk of Min, who was in a non-bathing stage.

She lay still, allowing the awareness of everything that had happened last night to sink in. Tears welled up but she managed to quell them. Her parents were dead and they were all in danger. She could not afford to break down. She had already failed two young boys. She would not fail her sibs as well.

A knock on the door stopped her from wallowing in the thought of Wade and Antny. She managed to slide out of her sibs' grip, though they searched for her form and only calmed once they held onto each other.

She still wore her Apprentice tunic and pants from yesterday. They smelled of night and terror and blood but would have to do.

Mayer was outside the bedroom door, in the general living area with dozens of large cushions scattered around to sit upon. There was a full tea set steaming in the middle of the room. Mayer moved back and Lil stepped into the room, leaving the door open in case Min or Davi called for her. Before she could reach for the teapot, Holder Mayer grabbed it and poured for them both.

Lil froze.

"I apologize for sending you home last night, Apprentice."

She had no idea how to respond, but tried anyway. "There is no need for apologies, Holder." She slipped into more formal language to try and find grounding she knew. "If you had not sent me home there is no telling if my sibs would be alive right now." She paused. "What was it that attacked last night, Holder?"

Mayer gave her a shrewd look, aware of her attempt at distraction.

"It is not only Zebub that has been attacked."

Lil sat up straighter.

"The reason that Chayyliel wished to meet last night was due to reports that our allies were sending from across Corpiliu. Many places have been attacked in the last moon. Only now that they have failed to defeat it are they letting others know of the attacks."

"All the cities?"

"Not all, but enough. There is no correlation between places targeted. It seems random. The attacks are small as of yet but the only thing that seems to have any effect, albeit temporarily, is Babel. So we are safe here. Any building with Babel in its bones seems sacrosanct for now."

Lil's emotions flared at these attacks being called small. Many 'dants had lost their lives last night, perhaps across Corpiliu. Her parents had been lost. But that was it, 'dants did not matter to the Ruling Courts or to Mayer, apparently.

Mayer continued talking. "As for what it was, that's the reason we were brought here. There are mentions in the oldest of the records inside Kandake of the creeping dark, but mentions are all we have. The Ruling Courts have decided to allow us into the Ossuary so that we may find a way to stop it. Chayyliel has graciously allowed us to stay within the Hive of its Court."

Lil's eyes went wide though she was able to keep the rest of her face controlled. No one entered the Ossuary. Had not since the Traitor Court had been destroyed millennia ago. Rumor said that the Ossuary had been destroyed alongside them. Lil knew from Holder Mayer that before they were all killed, the Traitor Court had managed to seal the Ossuary completely against entrance by Antes. Since none of them could enter, no one was allowed to. After all, what 'dants would they trust?

They must be worried.

"But why would they think there was something in the Ossuary involving this creeping dark? Why not have us search the Athenaeums for more information? The attack only happened last night. Unless . . ."

She looked up at Mayer, his face blank, head tilted in interest.

"They have a clue what the creeping dark is and are sure there will be no information in any of Athenaeums," she guessed.

Mayer nodded.

"Except. You said we were safe because this building has Babel in its bones?"

Mayer nodded, but slowly, as if he saw the direction her thoughts went in.

"Yet, this Hive is the newest, is it not?"

He nodded again.

"So how does it have Babel in its bones?" There was only one answer but she hoped for something else, anything else.

"I laid the protections myself, in the foundation."

She studied the man who had for all intents bought her and trained her and raised her for the past twelve cycles. He was simply meeting her gaze casually, not angry at being caught out in a lie. He had always said he was never summoned to the Ruling Courts, but now she wondered. How often were her evenings away used for business he simply never shared with her?

His face dared her to venture further. She was still his Apprentice, she had no power. She nodded and took a sip of tea, hoping it hid her anger. He continued as if their exchange had never occurred.

"Do you understand now? Not only must we find out what the dark is, but the Ruling Courts will be wary of what we may learn and our fellow Holders will be looking for anything to give them leverage."

She looked back at her sibs worriedly.

"Yes."

Her head whipped back to Mayer as he spoke.

"You see the trouble. You cannot focus on our work and watch them at all times. Luckily, a solution has provided itself. The two members of Chayyliel's Court who escorted them last night have offered to act as guardians while we are in the Ossuary and for the duration of our stay."

Lil stood up and turned her back on him.

"Holder, are you serious? You say that we are all under threat from Antes while we stay here, yet you want me to leave my sibs in the care of the two Antes who brought us the horrible news."

She turned back and Mayer watched her with a focused stare of disappointment. She tried to calm herself and sat back down. She did her best to school her expression but knew some of her anger shone through.

"I know you have no reason to trust Chayyliel or its Court, but they argued to bring us in long before the other Ruling Courts wanted. They saw the signs and worried about the coming of the darkness. I truly believe Queen Chayyliel wishes to stop the creeping dark. Arel and Jagi are its vassals in charge of the Hive. If either wished to do us harm, they could do so easily."

Lil acknowledged the truth but was still not happy. Holder Mayer seemed to sense this and his voice grew harder, less cajoling, and his expression grew cold.

"And what other choice do you have, really? Would you leave them unguarded in the Hive, take them into the danger that is the Ossuary, or repudiate your obligations to me?"

Lil met his eyes for a long moment before she nodded, pretending any of this was her choice.

"I would still speak with them."

The coldness left his face so quickly anyone who did not know him as well as Lil might doubt they had seen it at all. She knew better.

Mayer smiled and nodded as he rose to his feet. "I'll get them."

He left and she hurried back into the bedroom.

There was a second door in the corner of the bedroom, which she discovered led to a small washroom. She cleaned up a little, scrubbing her face and trying to wash some of the filth from her hair in the sink. When she felt somewhat clean, she returned to the bed and gently shook Minnie and Davi awake. Usually they would be slow to rise, knuckling sleep from their eyes as they tossed aside the heavy mantle of their drowsiness. This morning they came up instantly, eyes wide and scared.

"Hey, it's okay, I'm here."

They were both tense but slowly relaxed under her petting hands and soothing murmurs.

When they were both awake and their attention was on her, she spoke.

"Okay, I need to ask you guys to be brave. Do you know where we are?"

"The Hives of the Ruling Courts." Minnie's voice wavered but her gaze was steady.

"Right. They brought us here so I could do some work for them but I don't want to leave you guys alone." They both shook their heads emphatically, Davi's small hands tightening painfully on her arm. "So I was wondering, what would you think of Arel and Jagi taking care of you while I'm busy?"

Both children went still and Davi transferred one of his hands to Minnie. Lil could not tell what they were feeling, the stiffness making it difficult to read their bodies or expressions.

"If you don't like them or they scare you, you can say so."

Slowly Minnie shook her head. "No, they were nice, just weird. They kept calling us 'little pups' but they gave us a lot of food."

Lil did not ask what kind of food because she did not want to know. The Antes were said to eat all kinds of specialties from the wastes and other, darker, harder-to-reach places. Other worlds and lands that her readings only hinted at. Things that most 'dants barely heard whisper of, but whispers were enough. They both seemed okay and that would have to be enough for her. She rose from the bed as she heard the door in the other room open.

"Stay here. I will be back soon," she murmured to her sibs and left the bedroom to face Mayer, Arel, and Jagi. She closed the bedroom door behind her. She needed to talk to Arel and Jagi, but she didn't want Mayer or her sibs standing there for what she was about to do.

"I am sorry, Holder, but this is not about Athenaeum business. This is personal, and I would like some privacy to speak with those you want me to entrust the care of my sibs to." Lil said it without thinking. She was still angry about the lies she had discovered, but she was not wrong. This was not Mayer's business and as such he had no place here unless she allowed it.

Mayer frowned but bowed his head.

"I will await you outside."

"Thank you."

He left without another word, but Lil fancied she could see the resentment in the stiffness of his walk. When the door had closed loudly behind him, she turned to face the two Antes. In the light streaming through the tinted windows she could see more of their forms than she had previously in the dim light of nightfall.

Only last night.

Her life had changed so much in such a short span of time.

They were not as pale as she had thought; their skin was not white but a soft-looking pebbled gray that shaded between light, dark, and iridescent. The blue and purple ropes were gone from their heads, revealing a thin stripe of wheat-colored hair that ran down the center of their skulls and the backs of their necks. A small crease centered above the normal two eyes marked where a third eye sat; other creases on the sides of their necks and running in a line down each side of their bare torsos hid other extras. Eyes or ears, wings or clawed arms? She had no idea.

They could be anything, but their bloodline often had cleansing tentacles, according to texts.

Arel was slightly taller than his fellow. In the light there were subtle differences in their shadings and markings. The patterns that led down their torsos were variations on the same basic shape.

She held out her hand palm up. "If you are to take care of my family I would have blood and a promise from both of you. Would you agree?"

Both hesitated, and she could not fault them. She asked for much and insulted the hospitality and protection of their Court. They both tilted their heads at her but she stood firm.

"They are the last of my bloodline."

Whatever emotions had creased their faces smoothed away and with no more hesitation they reached for the belt knives on their left sides. They both made shallow slices in their palms and then looked at her in question.

"Three drops each."

They nodded and carefully let the pale white drops fall into her palm.

She made a big show of closing her hand around the six drops. Inside she was trembling, still weak from her use of Babel last night.

There was also the fact that the penalty for use of Babel on an Ante, any Ante, was death. Technically, since the blood was no longer in their bodies, she was not doing this to them. She closed her eyes and hummed in preparation.

Shrugging off her worries, she formed the two words she wanted in her mind and pushed them forward. They struggled, clawing at her throat, but she shook them loose. She felt her throat growing more sore but at least she did not taste copper in the back of it. The words slipped from her tongue, twining about each other in the air.

blood. knowing.

And she was suddenly inside their minds, or a recreation of their minds when they had given the blood. She had not expected it to work so well, to recreate them so well that they would push on her own mind like storms, trying to batter her thoughts away.

She was met with a mix of mistrust and affection. Confused, she tried to pick up more details but could get nothing further. Satisfied that there were no immediate plans for betrayal, she took a deep breath.

Her many years at Kandake had not only been learning Babel. There were other magics, and once Babel had opened the path into their blood it was easy. The blood in her palm began to writhe as she used Sanguar, a magic from some of the frozen northern isles, to dive even deeper into it, writing oaths and promises of protection and the pain of failure into their very beings. When Lil finally opened her eyes again the blood was alight with the oath, casting shadows through the room.

She looked at Arel and Jagi and waited for them to hold out their hands once again. They could protest. While what she had done was technically legal, how often did the Ruling Courts care for technicalities or fairness when an Ante brought a case against a 'dant? Finally they both reached forward, the small cuts they'd made still white and gaping open. She turned her hand and carefully let three drops flow into Arel's wound.

She turned to Jagi and did the same.

The connection sprang to vibrant life and Lil was pulled under. If the false minds had been storms, their true minds were like the cracking of the world.

It was not their age or power. On those levels, she was surprised to find herself almost their equals. Their perspectives were what threatened to overwhelm her. No matter how powerful she became, what wondrous things she did if she took over for Mayer, she would live to see two hundred maybe, at the outside two hundred and fifty years. For Arel and Jagi those years, the length of her life, would pass quickly. They would be here long after everything she knew of Zebub changed and shifted. Even as slowly as the Ruling Courts changed their traditions, they would see things she could not imagine. It took everything in her to turn away from the idea of forever. Immortality called to her, said take me, use me, and she struggled against the urge to say yes.

As she finally managed to pull back into herself and minimize the connections so they did not overwhelm her, a word lit up in her mind, bright and glowing. It was Babel. She knew this somehow, and the meaning behind it was clear to her as if it was her native tongue. TRANSFORMATION—not simply the act but the flow of change, the way of water into ice and steam, the way of wood into ash with the addition of fire, transmutation and the rise and roll of the universe. She did her best to memorize the shape of it as it flowed away.

When she came back from having watched the blood twist promises of protection into their bodies, her clothes were soaked through with sweat from the effort.

Arel and Jagi stood watching her impassively but she could tell by the quickness of their breath they were as affected as well. She tried desperately to think of something to say, something to break the awkwardness between them, but nothing came to her mind.

She wanted to ask about the word in her mind, bright as moonlight from the three sisters or sunlight from the cousin, but fear held her back. She did not actually know these two, ignoring the tiny voice that argued that she knew them all too well now, perhaps better than anyone else except each other. Luckily the opening of a door and the scrape of tiny feet trying to be quiet provided a distraction. Lil turned to find Minnie and Davi peeking around the doorjamb. They ducked back when she met their eyes but she snorted a laugh out.

"Come on in here, you two little spies!"

"We're not spies!" They were the first words Davi had spoken since last night. Lil laughed out loud and grabbed him as he came around the corner, hands on his hips indignantly. She pulled him close and kissed his cheek.

"You're all sweaty and smelly."

"Am I? Well then I guess I shouldn't give you a big smelly hug!"

"No, stop it!" Davi squealed and laughed, flailing in the cradle of her arms. Minnie laughed and slapped at Lil's hands in an attempt to help her little brother. Other hands, soft and a mottled gray, came into her vision, tickling Minnie. Minnie stopped for a second and then reacted to the hands the same way she reacted to Lil by scream-laughing and struggling to get away and burrow deeper at the same time.

Another pair of hands came over her shoulders and gently disengaged Davi. When she met their eyes, one pair of softly glowing brown and one of bright hazel, they both looked apologetic but glanced at the closed door where Mayer still waited.

　　　　　　　　　　　　　　　　NA'AMEN GOBERT TILAHUN

They could not harm her siblings either by action or inaction. They were bound. To break the binding would take mutual agreement as the original deal had.

"Okay, you two be good for Arel and Jagi. I'll see you tonight." Both of them ran forward for one last hug and a kiss on her cheek. She walked out to join Mayer, ready for the tongue-lashing she was sure to receive.

He waited patiently outside, but as soon as she appeared he turned and began to walk without a word.

She was confused. The lie was ready on the tip of her tongue—a simple truth-sensing cast on herself and a questioning of the two Antes. A little insulting but not worth true punishment. The first lie she planned to tell her Holder and it was unnecessary. He should have felt her use of Babel even if he didn't discern its exact purpose, but he said nothing. Had he not felt it? Or did he still trust her?

Lil longed to discuss the word that she could still remember the shape of with her Holder, but she understood something as she studied the stiffness of his back, remembered the lack of interest in her sib's well-being.

For the first time that she could recall they had different priorities, and she could not trust Mayer completely. They both wanted to solve the mystery of the dark, but he must think of the Athenaeum first and she had to think of her family.

The fact that she now trusted two Antes more than her mentor of twelve cycles did not bear thinking about.

AREL & JAGI

Arel grasped the squirming Davi while Jagi crouched down to Minnie's height and asked her what they wanted for morning meal.

"Cake!" Arel pushed Davi out to arm's length too late and his left ear rang from the boy's yell.

Jagi shared a worried look with Arel. Perhaps introducing the little pups to baked goods had not been the best move. In their defense they had no experience with children and their own memory of childhood was brief and blurred. Most Antes were born already capable of caring for themselves; even the slower-growing bloodlines were fully mature in a few cycles. The sweets had been the only things they could think of that might calm the sobbing children as they waited for their Holder-Apprentice sib.

"No cake for breakfast, Davi." Jagi tried to keep his voice firm but the little boy turned wide eyes on him and his bottom lip trembled. Jagi and Arel shared a distraught look.

Jagi quickly amended, "If you're a good child, you can have some after lunch."

Davi tilted his head, contemplating the compromise. He looked down at Minnie, who nodded. Davi immediately nodded as well.

After a breakfast of fried luta root and one huge ermi egg split between the four of them, they spent the first half of the day running around the Hive with the kids, taking them to the unexplored levels, ones still devoid of Antes. These levels would fill as the Court rose in status and they gathered more members.

Always one of them kept an eye out for any other Antes. Just in case. When they noticed Minnie and Davi yawning a couple of hours after a lunch of calla salad and cake, they took them back to the room to nap.

Leaving the door to the bedroom where the children slept open, they settled on the couch side by side. They let out a slow breath of release and the feeling of tightness in their bodies flowed out as the apertures on their necks and torsos opened. Quickly dancing, delicate gray tentacles emerged, wasting no time in connecting, braiding and wrapping themselves about one another.

When fully entangled they finally began to speak.

"Did you feel—" *her/it/everything/the power that rushed through her and into us.*

"Yes, what does it—" *portend/foresee/what will the results be.*

"I do not know but—" *the power/the fire/the scouring is something they will want.*

"Will Chayyliel—" *know/suspect/wonder that we are no longer bound to him.*

"Perhaps but it cannot—" *say/mention/let it be known that the power it used has been overwhelmed.*

Communicating this way was slower but allowed for more nuance and shielded most of what they said from the ears of enemies or curious allies. It also brought comfort, separated as they were from most of their bloodline by their "choice" of House.

"What are you doing?"

Their eyes snapped open, even the third ones they usually kept sealed. So it was six, wide surprised eyes that looked at Minnie crouched in the doorway. Neither understood how she had woken up, left the bed, and made it to the door without either of them noticing the sounds of her movement.

Arel replied as they hurried to disentangle and struggled to calm themselves enough to withdraw their tentacles and close their apertures and third eyes.

"We were talking."

"Then why'd you have all those thingies coming out?" Davi was hidden behind his sister and the finger in the corner of his mouth muffled his question just a little.

Arel had managed to withdraw his extra appendages and seal them off, so he knelt down and gathered Davi in his arms while Jagi kept trying to bring himself under control.

"It's a way for us to communicate differently."

Davi's small forehead and nose scrunched up while he thought about it. Then he simply shook his head, shrugging off the question. "Can I play with them?"

Arel started in surprise. "Maybe another time, little pup."

Minnie had crept onto the couch near Jagi and was moving her hand slowly, steadily toward the last tentacle Jagi was still trying to pull back inside.

"Minnie, leave Jagi alone."

She frowned at Arel, but looked at Jagi's face still creased in strain and slowly lowered her hand back to her side. Her lip trembled a bit and she looked as if she might cry.

"Minnie?"

"Stop calling me Minnie!"

Arel jerked in surprise. It was all he had heard Lil call her as well as Davi. "Okay, what do you want to be called?"

"Min." She stated this as if it should be obvious.

"Okay, we will try to remember," Jagi said.

The tremble disappeared and Arel and Jagi looked at each other. The change of mood was sudden and sharp and neither knew how to deal with it. A more honest pout made an appearance on her face. Arel crouched so he was face to face with her, balancing an equally pouting Davi on his hip.

"How about we go flying?"

The distraction worked and both of their faces lit up and they began to nod so hard Arel thought their heads might fly off the stalks of their necks. Minnie leapt up from the couch and took the hand that was not busy supporting Davi.

Jagi finally succeeded in calming himself and followed them out of the room.

LIL

She followed Holder Mayer out of the Hive and into the center courtyard and nearly froze at the sight before her. The courtyard now buzzed with activity. They had been allowed to sleep in, and Yanwan's journey across the sky was already half over. One of the Hives in the process of being built was obscured by the constant movement of the 'dants and constructs building it. The other Hives had Antes constantly streaming in and out, the larger ones using doorways specially built for them. Crikes and dragons carried passengers all over the place.

Two dragons almost collided in midair, their delicate translucent wings tangling for a terrifying second. They swiped at one another and stabbed with their proboscises, but finally pulled apart with no damage to either the proboscises, or their delicate wings. She saw some crikes begin to nuzzle and mate as soon as they let their passengers off.

As they crossed, some of the passing Antes, the ones with things she recognized as eyes, gave them looks but she could not truly read the emotion in all the different beings they passed. She was obvious in her traditional, if stained, white tunic and pants, and Mayer wore the gray scholar robes that marked him as a Holder. They were soon joined in their march by Krezida and Haydn.

Now that she was no longer in shock she took them in. Krezida was medium height. Her blonde hair had been altered, turned bright jade green, perhaps to match the paint on the tips of her fingers. The only reason Lil assumed blonde was her natural color were the roots that were growing out. Her robes were also multicolored, shades of blue and black the most dominant but sprinkled with other colors near the hem. Her skin was a light tan, cheeks hollow and thin. Next to her Haydn was just as thin, his hair limb brown that instead of shining in the light took on a dirty mud sheen that made his sallow skin look even more yellow. His tunic and pants looked older. There were ruffles about the neck that almost hid the torc that covered his entire scrawny neck. There were ruffles where the pants ended at his knees and a pair of lace-up white sandals with straps going all the way up his shins completed the look.

Riana and Razel joined them a second later; their outfits altered into sleek jumpsuits that hugged their bodies and covered most of them. The white of Razel's suit made her dark skin stand out even more and the scars adorning it even more obvious. Riana's jumpsuit was a brighter white than Razel's, with silver accents. It made her skin shine gold and her long dark hair was pulled into an intricate knot at the back of her head. They both wore boots with heavy soles and wickedly angled toes.

Lil had assumed the others were also staying in Hive Chayyliel on different floors, but she had seen each emerged from a different Hive. Riana and Razel emerged from the Hive that resembled the pink living tissue of her parents' old apartment building and most of the buildings in Zebub. Sorrow and Riches, the oldest of the Courts, had built most of Zebub, then lost it piece by piece. They enjoyed building with flesh, the way it could heal itself, grow as needed. It made sense for them to stay there, since Hypatia was in their district.

Krezida and Haydn emerged from a Hive that looked like pulsing light. Hive Inyades, the second youngest Court. Which made no sense. That Court's holdings were all outside the city, none of them anywhere near Enheduanna Athenaeum.

Lil mulled this over as they moved directly toward one of the gaps in the circle of Hives. It was right next to the second oldest; the one that resembled a spiraling forest and belonged to the Court of Pain and Solitude. Unlike the other spaces in the circle that were kept bare and ready for building, a forest had been allowed to thrive on this patch of ground. Brown and gray scrub grasses turned lush and green the closer they got. Trees with dark foliage grew close to one another, shading the ground with their high and widespread canopy.

As she stepped into the shade, Lil's stomach twisted in knots. Bile gathered in the back of her mouth and she struggled not to vomit. Lil knew where they stood. The place where the Hive of Traitors had stood. It made her stomach roil as the remnants of Ante power still lingered from a fight over fifteen thousand years past, now turned into a nauseating miasma. The others made various sounds of distress. Haydn was groaning lightly and clutching his stomach while Razel stood straighter and walked more precisely with every part of her body suppressing what she was feeling. Lil only knew Mayer felt it because of the clenching and unclenching of his left fist, a sure sign of his discomfort.

She was sure Riana and Krezida were feeling it too, but she didn't know their tells. They looked as if they felt nothing but the wind. The discomfort grew the closer they got to the center, where one tree stood apart from the rest. With each step her stomach turned over again; each breath felt like it was preparing the path for a stream of vomit. When they reached the tree, everyone was visibly feeling the strain. The Holders all had the sheen of sweat coating their foreheads.

"Lil, come forward."

Lil moved slowly until she was standing next to Mayer and not coincidentally blocking the sight of what he would do from the other Holders. He met her eyes and the fevered glow in his nearly made her step back.

"Pay attention." His voice was sharp, sullen.

Lil nodded and watched as Mayer reached forward and deliberately cut his finger on the rough bark of the tree. With his bleeding fingertip, Mayer placed blood in three different small hollows in the wood. They immediately lit up with words: TRAVEL, HIDDEN, SACRIFICE. Lil knew Mayer could see the words as well as she could, though he would have no idea what they meant.

She did. It was as in the binding of Arel and Jagi. She was now somehow able to read Babel, where she had not been even a day before. What had changed? She opened her mouth to tell her Holder.

"Holder Mayer—"

"Silence," he snapped. She narrowed her eyes but nodded. "Now move back and let them all see."

Lil did as he directed but did not take her eyes from the glowing sigils, could not in fact. From the gasps and growls around her as others caught sight of it, they could not stop looking either. Slowly the world in peripheral vision faded into a sea of red, the three words pulsing in the middle of it all. They were everything, nothing else mattered, not those around them, not the constant anger and tears behind her eyes. Only the words.

Until slowly they faded from sight and they were all somewhere else.

The new place was a shock to Lil's senses. There was no place in Zebub where the air did not hold the faint smell of life, of biology, of meat. There was not a place that did not buzz with power and where the colors of some House were not painted in ownership. She had doubted there was any place in all of Corpiliu that was free of these things.

Yet here she stood in a black-walled room lined with silver boxes that looked like bookshelves and yet were not. They went on much farther than she could see, even with the strings of wires crisscrossing the high ceiling with hanging balls of light. She could smell nothing but herself and the others around her and an odd sharpness that made her nose burn. There was no thrum and threat of constant surveillance or power in the room, no overwhelming fear.

No wonder the Ruling Courts had no love for the Ossuary.

It drove home how desperate the Courts were. She glanced around and saw that the others were nervously looking about, having similar realizations. Before either of the others could recover and wrest leadership of this mission from her Holder, she stepped up to one of the shelves. They resembled silver metal bookcases but each shelf held only a single block of solid metal, all with the same small round depression in their center.

The Babel from before lit up to her again, SACRIFICE, and by instinct she pressed two fingers into the small hole and endured a shock of pain. The smell of blood filled the air as she pulled her fingers back. Blood continued to pool in the depression but none spilled, even as it reached the rim. Another word appeared in the darkness of her mind, burning with a cold light. It curled around and around itself, making it almost impossible to read, but she wrestled it, struggled to hold it still so she could finally grasp its meaning.

OPEN, shades of meaning, open for help, open for aid, open for truth, the word tested her own worthiness as she studied its subtlety. She felt her mind bend under its regard and sweat gather on her brow.

On the verge of breaking completely, she felt the pressure of the word give way, just a little at first and then fading like morning mist.

A loud click echoed through her and she was back in the room, aware of her body again. She looked down and saw every shelf trembling, all the locks clicking open in unison. They were drawers.

"Well done," said Holder Mayer.

Lil turned toward him and saw his eyes were calculating and shrewd. He studied her, his mouth still before turning toward the others.

"Each of these drawers contains valuable information, but the only things we are interested in now is any mention or representation or weapon against the creeping dark. Anything at all that pertains to what it is, where it comes from, and how to defeat it. I have been promised by the Ruling Courts that if we discover the answer to this we will be allowed time on our own to research personal pursuits."

Lil did not need to see his face to read that lie.

RAZEL

Holder Mayer smiled as if he believed what he was saying. The only thing that stopped the Ruling Courts from destroying the Athenaeums was that threat that they might unite and unleash as much hell as possible. Although none were sure if the Athenaeums could actually be destroyed. The Athenaeums here and in other cities were the only things that challenged the Antes' complete and utter control of Corpiliu. They hated them but it would cost too much to attack. And the Athenaeums could not risk an open confrontation either.

Antes feared death more than 'dants, faced with the loss of a thousand years or more rather than the couple hundred.

They would never allow them the time to research and perhaps obtain more power.

Razel would have laughed if she weren't still holding her stomach together from their journey. If they did discover a way to defeat this creeping dark, they would all have targets on their heads. Once the common 'dants learned the Athenaeums were the reason everyone was safe? Revolutionaries would use them as figureheads and the Ruling Courts would see them as a more credible threat.

Holder Mayer had to know this. No one who'd found a way to be Holder as long as he had was stupid. Which meant he must have some plan to survive.

"Every one of us will be searched when we leave here in the evening and anyone found trying to smuggle something out will be executed," he continued.

Razel smiled. She and Riana had expected no less.

They nodded at one another and then separated as planned. Razel moved to a far shelf where none could see her and opened a drawer to find a random assortment of wood piled inside it. Only as she pulled one out did she realize they were carvings; the drawer was filled with wooden sculpture. She looked at the one she held, a woman writhing against a huge split tree trunk. Something crawled over the carved figure's thighs and wrapped around her waist. It looked like a serpent but something in the form was rough, with edges burred. The figure's head was thrown back and her mouth open in ecstasy and pain. Razel rubbed her hands over the form but quickly grew bored when she stumbled upon no secret.

"Holder Krezida, Haydn. I believe this drawer is more your speed." She held up the statue she had uncovered and both of them rushed over.

"Yes, this is from the era right before recorded history." Haydn took it from her hand without even a thank you.

"Or possibly later in the same style, do you see the way the wood is worked? The burring of the edges of pieces did not get popular until over 170 years afterward."

"True, it wasn't as popular, but the technique likely existed."

Razel moved on to another drawer, leaving them to a pointless argument. The next was filled with jewels, both those worked into jewelry and uncut specimens still attached to gray stone. She reached out for one of the pieces, a choker made of overlapping rubies sliced so thin they were translucent. As soon as she touched it a horrible spasm shot up her arm and she cried out in pain. The progression of the feeling stopped as soon as she released the necklace, but the tingling aftermath remained. Her skin felt like it was moving without her consent, her fingertips like ice, numb and insensitive. She was glad she had not grabbed with her torc; who knew the reaction that would have resulted.

"What happened?"

To Razel's surprise it was not Mayer or Riana asking but Liliana, with the other two gathered behind her. Haydn and Krezida had not even looked over, still pawing through their treasure of wooden statuettes.

"I touched a necklace and something shot up my arm."

"Can I see?"

"Why?"

"Because I may be able to tell what's wrong with you and if there will be any other effects."

Razel studied the girl in front of her. Mayer was shooting his Holder-Apprentice an odd look from behind her back. He obviously had expected the girl to defer to him. The fact that she hadn't was something he did not know how to deal with, which interested Razel and convinced her to hold out her arm.

Liliana took the arm gently, so gently Razel could barely feel it. Liliana traced her finger over the arm, making some sort of shape and then watching closely. Finally she released it and looked up at Razel.

"It's burned clean some of your nerves, but it should be only temporary."

"I don't know what that means."

Liliana sighed. "You know how when skin is new after an injury it's sensitive to everything, things you could handle before suddenly feel odd and disturbing?"

"Yes." Scars and new skin were things that Razel knew very well; not a week went by when she did not acquire a new injury.

"Our whole bodies are like that, we build up resistance. Yours has been burned away on this arm. It should return in less than an hour. Until then I would try not to touch anything with it."

Razel looked back at the drawer, curious.

"Why would someone invent that?"

Holder Mayer answered. "I imagine it was for some of the Antes who have issues with armor-like skin or sensitivity, to allow them to feel again for at least a limited time."

Razel nodded. That made some sense, but if it was only useful for Antes, why was it here? In a place Antes could supposedly never come?

Everyone went back to the drawers they had been ransacking and Razel closed the drawer of jewelry, marking it with the red stickers they had brought for just that purpose. They meant that Mayer or Liliana had to go through and identify the contents. She moved on to another drawer, allowing her sensitive arm to hang loose and move freely. It still ached, but if she tensed none of her muscles it was dull and manageable.

The next drawer was filled with odd gray/blue paper. She pulled on the edge of one cautiously with her torc. Her silver fingers closed around a corner and she realized that they were folded numerous times. When she yanked the edge free and part of a diagram met her eyes, she could not help smiling in delight. These she understood. Pulling out the one she'd grabbed, she lay it out flat on the ground so she could study it with one hand.

The lines had words next to them that were smudged out of existence or unintelligible to her, but the lines and shapes made perfect sense. It took her only seconds to realize they were plans on how to build some kind of weapon, a combination of gun and bomb, a gun that launched small bombs? She smiled and focused on committing the shape of it to memory.

MAYER

He stuck close to Lil as she moved past Razel.

"That was well done, Apprentice."

She turned to face him and nodded. "Thank you, Holder."

"Where did you learn to read her injury in such a way?"

"The Book of Numbers by Queen Jezebel."

"Ah, an excellent resource. However, that text requires parchment for its enchantments."

Liliana nodded. "Yes, since I was in a hurry I combined it with the hands-on techniques detailed in Hougan Orin's journals."

"Ah." He studied her expression. The Liliana of a week ago would not have felt confident in mixing two distinct branches of workings on the fly. The loss of her parents and the responsibility of her sibs had changed her. He nodded at her to go on her way and she nodded back before moving off to examine another drawer.

"She is skilled."

He had noticed Krezida moving up behind him. She spent so much of her time mixing potions, paints, chemicals, and herbs that she always had a strong scent about her. She had not come within touching distance and so he had not given her the satisfaction of reaction.

"It is why she is my Apprentice."

"Hmm . . . I wonder." She turned her body so they were side by side, both watching his Apprentice looking through a waist-high drawer. "She is the one who unlocked the drawers. She does you credit."

Mayer merely nodded, waiting for the next attack.

"How much credit can she do you though, without doing herself more?"

Mayer took in a deep breath and smiled.

"Your plans are obvious, Krezida. Old Jadzia would be ashamed of you." The Holder before her, now there had been a formidable and smart personality. Able to twist you in knots almost before you'd spoken.

Krezida reached out and Mayer turned to face her, hand in the air in front of him.

Her fingers stopped two inches away from his face and he stopped his fingers in the middle of the final protection sigil. He could smell whatever was mixed into the jade green paint that coated her nails and fingers up to the first knuckle. It smelled sweet and yeasty, as if a bakery were sharing space with a candy shop. Her normally blonde hair had been dyed a bright green to match. Her warm sand-colored skin was lined with age, a thin sheen of shining powder covering her face. Her eyes were mismatched, one black and one yellow.

She narrowed those eyes at him before smiling. "Relax, Mayer, I'm only joking with you. We are allies. As allies we should trust one another."

"Trust is earned, not simply given."

Krezida let her hand fall to her side. "True enough. I start with honest advice. Watch your Apprentice. She has the care of her sibs now, she will betray you easily for them. You have held your place longer than any Holder, but I would worry for it if I were you."

Before he could respond, Krezida marched off to rejoin her Apprentice. He watched his own Apprentice a while longer before moving on himself.

LIL

il was exhausted. She did not know how long they had spent going through the drawers, but her fingers ached from gripping and her back from bending. She had found a lot of interesting things, things that created more questions, but nothing she could connect with the creeping dark. The good news was there were yet aisles and aisles of drawers to search through; it was also the bad news. They did not have the years it would take to catalog everything in the Ossuary.

They at least seemed to be getting close to understanding the categorization system of the shelves.

Every case was grouped along relationship lines, like with like. The brace of drawers Razel first encountered had all been serpent themed. The statuettes featured serpents, the drawers above were filled with texts on serpents and medical designs based on serpent movement and anatomy, while the lower drawer was filled with plans for poisonous weapons.

They had little idea what they were looking for, but Lil assumed they needed older documents, because if there was knowledge of this dark it was something that had been erased with time. Therein lay the problem. Even the most recent records were ridiculously old by Zebub standards. The language was so archaic that Mayer and Lil could barely understand it. Krezida and Riana were running into similar problems; they could interpret the art and mechanics they found, but without the context of the times most of their theories remained exactly that. Though of course none were speaking to each other about what they had learned beyond stating they'd run across nothing referencing the dark.

At the end of the day, Mayer gathered them together in the center of the Ossuary where they had arrived and instructed them to look up. The same symbols that had been on the tree were carved on the ceiling directly above them. Mayer whispered the words in the repetitive chant and Lil joined in. They continued until, like before, all they could see was red and the writhing shapes of the words.

They were suddenly back in the forest, dizzy and not alone.

An Ante rolled back and forth in front of them, a thin wheel of flesh covered in eyes, each one closing as they approached the ground and opening again as they rose back into the air. Lil wondered what its field of vision must be to experience. The thought of it alone made her dizzy.

She used her hand to shield her head from the freezing mist of rain that had sprung up while they were in the Ossuary. The courtyard was as active as it had been that morning. One of the Hives being built was making excellent progress, already half as high as the others, although she could not see the material because of the layers of scaffolding around it.

Mayer turned to Lil.

"Did you remove anything from the Ossuary?"

"No, Holder," she answered truthfully.

Her Holder turned to each other person in turn and asked them the same question. After they had all answered in the negative, he turned to lead them away from the nausea-inducing grove. The Ante followed.

"Is it going to search us?" Haydn asked in what he believed to be a whisper, while glancing behind them. Krezida shushed him, but not before Mayer seized on it as a way to show up his fellow Holder.

"But he already has. Lil, would you care to explain to this child?"

The tone of his voice was pleasant enough but there was steel underneath. He did not expect Lil to let him down.

"Killi'ila is of the bloodline Ophde and as such can see through many things, including deception. When Holder Mayer asked us if we had removed anything from the Ossuary, Killi'ila would have seen through any lie and I assume killed us on the spot."

She looked to Killi'ila for its reaction. The eyes focused in her direction simply grew heavy-lidded in something like agreement.

"Oh," was Haydn's only response, but the look he shot her and Mayer was black and angry. Only a few days ago it would have cowed her terribly, but she had no time for any of that now. She met his gaze levelly and let no expression cross her face until he finally looked away. As they reached the center of the courtyard, Killi'ila stopped and its voice rang out from somewhere in the vicinity of the lower inside rim of the body. It rang through the night, running in tone from soprano to bass in the course of speaking.

You have all been invited to dine with the Ruling Courts tonight. Will you come now or must you freshen up first?

Despite the exhaustion lining their faces and the wrinkles marring every bit of their clothing, they all agreed to come now except Lil. She spoke up after the babble of agreement had finished.

"I must check on my sibs but I will come as soon as I have seen that they are well."

Mayer opened his mouth to say something but Killi'ila spoke again, drowning him out.

It is only right to check on your bloodline. We shall send someone to your rooms after Rona rises to escort you.

Lil bowed her head and thanked him for his acceptance before turning to head to Hive Chayyliel. She did not look to Mayer for his approval.

SAN FRANCISCO

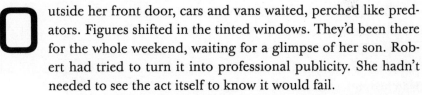

DAYIDA

Outside her front door, cars and vans waited, perched like predators. Figures shifted in the tinted windows. They'd been there for the whole weekend, waiting for a glimpse of her son. Robert had tried to turn it into professional publicity. She hadn't needed to see the act itself to know it would fail.

Though she *had* watched all of it on the CCTV in the kitchen.

At least he hadn't seemed to make things worse for Erik. His political career would probably never recover, though. She'd stayed inside. The need to go out and deal with idiots was not one she felt often.

She knew Erik would be home soon because Matthias had called.

"Where is he?"

She sighed before answering, not taking her eyes from the small television. Her fingers had already stained the black kitchen curtains with yellow fingerprint whorls of paint. She tried to angle the camera to see more of the front yard.

"I told you already, he's somewhere resting. He should be back soon."

"Damn it, Yida! He should be here now, dealing with this problem."

"I don't see where he did anything wrong." She shrugged, still not turning to face him.

"Are you kidding me?"

She heard him coming closer but only when he put his hand on her shoulder did she whip around to face him, knocking his hand away.

They'd always had a volatile relationship, screaming and jealousy and wild make-up sex, but the last three years had changed it from playful to serious. Robert looked at her and leaned back against the counter, his face flushed. She took in the wide shoulders as he slumped and put his head in his hands. She remembered the way his body had moved with hers when they still slept in the same bed.

Before he'd started to love the idea of fame and power more than her. For her part, she wasn't sure she'd ever really loved him. He'd been convenient and she'd liked him at one point. Now he had other uses.

"He defended himself. Everyone agrees those two little bastards were bullies who started things. Maybe he took things too far—"

"Maybe? He put them both in the hospital!"

"Well, the men in this family do tend to overreact."

Robert went silent and narrowed his eyes at her. He stood straight and tried to loom over her, which might have worked if she weren't a good three inches taller than him in flats. She stood her ground and watched him shrink back into himself.

"I am not overreacting. This is most paparazzi that we've had since Erik's earlier mistakes."

"Funny, I don't remember the mistakes being his." As she parried his words back, some of the tension in her shoulders lessened and channeled through her husband like a grounding wire. The build-up had been killing her and it felt good for some of it to flow out of her.

"If he had just—"

"What? Been what you wanted instead of who he is?"

"I don't care if he's a fag!"

The word echoed in the house. She tilted her head.

"I don't!" He crossed his arms over his chest. "I just don't know why he had to ruin his career."

"You did that, Robert, not Erik."

Robert sat back down and Yida turned back to her window. Her body felt loose and relaxed, ideas for painting crowding her mind, but she wanted to wait until Erik got home before heading back into the studio.

"I was trying to do what was best for us."

Yida froze. This was not where this conversation usually headed.

"I wanted us to have an easy life. It was so hard when we started out. What with you getting pregnant while we were both undergrads.

We couldn't afford anything for years. Scraping by on stipends from internships and loans. I fucking hated it."

Yida turned. Robert was back at the table, his body limp as if his bones had been removed. He looked raw and weak.

He continued. "Then Erik's acting lessons paid off with those indie movies and your paintings were selling and all of a sudden I was the background."

She approached him slowly and sat in the chair across from him. His face was buried in his hands and she wanted to say something comforting, but she'd too long been in the habit of speaking her mind to lie now.

"You were never in the background, Robert. There was never a background in this family." She stopped short of saying all their problems had been due to his ridiculous pride.

"It still felt that way, damn it!" He slammed his hands on the table and immediately Yida's sympathy shrank and her anger flared.

"And who made you feel that way? Certainly not me or our son! But who did you take it out on?"

He stared at her.

"We already loved you *and* we trusted you with our careers."

"Not Erik, he was letting that damn kid talk him—"

Yida took his hand.

"You've been blaming Daniel a long time but how many times did Erik say he didn't like the way his career was going? That he had no interest in the Disney-kiddie guest spots or TV series? But what roles did you keep making him take? He was going to leave with or without Daniel."

"They paid great. I wanted us to be steady. He wanted to take those arty roles that barely paid. I—I just wanted him to have a better childhood and teen years than I did. I didn't want him growing up wanting and resenting. And what about you?"

She sighed. They had never talked about the fact that she'd fired him as her manager as well. Maybe it was time.

"It wasn't just what you did to Daniel and Erik. I found out how you did it."

Robert went still.

"Why didn't you tell everyone?"

Why didn't she? The question had haunted her for the last couple of years. Why not get that poor boy out of jail and send her husband in? She didn't love him.

Was she accustomed to him?

Was she used to the relief he provided?

Was it just to avoid more shame and attention?

She had picked up the phone so many times, ready to tell all, but never went through it. Whenever Yida thought about that child in prison it made her guilty. So she tried not to think of it often.

"I don't know."

"What do we do now?"

"I'm going to wait until our son comes home. You're welcome to wait with me."

Robert nodded jerkily and they sat together, in silence, waiting.

ERIK

Erik felt like he had spent most of the last three days either asleep or passed out. It was not a trend he wanted to continue, so when he woke up exhausted the first thing he did was curse, a lot.

He felt as if he hadn't slept at all. The thought of changing his clothes seemed like too much effort and the smell of food was calling him. He needed protein, maybe then he could shake off the dreams that clung to him. Slowly he rose out of bed and made his way down the hall, back to the cafeteria.

The exact same setup as last night, down to the empty chair where he had been sitting, greeted him. He froze.

"Erik, how are you doing?" Matthias rose from his chair and approached him.

"What?" The fog of sleep was still affecting his thoughts.

"You've been asleep for twenty-four hours."

"Wha—Why?"

"It's my fault." Matthias looked down even as he ran his hands over Erik's body, checking him for any injury, though Erik couldn't understand how he could have been hurt in bed. "I should have gone easier on training you to call up and dismiss your power. It's been so long, I forget how tired you are when you first awaken and your body changes. It exhausted you." Matthias took a step back. "I'm sorry."

"It's okay." Erik reached for the chair and sat down in it. "No harm done and at least I know it's not some weird tapeworm or something. Now if I can just shake that dream."

"What sort of dream?" Patrah was staring at him. They were all staring at him.

"Nothing really specific," he said cautiously as a bowl of pasta mixed with veggies and oil appeared in front of him. "I was fighting for my life, I couldn't see anything. Some—other people were there with me. Then it was over."

"How did you feel during it?"

"Um . . . like I was fighting for my life?" He shoveled a forkful of pasta in his face. It was true and not as nuanced as he could have been. He didn't want to share that he'd felt responsible for it all. A weird arrogance or a guilt complex? He didn't feel like sharing either option with the group. "Why are you guys so anxious about this?"

Patrah looked at the others, but none of them opened their mouths to explain. Casting a sideways glance at Matthias, she started, "Whichever of the dozens of origin stories of our kind that you believe to be true, in most of them all our parents were betrayed by their other children and killed."

Erik nodded, shoveling more pasta in his face.

"But can beings that powerful really die? Their bodies were destroyed, true, and their minds were broken, stripped of power but still left—in some sense of the word—alive. Or at least not completely dead."

"What the—?" Erik started to interrupt.

Patrah shot him a look and he clicked his mouth shut on the food in it.

"They may be bodiless, powerless, and at this point quite mad, but we are still their children. They still recognize us. The children who did not betray, the ones who tried to protect them. When we are exhausted and the well of our power is dry, that is when they can reach out to us."

"How?"

Patrah sighed. "No one knows for sure but . . . where do you think your power comes from?"

"Inside myself."

"Yes, you feel it there, but where does that come from?"

Erik shook his head and swallowed. The food was slowly bringing him fully into the waking world. "How the hell should I know? I'm new to this. You people are the ones who are supposed to be telling me things, not giving me a damn pop quiz."

"Well . . . anyway, though they may be dead and powerless, that doesn't mean they are useless. We believe they are the conduits to the power that fills us, to the power of creation."

"Oh-kay." It was a lot; not only was he descended from something he still hesitated to call a god, but despite its being dead he was still connected to it. "So I'm guessing we're constantly reenergizing a little at a time, all the time, but when we're exhausted we're pulling so much that some sort of deeper connection is established?"

They stared at him and he rolled his eyes. Just because his power happened to involve beating down fools did not mean he was stupid.

"Yes," Tae answered, looking less surprised than anyone else.

"So does it mean anything?"

"Maybe. Sometimes we dream the past where we play their role in some memory they're reliving, sometimes it is a bit of our own future, sometimes it is simply scenes happening to others of your bloodline. It's usually impossible to tell."

"Well, isn't that just useless." Nobody contradicted him, so he turned to Matthias. "So it's Sunday night, right?"

Matthias nodded.

"Is it time to go home yet?"

"Yeah."

After hugging Melinda and exchanging numbers with her and Tae, he followed Matthias to the elevator next to the cafeteria, another thing he hadn't noticed. As they descended, they passed a number of floors and he wondered. The whole weekend—well, the parts he was awake—had been spent on that one floor. He had assumed it was the only one.

The doors opened in an underground garage. All the cars were small and compact but in excellent condition. Erik saw two Mini Coopers, both black, two Smart cars in a deep purple and an electric blue, and a number of classic VW Bugs in a string of rainbow colors going around the corner.

Matthias rolled up to one of the Mini Coopers and opened the door, gesturing for Erik to join him. As he walked between the cars, he noticed that they all had the keys just hanging out in the ignitions.

"Are these all just for anyone?"

"Technically they're for any member of the Organization, but they can be pretty okay about letting independents use their resources." Matthias climbed into one of the Mini Coopers. When Erik joined him he started the car and drove them out of the garage. "As long as they aren't actively working against the Organization. They see it as cultivation, you know, show them a little of what they could have if they join us." The odd industrial parks that filled this part of Brisbane surrounded them, lit by the moon and the occasional streetlight. Erik felt power rise in the car, pressing against his skin but also enveloping them all. He looked at Matthias and his mentor grinned at him. "I see it as a chance to play with a whole bunch of toys I don't have to replace if I break them."

The car jerked forward as Matthias pressed down on the gas. They sped through the twisting, empty streets. As he had when driving with his parents, he felt the pressure of the wind on the car and the jolt of the undercarriage. Every time they left the ground for even a second, Erik felt the slow gentle pull of gravity bringing them back down. He closed his eyes as they turned onto the freeway ramp, almost invisible to the naked eye, thanks to Matthias's power.

MATTHIAS

"You did well this weekend." They exited the freeway and Matthias let his power fade away, which let the car become visible again as he slowed and entered the more active neighborhoods of San Francisco.

Erik looked at him before he shook his head and smiled. "Thank you." Then he frowned. "I still have questions."

Matthias hesitated. "Of course you do. You can ask me any of them, but know that there are some I might not answer yet."

"Hmm." The sound was neither agreement or disagreement. Matthias nodded.

"Where is your family from?"

Matthias paused. He had not expected personal questions. He was tempted not to answer, but Erik had learned a lot of heavy shit this weekend. A distraction could be useful.

"I was born in San Francisco but my father was originally from Thessaloniki, my mother from New York. "

"Do you see them often?"

"No, they died when I was thirteen."

"Oh."

He answered the question packed into that one word.

"They were Agents and died on a FUBAR mission. I didn't blame the Organization at first, not till later."

"Where do you live now?"

"Not in any one place. I move around a lot, rent an apartment for a few months, see what good I can do in a town, and move on."

"Why?"

"It's easier." He doesn't think about the answer before it's out. "How about you, do you want to stay in San Francisco forever?"

"Hell, no." Erik laughed and lowered the window, putting his face into the wind. He could still feel the forces on the car but they were gentler now, easier to parse and ignore if he wanted. "I want to live everywhere in the world. Shanghai and Paris. Mumbai and Toronto. Kyoto and Addis Ababa. I want to see them all. I might settle down back here, though, after a decade or two. Who knows?"

Matthias pulled onto Erik's street and noticed his charge stiffen in the passenger seat.

"What is it?"

"Hell."

Matthias peered through the windshield. The dark street was littered with vehicles along both sides of the street, some of which had large satellite dishes on the top of them. Men and women leaned on the cars and trees, watching them at the end of the street. Paparazzi.

Erik did present unique challenges as an aspirant.

"Should I let you off here?"

Erik shrugged. "Six of one, half a dozen of the other. Either I have to beat my way through a sea of them or I have to deal with their questions about you."

Matthias was confused by what Erik meant, as he rarely had a television. But then he remembered the motel he'd stayed at in Akron over a year ago. He'd caught a TMZ marathon and been hypnotized by the aggressive paparazzi, the yelling, the need to know. Somehow it seemed less entertaining and more threatening when it was someone he knew and liked. He pressed on the gas.

He was tempted to use his power to shield them, but he would need to join Erik inside to hide him, at which point the car would suddenly appear.

Or he could let Erik suddenly appear in their midst.

Either way, he didn't think it would work in terms of keeping a low profile. So he drove steadily and without stopping, despite people standing in the road. Every time it ended in them diving to one side or the other. He pulled up directly in front of Erik's home and looked up.

Yida met his gaze through the kitchen window on the side of the house and he nodded as he read the worry in her eyes. She smiled and the curtain she was holding back swung shut. He turned to Erik and waited.

ERIK

"This'll be fun." Erik frowned as he looked out of the window.

"Should I come with you?"

The offer was sweet but it would only make things more difficult.

"No, that'll just make it worse."

Matthias nodded. "I'll pick you up Friday afternoon for next weekend's training."

Erik returned the nod and opened the door.

Who's the new boyfriend, Erik?

At least you're eighteen now, right?

Do you call him Daddy when he's inside of you?

You like them older, huh?

He had expected his reimmersion in this world to bring his anger surging to the front and he was ready to control himself. Surprisingly, he didn't feel any anger. Instead a calm enveloped him because, unlike everything else this weekend, this he knew how to deal with. He knew what they tried, the things they would say to get a reaction from him. Any reaction. It was helped by the fact that what they were yelling was absolutely ridiculous. There were barely five years between Matthias and himself, if that.

One man tried to block his path up the walk.

By instinct, Erik stepped forward and hooked his foot around the man's ankle. Knocking shoulders with the man, he tripped him off to the side into the crowd of paparazzi. It was simple and smooth and he knew the man wouldn't be injured. They crowded closer and he steadily made his way to his door.

He could feel the crowd around him, not who they were or what they were doing but the mass of them, the force that held them all together, himself in the center, their attention focused on him. He could feel the edges of the crowd, the way it petered out as some paparazzi gave up and left. He cut through the crowd, reading the weak men and women, those less rooted to the spot, and knocking them into their compatriots, careful not to actually hurt them.

Careful to make it look like an accident.

Suddenly two other presences impeded on his awareness; they were warps in the weave of the mob, not smoothly cutting through like himself but disrupting the flow, causing snarls and tangles. He came closer to his normal awareness as they reached him. He could still see the currents and waves of the crowd but not nearly as clearly. Erik recognized the warps as his parents as they moved in and took positions on either side of him. The three of them made their way through the remainder of the mob. The flashes of light were still there, and the yelling voices, but for the first time Erik had his parents bracketing him as he went through it.

They pushed through the last few people and Erik enjoyed the feeling of unity while it lasted. As soon as they were alone he would be on guard again, but for now, surrounded by enemies, they were on the same side. He didn't have to worry.

ROBERT

H e didn't know what to say to his son. He never knew.

They'd opened the door and pushed their way to Erik, who was patiently making his way through the crowd. They came up on either side of him. Erik looked over to Robert in sur-prise as he took his son's arm. Erik almost pulled away but paused, his gaze lingering on Robert, and instead of shaking him off as he half expected, his child merely nodded and allowed them to guide him the rest of the way into the house.

The voices formed a wall of noise and Robert did his best to let it blur so he couldn't hear the individual questions they were yelling. When the door closed behind them, the wish became blessed truth and he could no longer hear snippets of people talking about his son having sex and . . . he shuddered . . . other things.

"Erik. I need to talk with you." Robert knew it was not the best or most appropriate time, but now it felt as if the apology had been welling up in him for the past eighteen months or lon-ger. Even yesterday he would have said he didn't feel guilty over his actions, he had only been protecting his family, but now he saw it for the lie it was: he had not been worried about Erik, only himself, how it would make him look.

"I'm—I'm sorry," he blurted out.

"What?" Erik was looking at him, wide-eyed and suddenly young. He looked like he was ten again, not eighteen and grown.

"I—"

"No." Suddenly the child was gone from Erik's face and it was hard as granite, not an ounce of forgiveness in his expression. "Not right now."

Erik walked away from the door, putting distance between himself and Robert. He leaned against the counter and tried to gather himself. "Maybe not ever."

Robert felt anger roll through his body but he refused to bow to it, refused to let it make him yell. He'd lost too much because of his anger. The hardest thing he'd done in years was to not snap back, not start another fight.

Instead he stayed silent and looked at Dayida.

She was breathing hard, wheezing through her clenched teeth, eyes closed, fingers curled against the door as if they wanted to claw through the wood.

"Dayida." He reached for her wrist. She pulled away right away and turned to face him, eyes flaring open and trapping him in their anger.

"Don't. Touch me."

"I just want to—"

"Not right now." She turned and began to stalk to her studio without a word for either of them. As she moved past Erik, he reached out and grabbed her wrist. She tried to tug out of the hold at first and then went completely still.

Erik looked less exhausted all of a sudden. Ignoring the byplay, Robert approached his son.

"Erik, I really need to talk to you, even if you don't want to hear it. I need to let you know how I feel."

Erik turned to look at him and it was a stranger's face.

When had that happened? When had his child become a stranger to him? When he'd let his anger and jealousy drive him? Or even before then? Erik had always looked more like his mother, brown skin only a shade lighter than her own chestnut hue, the dark curls of his hair when it wasn't shaved as he'd recently started to do, dark eyes and long thick eyelashes that had him mistaken for a girl as a child. There were only two things that Robert could directly pinpoint as having come from him in Erik's face. The slightly crooked Cupid's bow of his lips were twins of Robert's own and the way his ears were jug handles. He smiled at these things.

The smile seemed to confuse Erik and he sighed and some of the stiffness left his cheeks.

"I need to talk to Mama."

"Erik." Robert opened his mouth to ask again.

"Robert, I get it. You're sorry and you want to talk. Honestly, I don't want to talk with you tonight, but we can try soon. Just not now." Erik looked uncomfortable as he said it but Robert ignored the tone and smiled.

"OK, son. Soon." He rested his hand on Erik's shoulder on his way out. It was tense and hard as a rock.

Robert had a few faults he would admit to, a number that he wouldn't, and some that had been attributed to him that he was actually innocent of. Spying was usually one of the latter, but the interaction between Yida and Erik was too odd for him to ignore.

He stayed around the corner to listen.

"I finally figured it out."

"What are you talking about?"

He peeked around the corner. Erik still stood near the door, not looking at Yida even though his body pointed in that direction.

"Don't try it, mama. You know I always wondered why you kept Robert around."

"Don't talk about your father that way."

Erik didn't even reply. Just looked at her.

"It's not the only reason, or at least wasn't when we first got together. I didn't even realize his use until after we were married."

Robert had no idea what they were talking about.

"Who knows you're actually awake?"

"Matthias. No one else."

"Why?"

Erik moved and Robert ducked his head back around the corner.

"I saw my parents die. Watched the power eat my mother alive and drive my father mad."

"Grandma's not dead."

There was silence. Then, "How did you do that?"

"Drain the force out of you? I didn't know I could but I saw Matthias and Elliot do something similar. When I felt the force under your skin I decided to try."

"Has Matthias traced your bloodline?"

"He tried." There was a long pause. "The Organization thinks it might come from Dad's side."

"What!"

The shock in Yida's voice was loud and ugly, but Robert froze for a different reason. It was the first time Erik had called him Dad in years.

"They think Robert is a Blooded who never woke up."

"Why?"

"Because I'm a berserker."

The gasp from Yida was loud as hell and the worry in her voice made Robert's heart beat louder.

"I . . . assumed you would be of Ogun's line but that makes sense. I never understood why I could use your father the way I did."

Erik made a disapproving sound. Robert didn't know what they were talking about, but it involved him and he wanted to know.

"Mama, it's not right to use Robert in that way."

"I know."

"Did you ever think of how it would affect him? Maybe, maybe—" Erik's voice broke and there was a beat of silence before he went on. "It has to stop."

"Well, now that you're here I won't have to use him anymore."

Robert dared to peek around the corner again. Erik was standing in front of his mother, close but not touching. They were looking into each other's faces and Robert read something in Yida's face that he had not seen in a long time. Fear.

"You have to learn control. I can't just drain off your power every time it fills you. What if I'm out? Or it's an emergency? Or I'm gone one day."

Yida moved around him and toward the door.

"I'll think about it."

Robert could try to silently scurry down the hall and hide quiet as a mouse or he could actually ask the questions that were now boiling up inside of him. He stepped out from around the corner and found himself only inches from Yida, who stopped in her tracks.

"What's going on? I think I deserve an explanation."

Yida's eyes were wide and her hand hovered near her mouth.

Erik watched them both from farther in the kitchen, his eyes dark as he nodded behind her.

DAYIDA

The explanation took a while. Erik left early on, and there were a lot of things she had to repeat more than once and other things she didn't have the answers for, since they involved his family history, not her own.

"Another secret you've kept from me." He shook his head.

"We can spend time going back and forth on who kept what from who or we can actually talk to each other." She looked away from him. "Lord knows we haven't talked in years."

Robert took a deep breath and rested his head in his hands.

"So at some point in the past my ancestor was a god?"

"Well, a being that was believed to be one of those things, for sure. She could have been a reborn but it's basically the same thing."

"So why don't I have any power?"

"Sometimes it skips whole generations, sometimes every one with the least blood connection ends up powered. It might have something to do with personality and environment, but we don't really know."

"But how does your history work at all?"

"What do you mean?"

"Different beliefs existed at different times in history. It doesn't make any sense that all these things happened at the same time."

She sighed. "The world is very old and in the beginning the old ones lived in harmony among humans and the other living things on the planet. Then they went to war. The details are lost but we know most of them survived.

"That's when the Tower of Babel fell. That is when the people of the world were split into many peoples and languages. That's when the old ones traveled, established themselves among the different people, formed different aspects, different personalities, and mingled with their people.

"Then the second war came when many of their children turned on them. That war destroyed the world."

"Destroyed it?" His voice was muffled by his hands but she could detect a wild note of panic in it.

"Every culture has a flood in its mythology or a different story of the world's death and rebirth. Things are lost, things are reborn, things change, and the world renews every time. Some believe the first world was destroyed after the faithful children of the old ones rose up and banished their siblings from the world. Many bloodlines were lost in the chaos. Those that survived kept the memory of the old ones alive, many of them awakening to the power and becoming Blooded themselves.

"And every so often there are those that are . . . more than awakened. The Reborn. They are . . . different. They usually appear in threes, sevens, or thirteens—mystically significant numbers. They're not the actual old ones but are the source of most of the earth mythologies—the stories they tell, the things they do."

There was more, much more, but she could see the fine tremors running through Robert's hands and when he lifted his head, his eyes were wide and watery.

"What did Erik mean that you were using me?"

She sighed again. He was trying to change the subject but she doubted it would have a happier outcome. "I don't . . . like that I'm awake. I don't want to be, so I've been bleeding off my energy so that it doesn't become so much that I have to use it or anyone notices. I mostly do it through our fights, dissipating it through your body."

He looked at her silently, his brow wrinkled, probably thinking back on their long history of screaming matches. Then he laughed. "Is that all? Considering everything else that seems like a small thing. I can't even really blame you, can I? Not like I didn't give you plenty of reasons to fight with me." He shook his head. "Why didn't my family tell me?"

"It depends. Some families don't reveal it to those who don't awaken to try and save time and drama. I've known since I was a child."

"How old are people when they . . . wake up?"

"Usually teens to thirties, though there have been Blooded who woke up as early as five and as late as eighty-seven. It's one of the reasons we think it has to do with personality and environment. Some simply have to grow into it, others never will."

"So Erik is what?"

"Our son."

He nodded. "No, I mean is he in danger?"

She softened at the actual affection in his voice. She didn't want to worry him further, but he had been lied to enough.

"Yes. Even if he chooses not to fight the Angelics, he'll still be in danger from them."

"So is that what this Organization does? Keep the world safe?"

"Helping to keep it safe, yes. The war against our siblings and their descendants is long and slow but continues on to this day. But it's possible Erik will choose not to join the fight. Some Blooded do try to stay out of it, choose to stay in the civilian world and find a job that they can use their abilities to augment in some way."

"How likely is that?"

She shrugged in response. She hadn't actually talked to Erik about it, but she doubted he would turn away from this. Even as a child his priorities had always been going after those he viewed as bullies, and this was the most animated she'd seen him since Daniel.

"Is that why you're so afraid of . . . being awake yourself?"

Yida pulled away and stood.

"You don't know anything, Robert. You always look at power and ignore the cost of it and that cost is often too high. You lose people, you lose places, you lose memories."

Robert had gone quiet, staring at her face. She stood from the table and paced the kitchen. The whole thing was done in simple black, white, and chrome—Robert's pseudo-intellectual design plan. She leaned against the cool chrome double oven.

"I watched my mom become someone else. After my father went mad and died, she gave into the power inside her, always in full-blood. I watched her become something more powerful but less human."

"I've always liked your mother."

"Yes, I know. She has a lovely mask, but she's not the woman who raised me anymore. She became harder, like she became a conduit and nothing more."

"You're scared of change."

She snorted but didn't pull away as he came to stand behind her and placed his hands on her shoulders.

"I'm scared of being changed, not change. There's a big difference."

"But every change is in reaction to something. No change happens without something to start it."

She laughed. "You make it sound simple, Robert, but it isn't."

He was silent for a time.

"I should go to bed. I have a lot to think about."

"Yeah, I'm going to go paint."

They walked away from one another and the silence that filled the house was the same, but now full of uncomfortable truths rather than lifelong secrets.

MATTHIAS

He had not been back to San Francisco in five years. The old boarding hotel he'd once known now long gone. He was staying in the new high-rise in the Mission that had replaced it and was half empty. His powers made sneaking in and out of one of the penthouses a piece of cake.

The walls were an inoffensive light khaki brown, every appliance top of the line three years ago. A large sleeping bag in red so faded it was pink formed a makeshift bed in the corner of the living room.

He had spent the last few days after dropping Erik off at home reacquainting himself with the city of his birth.

And doing research on Erik's father.

He had not been in San Francisco for so long and much had changed in the last sixty-two months, but the Mormons still kept awesome records. Many of his contacts were no longer in the city itself, having moved to various surrounding cities. Mostly Oakland.

Esta Noche, the iconic gay Latin bar that had been his underage watering hole was also gone, so he'd had to find another place. Luckily there were still some dark bars mixed in among the hipster preferences for organic, white, and expensive. He'd already hit one up tonight and a shot of whiskey and the still-sore feeling of his lips from an epic make-out had relaxed him.

He was lying on the sleeping bag preparing to sleep when his boot began to chirp. Cursing, he pulled the boot close and fished his b'caster from inside. His night was about to be shot to shit. There was no need to delay it.

He placed it against his face and endured the uncomfortable sensation of the wet cords wiggling out and encircling his eye and mouth and entering his ear.

He closed his left eye.

"Answer."

Hu's smug face expanded in front of him.

"Ugh. What do you want Hu?"

"We've done it."

"What?" Matthias sat up. "You found Erik's bloodline."

"No." Hu's face twisted a bit. He didn't trust Hu, he didn't trust anyone in the Organization really, but it thinned even further the higher you went into their bureaucracy. The Maestres were the lead bullshit artists. "We are still looking into that. We do however have an empty way-station near you."

"Really." Then he paused. "Did the other Maestres agree with this, or just you?"

Hu's lips thinned and that was all Matthias needed to confirm his suspicions. Technically Hu was doing nothing wrong; as a Maestre he was trusted to direct the resources of the Organization as he saw fit. The favor Matthias had traded to them made him such a resource *but* a rare resource, a one-time-use-only resource, and usually there would be endless debate over what to do with him.

His orders should have been weighed to help the Organization and also to try and convince him it was in his best interests to join up.

"It's south of the Mission and currently empty. We need to move on this now."

Matthias nodded.

"Do recon along with your berserker."

"His name is Erik. And aren't there teams with more experience that are also more familiar with the territory?"

"Yes, but none with your unique power combination. You can sneak yourself and your companion around and if worst comes to worst he can fight your way out."

Matthias didn't want to admit it but Hu had a point. Some of their best leaps in technologies and medicines, sciences and weaponry, had occurred when someone had managed to raid a way-station or base. And since both were usually built around portals they were often able to destroy those as well, and a watch set on those narrow points between their worlds could make sure no other portal was allowed to manifest.

"Okay, where is this way-station?"

Hu rattled off the address and Matthias wrote it down on the back of a take-out receipt.

"When do you plan to attack?"

Matthias squinted his eyes at the Maestro.

"Why?"

Hu blew out a frustrated breath.

"Because we intend to have other teams in the area to keep it quiet and safe in case of trouble. We don't need non-Blooded getting hurt or seeing something they shouldn't. The clean-up is always more trouble."

Matthias went cold. He knew what might be meant by clean-up.

"I'll pick up Erik and be on my way now."

"Good."

The Maestre disconnected the call before Matthias could do so. He grimaced at the slight sound distortion it left behind and pulled the caster from his face, shoving it into the pocket of his rumpled jeans along with the take-out receipt. He sniff-tested and pulled on a black T-shirt and socks. Jamming his feet into his favorite pair of gray leather boots, he was out the door.

As he jogged to the car, he nodded to a homeless man while avoiding the arms that were outstretched for a hug. He couldn't deny that he was excited to see Erik again. There was something about the man, a combination of sarcasm and optimism and practicality that Matthias had only seen rarely. Erik had seen the worst of the people around him yet still wanted to help others.

Nothing could happen between them. It would be entirely too complicated on both ends. Despite repeating these things to himself, he still found himself smiling as he pulled the car out of the parking space.

ERIK

Erik was bored out of his mind. He had been expelled from school, which was fine by him, but the fact that the two bullies hadn't been really pissed him off. Those little assholes had terrorized the school for years but they were perky and White, so of course they never paid for it. Bringing up the image of them after the fight always made him feel better though.

He would take the GED as soon as he could and get it out of the way, then apply for colleges. Still, at least school had been something to fill his days with. Now he spent most of his at home watching TV, not really able to leave because of the few trucks and cars still waiting outside.

Add to that that the conversation with Robert had not gone well.

"Son, can we try to talk now?"

Erik sighed. It was only the next day, much too soon, but Robert could not wait.

"Yeah, okay."

They were sitting in the living room, Erik muted the reality show that he'd been using to distract himself.

"Your mother explained about the whole Blooded thing."

"Okay."

"It must have been quite a surprise."

"Yeah, it was. Still is." It wasn't as bad as Erik had feared.

"Do you know anything about my bloodline yet?"

"No, but both the Organization and Matthias are looking into it."

"Okay . . . well, let me know what they find out."

Robert stopped and Erik waited, looking at him.

"What's it like?"

"What?"

"To have those abilities? To feel that powerful?"

"Are you kidding me?" Erik voice was quiet but he couldn't control the disbelief that shot through him.

Robert was up and pacing.

"I can't stop thinking about it, ever since your mother told me. How amazing it must be! I can't believe she has it and doesn't want to use it." The bitterness in his voice did not surprise Erik, but he was surprised at the disappointment he felt. He had thought he'd given up on his father long ago, but apparently not. While Robert was facing the other way, shooting questions at Erik, not waiting for answers, Erik rose and went to his room. He locked himself inside for a full day and hadn't seen Robert in the two days since.

There was nothing good on television this late at night; he'd grown tired of the trite suggestions Netflix had for him. He couldn't sleep at all. His mom was in her studio, seemingly unconcerned with Robert's disappearance, so when the doorbell rang he hurried downstairs, anxious for any kind distraction. Matthias was standing on his front stoop.

"Thank god! Tell me there's something to do."

MATTHIAS

M atthias froze, then burst into laughter.

"What is so funny? I'm ready to rip out my nails or actually watch the midnight late-oeuvre M. Night Shyamalan film festival on TV. Not sure which would be more painful. Plus Robert found out about the Blooded thing and was full of questions and then he left a couple nights ago and hasn't been back since."

Matthias stopped laughing.

"I'm sure your father is okay."

Erik nodded and waved it off, but his eyes remained worried.

"We have the mission from the Organization."

"Thank goodness. Something to do. I assume this is our favor?"

"An Angelic way-station in the city is unoccupied. The Organization wants us to do some recon, and destroy their portal."

"What's a way-station?"

"Usually a house that Angelics use to come through to our world or trade goods, back and forth—including people. They're built where the walls between our worlds are easily breached. Usually heavily guarded."

"That seems dangerous. I mean, correct me if I'm wrong, but y'all said that most Blooded can't stand up to an Angelic, right?"

"True."

"Then this seems like a suicide mission for most Agents." Despite his arguments, Erik had already pulled on his shoes and reached behind the door for a small duffle bag, locking the door behind him.

Matthias raised an eyebrow at the bag as they moved toward the car.

"I packed for the weekend early. I told you I was bored."

They slid into the black Mini Cooper.

"Well, the information says the way-station is empty right now so we should be fine, but also . . ." Matthias trailed off.

"They're using me."

"Yeah."

Erik shrugged like it was no big deal but frowned down at his hands in his lap.

"Just this once, though, and we get to shut down a place that they use to take people off to their world." Matthias pulled out of the driveway and turned down the street. Erik went stiff in the passenger seat and his voice, when he spoke, had an odd dreamlike quality to it.

"So we're going to save someone?"

"Maybe." Matthias didn't want to get his hopes up. More than likely if the place was unguarded there was no one left to save, but they could at least shut down the portal. He noticed the numerous cars pulling out behind to follow and waited until he was on a major road and a SUV was between him and most of the paparazzi vultures before letting his power loose and camouflaging the car.

The traffic was fairly light since it was 1:37 in the morning. He made his way back to the Mission district.

"In addition, we're looking for any technology, or papers with notes on them. You probably won't be able to read the language, just grab it if it looks important."

Erik still had a faraway look in his eyes and he squirmed in the seat, but he nodded.

"What about if we run into an Angelic?"

Matthias reached for the glove compartment and pulled it open. The three boxes of ammo were color coded, one red, one black, one white.

"So the Organization was being a little facetious when they said Blooded could not stand up to Angelics. One on one, they're right, but we each have our toys, don't we? The Angelics aren't fully physical."

"They felt physical," Erik said.

"Well that black thing was not a normal Angelic . . . still don't have any idea what it actually was. The other one, the Al-Kutbay? Well we've talked about how you're an advantage.

"So the white box just has regular lead bullets; we find that heavy metals do more damage on Angelic flesh. The red box has rubber bullets, each of which contains a small charge and reservoir of donation from a Souyoucant Blooded. They will explode and the blood will stick to them and burn. The downside is it'll fuck you up too if you inhale too much or get enough on your skin. Well, maybe not you."

"What about the black case?"

Matthias tensed. "That one can kill Angelics, but you are only to use it in the most dire of times. It's something special the Organization created—it eats through matter, living or dead. They only stop when they've devoured enough to be satisfied. They're horrible things. But effective. There will be some guns in the trunk, so we'll get you one too."

"Well, seeing as I don't actually know how to fire a gun, that seems like a stupid idea."

"Oh." Matthias pulled the white case from the glove compartment while they idled at a stoplight. "Well, then one gun for me and none for you. I'll have to take you out to a range."

"Maybe." Erik shrugged, still loose-limbed and relaxed, but his face was now wrinkled in thought. "Any chance of a non projectile weapon?"

Matthias was silent as he steered the car past Cesar Chavez Street.

"Any particular reason why?"

"Black man in America carrying a weapon, even with permits, just doesn't usually end well. Even if I'll survive it, I feel like the secret might get out."

Matthias froze as he turned off onto a smaller, quiet side street. Erik's voice was still vague sounding, but the request was one Matthias should have been able to figure out on his own.

"I'll figure out something else."

Erik nodded.

He pulled up in front of a narrow two-story with a few small square feet of yard in front. A chain-link fence on either side separated it from near-identical houses. The dull neutral tans with a bit of drab gray was peeling a little, the gate stood halfway between functional and broken, the lawn was a mix of brown and green that spoke of good intentions if not good time management.

"It feels different."

Matthias swung his head around. Erik was close, leaning over his shoulder, and Matthias could smell the slightly sour body scent coming from him, pungent but not unpleasant. He cleared his throat and then deliberately shifted his shoulders back, forcing Erik to put some distance between them. He'd been distracted by proximity but the words finally filtered through.

"Feel?"

"Yeah." The dreamlike quality was still in his voice but it felt more focused now, as if Erik were both daydreaming and concentrating on something. "It feels different from the other houses. That one is empty"—he pointed to the one next to their target—"no one's lived there for months. The others all pulse and shift with light, with people, with heat and life. This one pulses but it's different, irregular, painful."

"At least we know we're at the right place." Matthias grabbed the white case from Erik's lap and unsnapped it, pulling out a couple of magazines of ammo. Replacing the case, he climbed out of the car to put some distance between himself and his aspirant. Erik's powers were growing in odd ways and Matthias could somehow smell him everywhere, as if he filled the space all around them. Going to the trunk, he pulled a gun from the steel case. The car door opened and closed again. Slamming one magazine home and placing the other in his pocket, Matthias looked over at Erik.

He was more alert, watching the house with his head cocked to the side, eyes clear but wide.

"It's wrong."

Matthias rolled his eyes. "Can you tell if anyone is inside right now?"

Erik finally turned to look at him smiling. "I don't think it works like that."

Matthias raised an eyebrow. "Really? Then how does it work?"

The confidence fell from Erik's face and the space between his eyes and his mouth wrinkled. "It's like reading the history of something but not the present. Like the energy, the force we use to live has soaked into these houses so I can tell that things live here but I can't tell if they're here now 'cause I'm not reading them exactly but their long-term effect on the house. Does that make sense?"

"No." Matthias was as confused as ever, but a Blooded was usually the best guide to their own powers; their feelings rarely led them astray. Very few killed themselves exploring their powers and a large majority of those happened during the awakening itself. "But I trust what you're saying. Let's go."

He moved up the walk.

"What, we're just gonna walk in the front door?" Erik sounded impressed.

Matthias shrugged. "If there is an Angelic here, odds are they know we're here already. Their senses are usually much better than ours. I'd rather go in the front and have a fast and straight path to the exit if necessary."

Erik grunted but said nothing else as they reached the door. Matthias tried the knob and the door opened silently on its hinges. The hallway was painted an ivory that was yellowed and faded in spots. A set of stairs led up immediately on the right; on the left a hallway led to the rest of the first floor.

Erik moved toward the stairs before Matthias stopped him with a hand on the shoulder.

"It's upstairs," he argued.

The faraway look was back in Erik's eyes and Matthias nodded to show he had heard and understood.

"We need to clear the downstairs first. I don't want to run into any problems if we have to book it."

Erik nodded and they moved through the downstairs with Matthias in the lead. Matthias wrapped his power around both of them, softening the sound of their footfalls, blending their shadows in with the background, turning their breath into the soft rustle of wind. The entire downstairs was empty, not just of Angelics but of everything; there was no furniture, no appliances, nothing. The place was clean but the paint on the walls was faded, the violet wallpaper in the kitchen peeling and falling apart. It looked like a brand-new house that had been left empty for twenty years to acquire the dank mildew smell that came from deep in the walls and filled the whole house. After they'd circled the entire downstairs and gone through every room, Matthias led them upstairs.

Halfway up, Erik tapped him on the back. "The smell is gone."

Matthias took a deep inhale. He was right; the dank scent of mold and disuse was gone. Instead the air was fresh and sharp like right after a rain. Matthias kept on, Erik falling in behind him.

The downstairs was a warren of small rooms leading to and through one another, and the upstairs had probably looked like that once. Now it was one huge space, the walls that had separated the spaces ripped to rubble and left in piles on the floor. The ceiling was a spiderweb of cracks, and small piles of plaster dust attested to the fact that none of this was stable. There was no one he could see.

Erik gasped and grabbed Matthias's arm. He pointed down at the floor.

There was . . . something on the ground that had most likely been human at one point. It lay flat on the floor, gaping open in places like clothing worn and tossed aside. The tangled mass of dark hair looked like a mop, raw and ravaged in knots; the skin had most likely once been peaches and pink but now was grayed leather yellow. The face was in four pieces, split in a cross that with its haphazard toss gave it a manic full-face grin.

"Jesus."

Erik moved over to it. Matthias made a grab for his arm but missed and stayed rooted to the spot. Erik leaned down and touched the skin, jerking his hand back quickly.

"It feels weird."

"No fuck."

Erik looked back and rolled his eyes, the blood and horror of what was in front of him barely seeming to affect him. He reached down again and took a corner between his fingers and lifted it slowly.

"It's not real, right?" Matthias knew he was acting ridiculous; he'd fought his first Angelic when he was only sixteen and he'd survived. He'd killed his first collaborator at eighteen, his first "innocent" normal human at nineteen. This was something else, though; no matter that the face flopped and opened and closed with every bit of Erik's movement, he still was imaging the look of torture and pain on whoever's face it had been when this had happened.

"No, it's real." Erik prodded into the cut area and felt along it. "It's just been changed. It doesn't feel like flesh anymore, it's stretchy and malleable but with a weird powdery dryness."

Matthias finally moved forward to kneel by Erik's side, but he made no move to touch the thing. Closer, he could see it was a human hollowed completely out; the gap flapped open obscenely. There was the off-white of bone. Matthias stood.

"Why?"

"The most obvious answer would be a disguise but also maybe . . . food." Erik finally looked nauseated at his own theory.

"I want us both out of here now." Matthias shivered as he thought of it but said it anyway. "Bring the meat suit. Maybe the Organization can figure out more about it." He watched Erik gather the flopping thing in his hands, look around for a container, and finally shrug and tie it around his waist like some horrible sweatshirt designed by del Toro with help from Giger. Matthias looked away.

They scoured the rest of the broken room quickly, looking for anything else of value.

"I didn't find anything. You?"

Erik shook his head.

"Good, let's blow this place and get out of here."

"Blow?"

"Yeah." Matthias reached into his pocket and pulled out the bomb. It resembled a silver pen that had no cap or nib. He'd grabbed it from the car trunk as well; there were plenty of toys in there.

"Wait, we're actually going to blow this house up? In a crowded neighborhood?"

"It's not actually a physical explosion. I mean, it will blow out the windows but not much else. It's an energy thing, it'll rip the portal from their world to ours wider and wider until it's no longer sustainable and collapses in on itself."

"Okay." Erik sounded uncertain but he would learn; the Angelics had technology beyond anything that Earth had seen since the Betrayal, and the tech the Organization scrounged from them allowed it to stay a few steps ahead of Earth. Grabbing both ends of the bomb, Matthias pulled until a small gap of black appeared as they slid apart. He turned the sides in opposite directions and then pumped them twice. The black in the middle flashed cerulean blue and the whole thing began to whine. "We have five minutes, so let's get out of here quick."

Erik turned to head for the stairs and Matthias followed him. Erik froze, one foot on the step below, and this time Matthias felt it too. Something was building in the room, something other than the bomb. Behind them the room exploded.

TAE

His bedroom was the only room in the house that was Tae's alone. His parents tried and they were mostly great, but they weren't perfect and sometimes the rest of the house felt like a constant reminder of how far from their expectations he'd ended up. School was better. The people there had only known him for a couple of years. There was no past for them to remember. No expectations to hold him to.

His mother was out working on a case. Even having the level of sight his mother did didn't mean she could just look at the evidence and have the answer pop into her head. However, it did let her disregard dead ends and false leads more easily, and once she was on the right track, nothing could turn her from it. Tae's dad was so below his mother's level it was more a gut instinct than him seeing anything. It was really helpful in the kitchen of his restaurant, though.

Tae was far, far stronger than his mother. His problem was seeing too much.

Ophanim had eyes all over their bodies. It was less that Tae's eyes could see better and more that when he wished it, his whole body was eyes, sometimes even when he didn't wish it. How did one see with one's knees? Try and interpret that for a human brain. It was hard and confusing and right now his heart hurt in his chest.

Something was wrong and he'd been lying in his bed for the last hour trying to figure out what his heart saw. He closed his eyes and pressed his hand to his chest, trying to open his senses.

His heart beat because he was in a dark room.

Two people lay on the floor at his . . . feet, no, he didn't have feet.

Something is spreading through the room, something that can feel him.

Outside the window the moon is high in the sky, halfway done with her journey.

He rose from the bed quickly and grabbed the chest binder hanging on the back of his desk chair and struggled into it. Heading to his closet, he pulled on a pair of leather pants—rudimentary armor—and then a tank top and a T-shirt over that. Before he pulled his jacket out and on, he reached between all the coats to the back of the closet. He pushed between them to the safe and quickly typed out the combination.

Inside were three guns: a Glock 17 Gen 4, an M1911A, and the most illegal of the bunch, a sawed-off Remington. His mother had insisted, and so from the age of ten on Tae had trained with guns and other projectile weapons. The gun safe had been a gift from her to appease Tae's father, who did not like the fact that both his wife and son kept guns in the house. Tae pulled the harness from the safe and strapped it around his chest. After loading the Glock he put it in the holster and closed the safe. The weight was comforting as he pulled on a thick leather jacket to conceal the odd bulge and left the house.

His dad was not back from closing the restaurant yet, so there was nothing to worry about as he entered the garage. Sure, he didn't have Maestra Luka's permission to be out but he wasn't actually part of the Organization yet, so her orders only had as much power as he allowed them.

The small light blue jeep was technically Tae's, though it was in his father's name and he wasn't supposed to drive it without talking to them first. He shrugged as he started the car; he didn't want to worry his parents, though, so he plugged his phone into the jeep's Bluetooth.

"Call mother."

After only a couple rings his mother picked up.

"Tae, what's wrong?"

"I don't know but something is. I'm taking the car out to figure it out."

There was silence on the other end of the line and he knew she was using her own sight. There was a frustrated sigh and then she spoke.

"Are you carrying?"

"Yes."

"Be careful. Call Elliot, Daya, or myself if you need backup."

"I will."

"Okay."

A small pause.

"I love you."

"Love you too, Mom."

She clicked off and he pulled the car out of the garage and into the driveway. He turned left at the end of it and immediately knew he'd made a mistake. The pounding in his chest grew weaker and moved toward his back. He pulled a tight U-turn as he said, "Call Elliot."

He drove while the phone rang and rang. Finally a tired voice answer.

"Hello."

"Elliot, it's Tae. Something's happening."

The voice was suddenly more alert. "What is it?"

"I don't know." He let his frustration slip into his voice. "I'm trying to track it down now. It's somewhere in the south half of the city."

"Okay. I'm getting ready. Stay on the phone. Guide me to where you're going. I'll meet you there with Daya."

Tae did so as he steered the car into the Mission district. He arrived at the house and it was like a fire in his chest. He rattled off the address as he stumbled out of the car.

"Okay, we're only a few minutes away. Stay outside until we get there."

Tae disconnected the call without answering and headed up the walk. He couldn't wait a few minutes; a few minutes could be too late. The front door opened under his touch and he pulled his gun as he entered. There was a flash of light from the top of the stairs and Tae hurried up. Near the top he was almost blown back down by a huge gust of wind. He dropped to his belly and yelled when his chest slammed into the edge of the stair.

"Damn it." He breathed through the pain and began to crawl up the steps.

Peeking over the top step, he saw an Angelic appearing in the center of the room. At first all he could make out were teeth, a hundred teeth, all glowing pearl white and long and sharp and serrated, reaching for them. Then he saw the blue pulsing skin between the teeth. A groan drew his gaze to the floor, where Matthias and Erik lay moaning and pushing themselves to their feet.

He didn't know where this fell in his orders, but if there was one thing Tae trusted it was his power. He didn't know why, but Erik was important and he would not let him die.

The Angelic swelled bigger, teeth yawning open and releasing long ropes of dripping black tongues. The tongues fell to the ground and through the curtain of black he spied the silver of metal and a flashing blue light.

"Fuck."

He crawled forward quickly and immediately began to feel nauseated. The ground swelled and moved around him, becoming the ceiling, becoming the wall. Tae swallowed the vomit that wanted to rise up and crawled forward. He reached them and began to pull on Erik's arm.

"Come on, we need to get out of here."

Erik lifted his head. The capillaries around his eyes and lips had burst, giving them a bruised look. His eyes whirled in his head and he was breathing too hard, as if he wasn't getting enough air. He stared at Tae as if he did not recognize him and then shook his head to clear it before nodding slowly. They moved over to the corner where Matthias had been thrown, Erik moving slowly and delicately as if he hurt. They had to avoid several of the tongues that were spreading about the room, but none were actively seeking them so it was a fairly simple if disgusting game of hopscotch.

Matthias was already on his hands and knees but holding one leg up gingerly as if it couldn't take his weight.

"Get on his other side."

Tae obeyed and both he and Erik hooked their shoulders under Matthias's arms and lifted him. As soon as they were touching him, some of the tension began to leak from his body.

"Let's hurry."

"Yeah, I saw the bomb," Tae stated.

They were hobbling toward the landing, Erik wobbling dangerously but holding his own, when he gave a yell and fell to his knees. Matthias tilted and Tae staggered, trying to keep the man stable. He glanced back at Erik. One of the tongues had spiraled into a point at the end and was now stabbed through Erik's side. He had bloody hands around the point, tearing at it, but barbs had extended and dug into his flesh around the wound.

"Motherfucker!"

Tae heaved Matthias toward the stairs. "Go."

Then he pulled his weapon from the holster and struggled to move around the flailing Erik. The tongues were moving with more purpose now and that purpose was to get in his way. He darted around one and hopped over two that were trying to tangle his legs until he had a better line of sight.

He took careful aim. This was an Angelic like he'd never seen before and he didn't know how susceptible to lead it would be. He had to make every shot count. He fired one.

And the tongue exploded into chunks.

Tae froze but jerked out of it as Erik stumbled into him, something large and white grasped in his hands. Another tongue came for them and it exploded in air as Tae caught it with another shot, even as he crumpled under Erik's weight and it took them over the edge of the stairs and down.

ZEBUB

MIN

Min was worried. She liked Arel and Jagi; the other Antes terrified her, but they were more like 'dants and they had played with her and Davi all day. It was night, though, and Lil still wasn't back. All three moons were full, up and shining. Mom and Pop were gone and she didn't want to sleep. Even during her nap with Davi she'd felt too alone and woke up crying with Davi staring at her, never having fallen asleep at all. The dragon flying had occupied their attention for a bit after their nap. They'd headed to the roof of the Hive, where Min and Davi were distracted by the floor. The ground was a dance of light, a massive glowing shadow puppet show. Once Min heard the buzzing of the wings, her eyes snapped up and right to the pens. Two dragons flew in the air, kept chained to the roof by the leather harnesses around their thoraxes.

"They're so pretty," Davi had whispered.

Arel and Jagi had smiled down at them and whistled in unison, calling the two dragons down and removing their harnesses. One was a shimmering blue-green, while the other was a pretty pink. Their eyes were like faceted jewels and bigger than Min's head.

"Stay right there." With those words Arel and Jagi mounted the backs of the dragons and eight shimmering, see-through wings started to beat the air. Min and Davi stared as the two rose into the air so smoothly. Then all at once they had both been swooping down toward Min and Davi, and each of them was suddenly caged by the many legs of a dragon.

They had spent the rest of the day swooping about the Ruling Courts.

That had worked until it was time for bed.

She didn't know how much Davi understood and wanted to talk to him about what had happened to their parents, but she was scared to bring it up. Also, Min didn't want to think about it. They weren't coming back.

She was tired, barely able to keep her eyes open, but she didn't want to sleep without Lil. Arel and Jagi seemed to understand, and after they put Davi down to sleep she sat on Arel's leg while Jagi told them a story. His tentacles were out and moving all around him, casting elaborate shadows on the walls that represented castles and villains and whole crowds of 'dants. It reminded her of the roof.

Min laughed and clapped as Martes, the hero of Court Murielle, earned their new name—the Court of Feedings—and conquered the spirit of the Destrei, even though it tainted the surrounding lands, turning them into the badlands south of Zebub.

A throat cleared behind them and Min stood and turned in Arel's lap.

"Lil!" She launched herself from Arel's lap, through the air. Lil ducked forward and caught her just before she hit the ground.

"Minnie, don't do that." Lil sounded tired but she lifted Min up to her face. "What if I didn't catch you?"

Min reached up and patted Lil on the cheek and giggled.

"You wouldn't drop me, Lil."

Lil's face did something weird, scrunching up in the middle, and then she blinked a whole lot and clutched Min tightly to her chest until she squirmed to get down. When Lil set her on the ground she slipped her hand into Lil's and looked up at her sister.

"Can we go to bed now? I'm tired."

"I'm sorry, sweetheart, but I have to go out again."

Min's eyes got hot and her face felt like it was melting. She tried to hold back the wail but it came anyway and tears streamed down her face. Lil picked her up and tried to soothe her.

"I'm so sorry, dear-heart, but I'll lie with you until you fall asleep and then Arel and Jagi will watch you until I return. I promise you'll wake with me next to you."

Min kept crying, unable to stop the sobs right away, but she looked over Lil's shoulder at the two Antes.

"But what if I need you?" Min gasped out the words. She knew she was acting like Davi, like a baby, but she couldn't help it. She didn't want to lose Lil too.

Arel came forward at her question and lay a hand on Lil's shoulder that wasn't currently playing pillow for Min.

"Not a problem, little one. There is a bloodline called Turms who are connected to one another at all times. We shall ask for one to station outside the door and there will certainly be some at the party, so should anything happen your sister will be told immediately."

Min had finally stopped crying but she felt shaky in her chest and her breath was way too quick. She turned to Lil.

"And you promise you'll come right away if we call."

"Yes, Min, I promise."

"Okay. But you still have to stay until I fall asleep."

"Of course."

Min wriggled until Lil let her down on the ground again. She grabbed Lil's hand and led her to the bedroom to curl up around Davi.

LIL

il was tired but Minnie must have been exhausted. She had not ever seen her sister break down like that. Her sister had always been the type more likely to sulk and pout than to cry. Minnie fell asleep almost as soon as she was lying down with Lil's arm over her. Lil considered passing out, but she doubted the consequences of skipping a dinner invitation from the Ruling Courts would be pleasant. When she was sure neither of her siblings would wake, she rose from the bed and crossed back into the living area.

Arel and Jagi were waiting for her alongside a rack of clothing she'd never seen before.

"What's this?"

"Clothing for dinner."

Lil looked down at herself and closed her mouth on the question of why she had to change. Her white tunic was filthy, sweat-stained, and in disarray, and after a discreet sniff she could admit that she was also a bit ripe. However, the others had gone to dinner as they were and the clothing arrayed on the curved rack of bone was of a higher quality than Lil had ever seen with more elaborate fastenings than she'd ever used. Lil had never developed a taste for more expensive raiment; her loose pants and tunic uniform were more than enough for her.

Arel read the look of distaste on her face and continued.

"Even if they are not to your taste it is best to impress the Ruling Courts while you are here, especially if you are going to show up late. Everyone's attention will be on you when you enter."

Lil bit her lips and approached the rack of clothing. She was happy to see that only half of the things on the rack were skirts or dresses. There were robes with pants to go underneath and jumpsuits in a beautifully elaborate chained design that would still leave her legs relatively free to move.

She actually became excited by some of the things and ended up choosing a beautiful pair of gray leather pants. She could not tell the animal, but they were soft and had a slight reflective shine to them. The stitches had been kept small to make it seem like it had been cut in one piece. The shirt was a simple white but with a texture that made it seem rumpled stylishly and the places it was folded shone with blue where the light hit it.

"The bathing room is down the hall, the third door on your right."

Lil nodded, remembering steam coming from the threshold on her way through the building earlier. Arel handed her the softest robe she had ever felt, the loose fabric wiggling in her grasp like jellied water. She slowly stripped, leaving her torc of office on, and draped the cloth over her shoulders. It spread down her body like rain, clothing her form in something that resembled peach glass. She headed to the bathing room.

Opening the door, she was greeted by a wave of steam and heat. Her skin flushed and the material of the robe thinned in response so that her skin was cooled by the slight breeze moving through the room. Her feet moved over warm, rounded stones that massaged her soles as she walked. The bath itself consisted of two round inset pools next to one another. One bubbled and released the steam and delicious chemical scent of a hot spring and the other was chilled. She could see the fog that rose from it's surface and was dissolved by the steam.

She pulled at the neck of the robe and it peeled from her body slowly, reluctant to let her go. Lil resisted shivering in pleasure as it left her body with a *schlurp* sound and a delightful pulling sensation. Slipping into the hot water, her whole body unknotted. Muscles she had not known were tense turned languid. She wanted to soak for hours but was already late for dinner, so she grabbed a handful of the rough, granular soap in the dish by the edge of the pool and began to scrub her skin and hair.

She thought about Arel and Jagi and the help they were providing. She would be more suspicious had she not seen the inside of them so clearly during the binding. Even still, she wondered at their angle. Just because they bore her no ill will did not explain actually helping her, but she was in no position to throw away potential allies no matter their motivation. The Holders and Holder-Apprentices were the only 'dants within the Ruling Courts' Hives other than Min and Davi.

She would have assumed their isolation would make them more reliant on one another. Then she had seen the Holders together. Never had she seen her mentor act so petty and angry. Even while in the Ossuary, they had been taking shots at each other's positions and reputations. She believed they needed to be working together. If there was a clue on how to defeat the creeping dark in the Ossuary, better to work together to find it. Lil still believed that it was an attack from a pocket universe, that it was a group that had disappeared long ago and was now returning to make a bid for power.

Perhaps even the Traitor Hive themselves. The Ruling Courts said they were all dead, but if any had survived would they allow even rumor of that to escape? She would love to talk this over with Mayer. And yet.

In the space of two days she had gone from trusting Holder Mayer with her life to being wary of his anger and moods. Their relationship, always sheltered by the Athenaeum walls, was different in the Ruling Courts. Mayer was different. Was this why he had never brought her along when he came to the help with the Hives? Was this angrier and more secretive version of her mentor a mask he put on when he entered the dangerous political waters of the Ruling Courts, or was it his true face?

Mayer said one of their main jobs was to maintain the precarious peace between 'dant and Ante, but how was she to help if he kept things from her?

She rose and scrubbed her skin to a glowing dark topaz and then leapt into the ice pool. Her breath froze and her whole body tightened. She felt too large for her skin, as if she might split open right here and emerge into the icy water a new being entirely. Her head felt clearer and though no answers to any of her questions miraculously appeared, she at least felt confident in remembering Arel and Jagi could not harm or allow harm to come to Davi or Min.

She could simply take the help they offered, and as for everything else she would be wary and watchful. Even of Mayer.

Lil bobbed to the surface of the cold pool, spraying water everywhere, and pulled herself onto the warm stones of the floor. Rising to her feet, she delighted in the feel of her heavy brown curls resting on her shoulders, water dripping down her back. She reached for the pool of peach shimmer that was the robe. As she once again draped it over her shoulders, it spread down again, this time also forming a hood that came up over her hair. It sucked up all the moisture into itself, leaving her skin and hair only slightly damp.

Back in her room she was greeted by Arel and Jagi sorting through a small wooden basket of jewelry. She looked at it warily, thinking of the necklace that had given Razel such a shock in the Ossuary. The rack of clothing was gone, the clothes she had chosen laid out on the couch.

"I already have my torc." She rose a hand to touch the piece, warm and vibrating against her neck.

"True, but we need other pieces to go with that. Since the clothes you chose were neutral we're going to add color through red accessories." Jagi did not look up as he said this, focusing on the wood trunk that contained the pieces.

Arel and Jagi helped her dress. They stripped her of the robe and pulled out a tub of what looked like black sand, took handfuls, and starting at her shoulders began to rub it into her skin. There was no sexuality to their touch as they covered her body. She looked down and saw the rough substance diminish and sink into her skin as it was rubbed. Her skin was left smooth and almost glowing in the muted light from the vines wrapped around the roof rafters. The small buds she had noted earlier had now opened and revealed multilayered flowers of pink, whose stamens hung further down and gave off a light of such pale rose it looked white.

More light came in through the open window where Lil could spot Shelgig, Rona, and Rythi high and bright in the air.

Once every bit of her had been oiled, including the tight kinky curls of her dark brown hair, the two Antes removed the clothes from the hangers and the pins from the fabric and helped her step into them. Then the cosmetics came out and she flat out refused.

"No. I will not paint myself for their pleasure." Most 'dants did not wear such powders and liquids; most could not afford it. Only those who worked freely with the Antes sported such things.

Jagi crouched on his haunches before her, holding a thin cone of metal in one hand and a lump of some mineral in the other.

"It will not be too much, but cosmetics are ingrained in the Ruling Courts, for those who can wear such are usually those who look like 'dants . . . or are 'dants. To wear nothing would be like declaring yourself nothing. Luckily the current trend is for subtle powders. If this were two seasons ago, we would all be caked from brow to upper lip in symmetrical images of dragons."

Lil bit her lip but finally nodded. She winced at a particularly tight curl of Arel's fingers as he pulled back her hair and, using the oil, began to twist it into a complicated, high bun.

"You must keep still and close your eyes for the first portion."

Lil did as he asked and a soft grating sound started. She felt light pressure falling onto her eyelids. It reminded her of the time Mayer and she had made a day trip across the Drylands to the southern city of Dis and been caught in a sudden sandstorm with no protection except for the thinnest shell of power. She felt powder cover her eyes, cheeks, and the bridge of her nose. Then the metal was pulled away and she felt the cool wind of Jagi's breath—it smelled of copper and roses. Then something damp covering the powders.

"Now you may open your eyes, but keep perfectly still."

Jagi held a long thin metal spike in his hands poised near her right eyeball.

"What are you doing?" She tried to jerk away but Arel's hands held her firm.

"Would I tell you to open your eyes if I were going to harm you?"

She stopped struggling but still watched the pointed end of metal warily as it approached her face. He lowered it, scraping against the powder he had put on her. Occasionally he would rub the tip against a small white piece of fabric, cleaning of clumps of black, red, and yellow paint.

When he was finally done she stood and turned to the mirror in the sitting room.

Lil looked at herself. The pants clung to the muscles of her thighs, showing the power in them usually hidden by the drape of her tunic. The shirt was loose and light and the way it swung about her as she shifted from foot to foot caught both air and light made it look like wings from one angle and a veil of fog from another. She vetoed the earrings, not used to the weight of them, but allowed them to include a blood-red jeweled bracelet in addition to her choker. She was initially resistant to the three rings they picked out, a matching set of three red jewels carved into circles, each one darker than the last, but allowed herself to be convinced.

The makeup took her breath away. Her eyelids and the surrounding skin were the darkest black with subtle speckles of red as if filled with embered coals, those that tricked you into thinking they were safe to handle. The bridge of her nose was a yellow that turned to orange, then red as it spread out across her cheeks. Into the red and yellow Jagi had carved pathways so that her own topaz skin was revealed in the shape of flames. Not some vulgar, literal interpretation, but abstract angles and peaks.

The idea of fire.

She stood in front of a narrow mirror catching small glimpses of the two Antes that flanked her. The skin of her face, neck, and hands—all that was revealed by the outfit glowed. The shirt only accentuated her brown skin. The gray pants stood out against the white of the shirt like stone. For shoes Arel and Jagi had managed to scrounge up calf boots in the same gray as the pants. They had a slight heel, more than she was used to but not enough to hinder her movement. As soon as she had put them on they seemed to merge with the pants legs and mold to her calf.

Lil still recognized herself in the mirror, but she was more somehow. She was not the shy, smart girl everyone thought of her as. Or she still was that girl and would always be that girl, but was just more than that now. Power and confidence radiated from her and the makeup highlighted the strength in her face, the strong bones and deep eyes.

"Lovely." It was said so softly that Lil could not tell if it came from Arel or Jagi. She smiled either way.

"Now you must be off."

Arel guided her to the door with a gentle hand at the small of her back. As he opened it, two Antes were revealed. One was a long, flat rope of a body, its skin sparkled with green, blue, and red jewels. It was coiled about itself in an impossible-to-follow tangle, taking on the vague shape of a cylinder with an explosion of legs below and above. The other one was a glittering cloud of mist, the edges of its body clearly marked by a more solid edge of white. Within the amorphous shape little sparkles of gray and white flickered and died, merged and separated, formed things that looked like eyes to stare down at her and things that looked like mouths to laugh at her.

They stood silent and Lil wondered if these were some of the Antes who could not or would not speak to 'dants at all. Were they angry they had been sent to escort her? She stepped forward and then they were facing the other way. They did not turn; instead, it was as if they melted and reformed facing in the opposite direction. Both began to move forward and Lil followed. Though she did not look back, she could feel Arel and Jagi's eyes on her back all the way down the hall.

AREL & JAGI

"**W**ill she be all right?"

Arel met Jagi's gaze and the ridges of bone that were his eyebrows conveyed uncertainty. Jagi mirrored the gesture and Arel lct out a sigh.

"Not if they suspect what we do."

"But they have no reason to suspect. Would most even understand?"

Arel sucked on his teeth and his torso orifices opened and closed in agitation. He barely managed to keep his tentacles from emerging.

"No, most don't know the stories, but if they see something threatening they will still not hesitate to strike her down. They will all be watching tonight."

Jagi's more emotional agitation was obvious from the noise his tentacles made as they emerged and then retreated.

"What will we do?"

"We will keep our eyes and ears open, we will try to give her warning, and above all we will do what we promised and protect her sibs from any harm."

Jagi nodded and they both turned to watch Min and Davi curled into one another on the bed. There was nothing more that could be said about it. They could only circle around the knowledge they already had. They had written to Hina, the only member of their bloodline they still spoke with, to see if she could research further. She had replied quickly, telling them she would send any information as she found it.

Even though they still spoke with Hina, neither trusted her fully. She belonged to the House of the Unseen and they viewed everyone not of their House as a pawn for their own advancement. They at least knew where they stood with her, and in this she would wait to be completely sure before she told anyone.

To be the one who prophesied the end of their world was not a role anyone wanted.

RAZELL

Razel wished she had some excuse to miss even part of this dreadful affair. Dinner was in the central courtyard tonight, so no Court could claim prominence. The wind and insects were being kept out of their area by a barrier of power, marked by a small ripple in the air that surrounded all the tables. The Ante that were always airborne stayed so far above that she could only catch glimpses of them when she strained her vision upwards, so she assumed the protection went all the way up. Not a dome but a cylinder.

It would take a lot of power to heat and protect an open cylinder. She amused herself trying to figure out how much energy exactly, though she was missing quite a few necessary components for the correct equation. This at least kept her attention for a few minutes before she gave up. Anything was better than this. She would rather be in that horrid basement in the Hive of Sorrow and Riches, improving on her creations, than doing this. As much as she hated that place and herself when she was there, at least that was progress being made.

The conversations going on around them had not involved her or Riana much at all. Krezida and Haydn were also ignored. Mayer, seated at another section of the table, was much in demand, speaking to this Ante and that one. The other two Holders obviously had no intention of speaking to one another unless they had to, and the Holder-Apprentices did not wish to disrupt the atmosphere their masters created. They were surrounded by chatter but their section of the table was silent.

The tables were spread across the length of clear space, all made of the same dark green black-flecked material.

It did not escape her notice that she and her mentor, as well as Haydn and his, had been seated with mostly 'dant-resembling Antes. It was easy to take this as an attempt to offer them dinner companions they could actually converse with, but she knew it was actually an insult. Any Ante could rise high in the Ruling Courts, could form a Court of their own, build a Hive, and speak on various councils. Technically.

But it was harder for those who looked too much like 'dants.

Much in the way that 'dants became even more nervous around Antes that were closer to their inhuman predecessors, Antes did not enjoy being reminded that they could look like 'dants at all.

There was movement to her right. She turned to see Lil step through the barrier. Razel was caught and reminded how rough the rest of them still looked. All of their clothing was stained; luckily her shorter hair was fine, but the longer, more elaborate hairstyles of Holders Riana and Krezida were both in noticeable disarray.

Lil was not an extraordinary beauty by any means, though she was nice to look at. The allure tonight came from the fact that that she was so 'dant. So mortal. And unashamed of that fact. Her brown skin shone lightly through the shirt, the makeup on her face reminded all seated of the spark of 'dant life, quickly gone but burning bright, instead of attempting to hide the minuscule wrinkles and signs of age she had even in her youth. The powder settled into those cracks and highlighted them. Her face looked older, yes, but it also reminded all of those assembled that she would age and die, that everything she did was ephemeral and important.

Meanwhile her pants hugged the muscles of her legs and her stance was one of uncaring. At first Lil froze and shrank in on herself at the attention. Razel saw her take a deep breath and then stiffen her back and neck; her head came back up and she met the gazes head on. Her brown hair, which Razel had only seen pulled back in a puff or wild about her face, was oiled and shining, arranged in tight braids halfway down her skull before exploding into a curling high crown-like bun. She straightened her body and jutted one hip to the side, craning her head from one side to the other to take in all of the room.

Many of those seated had fallen silent and still and watched her walk into the room. That limit of life, of their life, was what drew Antes to 'dants. Whoever had made her up knew that this reminder of their fascination with 'dants would both attract and repel them.

Mayer did not even glance her way, though it would have been impossible for him to miss her entrance at the angle he was seated. Riana leaned over.

"What is that old man playing at now?"

Razel lowered her voice to a shade of sound, noticing that Krezida and Haydn were in conference as well.

"You think that Mayer is behind this?"

"Yes. Look at her. So confident in the Ruling Courts. Why? It is like a mizzene dancing among the bone-wolves of the wastes."

The shy and elusive mizzene danced under moonlight among themselves, furry feet and tails raised high, beautiful, but a pack of mizzene had also been rumored to take down an Ante when they put their mind to it. Razel found it an apt metaphor. "True. But Mayer will not look at her."

Riana turned and observed, making a humming noise in her throat. "It is almost as if he views her as a threat. That is an opening we should exploit. Make friends with his Holder-Apprentice. See if this is a plan or a rift."

Razel nodded and then gasped.

A flood of black fell from directly above Lil as she hovered at the barrier, unsure of her welcome with her Holder. The mass slowed as it fell until it hovered gently in the air, then it started to separate. A thousand perfect black butterflies peeled away and fell to cloak the young girl.

"Nif?"

Razel heard the question in Haydn's voice but did not answer. She was too focused on what was happening before her.

LIL

Fear froze her feet to the floor. She wished to turn and run but knew it would be no use. She had everyone's attention, as Arel and Jagi had said, and if she was to make an impression one way or another, let it be a good one. She took a breath and tried to recover the calm she had felt as Arel and Jagi had worked on her hair and face. Her body relaxed as she focused on the feeling of comfort and safety. She felt her fear settle. Her position protected her more than most. She would not shame it or her parents by acting as prey.

Her head came up and she scanned the room. Her gaze lit on Mayer but he was paying no attention to her. She knew that her decision to check on Davi and Min before dinner would anger him, but to visually repudiate her in such a manner? Her confidence began to crumble at the public humiliation, but suddenly she felt a feather light touch on her shoulders. She was surrounded by butterflies. They sparkled in the pale light of the three moons as if made of onyx. They covered her shoulders first, and then she felt their coolness as they fell along the line of her body like a cape until they brushed the floor.

She recognized them as Nif right away, though she had never seen them take a form other than the small humanoids or pools of shadow they preferred. They radiated a soothing cold and she felt her fear lessen further. They shivered and she felt pressure on the small of her back and stepped forward, the butterfly cloak fluttering and flaring behind her as she moved.

She saw the other Holders and Holder-Apprentices in one place and would have joined them, but the Nif pressured her the other way. To the seat beside Mayer. Even as she neared, he did not turn to face or acknowledge her at all. She sat in the empty chair beside him and released a sigh when no one objected.

The tongues that flew around her were nothing like the language the 'dants of the area spoke. Mayer was conversing somewhat freely, gesturing for the words that were too complicated for his human tongue to curl around or too broad for the width of his throat. Lil was not nearly as skilled, could not converse in nearly as many of the dialects, but she could understand well enough.

As she sat in the seat, the Nif parted around her body and draped to the floor on either side of her chair. She picked up her spear and knife and began to cut away at the huge slab of meat on her plate. The leafy vegetables she also speared, but the odd squishy white block she pushed to the edge as politely as possible. The babble of their voices fell over her as she ate.

"The idea of allowing 'dants into the Ossuary is horrifying. The longer you find nothing, the more suspicion will fall." The language sounded like running water and the literal translation would actually be four times as long because of the nuance and many, many metaphors. It came from the bulbous Ante across from Mayer, a oblong ball of blue flesh that had additional globules of various colors attached to its outer layer.

Mayer replied in the same tongue, a tiny trickle of drool escaping the corner of his mouth as his lips struggled to flap properly in the wind of his breath. "True; however one cannot expect the tadpole to mature in minutes."

The reply sounded like 'dant laughter but was actually a lengthy description of how the speaker had amused them. Lil smiled politely in case the Ante looked in her direction. A number of Antes at the table snuck glances at her, or took information about her in through other senses. She could feel sensory apparatus pointed at her and it made her shiver. The Nif thickened around her collar and warmth suffused her body.

The scent of dead eggs wafted to her, followed by the crush of roses and then the fading scent of general decay. An Ante of the Muriil bloodline intruded into the conversation. Lil, through a mighty effort, kept chewing through the volley of smells Mayer and the Ante threw at one another until something hit her nose, sharp and commanding without an actual scent attached. It was like there was something that should have been there, a scent so unobtrusive it was obvious among the stronger ones simply for the relief it provided.

It was asking about their progress in the Ossuary, but the scent itself reminded Lil of the feeling of the darkness as she and her family stood there frozen waiting to be devoured. The fear shook her into speaking.

"Have there been more attacks?" Mayer and the Ante froze and Lil bit her tongue. It was a mistake to interrupt a conversation in the Ruling Courts, especially when you had no formal title. But her heart was in her throat as she remembered that ever-creeping dark and how it had swallowed 'dants and places she had known all her life. She had to know how many more had suffered as she had.

Some of those around her understood but it was obvious some did not. Antes who did not have much contact with 'dants never bothered to learn to comprehend their language. Those who did not understand turned to Mayer, waiting for a translation. He grimaced and his face froze. She knew him, knew he was calculating how much it would hurt his own status to ignore her.

He had not started to translate when a scent rose up around her, from her. The musky marking of a desert cat and then the same dark scent of nothing she had just experienced. A small fluttering sound made itself known, and she cocked her head in shock to see that the Nif butterflies that covered her shoulder were emitting the scent and flapping their wings steadily to spread it.

The table erupted into a dozen conversations conducted in so many different manners Lil could not keep track. Scents exploded, as did voices in dozens of different dialects; skins flashed through colors; and fingers and tentacles and appendages Lil had never seen before beat questions onto the tabletop. The babble did not pass their immediate vicinity but it became clear that something was happening, and other sections of the table fell silent as they tried to figure out what it was.

Lil was frozen, trying to concentrate on picking one "voice" out of the din to find out what happened. The idea and answer that was repeated over and over through sight, sound, smell, and touch was Nif. Lil realized none of the talk had anything to do with her asking a question or interrupting—it was all about what the Nif had done.

Mayer leaned over toward her, his usual pale cheeks flushed an uneven, shiny red, making the dark stubble on his cheeks stand out. He hissed at her in a voiced designed not to carry.

NA'AMEN GOBERT TILAHUN

"What have you done?"

Lil was shocked by the way his face turned into something monstrous, the thinning of his lips, the deep valley that appeared between his narrowed eyes. He had never spoken to her like this, not even when she disobeyed, not even when she had to be punished. Lil could see the fear that was driving the expression across his face but the Antes did not seem angry, just confused and curious.

"Nothing." She hissed it back trying to fit all the injured dignity and indignation she felt into the word, though she could not suppress the thread of fear. It was automatic on some level; Mayer had been her protector and teacher for years, and his fear triggered her own. The few times he'd shown fear in the past had been her cue to feel the same.

Slowly the fervor died down and conversation continued in its myriad different ways. This time, however, Mayer was forced to include her in the conversation at the insistence of others. Though he was now unnecessary, she could already understand most of the dialects around the table, and the Nif took care of expressing her thoughts in the languages she had yet to learn to "speak."

She was asked about her training and managed to be vague, mysterious, and threatening all at once. It was the first time she'd received a smile out of Mayer all evening. The Antes murmured approval.

When asked about her family, she was able to remain stoic and discuss how happy she was to spend time with her sibs, while steering clear of any mention of her parents. They all knew of her parents' death. Little remained secret from the Courts, but to mention them would show weakness and she could not afford that. However, by focusing on her devotion to her remaining family, she showed how much she cared for her bloodline.

For conversations conducted in sound, whether voice, grunt, or rhythm, she was able to hold her own. When the conversation turned to lights or smells or the creating of wind currents, languages in which she had understanding but which she had not yet been taught to manipulate, the Nif still cloaking her conversed for her, reading her intentions and relaying them more or less intact.

Her anxiety flared when the Nif added a scent of flirting in a reply to an Ante that was nothing but a mound of moving, grinding fingernails. However, it collapsed all over itself in an ear-melting grind-shriek of what she took to be laughter, so she smiled along. They broke into smaller and smaller conversations as the night wore on and the guests moved from table to table, switching chairs in some complex dance they were excluded from but surely had something to do with power and hierarchy. She sighed. She would have to learn it all if she was to become Holder herself one day. Why had she not already learned it?

"Why do you sigh so sadly?"

Lil nearly jumped at the voice, calling on her training to maintain her calm outward facade. It was a dialect she knew, but the accent was something she had never heard before, a blurring of the consonants so that all the words were soft and welcoming. The Ante who had spoken was shaped like a 'dant superficially, except that their skin looked like smoky glass. Things floated through them, diffuse lights and vague shapes and colors traveled across forehead, then down neck and through uncovered androgynous chest. Soft and hard and beautiful, but neither male nor female. Their pants hid whether the effect covered all of their body, but Lil was sure it did.

She shook herself from following a particularly beautiful teal pulsing light across their cheek and pulled her mind back to what had been said. Before she could think up a suitable reply, they spoke again.

"I have never seen the Nif act so for a 'dant."

She snapped her attention from the gold traveling through two plump pursed lips and said casually, "They have acted this way before, though?"

"Yes, it's not that unusual. They are sometimes forced to act as interpreters for Ante without the ability to represent some of the languages." They waved it away with a perfect hand. The nails were hard and white, opalescent in the light. "However, them doing the same for a 'dant, and of their free will? Now *that* is a surprise."

Lil felt as if there was something she was supposed to remember, but the color of their eyes was fluctuating so fast that all her focus was taken by identifying the color they were at that very second.

The Ante leaned forward and reflexively she began to do the same, but something outside held her back, a tightness in her shoulders. Still, even that little bit closer she felt as if the lights under the skin were brighter, moved faster.

"You have half of the Ruling Courts more fascinated with the Athenaeums than they have been since the war."

That sentence snapped her wholly out of whatever trance she had been falling into. Now she understood at least some of Mayer's anger at her. Tensions between the Athenaeums and the Courts were always

NA'AMEN GOBERT TILAHUN

ready to explode. If not into all-out war—they had not had a true warring conflict in over five thousand years—then into something almost as unpleasant. Sanctions, hassles by the Courts agents, both official and unofficial, up to and including vandalism of the Athenaeum.

Only five years ago Mayer had done something that had set the Courts up in arms. Lil had never learned all the details, but she had arrived at Kandake one morning to find the building sunk into the suddenly softened ground up to the top of the first floor windows. She'd spent two weeks living muddy on the second story and translating texts for the Court of Feedings so they would raise it again.

"Why?"

"There is power in you. Anyone with sense can see it."

"It is only the same ability that Holder Mayer possesses, nothing new." He had taught her everything she knew, so why did her words feel like a lie?

"Perhaps not." The Ante shrugged and looked away. "However, you yourself are new and that is enough to make you interesting to some. Do you have a special relationship with the Nif at your Athenaeum?"

Lil thought about the quick broken shadows that moved through the lit halls of the Athenaeum, that appeared without request to help her. The ones she had give names to—lugh and eri, iles and ayl, coo and woge, xex and defi—acts that were not unnatural, but odd all the same.

The lies died on her tongue as a shooting star of silver light cascaded across the Ante's forehead and down one cheek; it exploded and reflected through their face. Suddenly she felt comfortable, relaxed, as if she might slip out of her chair. The Ante was no longer a stranger but an old friend.

She smiled and opened her mouth, happy to answer all their questions. There was a tightening around her neck and shoulder and her tongue twisted in her mouth, against her will, a single word falling from it before something freezing cold spilled down her back. She leapt to her feet, just managing to refrain from calling out. She turned around and found a Turms, identical to the one that Arel and Jagi had summoned up to the room upon her exit, holding a small glass of liquid that sparkled, leftover drops crawling up the sides as if it were alive and wanted to escape.

It bowed its head in apology and Lil tried to indicate it was no problem but the Ante she'd been speaking to spoke up for her.

"No, I believe I am the one who owes the young lady an apology. We so seldom see 'dants in the Ruling Courts that I forget the effect that I tend to have upon them. I take my leave of you, young Holder. Until we meet again." The Ante stood and bowed low.

Lil begged exhaustion and Mayer seemed delighted to see her leave; at least now she felt she knew why. She made her way back to her rooms, walking slowly, nervous, thinking of the word that had slipped past her lips. She had felt the others lined up behind it, a string of words that had burned with power in her throat, but what had caused it? Was it Babel itself? Mayer had warned her that Babel was not like any other tongue; it was a living, willful language. That was why you had to fight to shape it, but nothing like this had ever happened before, Babel coming without her call. She longed to ask Mayer about it but hesitated to share anything with the 'dant he'd become.

What effect would the entire phrase have had? She shivered at the thought of calling up any Babel at all among such a large group of Antes.

Arel and Jagi were pacing, a million questions and explanations swimming in their eyes. She was too tired for any of it.

She raised her hand and the two of them subsided. She ripped off the clothing they had so carefully placed on her, threw it on the couch, and moved into the bedroom. She shut the door and crawled beneath the blankets, wiggling her way between her two siblings. When she was surrounded by the scent of family and the heat of two small bodies, she tried to drift off to sleep.

However, she could not stop thinking about that feeling, her own body betraying her will. She stayed up long into the night, trying to understand the word of Babel that had slipped past her lips, but it was beyond her lessons. She fell into an exhausted sleep much, much later, her body betraying her once again.

AREL & JAGI

They stared at the closed door.

"Why is the white snake involved?"

"Your guess is as good as mine but it is most certainly nothing so straightforward as belonging to a side. The white snake has its own plan in all this."

"And other than that?"

"It could have gone better."

"It also could have gone worse."

"She did not inadvertently reveal herself."

"If what we believe is true."

"Let's hope it is. Then we may have some chance against whatever the creeping dark is."

They slept in the small front parlor, wrapped in each other, alert for any movement or danger.

SAN FRANCISCO

MATTHIAS

He lay on the ground outside the house beside two unconscious bodies, Erik still with the gruesome remains of someone else tied around his waist, a white skull held in his palms, and blood slowly dripping from the place one of the Angelic's tongues was still lodged in his side. He had been waiting at the bottom of the stairs when Erik and Tae had been launched down them and directly into him. He'd dragged them outside and only a minute later all the windows on the second floor silently exploded and showered them with glittering glass. Now they simply lay on the tiny scrap of grass in front of the house, his power covering them from wandering eyes. His body healed more the longer he lay near his aspirant.

He tried to figure out how the mission could have gone so badly. The build-up to bring through an Angelic that large should have been noticeable for at least an hour before the thing came through. Alarmers should have notified the Maestres in the area, who in turn should have spread the word and sent Blooded out to monitor the situation.

The sound of a roaring motor and the skidding of brakes finally forced him to raise his head. The small crotch rocket came to a sudden stop on the sidewalk only feet from them. As soon as he saw Elliot jump off the back and Daya kill the engine, he flopped back down to the ground and let his hold on his powers dissipate.

"What happened?" Elliot's voice was shrill and Matthias could feel his power roiling around him looking for some direction, something to do. He held his helmet in one hand, visor up, almost as if ready to use it as a weapon. Daya had placed hers on the bike itself.

"A way-station. An Angelic came through right as we were leaving."

The silence was answer enough and he opened his eyes to find the two partners staring at each other worriedly over his torso. Meanwhile, Elliot was running his hands over Erik as Daya did the same for Tae, trying to suss out any injuries.

Tae came awake with a start and smacked Daya's hands away from his body.

"What's going on?"

"What's going on is you disobeyed a direct order from your *Counselor*!" Daya yelled as she tried to check him over again. He pushed her away and sat up.

"There was no time and I'm fine."

"He probably is, I had him in contact with Erik this whole time and his powers are running high healing him up. There's a lot of spillover."

"No wonder." Elliot leaned over Erik's side where the pointed tongue had gone limp and flopped back onto his chest.

"Don't take it out until we get to Brisbane. It's stopping him from bleeding out and even with his healing ability I want him near a facility when we cut it out."

"Let's get going then." Tae sounded enthusiastic but his voice was strained as he rose to his feet. He swayed on his feet before he locked his knees.

Elliot and Daya looked at one another. "Yeah, I don't think you can drive," Daya stated.

"I'm fine. Besides, you need three drivers. One for my car, one for Matthias, car, and one for your bike."

Daya shook her head. "Nope. Matthias's loaner will be fine here for a few hours. It has protections, we'll summon it back to the garage. Elliot will drive your car to Brisbane with all of you piled in and I'll ride my bike."

"But—"

"End of story." Her voice was hard and full of the warning that he was still in trouble for entering the house in the first place. Matthias smiled; he remembered that tone from years ago, and Tae seemed to have learned it quickly enough since he just dropped his head and handed his keys to Elliot. Daya picked Erik up bridal-style while Elliot helped Matthias to his feet. He was mostly healed, but his leg still ached and he was glad for the help.

They piled in to Tae's powder-blue SUV, Matthias and Tae both in the back to help stabilize Erik's form during the ride.

As Elliot pulled out of the parking space, his own b'caster chirped loudly. He inserted it into his ear.

"Answer."

He listened, then let out a laugh.

"Yeah, no shit, Sherlock." He threw it down on the empty passenger seat, glancing into the rearview mirror. "That was a notification call that an Angelic had been registered as entering our location minutes ago."

Matthias met his eyes grimly in the mirror. They both looked at Tae, who was staring determinedly out of the window. One of Ophde's spawn probably already knew too much, especially if he was as powerful as Matthias suspected. He smirked and allowed his power to furl out. With the delicate surgeon scalpel of long practice and a long time on his own with nothing to do but practice, he surrounded himself and Elliot in the bubble of his power, cutting Erik and Tae out completely. He wasn't sure it would work against Tae's vision until the child's head whipped around viper-quick, eyes narrowed.

"Something's wrong," Matthias said, ignoring the teen's searching gaze.

Elliot rolled his eyes. "Yeah, no fucking duh."

"Hu?"

"Maybe . . . but wouldn't that be completely obvious? I mean, he sends you on the mission and you die? How could he even make sure you would be there as soon as that thing made its way through?"

Matthias nodded reluctantly. Hu was an easy target, but there were at least a dozen factions in the Maestres and he'd managed to piss a whole lot of them off over the past few years.

"We need to find out who gave Hu the tip," Matthias decided.

"I could ask, but he'll know the question is from you and will probably demand you come to him. You know how he can be. Especially after your aspirant embarrassed him so thoroughly in the training room." Elliot smiled wide.

Matthias returned the expression. "Yeah, but I need to know, what if it wasn't an attack against me, what if it was against—" He stopped himself in time, but Elliot's eyes flashed to Erik and Matthias looked away from the mirror.

"You really like him, don't you?"

"Don't be stupider than usual. We just met and I'm four years older than him."

Matthias saw Elliot shrug out of the corner of his eye. "Four years isn't much and sometimes a week is all you need." His voice had gone wistful in a way that Matthias knew meant he was thinking of losing Elana and Daya choosing his sister over him. Matthias dissipated the bubble around them and went silent, holding on to Erik as they sped down the darkening streets.

ERIK

He didn't have a legitimate reason to be mad at Matthias. Okay, not exactly true, but he didn't have a reason for how angry he was at Matthias. Some of it was because everyone insisted he rest for the last twenty-four hours, even though he was perfectly healed. At least Melinda had come to visit and spend time with him. The rest was because of the sudden distance Matthias seemed to be deliberately placing between them.

Either way, he was done sitting around. Tae and Matthias were fully healed thanks to him, but they all still insisted that he was still convalescing for some reason.

It was really ridiculous.

He got up from the bed and carefully pulled his clothes on. He winced; he *was* healed, his side was just tender as fuck. He peeked into the hallway. There was no one, but he suspected that was because everyone would be in the cafeteria. His stomach was telling him it was mealtime.

Matthias had let him know they were just going to stay here through the weekend. Erik had called his mother so she wouldn't worry and she'd let him know that Robert was definitely gone. His bag and some of his clothes were missing from his room. In their place was a note saying he needed time alone to think and talk to his family but he'd be back in a few days.

He still didn't know what his mom saw in Robert, other than using him as a waste-gate for her own power. If he was being charitable, they had had some good times when he was a kid, before Daniel and the trial, but that was long ago and a different man. Erik was feeling more sympathetic toward the man since his conversation with his mom and Robert's attempted apology. Even if Robert had completely fucked up the conversation when they'd had it, there was a part of Erik that appreciated him trying.

He moved down the hall at a smooth pace, careful not to show his discomfort even as every move tugged on the new pink puckering skin that took up a good portion of his back and stomach on his lower left side. He heard the chatter before he reached them and smiled. He needed human, or in this case Blooded, company before he lost his damn mind. He entered the dining room and the conversation around him stopped.

"Erik! Come sit by me."

He smiled at Melinda and moved around the table to take her up on the offer and sit between her and Maestra Luka, who turned to him.

"How are you feeling, Erik?"

He smiled too brightly and brought it down a notch. "Fine, good as new."

"Remarkable."

Erik began to dig into the food that appeared in front of him. A hearty soup of lamb, potato, and greens. He reached the bottom of the bowl in no time.

"At least your appetite wasn't affected." Even though the words were joking, when Erik looked up Matthias's face was creased in worry. He scowled at his Counselor. If the man cared so much, why had he avoided Erik for most of the past day?

"If you are healed, perhaps you would be willing to spar with Tae, as he requested last week?" Hu's voice held a smirk, though Luka didn't look displeased with the suggestion at all.

"I don't think—"

Erik interrupted Matthias. "Sure, sounds like fun." He refused to meet Matthias's hot gaze of disapproval.

"Excellent."

"But is there somewhere outside we can do it? Being cooped up inside is driving me a little crazy." Erik looked over at Matthias as he said this.

Elliott spoke up. "There's a rooftop bowl."

Erik nodded and followed them from the room, bringing his second bowl of stew and draining it on the way.

They all crowded into small metal elevator and jerked as it sped faster and faster. It finally slowed and Erik lost his footing as it came to a stop. Matthias reached out to steady him and he could feel the unnatural warmth of Matthias's hands through his shirt. Erik let them rest there for only a second before shrugging them off.

The doors opened and they were welcomed by cool night air. Stepping out onto the cement roof, Erik looked around. They were in one of the almost identical industrial subdivisions that littered Brisbane. There were buildings off in the distance, but the curving roads and rising hills meant almost no one would have a direct view. Three lamps sat on the roof, all glowing a soft white that made the whole rooftop visible.

Erik walked over to the edge of the roof and looked down. Matthias joined him and leaned close. The warehouse was only two stories off the ground, not nearly enough to account for the length of their elevator ride. Simply being outside was calming Erik. He was still mad, but cutting off his Counselor would be the height of stupidity. He trusted Matthias more than the rest of these people, which granted wasn't much, but it would be foolish to alienate him.

"There must be more floors than the one we are on. Why waste all that space?" Erik said, eye trained on the street below them.

Matthias snapped his head around and caught the small blush coloring the brown cheeks. He recognized the comment as the olive branch it was and smiled in return.

"I was just thinking the same thing."

"So maybe we should have a look around?"

"You know the whole place is under surveillance, including your room, right?"

Erik rolled his eyes. He was still angry at Matthias for ignoring him, but the more fresh sunset air he took in, the more forgiving he felt. Until they were alone and he had a chance to grill the older man for answers, it seemed prudent to just let it go.

"No. I'm a complete idiot."

"Are you ready, Erik?"

Erik turned to face Tae. He had no great expectations of winning this fight. Tae's intervention the other night had caused Erik to firmly move the young man to the friend column. Even if he still didn't completely trust Tae, there was little chance of slipping into his power accidentally and he had no intention of doing it on purpose. He knew Tae had come here to train more physically, which meant he wasn't great, but he was still probably better than Erik, who had zero conscious training in anything but street flail fighting, no matter what the others said.

Without his power, he was no great fighter. The lessons his mom had given him were automatic, even easy to remember, but they weren't instinct for him when unpowered.

"So what are the rules?" Erik widened his stance so he couldn't be knocked over immediately and faced Tae within the loose circle of everyone's bodies.

"Since we're not doing edged weapons, I would say two touches out of three?" Tae smiled.

"Any kind of touch?"

"No. Just the landing of a blow or a hold you can't get out of."

Erik nodded.

"Begin!"

Hu's voice rang out and Tae came at him right away. Erik could see where he was a little clumsy, but he was fast. Erik ducked low as arms came toward his torso, so he was almost caught by the unexpected kick that came toward his face. He managed to get an arm up to block it but it unbalanced him enough that he fell backward and scrambled out of reach. Before he could get to his feet, Tae barreled into him and locked his arms against Erik's chest with a surprisingly strong embrace. Erik tried to wriggle free but that simply brought their heads closer together. Tae turned his head and Erik could feel the warmth of his breath as he whispered.

"Trust no one."

Erik jerked and Tae said, loud enough for everyone to hear, "Do you concede?"

"Yes."

All of a sudden Erik was free. He groped for his balance, fell, and his palm slammed into Tae's hip. The other boy hissed but it quickly cut off.

"You okay?"

"Yeah, just my injection site, I thought it wouldn't hurt since it's all healed up, but it's still sensitive."

"Injection site?"

"Testosterone."

"Oh, got it." Erik smiled and nodded.

Tae reached back and fiddled with the loose bun his hair was pulled into as he stood.

This time as Tae came at him, Erik watched his face, trying to predict where the attack would come from. Tae's eyes flicked to the right and he moved to the right himself, moving closer to Tae rather than farther away. He moved inside the swing of the other man's arm and slammed into his chest, wrapping his own arms around Tae's upper arms to try and keep them still. Erik's heavier body tipped them both over like a huge redwood and Tae twisted so the fall didn't break his tailbone. They went down face to face. Tae's longer hair pulled loose and shielded them from the eyes of their audience. As they struggled and writhed they held a whispered conversation.

"What do you mean?"

"There is more going on."

Tae's right arm broke free before point could be called and he grabbed at Erik's ear, pulling him up and back. Erik yelled and twisted his body to the side, going with the pull but also slamming his whole weight into the arm and between himself and the rooftop. Tae yelled and Erik kept rolling off the limb and to his feet.

"Point for Erik."

Tae was favoring the arm as they circled for the third time. Erik rushed Tae and only had a second of realization to throw himself to the side as Tae dropped to the ground. The blow that would have knocked his legs out from under him instead just clipped his shins as they passed each other. Erik landed hard on his side and felt his breath leave him in a whoosh. Instead of panicking and struggling to breathe, he imagined he was underwater and allowed his breath to be gone while he crawled to his knees. A weight took him down and surprised him into breathing and choking, but he still folded forward and tried to throw over his shoulder.

It didn't work. Tae clung like a limpet and they fell forward. Tae's breath fluttered against Erik's ear, sending a shiver through him.

"Everyone has an investment in our origins, and who is right or can make everyone believe they are right will lead us. The dark is coming."

Something in those last four words triggered something in his chest and Erik felt a rattle inside of him, almost as if something were shaking loose. He shuddered and his whole body went limp.

MELINDA

"**G**o Erik!" She felt bad as soon as it was out of her mouth, so she yelled, just a little bit quieter, "Go Tae!" She didn't want Tae to lose; she just wanted Erik to win more. Patrah was whispering things under her breath as she watched, and Melinda went quiet to listen.

It was fighting advice. As she looked around, she realized most of the adults were doing the same. Erik wasn't using his powers. Melinda could tell because he wasn't winning. She'd seen Erik in action and when he was fighting no one could take him down. The others looked scared sometimes but Melinda didn't understand why—it was like being scared of thunder or rain. Being afraid didn't help, you had to understand it. At least that's what Mom and Mama had said.

She missed them, but knew she'd see them again on Sunday night and they would all sit around at dinner and Mom would ask her what she learned this weekend and Mama would tell them all a story about someone in her family history who'd been Blooded.

Melinda turned back to the fight. They were both quick and smart. It looked like Tae had Erik held pretty good when he gasped loudly and his eyes rolled back in his head. Erik went boneless, every part of him limp. Tae immediately scrambled to his feet and turned him over.

Everyone crowded around and because of how small she was Melinda was able to wriggle through the gaps between bodies and legs until she was kneeling by Erik. As soon as she touched him, she knew it was a mistake—she didn't even have to hear the faint "no" from Patrah as the whole world faded away.

MELINDA/ERIK/ MELINDAERIK/MERIKDA/ ERINDA

1 t's dark everywhere.everywhere.everywhere.
NONono, light, over there, over there, just a little light.
The lastLASTlAsT light?
Maybe.

Closer it is a small city, no not a city, it does not deserve that title, not even a town, a village—maybe. The houses are trash, literally garbage stuck together however they can manage. The people look dirty and angry, they circle one another like animals, rip into each other for meat, warmth, pleasure.

They shiver as they watch the display, time moves oddly, fast forward, then backward, then slow like molasses, then from different angles. One tries to comfort the other but it doesn't work they aren't two anymore, they are one and their one is horrified and scared. But if they were one how could they speak to one another.

They would not be the first being to speak to itself and receive an answer. LooklOOkLOOK!

The darkness—
it MOVES.
it attacks!
it laps at the humans like a tide

They zoom out and look at the light from farther away, as they pull back and back and back it turns from village to hamlet to farmstead to a tiny pinprick of light, no bigger than a pore on their pinky. The rest of the globe is a roiling mass of black, always hungry, always feeding on anything that tries to live and break through it.

There's another darkness, though, hovering above the devouring one, different than the one that frightened them. This one was the sheltering dark of home, the warm dark of a lover's arm in the middle of the night. This darkness was the reason the one spot of light was still alive, still fighting back. It was shattered and reformed, shattered and reformed until more of it was cracks than substance and still it fought on. It spoke to them.

do you see? do you know? you are a part in the chain.

TAE

This was epically bad. Tae had only meant to warn Erik about some of the hints he was getting from working with Luka and his gift. Instead he'd triggered a Cassandra and Melinda had been swept up in it along with Erik. He had no idea what the two of them were seeing, but he doubted it was anything good and it would only lead to more questions. Especially after the whole dream thing, the last thing they needed were more eyes on them, but it was now inevitable.

Melinda woke up first, her eyes opening so fast that Tae expected to hear a clink as they locked into place. She took a deep breath and then, without pause for an exhale, another shuddering breath and then another until her small cylinder of a chest was distended as her lungs pulled in more and more air. Tae worried that he was about to see a little girl explode when Patrah quickly knelt by the girl's side, turned her over, and slammed an open palm onto her back. The breath snaked out of her tiny body in a long sigh.

Hu and Luka started to pepper the girl with questions before she was fully conscious. She did not even look at them, having eyes only for the still-unconscious Erik and Patrah, who was now wiping her brow with a cloth she'd gotten from somewhere.

Finally Hu grabbed her face and turned her to face him. "What did you see?"

She immediately reared back to yank her jaw from his fingers and then snapped forward again. Only Hu's quick reflexes kept himself from losing fingertips to her small, sharp teeth. Hu scrambled back and Tae noticed that he and Luka were not the only ones trying to stifle laughter or hide it within coughs.

"None of your business!" The anger brought her color back to its normal dark sepia, though no one was happy with this answer. They all wanted to know and Hu's clumsiness might have messed it up for everyone. She turned to Patrah and said in a more normal voice, "That's what you were talking about, right? Getting drawn into someone's head because they're having really strong dreams?"

Patrah nodded slowly. "Not exactly, but like that, yes."

"So it was Erik's dream, not mine. So telling is like telling someone's secrets without their permission."

The nod was even more reluctant now, but it was there, and with a sharp nod of Melinda's head that was the end of it. Tae had no doubt that Hu would still try to get it out of her, but he saw the way she looked at Erik. She was loyal to him. Patrah's face was doing a weird contortion back and forth between annoyance and pride.

With a loud groan, Erik heaved himself off of his stomach and onto his side. He faced Tae, Matthias, and Elana full on and Tae could see that his mouth was open and panting with his tongue lolling out, his eyes circling independently of one another. His hands twitched at his sides as if they wanted to move. Matthias curved himself around Erik's head, placing his thighs between the ground and Erik's head as a cushion. He leaned down over his aspirant and wiped some of the sweat from his forehead with one hand.

His face came up with a snarl across his lips.

"Back the fuck up!"

Everyone aside from Tae took a giant step backward, though Hu and Luka hesitated before moving back. Matthias looked at Tae and opened his mouth for a second before shutting it and focusing his attention on the stirring body in his arms.

ERIK

Erik's body was not cooperating and so his mind panicked as he tried to get his arms to lift, as he tried to speak. His mouth spasmed open and closed repeatedly; his teeth chattered with no care for the damage they were doing to his tongue and the blood filling his mouth. His body flopped and shook and turned; he wanted to scream and the best he could push out was a sob. His body was not his own, and coming on the heels of his injury it was the world reminding him it could still fuck him over whenever it wanted, no matter how special he thought he was. Finally his body just flopped over onto its side and he panted, feeling slowly coming back along with control.

His limbs jerked with a flood of pins and needles and muscle cramps. Erik clenched his teeth against the cries that wanted to emerge and ended up groaning through them. His vision began to clear and he could see more than the burnt-out white sunbursts. Matthias's face slowly resolved, his strong Mediterranean features pinched in worry, his usually tan skin drained to blotchy yellow-white.

His hand reached out to stroke Erik's cheek and Erik's eyes shot to meet his own. At this sign of his awareness returning, Matthias quickly yanked his hand away and some of the worry disappeared from his face, though it still lingered at the edges. Erik did not focus on Matthias for long because his body shook again, coming alive, coming under his control. He closed his eyes, riding out wave after wave of cramps as they raced over him, each wave getting less painful.

When it finally ended, he did not bother to open his eyes again. Darting his tongue out to lick at his cracked and dry lips, he croaked, "What the hell?"

Immediately a babble of voices answered him, talking over each other. They blended into a mélange of tones. He could pick out words here and there but they made no sense.

". . . did you see?"

"Stay still."

". . . vision."

". . . Cassandra . . ."

"Cassandra."

"Cassandra . . ."

Finally Matthias roared, "*Silence!*" and everything fell quiet.

Erik realized he had heard nothing from Melinda and groaned, forcing his eyes open against what felt like a mountain of sand. "Melinda, is she okay?" He tried to turn and look, but all his muscles screamed at what they considered an unreasonable request. He let his eyes drop closed again. He felt a smaller hand slip into the loose clasp of his own. He smiled as she squeezed his palm despite the jolt of sensation, not quite pain, that shot through him

"I'm fine."

"Good."

"I'm taking him to his room."

As Matthias said this Erik felt himself lifted into the air bridal-style. It was an odd sensation; he could not recall being carried in such a way. It made him feel oddly vulnerable, a feeling he had tried to avoid for the last couple of years. Any hint of vulnerability was weakness and he refused to be caught by a surprise betrayal again. So he expected to hate the feel of Matthias's arms wrapped around him, but for some reason it did not make him feel weak so much as safe.

He could not remember the last time he had actually felt safe from attack. He curled into the embrace, just a little, just until they reached his room. The arms tightened ever so slightly and Erik's felt a small flip of excitement and fear in his belly.

He whispered, "Tae and Melinda."

Matthias paused in his movement and looked down at Erik's face. Erik didn't know what he saw but he nodded and called out, "Tae, Melinda, if you would come with us I think your presence would comfort Erik." Then he started moving again without waiting to see if they followed. As they entered the elevator, they turned and Erik saw Tae and Melinda inside. The ride down was silent, as was the trip through the hall to Erik's room.

As Matthias lay him on the bed, Melinda closed the door. With more effort than it should have needed, he sank into the mattress until he almost felt a part of it.

"So what was that?"

"Well, it's this effect where—"

Erik interrupted Tae, who he could tell was ready to go on for a while. "Short version. Please."

Matthias's voice rumbled and the bed shook lightly, letting Erik know the man was perched next to him. "A Cassandra happens randomly. No one can explain why. They usually show glimpses of the future, though they've been known to show the past as well. Most only have to do with things of a personal nature, but there have been a few massive Cassandras over the last century. Warning of wars, assassinations, et cetera."

"Okay." Erik thought about what he had just learned. The images were all jumbled and the meaning of it, which had been so clear while he was seeing it, now felt vague and unbelievable.

"You don't have to share it with anyone you don't want to. A Cassandra is considered private and personal." The words spilled out of Tae in a rush and then he fell silent.

"Good." Erik didn't know who to trust; even the people in this room had only proved themselves more trustworthy than the others. He needed allies and they were the safest options.

"I didn't tell anyone either . . . and now I barely remember." Melinda's voice was soft and Erik squeezed her hand once before his exhaustion took hold and he passed out.

He woke in darkness and even before he tried to pierce it by straining his eyes, he could tell he was not alone. There was one other person in the room, their breath was soft, and Erik could almost sense the heat they were giving off. He slowly sat up and slipped off the bed, heading in the direction of the presence. After a couple steps he could tell it was Matthias. He didn't know what that meant, that he could tell Matthias's body and presence even when he could not see him. He could even tell the exact point that Matthias started awake.

"Did you rest well?"

"Yes." Something of the darkness kept them from talking at normal levels. They whispered their words, relying on the stillness and dark to carry them.

"We're gonna be leaving the facility soon and not coming back."

"But I thought—"

"We can train anywhere and you're getting better at control already. You can bring the rage on at will."

"Yeah . . ." Erik could, but it wasn't the getting enraged that still worried him—it was not doing so.

"And I already didn't like Luka and Hu being here. Now with the Cassandra on top of the power drain dream, they'll be watching you even more closely. I don't like their interest in you."

There was a hesitation in Matthias that he could feel.

"There's something else." It wasn't a question.

"Yeah, the students from your first manifestation. They reneged, they want to sue."

"Those piece-of-shit entitled bullies." Erik was up and pacing the dark of the room before he knew it, in a tight circle so he didn't slam into anything.

"Well, there was enough evidence that they were the aggressors that is shouldn't be too much of a problem . . . but some actual legitimate newspapers picked the story up. It's drawing even more attention."

"Fuck." Erik had done his best not to draw attention to himself after the trial and cancellation. He'd appeared in public enough so they didn't speculate too hard and he'd said nothing and eventually he'd faded away except for the occasional "where are they now?" bit online. Then the fight, and now this.

Was this why Robert had actually left?

Sure, his fuck-up son was in the news again, but all publicity was good publicity and Robert might be out there right now, giving interviews, steering every conversation he could to his campaign. Which meant he should probably be out there doing damage control.

"Fuck me gently with a chainsaw. This is gonna suck even more." He put his head in his hands and sat on the bed, where Matthias soon joined him.

"Yup. We got you being 'homeschooled' now, so no more school. We'll train indoors during the day and we'll patrol in the early morning before dawn. Most of our training will focus on unarmed fighting and weapons as well as reaching a more full understanding of your powers."

Matthias's voice had gotten more and more cold and remote as the conversation had gone on. Erik wondered why. Then he wondered why he cared. If Matthias wanted to get cold and distant it was for the best; the less close someone was, the easier to see a betrayal coming. He pushed the whole thing from his mind.

"We have enemies. Not only the Angelics but their Suits within the government and without. As much as I hate to agree with Hu, you are a valuable weapon in the fight if you choose to join it. They may send people after you and we do not want you unprotected when you go out, so we ha—"

"Who's this 'we' you keep talking about? I thought you were an independent." Erik suspected Matthias of using the formal language in an attempt to place even more distance between them. The silence that answered him as good as confirmed it, as did the different tone and softness to Matthias's voice when he spoke again.

"I have a present for you."

A hand took Erik's in the dark and pressed his fingers close together. Something cold and metallic was slipped over them. The same was done with his other hand, though Matthias's hand lingered on his own for much longer than was necessary. Then the touch was gone and Erik could feel him getting off the bed and backing away to the wall.

"Close your eyes."

Even with his eyes closed, the sudden flare of light burned and left orange and pink starbursts dancing behind his eyelids. When his eyes had adjusted, he opened them and looked down at his wrists. They were both adorned with thick metal bracelets, bent and reshaped oddly, flat in some places and almost pointed in others. They were cold and sleek as he jangled his wrists; there was a weight to them, more than it should be.

He looked up at Matthias in question.

"Diamond coated in a layer of chromium, an easily hidden weapon."

Erik looked at them again, confused as to how they were a weapon. Matthias sighed heavily and stepped forward, once again taking Erik's hand in his own. Carefully, touching as little as possible, he slid the bracelet back up until the flattened portion rested in his palm and then closed his hand into a fist. Erik lifted his hand and admired the way that the weapon hugged the space between his first and second knuckles. The blunt edges and burnished surface would make his punches more deadly. He liked it.

"Or perhaps we don't have to do more weapons training at all."

"No. I like this one."

Matthias smiled lightly as Erik positioned the other weapon on his fist as well and made a few experimental jabs into the air.

"Good, well, get dressed and let's go."

Erik was startled out of playing with his new toys. "Now?"

Leaving in the dead of night was odd and made him wonder if Matthias was actually afraid of something. "Yes, I figured we could snoop a bit before we go. And I want to get you out of here as soon as possible."

"What about Melinda?" Erik was anxious to explore but he also wanted to say goodbye.

"You can go and say goodbye before we leave." Then he opened the door and was gone before Erik could say anything else. He stared at the closed door, then down at the bracelets that reminded him of Matthias every time he moved. He hadn't unpacked most of his things, a habit that annoyed Robert because he was always wrinkled, but he felt the time saving was worth it.

He had finally decided to venture out to Melinda's room when he heard footsteps converging from different directions in the hall outside. Then the low murmur of voices. Erik froze with his hand already turning the doorknob. Slowly he crouched to place himself below the immediate line of sight and carefully, cautiously, finished turning the knob, cracking the door to listen in.

"We apologize for coming at such a late hour but we did not want to miss your departure." Luka's voice was sharp, almost angry.

"Of course. Well, I regret to say that we will not be staying any longer; if you wish to contact me after Erik is settled back with his parents, feel free," Matthias replied.

"So you leave like a cockroach scuttling before the light?" Hu's voice was heavy with barely leashed anger.

"Let me remind you that we are only here as a favor to the Organization and in return we have almost been killed, most likely by someone on the inside. I believe it makes perfect sense for us to leave now and in secret." If Hu's anger was leashed, Matthias's was not. His rage was a well-trained attack animal held back only by its master's will.

The silence that filled that hall was heavy and Erik longed to peek out and see their faces, but he had no desire to get caught.

"In any case. We're afraid this news cannot wait." Luka pushed on, her voice slightly more conciliatory now.

"I don't know what you think you can say—"

"We've been contacted by Suit Byron."

Silence again. This time so complete and unbroken that Erik thought they were gone, that somehow they'd been spirited away to a private chamber. Just when he was prepared to chance it and push the door open further and try to catch a glimpse of the hallway, Matthias spoke, though his voice was quieter now. It sounded fragile, close to breaking.

"What, where has he been?"

"He neglected to fill us in on his last few years of his life—" The sarcasm was heavy in Hu's voice, and then it cut off completely with coughing and choking sounds.

"Put him down, Matthias, honestly. This is all just wasting time."

The choking cut off with the thump of a falling body.

"And what did the traitor want?" His voice was hard, without emotion.

"Our help."

Matthias laughed. Despite the growing attraction that Erik felt for the man, he shivered to hear the lack of sanity in that sound.

"Oh, does he?"

"Actually, he was contacting us on behalf of the Agency."

The silence again was long and deep, filled with secrets Erik had not yet been told.

"How much do they know?"

"As much as Byron did when he turned, but we've changed everything we could since then—passwords, safe house locations, gathering times. Everything that could be altered was, but we must still assume he told them much of our numbers, powers, the bloodlines we had located. And what the Suits know, the Angelics do as well."

"Not surprising, but most of his information is over five years old at this point."

"Yes, but we suspect he is the reason we've seen more and more missing potential Agents and suffered more losses of actual Agents." Luka's voice was quiet.

"So what does he want?"

"He says he has a warning and a proposition for peace. Not from him but from the Angelics. A chance for a cease-fire and maybe eventual peace."

"So why involve us at all? You have plenty of Agents who specialize in negotiation and diplomacy. I doubt either Erik or I would win any awards in either department."

"They are insisting on your and Erik's attendance."

Erik felt a huge shiver of unease go down his spine and then back up.

"Who is 'they'? Byron or the Angelics?"

"He did not specify." Hu said it stiffly, as if unused to answering questions.

"And why do we have any reason to believe this is anything but a trap?"

"We don't." Luka was blunt about it and shrugged her shoulders. "Byron will be there, though, in arm's reach for the first time in five years."

"Do *not* patronize me." Matthias went quiet after his statement and Erik really wished there were a way to see what was happening in the hall. "When and where?"

"There are no details as of yet."

"Ha, yeah, that's what I thought."

"Think of it this way, Matthias, even if it is a trap it is a chance to learn vital information, about the Agency, the Suits, the Angelics . . . Byron."

"Fuck." Matthias snarled it deep in his throat, the kind of fuck that comes from understanding you're screwed and there's no way out of it. "We will still leave the facility. I do not believe coming here will be of any more use to my charge. Already too much attention falls on Erik's absence."

"That is fine." The surliness to Hu's voice said it was anything but.

"You will call me with the time and place of our meeting and I will see if we can make it." Then his voice raised in volume. "That all right with you, Erik?"

He started at his name but he'd obviously been caught. Taking a deep breath, he stood and pushed the door open, stepping out into the light of the hallway. Luka and Hu looked at him with wide eyes.

Powerful Maestres his ass. He looked to Matthias, who simply smiled and nodded for him to speak.

"Why are they contacting us now? What kind of help can we provide that they don't have with all their fancy government approval and resources?"

"Excellent question, Erik. Well?" Matthias had his eyebrow raised at Hu and Luka, who looked at each other, some sort of battle of wills, until Hu looked down and away before he spoke.

"You've no doubt noticed the increase in Angelics showing up. Well, Byron implied this was something more than an increase in activity. He implied it was preparation for an invasion. This could stop that."

Erik bit his lip to stop the growl that suddenly rumbled in his own chest. The idea of an army of things like he had fought that first night filled him with dread and worry but another part of him, a deeper part, felt a thrill. He wanted to face those creatures again, to show them what he could really do. He squashed the smile that threatened to take over his face.

"He implied? And you believe him?" Matthias did not sound impressed with the intelligence they'd received or the intelligence of their ancestors at this point.

"Not necessarily, but there is something happening, and it would make sense for us to find out what it is so we're not completely caught off guard."

"Yeah. Information." Erik could not deny the logic. "Who else will be at this meeting?"

"Well, we don't know who they will send—"

Erik interrupted Luka. "No, I mean who else are we sending?"

"You two plus Elliot, Daya, Elana, and Tae. They have the most experience working together, with the exception of Tae, and they're people you two trust. If we sent you in there with Blooded you didn't know, I doubt everything would turn out so well."

"I sort of doubt it's going to turn out so good anyway," Erik muttered.

"Also, you are better trained that you think. Your instincts are raw but well developed nonetheless." Luka spoke over him and could not hide a quick glance and smirk in Hu's direction. Hu stiffened under the regard as if feeling her taunting, even if he could not see her face. "Also, as a newer Blooded, they will have no intel on your bloodline or powers. And you will not be going alone. Patrah and Melinda will stay here at the facility, continuing their dream-training to hopefully provide some insight on your mission."

Erik nodded. He was no less convinced this might be some sort of trap, but at least they were not as stupid as they seemed. He turned to Matthias.

"I'm finished packing, but I would like to say goodbye to Melinda."

Matthias nodded and Erik turned his back on the lot of them, heading for the girl's room.

There was no answer to his first knock. He knocked a little louder and called through the door softly.

"Melinda, it's Erik. Are you awake?"

There was the sound of tiny feet and the door opened just a crack. She looked at him, then opened the door wide and hurried back to the bed, burrowing into the pile of blankets, searching for the warmth she'd left behind.

"I'm sorry to come in the middle of the night but I'm leaving and I wanted to say goodbye."

"Leaving?" The girl shot up in bed, the blankets falling off her head like a hood, revealing her wild mass of dark, kinky curls. "Where?"

"Well, I'm gonna go home."

Melinda stiffened and Erik could read the horrible memories of her last night at home chase themselves across her face. "Don't go."

It was a whisper and it broke Erik's heart that he couldn't do what she asked.

"I'm sorry, honey, I have to, but you have Patrah and she'll protect you for sure. And just cause I'm going home doesn't mean we won't see each other."

"Really?"

The hope in her voice undid him. She was the first person he'd rescued, one of the few people to associate him with only good things, with being saved rather than hurt by knowing him. She still believed people when they promised to stay in touch and he refused to be the one to teach her that more often than not those promises were lies.

"I promise. You have my phone number, right?"

Melinda nodded.

"You call or text me anytime you need and I will be here for you."

She still didn't look happy about the situation, but at least she no longer looked terrified, as if as soon as he left something would come for her. She hugged him, her small arms tight around his neck, and he leaned his forehead against her, taking in the scent of honey, cocoa, and child.

Untainted by the world.

She drifted to sleep in his arms and he slowly lowered her back to the mattress and covered her with the blankets. He turned to leave the room but something turned him back. He took in her smiling face and his hands curled into loose fists and he swore he would do everything in his power to keep his promise.

He slipped out into the hall.

"Don't I get a goodbye?"

Erik flung himself around to face the threat, haze of rage already coming up. He dug his teeth back into the wounds on his lips. Once the voice penetrated and he realized who it was, he let the power drain away completely. Perhaps Matthias and Luka were right? Maybe his control was better than he thought. He looked up at Tae.

"Don't surprise me like that."

"I wasn't worried." The simple truth in the statement hit Erik in his core. Tae trusted him.

"Didn't think you needed a goodbye since we'll be working together."

"Well, yeah, but it's still nice to be thought of." The smile on his face was just this side of teasing and Erik returned it.

"Well then." Erik held open his arms and Tae rushed forward, looping his arms around Erik's neck and turning the whole thing into the cover of a cheesy romance novel, the ones where they couldn't afford Fabio. They both laughed as Erik let Tae drop to the floor.

"I'll see you soon." Tae turned to leave but hesitated then turned back to face Erik. "Watch your back, okay?"

"I will." Erik had been watching his own back for years. He had no reason to stop now and every reason to be even more vigilant.

MATTHIAS

He waited in front of Erik's room with both their bags until his aspirant returned. They both wore broken-in jeans. Matthias had a plain black leather jacket over plain black T-shirt; Erik's shirt was mostly black with a drawing of a serpent emblazoned—"The Wrath of the One-Eyed Snakes" was scrawled underneath and over it he wore a dark purple hoodie.

"You ready?"

Erik smirked and picked up his duffel bag. "Yeah, let's do this."

Matthias nodded and led him to the elevator. He called the elevator but stopped Erik as he moved to get on. He let his power flow out of him, slowly controlled. He curled it around himself and Erik. Invisibility was not his power; it was not even Elana and Elliot's. Their powers were similar because they both came from different hunter-bloodlines.

His was the power of the skilled huntress, to make oneself part of the landscape, fade into the background in a way that mimicked invisibility. People knew he was there but it seemed normal, as if he should be there, and so they paid him no mind at all. It was one of the blessings Artemis-Agrotera had passed down to him, one of the few he was comfortable showing off in public.

He removed a long, solid metal bar from his bag and if it was longer than the bag it came out of, Erik said nothing. He carefully slotted the metal between the outer doors, then leaned in to press the button for the garage. The elevator whined a bit but the inner doors slowly closed.

"Be ready."

Erik nodded, The car began to move downward and as it disappeared he leapt for the roof of it, Erik right behind him. They crouched there, side by side, sneakered feet gripping metal through streaks of grease, getting used to the sway and movement of the elevator.

"This seems pretty obvious."

Matthias shrugged. "The Organization is slower to notice non-gods-power threats. Their number one line of defense is the Alarmers and they look out for aggressive power, not physical things."

"What are Alarmers?"

Matthias stood as the elevator came to a stop. Again he reached into his bag and pulled out a jack. Jamming the lips of it in the seam between the outer doors, he turned the crank around and around until the doors were wide enough for them to step through.

"Future seers. They usually can only see a few minutes or hours into the future, though, much less powerful than dreamwalkers like Patrah and Melinda, so most end up working for the Organization as Alarmers. Spending most of their days linked into nets of twenty or more, no sole identity, monitoring the currents of power around cities and Organization buildings."

"Well, that sounds . . . horrible."

Matthias nodded as he stepped on the floor above the garage. The hallway they entered was spacious, easily twice as wide as the one on the floor they had been staying on.

"This way." Matthias started down the middle hallway, power still wrapped around the two of them, but they saw no one as they walked. They heard no one moving in the rooms they passed. It was night but Blooded often had odd sleep patterns because of their connections to various forces of nature. It was odd to find no one about. This space had come into use after he'd left, but Matthias remembered the other centers he'd visited around the world. There was hardly a time when someone wasn't moving about, working on something.

Perhaps this was a subsidiary bolthole.

He caught a glimpse of something through the window of a room and turned to the locked door.

"Erik, would you mind?"

Erik met his gaze before smiling and nodding. He stepped forward, took a deep breath, placed his hand on the knob, and turned until the door cracked open against its will. Another deeper breath and Matthias could practically feel the power rush out of him. They stepped inside.

The room was dark and Matthias groped for the light switch, flipping it on and flooding the room with illumination.

On the stainless steel table in the middle of the room was the meat suit from the way-station. Splayed out and pinned open, the disturbingly plastic-looking red and white insides exposed. Except the face, which had been pinned into wholeness and looked disturbingly alive.

He recognized that face.

"Oh god." From the horror in his voice, so did Erik.

They both slowly came forward, Matthias keeping an ear out for anyone approaching.

"How did Elana die, Matthias?"

"An Angelic killed her."

He reached out but pulled his hand back.

"And her body?"

"I don't know. I wasn't with the Organization when she died and I never really asked for the full story. It felt rude."

"Rude or not, I think we need to ask and soon."

Erik's voice had already recovered its calm, but Matthias noticed he had moved away from the table toward the counter where the white skull he had grabbed at the last minute rested. Matthias stared at Elana's former body longer before he joined Erik. The skull looked expertly cleaned, a pure white. Erik picked it up and turned it over in his hands.

"Is it Elana's?" Matthias asked as Erik prodded at the various openings.

"I don't—what the fuck?!" Erik juggled the skull and Matthias could see the thing was shuddering in his hands. Slowly, the skull broke apart, or perhaps that was wrong—more like the skull came apart, separated into sections, still attached but showing their inner workings.

"Fuck me virgin goddess."

Erik's head snapped around and he laughed.

"Really?"

"She'll understand."

They grinned at each other and then went back to the skull. Exposed was the fact that this was no organic skull; the connectors between the pieces looked like gold filigree, small gears and joints shining in the fluorescent light. Then, just as quickly as it had opened up, it began to snap closed again.

"Fuck," Erik exclaimed. Matthias could see where a sharp edge had caught his thumb and cut it open at the base. As they watched, the blood stopped and the wound closed. Erik wiped his blood from the skull and replaced it on the counter.

"Let's get what we came for."

Matthias nodded. "Yes, this way."

He silently led the way to the main records room, his mind turning over the new information. What were the Angelics doing with Elana's body? She had died years ago, so had they preserved it this whole time?

The room was easy enough to find, always on the lowest floor, in the center, and here it was. He rolled his eyes but he supposed bureaucracy had helped him in this instance. He had never dared to do this before, but something about being in Erik's company made him more willing to take risks, to do the things he'd wanted to for so long but had hesitated. This was very near the top of his list.

"So what are we looking for?" Erik asked. He kept his voice quiet despite the fact that Matthias had told him there was no need.

"Information on you."

"Me?"

"Yeah, I don't believe for one minute they haven't already worked out your bloodline or at least have more hints than they were giving us." There was no need to tell Erik about the other things he was looking for. Again, they were faced with one of the oddities of Organization bureaucracy: all of their copies were hard copies. The records were in circle after circle of file cabinets.

Everything was labeled and Matthias was already acquainted with their filing system. By the time Erik called out that he had found his file, Matthias had already located the five files he wanted.

"Excellent." The files were already in his bag as he hurried over.

Erik already had the file open on top of the still-open drawer, flipping through the pages. There was a mix of papers, some handwritten, some typed, English and others that Matthias recognized as Greek and Latin. The materials were various as well: notebook paper, computer paper, linen parchment and slabs of pale leather, their ink the disturbing brown of dried blood.

"Shit," Erik called as he turned a page and revealed the illustration of a woman. She stood tall and strong, wearing nothing, her skin covered in small scars. This woman would not bend or break. The mountains behind her would shatter before her resolve. She had been drawn with her feet planted in a village to show her size. They stood frozen in shock as the drawing began to shift.

First the figure's hair began to move, to snap and curl like it was being blown by a powerful wind. Slowly the neutral expression on her face sank into one of anger and glee, the readiness of a fight. Matthias recognized the expression from Erik's face. This was his bloodline; this woman was the one he was descended from. She crouched down in preparation for some sort of fight and then leapt sideways out of the frame of the drawing. The background of the illustration blurred as it moved to catch the woman in the frame again. When the movement stopped, she was centered wrestling with a dozen figures less than half her size, winning easily. In the distance other giants of her stature were being taken down one by one by these smaller creatures.

Eventually only she stood, with the smaller figures piling on her until she fell under their combined weight, still screaming in defiance.

"What is this?"

"An interpretation of the Betrayal. Greek if I'm not mistaken, the Titans and the Gods."

"So who was she?"

Matthias shrugged and gestured for him to turn the page. The next piece of paper was ripped from a spiral notebook and covered in small block writing.

BIA IS ONE OF THE FEW OLD ONES (OTHER EX.—DAM-BALLAH, IDUN, TARA, ENKIDU) FOR WHICH OTHER ASPECTS CANNOT BE DEFINITIVELY NAMED. BIA WAS NOT SIMPLISTIC VIOLENCE. SHE WAS FORCE CONTAINED AND CONTROLLED. SHE WAS ONE OF THE LAST OLD ONES TO FALL. HER BLOOD-LINE WAS BELIEVED TO BE WIPED OUT SO NO EXACT EVI-DENCE EXISTS OF THEIR POWERS BUT ACCORDING TO MYTHS HER CHILDREN WOULD BE EXCELLENT FIGHTERS, BERSERKERS WITH CONTROL AND TACTICAL KNOWLEDGE. OTHER POSSIBILITIES INCLUDE AWARENESS/ABILITY TO READ VARIOUS FORCES SUCH AS GRAVITY, ELECTROMAG-NETISM, AND MORE. AS SUCH THEY WOULD REACT BADLY TO A SOURCE STRONGER THAN THEMSELVES MANIPULAT-ING THOSE FORCES UNNATURALLY NEAR THEM.

"That's why you took so long healing after the way-station—the Angelic disorientation affects you more." It also explained his fugue states while in the car.

"Huh." Erik flipped the file closed and handed it to him. "Can you put this in your bag? I wanna read the rest later."

The lights came on.

"We know you're here, Matthias."

Matthias rolled his eyes at Hu's voice.

"There was no need for this deception. All you had to do was ask to see the records room." Luka sounded offended.

He dropped his power and instantly they were the center of two gazes.

"And give you the chance to remove the information we wanted to find? The information you kept from us?" Erik's voice was angry, each word almost a yell.

Luka looked confused while Hu looked guilty. Erik let out a snarl, calming only when Matthias placed a hand on his shoulder and moved in front of him.

"You knew my aspirant's bloodline but you didn't reveal it despite our upholding our side of the deal we made."

Luka was immediately staring at Hu. "You idiot! Is this true? You broke the Organization's deal?"

Hu was silent but the color was rising in his face.

"I will have to talk to the other Maestres. There will be repercussions for Hu and reparations offered to you. On my name," Luka said to them formally.

Matthias nodded and Erik followed his lead, though he could see the young man's feet start to step in Hu's direction before he grabbed his elbow.

They exited the room and found a stairway down to the garage.

"Well, that was fucked up. What do you think Hu is up to?"

Matthias shrugged. "Who knows? The Organization has a lot of different factions inside of it. It could have something to do with your bloodline being Greco-Roman or your race or your sexuality. Don't ever think because we're descended from the old ones that we aren't just as flawed and fucked up as humans."

"Well . . . that's lovely, isn't it?"

Matthias shrugged. "It's the truth." He opened the door to the same Mini Cooper as before and Erik climbed into the passenger side.

"Well, bad luck they caught us but we came out of it okay, yeah?"

"I thought they might catch us."

"You did?"

"Yeah." Matthias shrugged. "I mean, if they were hiding something they would have to be watching it pretty closely to keep us from stumbling on it."

"That reminds me, why would you keep the evidence in the building we were staying in? Seems stupid."

Matthias smiled. "Bureaucracy. Hu didn't do that research himself. Somewhere along the chain of information someone filed it and it just grew. All the files replicate in all of the research libraries as soon as they're filed in one. In fact, they've probably already replicated, so don't feel bad about taking this copy."

"I wasn't. I feel bad they still have a copy."

Matthias smiled and turned the car toward Erik's house.

DAYIDA

I t was late but Dayida didn't keep "normal" hours on an average day, and it was anything but average. Her son was injured and her husband was gone. The second of those affected her more than she liked to admit. She did worry for her son, but Erik was strong, she had tried to make sure he would be, and his father had inadvertently brought it all to fruition with his actions toward Daniel.

Robert was weaker. He always had been, though she hadn't been able to see through his bravado early enough. All that anger had been a mask for his weakness. He hadn't shared it with her and she wasn't a mind reader so she didn't feel guilty. But that didn't mean she wasn't worried. She didn't know much of Robert's family except that he'd had a falling out with them right before he left for college and never talked to any of them again, and that most of them were on the East Coast.

The front door suddenly swung open and Erik rushed into the hall. He leaned his back against the door. She came in from the living room and caught a flash of light through the part of the small window that his body wasn't blocking.

"They're still out there?"

"Yeah, just a few." Erik glanced back through the window, rolled his eyes and pulled the curtain down.

She took the time to study him. He stood taller. Over the past year she had watched him shrink in on himself until he looked like a hunched shadow of the young man he was. Now, in only days, his confidence was back. Dayida could actually believe that for him, awakening was exactly what he needed. She studied his face; it was as if all hints of his childhood had been washed away. He was a man now.

When he finally turned again, he took her in and smiled.

"Mama. How have you been?"

"Boy." She got up from her seat and he stepped forward to meet her. She clutched him in her arms. He had only been gone for a few days but she feared that his power would wipe away his personality and remake him into someone else. It hadn't and she was grateful. She buried her face in his hair and took a deep breath. The scent of him was different. There was now a hint of something spicy that overlaid everything.

"Are you okay, baby?"

"Yeah, I'm fine."

She pulled back to take a long look at his face and then nodded.

"Let me see."

He fiddled with his shirt hem before pulling it up. She placed her hand on the soft bulge of pudge that was his stomach and traced her fingers over the scar that now marred his side. It was the size of a baseball and she was sure it had been larger when it first happened.

"Any news from Robert?" He dropped the shirt as he said it. She knew an attempt at a distraction when she heard it. She allowed it. For now.

They moved into the living room. It had always been one of Dayida's favorite rooms; the walls were a shade somewhere between purple and red, and the couch and love seat were deep sea-green monstrosities you could lose a limb in. The tables were all glass-tops with drawings from her students and Erik placed under the glass. It had been her tradeoff for the kitchen. Robert could have that room but this one was hers.

"No, I've called all his cousins that live in state. They all say they haven't seen him. I think he's just sulking somewhere." She settled on the couch and he did the same next to her.

"I could have Matthias look into it. If you want."

She hesitated and then shook her head. "If I wanted that I would ask that boy myself. I've known him since he was a teenager." She paused, and then continued. "Robert will come back when he's ready. Besides, it's not like I don't have enough on my plate right now." She had a gallery show coming up in just a few weeks and wanted to finish a couple more pieces beforehand.

Erik looked at her and did her the return courtesy of changing a subject that she was obviously uncomfortable with.

"How exactly do you know Matthias, Mama?"

"He trained with your grandmother for about a year before being transferred to another Counselor. It was when you were working on the King Peggy biopic in Los Angeles and I was traveling back and forth. When I was up here I stayed with your grandmother sometimes. He was a lot younger than me but we became friends. He was easier to talk to than your Grandma Hettie. We just always stayed in touch."

"Do you know anything about someone named Byron?"

She sighed and made a move as if to stand. "Are you hungry?"

"Not really."

She stayed silent, almost hoping he would try to push her to reveal it. She would meet such coercion with an equal amount of contempt and push back, but this silent waiting slowly unraveled her resolve.

"It's not really my story to tell, but Byron was someone he cared about. The Organization messed with him and then he caused the death of someone else Matthias cared about very much. Matthias changed after that. First he hoped that she would return like some of the Blooded do. When enough time passed and that didn't happen he disappeared, went completely off the radar. No one could find him for four years. In fact I thought he had been killed . . . or killed himself, but then a year ago he just popped back up and got back in contact with everyone."

"Hmm."

She knew that look on her son's face. She had seen it before, whenever he looked at Daniel. Any attempt at warning would be useless but she might still try. Later.

ERIK

H e hugged his mama one final time, taking in the comfort of her scent. She promised to cook him a big breakfast before he went to his former school to clean out his locker. He knew it most likely wouldn't happen. His mom had a habit of promising things she never delivered on. It wasn't malicious on her part. She just tended to get engrossed in her next piece and forget certain things. Plus he was a better cook than either of his parents anyway. He pecked her on the cheek and headed upstairs to his room.

He still loved her for the promise.

He'd spent a lot of the last two days sleeping and wasn't feeling particularly tired, so he turned on the television in his room and it immediately came on to a local news station. His face stared back at him from the screen, two years younger, smiling with boundless enthusiasm.

"Local celebrity Erik Allan has been expelled—"

He turned the channel immediately. How was he still news? He'd stepped away from it all over a year ago. He just wished that they would forget him. He found a station playing a marathon of Elvira and lost himself in cheesy black-and-white horror films until he drifted into restless sleep.

He did not want to wake up but he could feel something getting closer and then there was a knock on his bedroom door. He was up in a flash, his mind still working to catch up to the rapid movement of his body.

"Erik, breakfast is ready! You better hurry, Matthias called and said he'll be here in thirty minutes."

"Okay, Mama." His voice was shaky because of the adrenaline still shooting through his body.

He checked his phone while doing his best to ignore the cracks in the screen; the results of his tantrum after his failed attempt to call Daniel last weekend. There was a missed call from Matthias and a text from Melinda that read "good morning" with a ridiculous animated face smiling and dancing next to it. He smiled in spite of himself and sent a reply about how he missed her with an equally ridiculous animation of a heart breaking.

He pulled on a pair of dark blue jeans along with a long-sleeved brown shirt that spiraled into blues and blacks and whites on the edges, like a nebula. He didn't have time for a shower if he wanted to eat breakfast. He shoved on a white beanie with the words Bow Down B*tches embroidered in black thread across the front. He made sure he was wearing his bracelets.

He smiled as he entered the kitchen. His mother sat at the table, two plates in front of her. Eggs, bacon, and toast waited for them. He ignored the smell of burning that told him this wasn't the first breakfast she'd tried to make this morning. It explained why she was waking him up with so little time to get ready. His mom looked at him with the same combination of pride and fear that had showed in her face any time he left her side for an experience she could not join him in—elementary school, the show's set, and now this.

They ate in relative silence and quickness. He heard a horn honk outside and stood up, reaching down to grab the almost empty backpack he'd carried downstairs. His mom stood to say goodbye.

"Good luck today, sweetie. Pay attention to Matthias, he'll keep you safe. And call me with updates. I might not answer cause I'll be in the studio but I'd like to know you're okay."

"Yes, Mama." Erik smiled and leaned up to return the kiss. Her cheek was soft and he could feel her smile through its movement, though it was gone when he pulled back. She left the kitchen, putting her dishes in the sink, already mumbling softly to herself as she moved toward her studio. He turned to the window in the side door and took a peek. Angling his head, he spotted two paparazzi right away and he was sure there were some others hiding about.

Matthias had his car in the driveway and he was staring at the house, not noticing he was already being photographed. Erik didn't want to imagine what the blogs would be saying tomorrow. In fact he didn't have to imagine; he knew exactly how they would spin this. He took a deep breath and opened the door, determined to give them as little fodder as possible.

Erik couldn't help thinking how he wished the stories they would print were true. But he shoved the thought aside. Matthias had put distance between them for some reason and he wouldn't fight for someone who didn't want him.

ZEBUB

LIL

She fell into a rhythm over the next two weeks. Every day was spent researching and gaining tidbits of knowledge that Lil savored. They found statues hinting that Antes and 'dants once lived on equal footing, books detailing animals they'd never heard of, scrolls locked behind powerful blood wards. She longed to spend years studying these things. Things she was not allowed to carry from the Ossuary. The others shared her disappointment every day, not only in finding nothing on the creeping dark, but disappointment in being denied the spark of rediscovery that was right on the tips of their fingers.

The rhythm of her new schedule was not completely smooth, though. More and more she had noticed Babel coming to her tongue, mostly when she was annoyed and too tired to control it. So far, she had been able to regain control of her tongue before completing any of the words. But even those few syllables should have burned. She was worried and had been subtly trying to ask Mayer questions. Unfortunately, they had no time and he refused to speak with her.

Every night was a dinner that Arel and Jagi helped her dress and make her face up for. None of their dinners were as large as the first. They shuffled from Hive to Hive and were not a gathering of the full Courts. Some treated their group of 'dants as nuisances, others treated them as beloved pets, which was the best they could hope for sometimes. During the nightly dinners she heard talk of attacks reported from the outskirts of Zebub as well as nearby Dis and Tarus and as far away as Hannam and

Raka. Thankfully none had penetrated Zebub as deeply as the initial attacks, but they were becoming more frequent and longer in duration. Some Antes had been lost in addition to many, many 'dants and the Courts did not like that at all.

All the Holders and Apprentices put on brave faces every night and spoke in vague hints of potential weapons against the creeping dark to stem the tide of impatience that grew against them every day. Lil and Mayer understood best what was happening, being able to understand more of the angry gurgles, scents, and wind patterns as they were.

The Nif came to her every dinner but there was no more startlement, even if she still felt herself being observed every night. Mayer and the other Holders did their best to push back against the rumors that said the 'dants had caused this somehow and that the Holders were deliberately holding back information. They all called in favors and still Lil felt the danger grow more and more every day she was in the Courts.

The days and nights blended into one another until the night the white snake came back. Lil had not seen them since that first night and had done her best to forget how easily she had lost herself in the colors of their skin. Arel and Jagi had tried to explain something about the Ante the next morning, but she had changed the subject until they'd gotten the hint and talked of other things, though the kicked-puppy look had lingered on their faces when she'd returned that evening to check on Davi and Min and for them to dress and make up for dinner.

The next morning, she remembered her vow in the bathing room. She could not afford to turn away information simply because she was embarrassed the Ante had gotten the drop on her.

"Fine." She spilled out the entire story and finished with, "Tell me."

Arel and Jagi both let out deep sighs.

"Thank the seven sisters. The white snake is named June and belongs to the House of the Madame. So they knew exactly the effect they were having."

"Hmm." Lil had suspected as much.

"This white snake, June, is ambitious and will do almost everything to get their way. No one knows where their true loyalty lies. June is high in their House, not quite in the upper ranks but climbing fast."

Jagi finally took over. "It is possible that June is working for one of the Courts but more likely for their House or some private agenda. Stay alert."

She nodded. She was no fool; she knew there was more to their loyalty than the binding she had laid on them. They had both gone above and beyond the letter or spirit of it. She trusted them. It felt odd, to trust an Ante rather than fear them or hate them.

Now, she was glad she had asked. She sat at a table with the other Holder and Holder-Apprentices. Everyone was aware of the impatience that filled the Hive, which was directed at their table. That evening they were hosted by the Court of Decayed Thought and they sat at many small separate tables in a line on the back of an animal, the likes of which she had never seen before. It filled the dining hall they had been escorted to. A giant limbless worm circled around and around in a large ring, almost nose to tail, yet somehow the scenery around them changed from forest to city to desert to beach to ocean. They skidded along, all on the steady back of their calm pet.

It made Lil sick to her stomach when she thought about it too much.

The Holders and Apprentices had been seated at one table together. It was the first time that she and Mayer had been seated alongside their more shunned brethren. Mayer was fuming.

Someone laid their hand on her shoulder over the Nif cloak. She jerked forward and looked back at June. A splash of red and purple lit their nose and mouth from the inside.

"There she is. The most lovely 'dant in the city of Zebub."

Lil started. Never had she heard an Ante compliment a 'dant at all, let alone in such a manner. To call one lovely. It would be foolish to pretend such assignations did not happen between some of the more physical Antes and the more daring or powerful 'dants, but to speak or even imply such a thing in public usually brought immediate censure and punishment. Yet here this Ante was talking about it in the seat of the Ruling Courts themselves.

More surprising, other than some looks of mild discomfort from one Ante, which might have counted more, as his skin was dotted with hundreds of eyes, anyone else who had heard had obviously chosen merely to ignore it. It made her more nervous. Who was this white snake that they had such power?

"Hello." She greeted them politely but turned back to her meal. As before, she pushed most of the unfamiliar lumps of yellow and white to the side of her plate and dined on the nuggets of meat, on the bed of bright blue phai leaves. The sauces added back the flavor that was lost in the cooking of it. It seemed like a lot of wasted time to her.

"I had worried you would be . . . gone when I returned. Or too busy in the Ossuary to come out for supper." June shifted around to come into Lil's view.

Lil faced the Ante with a tremble of fear in her chest and a false smile. She kept her eyes roving across June's face and the wide expanse of chest displayed by the shirt, never allowing her gaze to stay on one pattern of lights for too long. She felt the attention of others at the table on them, sharp and hard.

"We have no intention of leaving before the creeping dark is defeated." Lil lifted a glass of dark wine to her lips, unsure how to approach the other question. The implications that they were delaying on purpose, that they were not working hard enough, and that they should be made to tell everything they had learned all swam in the depths of his words.

"As for the Ossuary . . . it is a trial. Much is without context and therefore unexplainable or, more accurately, undecipherable. It is like trying to read something in a language that is long dead by picking out remnant words and images you recognize from your tongue millennia later."

"Ah, but are languages not the stock in trade of all Holders?"

Her nerves fell away as she fell into teaching mode. "Yes, in some ways."

She could not outright contradict an Ante. The white snake blinked, and for just a second the lights in the face went dim. It made Lil suspect the patterns and brightness that swirled within were more under control than they liked to imply. Before June could take control of the conversation again, Lil took up the thread, finishing her answer.

"We study communication. The way that thoughts are passed on and changed, the way they are expressed, whether that be in words, dance, or mathematics. Everything is an expression of ideas and we wish to understand the ideas through their many interpretations."

Lil saw that the Ante was still confused, but would June admit it?

"Fascinating. Please tell me more."

Lil saw through it, suspected others did as well.

"Of course. Please do me the favor of picking an ideal or a powerful thought in history."

"The crike."

"Not exactly what I meant." She had wanted something more abstract. "However, I can make that work. We know that the crike was tamed and bred as transport, but before that it was a food animal. What were the thought processes that led to their taming? When did they change from food to transport in the minds of everyone? Is there an easy way to say this is the moment, when the first one was tamed, when the first one was deliberately bred, when public crike became available? You can examine the art of the time, the novels and the dance, the messages sent from one being to another, or anything, really, that lingers from that time. If you have enough of the surrounding information you may be able to discern the answer to a question by what surrounds it. That is what we do. Though we all do it differently and have separate focuses."

"Fascinating." June waved their hand for her to continue. The explosion of purple in their palm distracted her.

"As you can imagine, since we know absolutely nothing of the creeping dark, no date, no hint of its nature, or even if we are looking in the right place, it is much harder than usual. We examine every piece and try to divine its purpose, knowing that what we find could be the key to success, though it is most likely simply another dead end. We are disappointed often but we continue to try for the good of Corpiliu."

Lil was surprised by her vehemence, but she was tired of the looks and the whispers and the commentary and the suspicion that followed her everywhere she went now. She stopped herself just short of saying that if the Ruling Courts had not obscured their history so well, buried and hoarded the knowledge they had, then maybe progress could be made.

She bit at her tongue until she tasted blood; she had no wish to die today.

There was a smile on June's face and Lil noticed some of the tension in the hall had melted away. She still felt the prickle of danger up her spine but it no longer felt like a knife was constantly aimed at her. June wandered away and the rest of the dinner was better, though she noticed Mayer frowning at his food and Riana and Krezida fiercely whispering to their Apprentices.

As she left the Hive and entered the chill of the courtyard, a voice called out behind her.

"Liliana."

Lil sighed and turned. It was Razel. They had gotten along quite well in the last couple of weeks with the exception of Razel's insistence on calling her by her full first name.

"Yes, Razie."

Razel frowned.

"How did you know what to do in there, to calm everything down?"

Lil studied the woman in front of her. Just because they had been getting along was no reason to trust her. Lil sighed. She felt like she was on a tightrope at all times. She couldn't give the other Holders a reason to believe she was turning on them or attempting to hoard power. She had to appear competent so they wouldn't turn on her to rid themselves of something weak. Normally she would not worry as much, knowing Mayer was there to help, but right now she knew nothing of the kind.

Her Holder had only spoken a few words to her at all in the past two weeks. Her overtures had all been ignored and after the first few days she had mostly stopped trying.

She made her decision.

"I didn't. I think it was all that Ante's plan, to be honest with you."

"Really?" Razel looked skeptical.

"I believe so. Either way, I swear, I had no plan coming into dinner tonight."

Razel studied her face and whatever she read there convinced her. She nodded and slipped back into the Hive and to the dinner without a goodbye. Lil rolled her eyes. For someone who could read most 'dants so easily, Razel sometimes had no manners whatsoever. She shook it off as she made her way back to Hive Chayyliel. She had more important things to worry about, like what was the endgame of June's plan?

To win her trust?

She was more suspicious now. She was exhausted, but still managed to brief Arel and Jagi on what had happened before crawling into bed between her sibs.

The next day she said goodbye to Min and Davi, leaving them in Arel and Jagi's care. As usual they were sad to see her go, but she had made sure to rise earlier than necessary so she could have some time with them this morning. Besides, the separation was not nearly as traumatizing since Arel and Jagi were quickly becoming favorites. Especially for Davi, who had taken to drawing little circles on his sides in soot to imitate their bodies.

As soon as she closed her room's door behind her to head to the courtyard, the same voice as last night stopped her. "Liliana."

"Razie." The girl frowned in annoyance but still nodded in greeting.

"We are not going to the Ossuary immediately today. Instead we are to meet at the top of Hive Chayyliel."

"The top?" Lil cursed herself for the question as soon as it left her lips. There were ears everywhere, or so Arel and Jagi said. She smoothed all emotion from her face. "Very well." She had questions, but asking them would give Razel the upper hand and Lil had no intention of giving up any ground to her fellow Holder-Apprentice.

They were unfortunately joined by Haydn as they reached the foot of the great stairwell that climbed in a spiral up the center of the Hive.

"What do you suppose Queen Chayyliel wants with us?" he asked.

Lil, who had not known that Chayyliel had called the meeting, only shrugged her shoulders and made sure Razel was between them. Haydn had shown himself to be both easily distracted and unconsciously cruel. A combination she had never thought possible but had learned was dangerous. She was never sure when he was truly lost in his thought or simply feigning it to glean what he could from careless lips. He was not smart but he was cunning, which could be twice as deadly.

"We won't learn anything down here, will we?"

Though the climb all the way to the top was hard and strenuous, none of them faltered, but neither did they have any extra breath for speech.

As they reached the final landing, the pits and necks and backs of their clothing were soaked almost clear with sweat. Two hallways led off from the upper landing but there was no clue as to which way they should go. They all stared at one another, unwilling to admit ignorance.

Suddenly the crack of stone sounded from above them. All their heads shot up, Razel leaping back toward the stairs while Lil and Haydn fell into crouches. There was now a square hole in the ceiling and Krezida looked down at them all with a frown while her rainbow of hair cascaded down around her. Lil could not recall ever seeing a pleasant expression on the woman's face, though what did any of them have to feel good about?

"Hurry up." Her head disappeared and a long knotted rope fell down to them. Again they froze, none willing to be the first to show their back to the other two. Finally with a sigh Lil moved forward. As if it were a challenge, the others moved to grab the rope as well. Lil was quicker, snatching it out of Razel's path and pushing it into Haydn's grasping palm.

"After you." She smiled.

Haydn was silent but his jaw tightened and he grabbed the rope from her and scurried up, quick as the rodent he was. Razel went next and Lil brought up the rear.

Yanwan blazed in the sky today and the world was bright. The roof shone around them, a gentle golden glow moving about their feet like a living thing. Over to the side two dragons lazed around in their pen, unwilling to move in the heat. Chayyliel stood with two members of its Court. Both were rapidly moving black clouds that whipped around and around in a cone shape. A small Turms stood near him as well. Lil wondered if it was the same Turms that always accompanied Chayyliel, or if they worked in shifts.

The Holder-Apprentices joined their masters in a semicircle facing Chayyliel. They stood behind and to the right, subservient and non-challenging. Lil stared down at her feet, watching the gold light circle them, billowing out into paler smoke, then coalescing into bright points.

"Time grows short." Chayyliel did not sound impatient or angry, only matter-of-fact. Nonetheless Lil could feel her Holder stiffen in front of her, and was sure the other Holders could sense the same. "It is not your fault, but in many ways fault does not matter. Powers in the Ruling Courts grow impatient, and allies turn against me."

"Would it be safer to move back to our own Athenaeums?"

Lil recognized Riana's rough tone.

"You would never make it. Some would see it as admitting defeat, some as betrayal. One of them would attack and whoever survived would retaliate. The city would not survive it. No, the only way out is to find some sort of answer and quickly."

"What do you think we've been trying to do?" Krezida's voice had an edge to it. She teetered between despair and anger daily and both laced her words.

Chayyliel shifted and Lil glanced up once, quickly, to see that it now stood with its multiple spindly arms crossed over the narrow stick chest, hands curved inward.

"Peace. I did not call this meeting to chastise, but so that we may figure things out together."

Lil slid her gaze back to the floor. The gold light was diffusing below her soles, spreading out and becoming dimmer but opalescent as it expanded. Then in the center a dot of complete darkness appeared.

"Are there any ideas that you may have?"

"We need more information." Mayer spoke for the first time. "I have done my best, but all of the Courts claim to have no knowledge of our history farther than twenty thousand years back. Though I know it a lie."

Chayyliel snorted, which startled all of them. It was odd for an Ante to use a gesture so associated with 'dants. "Most likely they all have crumbs they are desperate not to share with others even if it means their death."

The small spot of darkness in the light had begun to send out tendrils; it spread across the light beneath her feet like blood on hot stone, it bubbled and burst and spread. She noticed a star pattern that looked to be winking at her and then she realized it really was winking at her.

Nif!

They were inside the light somehow.

"Could we convince them to work together in this?" This from Riana. Lil would have thought her an idiot had her voice not held so much contempt and weariness. She did not say it because she thought it might actually work, but because it felt obligatory. Something that one of them should suggest before moving on to more likely solutions.

No one convinced the Ruling Courts to do anything. They were in charge and no one challenged them. Every once in a while a rebellion rose up and those who survived were the unlucky ones, as their tortured voices would ring out over the city for days and sometimes weeks, driving any surviving family mad with grief and pain. The Athenaeums were impregnable and spots of sanctuary. Many times they had sheltered 'dants and even some Antes without asking the reasons. The Holders would have been able to withstand the Ruling Courts from within their homes, but coming here had robbed them of that safety.

No one answered Riana.

"Would we be able to somehow induce them to share with us?" Krezida asked. Blackmail was a time-honored tradition, after all.

"I have enough influence left to force one or maybe two of the Courts, but how would we pick which ones had the best information? And they would then definitely be enemies afterwards. That is a last resort because it leaves us with fewer options." Left unsaid was the sinking feeling they all felt, that they were sorting through "last resorts."

The Nif were coalescing into a dark sinuous shape that slowly became longer. It looked like a long rope, or a drawing of a river seen from above, small threads of black tributaries still running from its main body.

"Perhaps some sort of *word*, to glean an idea of the knowledge they have?" Lil immediately felt the attention focused on herself and Mayer. She carefully kept her face blank, even though at the mere mention she could feel the Babel trying to form on her tongue. No one had noticed her problems so far but she was not fool enough to think that meant she was safe.

They all knew they were asking Mayer and herself to risk almost certain death by bringing this up.

"No." Mayer did not elaborate and no one said anything to try and convince him otherwise.

The Nif were clearly showing her a snake now. A serpent made of their darkness that looked poised to strike at the tip of her shoe. They were showing her an answer; just not one she wanted.

"We could extend our hours in the Ossuary."

"That would mean asking for extra protections and also any one of you missing a dinner could be seen as guilt on your part."

"Is there a way to contact the Athenaeums left in other cities? Perhaps they might have something?"

Mayer nodded. "I have sent dragons off to all the Athenaeums we know of, even the ones which are barely worthy of the name. So far none of the replies have been helpful. And to my knowledge no other city has the Ossuary. That is Zebub's prize alone."

"How about—" Krezida started.

The snake was staring at her and Lil found her mouth opening.

"Snake." It was more a whisper than anything but everyone heard and turned to her. She kept her head down and began to curse herself for a fool. This was not her place but she knew it was the only choice. The shadow serpent about her feet began to break apart, the Nif returning to wherever they came from.

"What, child?" Chayyliel did not sound offended that she had spoken, simply surprised.

And now she had no choice but to speak.

"The white snake—June."

"What about them?"

"I am told that the white snakes gather secrets and June seems especially powerful within the House of the Madame."

"Yes, those are both very true." Impatience entered Chayyliel's tone. "Look up, child."

Lil raised her face and met the gaze of everyone on the roof. Mayer was livid. She could tell by the way his lips had disappeared. The others looked angry as well or perhaps jealous that all of their suggestions had been shot down. Hers was the first that had gotten some consideration.

"June has expressed an interest in you. You would have to be the contact. No one else has interested them that much in a very long time. At least not to my knowledge. Would you be able to do this?"

Lil was so nervous she had to swallow several times before she could speak without her voice breaking.

"I don't really have a choice, do I?"

The anger on Mayer's face ratcheted up a notch and everyone else looked shocked. She did not know what possessed her and was instantly regretful. However, the Queen simply snorted again and looked her up and down.

"Not unless you have another idea that might work in that head of yours."

She shook her head. She felt guilty for taking credit for something that wasn't actually her idea, but drawing more attention to her strange relationship with the Nif could only make things worse.

"Holders Krezida and Riana, please take your Holder-Apprentices and leave us. I must speak with Mayer and Liliana about this plan and too many arguing voices will not do us any good." They all stiffened, but none did anything but slowly move to the roof hatch and lower themselves back to the landing.

Once they were gone Chayyliel turned to the two guards. "Patrol. Secure the area."

The two mini-thunderheads whirled off in different directions and circled the rooftop, looking for any enemies. Meanwhile, Chayyliel spoke a word, not in 'dant but in what Lil assumed was its own dialect. The light around them flared and grew so bright Lil had to close her eyes and cover them with her palm.

When she could open her eyes again, three chairs were on the roof placed in a triangle facing each other. They were made of solid light and glowed rhythmically.

"Please sit."

Only after Chayyliel sat did Mayer and Lil do the same, still nervous and wary.

"Now, there are two ways you could approach June. The first is seduction."

Lil felt her dark skin blaze with heat. She had no doubt that her cheeks were darker than usual. She had no fear of sex. She was no virgin, but the casual mention of her sleeping with someone for information made an odd mix of want, rage, and humiliation flare in her chest.

"Which I doubt would be the best choice, even if Liliana could pull it off flawlessly—" Chayyliel's voice was laced with doubt and it made the heat inside her climb higher. "—the reveal of seduction always makes a very deadly and permanent enemy. Most important, to have such an assignation in my Hive would cause me to lose large amounts of face and influence. The second choice I think is best. Negotiation. June would not have approached Liliana so openly unless they believed she had access to something they wanted. We can trade on that."

They spent the next hour laying out a plan. Although it would be more accurate to say that Chayyliel laid out a plan and Lil changed it to suit herself, and Mayer stayed silent and sour.

MAYER

He listened to his Apprentice and Chayyliel lay out a plan to help them all and stayed silent. He was gazing at Liliana, looking deep inside her.

There were a number of things that Mayer looked for in his Apprentices. Power was a nonnegotiable, but he also needed them to be generic. Power would eventually take on the impressions of the one who touched it most often. The less personalized the power, the easier for others to use it as well.

Liliana had a deep reservoir of power within her. He had always seen it as a large ball of clean blue slowly turning, its surface rippling. She touched it but her impressions were quickly wiped away, leaving her power core blank and clean once again. He'd never seen anything like it.

Now, though, when he gazed inside of her there was a deep purple invading the blue of the sphere. Like a bruise, it spread across the surface of her power. In its wake it left valleys and mountainous regions. It solidified the power. Already half of the globe was crystallized solid.

He wondered how to stop it, and what had caused it.

When Chayyliel dismissed them, Yanwan was already more than halfway done with its journey. The Queen had outlined all the possible deals that June might want, what Liliana was allowed to promise and what she wasn't, and where she had to use her own judgment. Mayer interjected here and there but mostly left it to the Queen.

They made their way back down to the base of the Hive in silence. He struggled to decide how much to tell her. It was the perfect time to talk since they had been given the rest of the day to rest.

He could ask her about the changes to her power, or suggest the moving of her sibs as he had been considering, or question her more closely about the evening of her parents' death. There were things he needed to say and things she needed to change. Perhaps it was time to take her on his next crafting mission. She would see what Holders truly had to do to survive, which would no doubt make her more subservient.

For too long he had been silent and allowed this change in their relationship to go unchallenged. At night he had wondered why. With any past Apprentice he had been very quick to correct them if they strayed from the path he had chosen. Perhaps he had a genuine affection for the girl? He had never taken an Apprentice when they were so young and so she had grown up around him.

Still, she needed to be reminded that while he wasn't her family, he had been the one to teach her and he was the one she owed loyalty to. It was time she remembered that.

Before he could speak up, they had reached the bottom landing and Liliana turned to face him.

"Since we have a day free of research I will spend the day with Min and Davi. Unless you have something you would like me to do?"

Bitterness welled up in him but he did not allow it to touch his voice "No. It's fine. Go and spend some time with your sibs."

He told himself he would do the research about her power himself. He told himself that he would speak with her soon. He told himself that there was no need to worry her until he knew something. He told himself it was for her own good.

No matter the lies he told himself, he could not make himself believe them.

DAVI

Davi screamed a war cry as he leapt from the top of the bed onto Arel's back. The Ante reached back to grab him but the boy avoided the hands, which weren't quite long enough. He hung onto Arel's neck while Min and Jagi rolled around on the ground to their side. Davi reached up with his small hands and grasped at Arel's face.

"What is going on in here?"

Davi let go in surprise and fell back onto the bed. Lil stood in the doorway. Her arms were crossed, but she was smiling. He slid down to the floor and ran to his sister.

"Uncle Arel and Uncle Jagi are showing us how to fight."

"Uncle?" She reached down to pick him up and set him on her hip.

Davi rolled his eyes. His sister always focused on dumb things.

"Did you see me winning? I was going for his eyes like they said."

Lil laughed and turned to the floor, where Min and Jagi were still rolling around.

"Min, stop," Jagi ordered.

"Only if you say that I won!"

She held on to one of Jagi's arms and kicked out at the other one.

"Why are you here? Are you staying here today?" Davi's voice rose in excitement—he never got to see his sister during the day anymore.

Lil nodded and a huge smile exploded onto his face as he squealed and hugged her.

"So what do you want to do today?"

"Exploring!" Davi yelled in her ear. She winced, then turned it into a smile.

"What's exploring?"

Min ran over, having gotten Jagi to admit to his defeat.

"It's when we go all over the Hive looking for secret rooms and passages."

Davi saw Lil look at Arel and Jagi. They looked at her but Davi could see the holes on their sides were closing and opening. Davi knew that wasn't normal; usually they kept them closed no matter how much he asked. He squirmed to be let down so he could get closer, but Lil held him tight.

"It is good for them to know their way around this place. Just in case," Arel said in response to nothing.

Davi looked from Lil to Arel. It was like this sometimes when they talked about things that didn't make sense to him. It was a grown-up thing and he was bored.

"Can we go do it now? Can we?"

Lil pulled her gaze away from Arel and Jagi and looked down at him with a smile. It reminded him of Mom's smile. He pulled himself closer to her at the thought of Mom and Pop-Pop. She hugged him back.

"Let me just change out of this and we'll go." She set Davi on the bed and he began to jump up and down, shouting wordlessly in excitement. He watched Lil go to the wardrobe in the corner and get dressed.

She turned back to them.

"Let's go."

Davi grabbed her hand and pulled her to the door of their room. He stopped in the doorway and turned to her. He held a small finger up to his lips.

"The first rule is to stay quiet and don't let anyone see you."

Lil nodded.

"The second rule is if they do see you, act like you belong there."

Lil smiled at him and Davi got the feeling that she wanted to laugh, but this was serious business and she had to focus.

"All right."

"Promise," he said sternly.

"I promise."

Davi nodded, took her hand again, and led them out into the labyrinthine halls of the Hive. It wasn't interesting like some of the other Hives he saw from the windows or when Uncles Arel and Jagi took him flying. The Hive they were in was just plain black stone. It wasn't fancy and magic like the others. Still, there were a bunch of weird magic things he and his sister had found on these trips. He still didn't know what any of them did and Arel and Jagi never let them keep what they found, but it was still fun. He looked left, then right, and turned right, carefully setting his feet so they made little noise. Min was doing the same. When they reached a set of wooden stairs both were careful to only step on the edge closest to the wall.

"Why are you walking this way?" Lil asked.

"It makes less noise."

"The stair is stronger at the place of joining with the wall, less likely to creak or make any noise," Arel shared from behind them.

Lil nodded and they continued on their way.

LIL

L il was shocked as she trailed behind her younger brother up and down through the floors of the Hive. So much of her time in the Hive had been spent sleeping in her room, she had not seen many of the wonders within it. They walked through a hall, the floor and walls of which were gold. No furniture littered the room except for a number of tall candelabras that threw their candlelight over the room, turning the gold alive and warm. When she looked up she could not see the ceiling, and she assumed this was one of the rooms set aside for the Antes who rarely if ever touched the ground.

From there they crossed into a small room that looked ordinary and plain. It had the same black stone as most of the other rooms, except that the floor was completely transparent. Beneath the surface lay a sea that defied explanation. Dark things swam beneath their feet. Fish that looked like a hundred jaws strung together slammed against their feet, trying to get through to them. Davi laughed and began to taunt the things by dancing around. Lil let them stay until she looked down and saw a pained 'dant face staring back at her, begging for help. It was distorted, skin stretched back to where it was stitched to the side of a fish that darted away.

They spent a couple of marks of the candle moving through the Hive and then decided to head back to their room for a snack. As they neared the room, Lil could hear Razel and Haydn's voices. As they turned the final corner Lil saw them, heads bent together as if sharing a secret, and she was immediately on guard.

"Take Min and Davi inside. I will see what they want."

Arel stared at her, then nodded. He and Jagi ushered the protesting kids past her two fellow Holder-Apprentices and into their room.

Haydn kept his eyes on Lil, but Razel watched her sibs with the spark of intelligence in her eyes. The Babel words came to her fast, a light sentence, a quick mutter. She was no longer surprised at the ease with which it rose up, only grateful. It flowed easily off her tongue as she spoke-sang it under her breath—there was no coughing, no raw feeling. She still did not know what it meant. Even Mayer, after his years of speaking it, still suffered through every use. Why had this become easy for her?

After a few words both their eyes were on her, no longer able to focus on her sibs.

"That's what we wanted to talk to you about."

"We?" Lil looked hard at Razel but the other girl simply met her eyes with no expression.

"Yes, the language you've been speaking."

Lil tensed up immediately. She had actually not spoken a full Babel word at all in the last few weeks, but if they suspected she had been using it all along, so did others. Not good. Babel was something only her Athenaeum controlled. Each Athenaeum had their own communications that they taught. Enheduanna, the language of philosophy and diplomacy, alchemy and the arts, how to interpret the creative and bring others to your side. Hypatia, the language of machines and technology, the suppressed arts of the distant past. Their inventions were popular with those that could afford them. And Kandake had the broadest range of knowledge and Babel, the first language before Babel themselves cast everyone—Ante and 'dant—down for their hubris. It was dangerous and wild and most had trouble speaking it. Most burned their tongues to nothing in the attempt.

"You know what it is. What question could you possibly have?"

Razel spoke for the first time. "I've been paying attention . . ."

Lil knew that tone from the past two weeks. Razel thought she had something that would corner the person she was speaking to.

". . . and you and Mayer aren't speaking the same language."

Lil felt some tension leave her shoulders, though she didn't fully relax.

"You haven't even heard me speak Babel."

"That first night as you ran for the Athenaeum and right now. And the whispers you thought that no one noticed."

Lil sighed. "Is that all? Of course we don't speak it the same. Babel is not simple, like learning another language. Everything about you and what you are talking about changes the words in the chain. The simple fact that I have sibs while Mayer doesn't means I have to use another form entirely." She might have shared a little too much, but she wanted this rumor shut down fast. She ignored the mention of the fact that Razel had noticed her slip-ups.

If the Courts started to believe she was using Babel all the time, it could lead to an investigation, which could lead to Arel and Jagi, which would lead to her death.

"It's not just that." Razel's eyes lit up. "You're acting different, less like yourself."

Lil kept her body from going tense all over. She pushed herself forward into their space. The final words for what she had started seconds ago hung in the air around her, ready to be spoken, ready to complete themselves.

"Firstly, you don't know who I was. And second, I think you're both jealous and scared." She turned to face Razel alone. "I think you have teamed up with someone you hate because you think I have some advantage now. Did you forget what we are working for?"

There was no reaction from Razel and Lil sighed and pulled back to look at both of them again.

"I will not let our whole world go down in flames because you are too invested in power games to put differences aside. I will not let you or anyone stand in my way of destroying the creeping dark. For everything I've—we've lost."

She turned her back to them, mouth ready to form the final word that would put them both into an immediate sleep, but neither attacked. She closed the door behind her and sagged against it. Arel and Jagi were immediately there hovering over her, hands reaching out to touch her and make sure she was okay.

She waved them off and walked over to where Min and Davi were already enjoying their lunch, hugging both of them to her chest. They froze, then turned and returned her embrace. There was a desperation to their smaller arms that she had not anticipated but should have.

They had spent all their days with Mother and Father. They did not have the distance and fear between them that she had. She was the only family they had left, and they were the reason she would not falter or fail. Her sibs would be safe, her world would be safe, no matter what she had to do.

NA'AMEN GOBERT TILAHUN

RAZEL

R azel liked Liliana. She did. But that meant nothing really, in the grand scheme of things. Lil was interesting; she understood power and its plays but retained an odd naiveté about what some would do to obtain and maintain it. She did not want their world to be devoured by this dark any more than Liliana did, but she also had confidence that a solution would be found, if not by them, then by one of the Ruling Courts.

Money and power found answers and when there weren't any to be found? It made them.

She was more concerned with what came after. Those who found the answers would have power in the new regime.

If the Ruling Courts didn't kill them.

Razel figured of all of them, Liliana and Mayer had the greatest chance of discovering something, not only because they possessed a wider base of knowledge than Haydn, herself, or their mentors, but because Liliana was changing. She was becoming something. Most had not noticed anything except for the sudden interest of the Nifs. But Razel saw it.

She left Haydn, and his disgusting suggestion she come back to his room, in the center courtyard and returned to the Hive of Sorrow and Riches. The sight of the pulsing, pink, alive Hive woke conflicting feelings in Razel. It was comforting in some way since she had seen buildings like this for most of her life. However, she also thought of the nights every moon when she had to attend and help Riana create beautiful horrors. Now that they were staying here, it was even more often.

She entered the Hive and walked to the center of it. There, hanging from the ceiling to the ground in the central well of the Hive, were dozens of bright red ropes in constant motion. Moving closer, she grabbed one as it moved upward, wrapping her arms and legs around it as it shot up through the floors of the Hive. It slowed at the platforms through the Hive but never stopped.

The floor they were staying on came up and Razel swung out, allowing herself to drop onto the lip of the platform.

As soon as she entered their suite of rooms Riana was on her feet.

"How did it go?"

"She did not seem worried, had an answer for everything . . . said she would do anything to save this world."

"Ha! Mayer has taught her well."

"Yes." Razel made sure the question stayed out of her tone.

"How difficult would it be to take her out of the equation?" Riana watched her with those beady eyes that saw everything.

Razel thought and then shook her head, trying to hide her relief at realizing it was not a feasible plan.

"She keeps her power close to the surface now. She said something to us and for the rest of the conversation I could feel her power all around us on the verge of coming loose. Plus, after our discussion this morning, I assume that Chayyliel will have her under watch and any attack on her would be investigated."

"True." Riana smiled.

Another test. Her life was a series of constant tests but she had passed every single one or she would not still be standing where she was.

"So what are our options?"

"To watch and wait for an advantage," Razel answered.

"And Haydn?"

Razel kept the disgust off of her face by force of will alone.

"Good, I almost believed you that time. Get to the point where even Haydn cannot tell that you think him lower than a worm."

"He already thinks that now. He is not hard to fool."

"Fine, until Krezida believes it."

"That day will never come. She knows what a loathsome toad she's chosen as an Holder-Apprentice."

"A loathsome toad unusually skilled in true names and alchemy."

"Yes." It burned her insides to admit the creep was good at anything at all, but she had seen the way he could figure out a thing's true name with enough study and contact. She spent all day trying to emulate it in the Ossuary.

Krezida and Haydn could sometimes tell the purpose of a thing. Blueprints were simple enough to guess at but the fully made mechaniques they found were nothing but guesswork. They could just as easily be a weapon as a harvesting machine or something they would not figure out even given decades. And they could not simply try turning each one on; the potential for disaster was too high.

"He is the weak link here, not Liliana. She has become more of a power than we thought. We risk her emerging from this crisis with too much credit and power."

Razel nodded, though she wasn't sure Riana was right in this case. The Holder tended to think everyone acted as she did, that everyone worked with the same motivation Riana oozed with. Razel had more friends, or had them at one point before coming to Hypatia. 'Dants were complex and contradictory. She believed that Liliana believed there was a chance the dark would take them all, that she was scared for the future.

Still, it changed nothing.

"What of your personal project?" Riana interrupted her train of thought, which Razel was grateful for.

"It goes well." The thought of her project made Razel smile for the first time that day.

"How many do you have?"

"Three completed so far." Razel was trying to reverse engineer blueprints based on some of the mechaniques in the Ossuary. Riana had taken the easier job of recreating the blueprints they found. Riana planned to rebuild some of them in Hypatia, where they could be studied in safe conditions.

"Excellent. Create as many as possible; most will likely do nothing, so the more we have the more potential advantages we have when this is over."

Razel nodded and kept her smile firmly in place.

"I will go and work on them more now, if it pleases you."

"Yes, do that. I will find Krezida and Mayer. Sleep if you can. We will be working downstairs after dinner."

Razel shivered but nodded, happy to leave Riana's presence. For all that she had been Holder-Apprentice for over three years now, they did not spend that much time together. Razel was under no illusion that

Riana had chosen her for anything other than her near-perfect memory. The fact that she was intelligent and, in her own opinion, a better mech than the Holder was not something that Riana acknowledged.

Razel knew it though and, more importantly, those that had contact with Hypatia knew it.

Riana's mechaniques were crude things. They worked well but relied on power and force. Razel did not deny such things had their place, but there had to be a balance of finesse and beauty. Mechaniques were not simply things to use but beautiful works of art.

She spread out her latest blueprint on the floor of the small room she'd commandeered as her studio on the first night. All the furniture was now gone. The pulse of the living walls of the Hive was comforting. She was used to the cold metal of Hypatia now, but she had lived in a building like this before Riana took her. The dark black paper took up three quarters of the floor; the only thing decorating it now was a diagonal streak of red. She stared at the red and the rest of the ancient mechanique began to flow into her vision. Grabbing her chalks, she began to mark down the things she remembered. Here was the moving arm in white and here the crank that powered it in yellow and the hinges and other joinings in cerulean.

She had tried to explain her process to Riana only once, and the look of blankness on the Holder's face plus the hint of jealousy in the curl of her lips stopped her. There was no way to explain it anyway. She had tried before but the combination of memory, visualization, and art made no sense to anyone but herself.

She drew what she remembered, the connections she imagined, the hope of it working. All of it went into her blueprints. The colors allowed her to know what to switch out first if it did not work.

When her arm was exhausted, she saw that the outline of the mechanique from the Ossuary was complete. As of now it was not a blueprint so much as an art project, but she would continue to study the whole creation little by little each day until she had more information on the inner workings.

Exhausted, she dragged herself up and next door to her bedroom. A nap would do her good; she would be refreshed for dinner and everything that came after.

NA'AMEN GOBERT TILAHUN

SAN FRANCISCO

MATTHIAS

When Erik burst out of his front door in a hurry Matthias tensed for an Angelic attack, but as he got closer Matthias noticed the way his shoulders were hunched up to his ears. Then he noticed the two people with cameras, one across the street and one in a neighbor's yard.

Matthias had assumed because the street was no longer choked with cars that the scrutiny of the photographers had ended for some reason. He should have known better. They were simply better hidden and fewer. Erik flung the car door open and threw himself into the passenger seat. Matthias asked no questions as he put the car in reverse and left the neighborhood as quickly as possible.

"So what's up?"

"Did you listen to my voice mail?"

"No. I knew you were on your way so I just figured you would fill me in."

Matthias sighed. "Luka contacted me. Byron has requested the meeting this morning."

"Okay, where?" Erik blinked as the soothing feel of the forces of the car came over him again. At least they knew why now. For some reason he had not expected everything to happen so soon.

"Their base downtown."

Erik paused. "That seems stupid."

Matthias just grunted in agreement. "We have an assurance of safety. Not that I think the Organization would do too much if they broke it."

"All right. I need to swing by my former school so I can pick up my shit. Do we have time?"

"Yeah, it's why I came by so early."

The silence was only broken by directions and affirmative grunts. They drove from the Richmond toward the south end of the city. They moved through the more suburban neighborhoods until they came to Ocean Drive. There in the hills, protected from sight by a line of private homes, sat his school. They pulled into the parking lot.

"Erik, is everything okay?" Matthias wanted to comfort his aspirant but also knew the distance he had kept during Erik's convalescence had done exactly as he wanted it to. Send the message that they could be friends, and nothing more.

"I'm fine." Before he turned to exit, Erik took a deep breath and the sadness and guilt left his face. The lines of his face got hard, the lips became firm, and he looked ready for anything. "I'll be back in a few minutes."

"Do I need to come with you?"

That surprised a laugh out of Erik though Matthias did not know why.

"No, there's nothing in this building that I can't handle."

He left the car but before he shut the door, he leaned down. "Hey Matthias." He met Matthias's eyes and for just a split second the hurt and vulnerability Erik had hidden shone in his face. "Thanks for asking." The hurt was gone again as he smiled, then turned to walk away.

Matthias knew a lot of things about himself. After everything that had gone down he'd spent a lot of time alone, with only himself for company. The longer you spent by yourself the less able you were to lie to yourself. He was pretty much incapable of self-delusion at this point, which was probably one of the reasons he came off as bitter. Looking into Erik's smile made him realize, without a doubt, that he was fucked no matter what he did.

ERIK

He barely paused as he moved through his school of a semester and a half. Classes had just started, so the halls were empty and the students that were there, on errands or skipping, didn't speak to him. They simply watched as he walked through campus. The school was a number of small courtyards and open-air hollow squares that held lockers and rooms around the edges. In the middle, works of art and fountains took up the space.

The courtyard with his locker was abandoned. As he entered his combination, however, he felt the force of someone's eyes on his back. More than one someone. He knew exactly who he would see when he turned, so he calmly pulled out his books, magazines, and one sweater he thought he had lost from the depths of his locker and shoved them into the empty bag at his feet.

Only when he was done did he turn to face Harry and Melissa. He was reminded by their bruises that it had only been a couple weeks since he'd beat the shit out of them. Melissa was favoring one leg, and he vaguely remembered kicking the other out from underneath her as she'd gone for his ribs. She had a cast on her right arm and her lower lip was discolored as if it had been busted and only recently healed up.

Harry looked worse off; a chunk of hair was missing from his scalp, both eyes were healing bruises, and the whistle when he exhaled meant more that one or two teeth were at least chipped if not missing from his mouth. He also had a cast on one arm and he shifted from leg to leg as if uncomfortable standing long.

Erik remembered a knee to the groin at one point and could not help smiling.

"Harry. Melissa."

Both of their scowls darkened and he could feel his own smile widen.

"Those aren't our names. It took a lot of nerve for you to come back here." Melissa was the one who spoke and took a step forward.

"Did it?" They hadn't been able to take him at full strength; they had to know they had no chance now and that he had nothing to lose. Then the smile froze on his face.

They weren't alone. His head turned to the right, to a corner of the courtyard. He had to force his eyes to look. There was a constant thrum running through his head telling him he should turn away. "Who are you?" He forced the words out.

Slowly the man was revealed. He appeared as if he had always been there and Erik had just refused to acknowledge his presence. Even cross-legged on the ground Erik could tell the man was at least six foot six. He had a very light bright brown complexion, with darker freckles sprinkled across every bit of his face. The rest of him was covered in a black-on-black suit, with gloves that were at the very least expensive pleather if not straight up leather. His hair was a frohawk, well groomed with huge dark curls with a red tint.

"Well, maybe Matthias has found himself a worthy aspirant this time?"

Something in the man's voice made his shoulders tense and rise around his ears. The smugness perhaps? The voice felt slick like oil against Erik's brain. The man rose to his feet and Erik saw his estimation had actually been off—the man was closer to six foot eight. He turned to Harry and Melissa and nodded at them.

"Thank you for your help, children."

Erik saw how they bristled at being called children and warmed to the man—just a little bit.

"You may go." The man turned his gaze from them and met Erik's eyes and Erik knew with a chilling certainty who this man was.

"What the fuck? What about what you promised us?" Melissa's voice was shrill and Erik suspected the only reason Harry was not yelling as well was that he would have sounded like a parrot, whistling each word.

Byron looked back at the two, but this time something in his face went dark. Harry and Melissa both jerked as if something had shocked them and their faces went blank.

"You will only remember trying to confront Erik again and that he scared you off anytime you come close to remembering me or anything you have heard this morning you will be struck down with a migraine so severe you must spend the next two days in bed if you continue you will slowly lose parts of yourself first your ability to speak then bowel control then hearing then sight and finally your life now leave." He said it all quickly, with no punctuation or pause for breath and without any emotion or tone, though Erik thought he could see a vicious pleasure in the curl of his mouth.

Neither Harry nor Melissa reacted to the threat in the words, simply staying still and listening to his instructions . . . orders? When he finished, they turned and marched away. As they crossed the line of the courtyard, they shook themselves and Erik held out some hope, but they simply looked back at him with terrified faces and moved as fast as their casts would let them.

"I apologize for the test and also for not introducing myself. I am—"

"Byron."

He smiled, pleased at having been recognized.

"Yes. Tell me, does Matthias still talk about me?"

"No. You just seem like the kind of person that would inspire that level of revulsion in people."

The smile dropped from Byron's face. Then it returned brighter than ever.

"So he does talk about me."

Erik rolled his eyes but kept Byron in his sight. He would not be surprised by a physical attack, but what worried him the most was the voice. How did one fight someone who could change your mind at will?

"Don't worry, it isn't as easy on the Blooded for some reason. Most can shake off my commands in a day if not sooner. It didn't even take you that long to see me."

"You mean you in the corner? Is that one of your tricks?"

Now the smile dropped from Byron's face and he took a step forward. Erik did not know why he was antagonizing the man, but it felt good to have a target he had no fear of hurting.

"What did you want to say?"

"How do you know I have anything to say?" The smug smile was back in place and Erik longed to bash it in with his fist. He could see himself doing it, the fist flying, the blood spray, and perhaps a tooth flying into the air. It calmed him.

"Well, why else would you be here? To attack me? That would be stupid—much easier to arrange an accident at the meeting place. And if you wanted to have a simple conversation, you could have waited until the meeting as well. No, you had something to say that you didn't want anyone from either side to hear, so what is it?"

"Well I can see you're going to be a fun one."

Erik gave him the thinnest smile in response and waited, letting the silence stretch on and on.

"They're not who you think they are."

Erik smiled in response and gestured for Byron to go on.

"They aren't the valiant resistance fighting a corrupt government or whatever. They're violent isolationists who don't want us to make any contact with another culture."

"Well, number one, I'm not part of the Organization, and number two, I'm pretty sure you already have contact. Also, wasn't that your group that was cleaning up after the Angelic tried to take that little girl?"

"We were helping her. Her parents were not happy with the knowledge that their child was . . . special, so we decided to take her in the night before her parents had the chance to hurt her."

"Really? You guys thought the best way to save a child from an abusive situation was to scare the living daylights out of her with a monster?" This leaving aside the fact that Erik was fairly sure Melinda's parents were nothing of the kind. Had heard from her own mouth how much she missed her mothers and how she loved family dinners. Though none of that exactly ruled out abuse. He resolved to ask her the next time he saw her.

Byron gave a wry smile. "I never said we were the smartest, I said we had good intentions."

"Yeah, well, you know what they say about good intentions."

Byron's shoulders slumped and he got a wry look on his face. If Erik didn't know better he would say the man looked pained.

"Look, it's obvious you don't trust me. Or us. Whatever. But I just wanted to ask you to keep an open mind for the time we're working together. They haven't shown you even a small fraction of what they truly are."

He kept saying that, they. Was he talking about the Organization? Or the Blooded?

"Okay." Erik had no intention of agreeing to anything this man said when the conversation started, but it was a simple enough request.

Byron turned to leave. The morning sun caught the red highlights in his hair, so that the glow reminded Erik of blood.

"Oh, one last thing."

Erik rolled his eyes. There was always "one last thing."

"Yes?"

"Have they told you why they're so angry with me? Why they hate me so much more than any other Suit?"

"Yeah, you killed an Agent." Erik didn't know this for sure but it was a fair guess.

Byron smiled and it was like the devil was getting a handjob. "But they never mentioned who or what came before?"

"No." Erik didn't find it that weird. It obviously hurt too much for Matthias to discuss. Even now.

"Ask Matthias."

Erik simply nodded and watched the man go. After a few minutes, when he was sure Byron would not return, he picked up the bag with all of his stuff in it and sat on one of the stone benches. When the bell rang and students emerged to move from homeroom to hurry off to their next period, Erik joined the moving crowds. Some spotted him and stepped away to stare or let him pass, but most of them paid him no attention whatsoever and he moved with the flow of students.

Erik made it out the front of the school without speaking with anyone and ran smack into a crowd of paparazzi. A small crowd of them, to be sure—even with the current dramas he wasn't a big enough draw to get the professionals up from LA. It was mostly the same hopeful, local amateurs as before, yelling more foul things at him as he waded through them.

Hey Erik, why you leaving? Caught sleeping with a teacher?

Is that what the fight was about?

Did you really beat up a girl? Guess we can't expect any better from faggots.

Have you talked to Daniel? Does he hate you for getting him put away for two years?

He ignored it all and kept moving. When they blocked his way completely he closed his eyes and froze, refusing to give them a different shot until they moved from in front of him. He made his way to the car and was happy to slam the passenger door between himself and the vultures. He wasn't really that angry at them. They had a job to do. People being callous and mean on the off chance they could turn a reaction shot into some money matched Erik's low expectations for humanity.

Matthias slammed the car into reverse and floored it. Erik watched two paparazzi leap out of the way before they became marks on the pavement. Anyone who tried to block them as Matthias took them out of the parking lot got the same high-speed treatment. It was Matthias's go-to answer to photographers. The first few minutes of their drive were silent.

"I have a question."

"Okay." Matthias sounded worried and perhaps Erik's tone had given a clue that he expected this interaction to be awkward.

"Who did Byron kill?"

Matthias was silent, but Erik clocked his knuckles growing white on the steering wheel, the way his expression froze into a rictus. They were headed steadily away from the Balboa Park area toward downtown San Francisco and Erik watched the neighborhoods fly by, refusing to ask again.

"Byron."

Erik turned at the name but nothing else was forthcoming so he decided to prompt the older man.

"Yeah, Byron. I get that this is hard for you and I don't want to pressure you but we're going into something really dangerous today and both our lives may depend on having all the information. Who did he kill?"

"Byron . . . that's who he killed."

"Byron killed Byron, like suicide? I saw him at the school."

Matthias head whipped around. "What?" They began to swerve into another lane and a loud honking brought Matthias's attention back to the road. He immediately signaled and pulled them over into one of the many tiny alleys that dotted the small bucolic side streets. "What did he say, what did he do?"

"First, what do you mean he killed himself? Is he a spirit now, like Elana?" Even as he said it he knew it wasn't the case; though Elana could look extremely solid, there was also something ethereal about her at all times, as if only a thin thread connected her to the earth and the living. You felt as if Elana could float away any time she wanted and Byron had not had the same feel.

"No. Whatever is squatting in his body now is not Byron."

"What?" He wanted to believe it was a joke.

"No. Tell me what happened in the school." Erik sighed, recognizing the stubbornness in the tone. Slowly he told Matthias everything that happened, from Harry and Melissa to the last comment about asking who he had killed.

Matthias was silent, his hands rested on the steering wheel as if they lacked the strength to move. His slump spoke of a whole body that was exhausted.

"I was once with the Organization. My Counselor at the time was an older woman by the name of Ruth. She was hard as nails and taught me all the tricks of dealing with the Organization and Suits and other Blooded. She was great. She'd been separated from her family during the Japanese Internment and after she got out of the camp it turned out her parents were dead. She was thirteen. She lived on the streets until the Organization found her at fifteen.

"I'd been her aspirant for over a year, just about ready to take my vows to the Organization, when some of the Maestres contacted her. There was another one they wanted her to take on, he'd just awakened. I'd only been placed with her because of personality similarities and because I had gone through most of the other Agents available in the Bay Area." Matthias looked down with a smile that slowly disappeared. "Byron and her, though; they shared a similar power. It's rare but she took both of us on. Everything was fine for about a month. We all got along great.

"However, he could not learn control. They were both charmers and his power would flare out of control. It would call people in from the street who'd never even seen him. It got to the point where he had to live in a shielded Organization facility. Ruth and I stayed there with him. We all got close. She started to work with him almost 24/7 and I stayed to take care of both of them. Byron and I grew close."

He stopped and Erik got the feeling he was editing out part of the story, the part too painful to share.

"The Organization took him for retraining. He was one of the lucky ones, one of the ones who came back. But it wasn't Byron, I mean it was still him, not like now, but they had damaged him in some way. He would never talk about what happened and trying to force him to talk about it just sent him into a catatonic state.

"Still, he could control his power now and every once in a while I would catch him acting like his old self. I left it alone. I thought he would heal on his own.

"I should have tried harder.

"Then I started to notice changes in both Ruth and Byron. They became more secretive and would shut up when I walked into the room. I thought it was just bloodline stuff. Byron started to spend most of his time alone in one of the safe houses. I thought he was recovering. Then one night I got a call from the Organization. The safe house Byron was staying at had been sealed somehow. Ruth was inside and some build-up of power was happening. That was all they told me, but I hurried over as quickly as I could."

Matthias was looking blankly ahead through the windshield, his hands clutching and squeezing the steering wheel desperately. Erik watched the man turn younger and younger. A broken innocence entered his face as he remembered and relived. He knew he was about to watch that innocence be shattered irrevocably.

"I remember it like yesterday. The safe house was this nondescript Victorian in the Haight district. It was painted blue and yellow but had turned a sickly green from the light spilling from the windows. Blooded were discreetly stationed all over the street. Somehow they had kept the Suits from noticing, but it sure wasn't going to last long.

"Suddenly all the light that was spilling from the windows went dark, not off but dark, as if they were radiating shadow. The stupidest and bravest thing I ever did was go up to that door and try it. It opened for me like it had for none of the other Blooded. The dark light was hard to move through, as if the air had turned to thick blackstrap molasses.

"Byron was on the top floor, unconscious, covered with blood, and . . . other things, herb pastes, markers, cuts, human waste. There were candles all over the room and what looked like some old pieces of silver. The Organization took everything so they probably have more details, but I was focused on finding Ruth. She wasn't there, wasn't anywhere in the house. I carried Byron out; he woke up as I was heading down the steps.

"I knew immediately something was wrong. Whatever was staring out of Byron's eyes wasn't him, wasn't even human. Then he spoke—"

Matthias broke off and the rage and pain in his face made Erik ache to reach over and comfort him, but this was not the time and it was not his place. This was not about comfort, this was about knowledge. He waited, silent and still, for Matthias to continue.

NA'AMEN GOBERT TILAHUN

"When he spoke, we did what he said without question . . . just sat there and waited for the Suits to show up and then he just walked off with them. No answers, no nothing. That thing killed Ruth and Byron and just walked away as if they didn't matter. The Organization was more occupied with getting him to rejoin the fold and learning about what he had done, and how his power had changed. They had no interest in the justice that that *thing* deserved."

"So he couldn't always control people like that?" It was comforting to think this wasn't a power running rampant in the world. On the other hand, it definitely lent credence to Matthias's deduction that whatever was in Byron wasn't Byron.

"No. He was a charmer, like Ruth. Uncontrolled it can be dangerous because of the obsession it can kindle in someone, but they were never able to control others' actions so directly."

Erik nodded and thought about what he had been told. In seconds Matthias had started the car back up and had it on the road again.

"I didn't mean to keep this from you. It's just not something I like to talk about."

Erik nodded. "I understand. There are things in my past I don't like to talk about, but I need to know what we're heading into. I don't really trust any of the people there except you and I want as much information as I can get, so when this all turns sour we can get out alive."

Matthias nodded and they were silent for the rest of the drive downtown. They pulled up to a building in the middle of San Francisco's financial district. It was huge, going up at least thirty stories, a mix of modern streamline and ancient gothic. The outside was a uniform slate gray, a diminishing rectangle as it rose higher into the sky. Every ten floors there were gargoyles leaning over the edges, each unique and monstrous in different ways. Some were human but with other legs, ears, arms, and bodies grafted on; others were giant snakes with screaming faces pushing out of their skin. One that hypnotized Erik looked like a mass of tentacles rising from a frothing sea.

The main doors continued the aesthetic, done in normal metal and glass. As they exited the car and stood on the sidewalk, it seemed to Erik the glass was frosted into shapes, with hidden stories trapped in its depths.

"You ready?"

"No. There's something I need to do first."

Matthias raised an eyebrow at him. Erik simply returned the gesture and waited until the older man smirked at him and nodded.

"Okay, I'll wait just inside."

"Thanks."

Erik watched Matthias climb the stairs and nod at the two Suits standing on either side of the door. They returned the gesture and opened the door for him.

Erik pulled out his cell phone and dialed.

"This is Daniel. If you have this number you know I might not be able to get back to you for a while. Leave a message, I'll do what I can. Don't text me."

"Hey Daniel, it's me again. I'm sorry. I should have taken the hint and stopped calling and pestering you a long time ago. I should have taken the hint when you refused my letters, and when you refused to see me on visitor's day. I certainly shouldn't be leaving you these voice mails. I just didn't know how to let go, and how to say sorry. I kept trying to get in contact with you because I loved you but also because I wanted to make my own guilt go away. But I can say I'm sorry until the stars wink out and it won't change anything that's happened.

"Anyways, I just wanted to say I'm sorry one last time. Have a good life, Daniel."

He hung up and ignored the feeling of his heart breaking in his chest. He ignored the pain that broke him from the inside out. He took time to lean against the borrowed car and take a deep breath.

Placing his phone back in his pocket, he climbed the stairs. The two women on either side of the door could have been sisters. Both had the same pale, freckled complexion and short white blonde bobs. Their eyes followed him in unison and the little wrinkled noses of judgment were identical as well. One of them opened the door for him but it was more reluctant than it had been for Matthias, as if they expected him to bite. He simply nodded and slipped inside.

His jaw did not drop but it was a near thing. The building was hollow. The ceiling was ten stories above, rooms and offices lining the walls all the way up. Everything was painted white and gold, like heaven as designed by mainstream Hollywood. On the ground floor in front of him was a garden crisscrossed with walkways laid out in golden brick.

"Follow the yellow brick road," he whispered to himself.

"Yeah, it's all a bit pretentious isn't it?"

Erik stopped himself from screaming or attacking but he did glare at Byron as he turned.

"What can I say? Though our visitors seem to like it."

"Mm-hmm." Erik turned back to the garden but took a step to the side so he could keep Byron in his peripheral vision.

"Can I take you through the garden? You're the last to arrive."

"I think I'll just wait here for Matthias, thanks."

There was silence and Erik could see that Byron had gone perfectly still.

"So he actually told you." The voice was soft and disbelieving.

Erik hummed agreement, seeing Matthias headed their way through the garden right now.

"Except it's not the whole story is it? How could it be since he doesn't know the whole story?"

"Are you offering to tell me what happened?" Erik didn't believe it for a second. Why keep it a secret for years and then tell someone he barely knew?

"Maybe. For the right price."

The conversation stopped as Matthias approached them.

"You okay?"

Erik nodded.

Byron interrupted. "Oh I'm fine too. This morning I had an egg and bacon croissan'wich and then I took a run through Golden Gate park—"

"And then you confronted my aspirant at his school, when you knew he wouldn't be around me." Matthias was in Byron's face now, fists clenching, but Byron just smiled that same wide smile at him.

"Guilty. But in all honesty I knew he'd tell you. I just wanted to test him a little." Byron moved past Matthias swiftly and to the edge of the garden. "And he did quite well. Now shall we join the others?"

He started down the path and they had little choice but to follow. A few steps in and Erik knew it wasn't a normal garden. The colors were the first clue, flowers that bloomed a true black with dark blue centers, bright red grass that moved independent of any breeze, the shimmering silver-gray bark on most of the trees.

"Many of these are specimens brought over from Zebub but some are hybrids we cultivate right here."

Matthias made a face at this. "Frankensteins? Really?"

Erik thought a lot of the plants looked lovely because they were so alien and odd. He liked it. The fruit that hung from the trees, for example, with colors that shifted with the breeze. Something chirruped off the trail, deep in the garden proper. Erik wondered what it was and felt a mild temptation to leave the path and explore.

"No. Contained experiments only. Nothing gets out of this facility unless we want it to." Byron's voice was stiff and formal.

Erik caught the threat in those words. How could he not? Also, the more he thought about this display of wealth and scientific knowledge, he wondered at the things they bred that they kept locked away. The things not for visitors' eyes.

The first experiments. The mistakes, because there were always mistakes in science. And he imagined the mistakes from mixing magic and science were spectacular.

He shivered, and any urge to leave the piss-yellow walkway left his body. He kept pace with both Byron and Matthias until they were through the garden.

They passed into what Erik thought was a circle of cables at first, and then he looked up. Each cable was being clung to by a golden elevator that swayed as they rose and fell. Byron whistled and one immediately started moving down, like a golden drop of honey falling slowly to earth. As it came closer, Erik could see it wasn't made of metal. Rather it looked like some sort of clear plastic, but there was something liquid in the way it moved.

They climbed aboard and the give of the material under his shoes put Erik even further on edge. The view from the inside was like looking through a champagne bubble; everything outside distorted to a swirl of gold. Byron signaled somehow and they began to rise. Matthias broke the uncomfortable silence.

"So what exactly is the problem you need our help with?"

"All will be revealed by our allies."

"You mean the Angelics?" Matthias was tense and Erik was worried he might bite off a part of his lips in the process of biting off his words. Erik did not blame him. His interactions with Angelics had been anything but welcoming, and he was not thrilled to be walking into a room of gods knew how many of them with the only assurance of safety from people he didn't trust. He wondered if this was just another setup.

"Of course. They aren't what you think though."

"Oh, you mean they haven't kidnapped a bunch of human kids or killed Agents while going about their business."

"All misunderstandings." Byron turned and smiled at them.

Erik did not comment. He didn't have enough history to say one way or another, but it sounded like Byron was spewing a party line.

Matthias snorted and they were all silent until the doors slid open on the top floor and they stepped out. The floor and roof were made of some glass that looked shaded black to Erik, but the light it was letting through shone a dull red. A table was situated in the center of the room. Tae, Daya, Elana, and Elliot were seated at the far end and at the near sat one human Suit and three Angelics.

They were not like the ones he'd first encountered. They resembled the inhuman monster of the way-station more than the human-shaped monsters he'd hurt. Though they were small enough to fit around the table, Erik still felt as if they were huge and towering over him. They filled the room while somehow not physically doing so.

Did the others feel this?

Or was this a force that only he could feel through Bia's blessing?

Matthias hurried around the table and Erik followed, trying not to stare. When they reached the stretch of empty chairs between Tae and the other side, Matthias pulled out the chair and gestured for Erik to sit next to Tae. He then sat in the chair on Erik's other side. Erik found the display of protection annoying, especially considering if things actually went downhill and became violent, Erik was their best hope of getting out of here intact.

Tae reached over and squeezed his arm in greeting. Erik turned and smiled in response. Byron had taken a seat next to something that looked like a giant bright blue dung beetle but covered in fine, white fur that had two human-looking faces on either side of its head.

"We are glad you joined us here today." The Angelic that spoke looked like a collection of sand formed into a pillar and lit on fire. The voice emerged from somewhere about a foot in front of it and sounded harsh and echoing. "You have the most of the empowered 'dants on this side of the veil. And we are hoping an alliance could be entered into."

"'Dants?" Elana was the one to ask, her voice's ethereal quality making the words seem to float. It was Byron who answered.

"That's what they call anyone human but I think they mean you have more diversity in bloodlines not more people."

"I mean exactly what I said." The voice got harsher, like sand grinding against glass. Then it softened, became conciliatory. "I apologize. I am unused to speaking with 'dants as equals."

That was all Erik needed to hear to know that one part of the myths Matthias had told him was true; they ruled over their land. He doubted any humans were treated with respect. Tae, Elana, Daya, and Elliot shared his reaction and reared back. The others around the table either didn't notice or didn't react visibly.

The Angelic went on speaking to Byron.

"You are powerful because of your connections with the government of your people, but many of your people are not truly of the bloodlines or are weak in their power."

Erik could see Byron and his companion stiffen, but before they could open their mouths to argue again, Matthias took up the reins of the conversation.

"What exactly is it that you wanted our help for? And why exactly should we help you?"

"And if this is between the Organization and you guys, why are Matthias and Erik even here?" Daya asked. She frowned at the two of them and Erik returned the expression.

"The berserker has been seen in action," the pillar of sand replied. "He has destroyed one of our most powerful warriors, one bred for fighting. If he could do this, then what else might he do?"

Erik growled under his breath. Everyone wanted to use him, see what he could do. He felt like he was a child again, unable to control his own life.

"As for the other one, our contact insisted that one would not come without the other."

Everyone looked at Byron, who merely smiled and remained silent.

"As for what we want." The Angelic turned to its companions.

The alienness of the things at the far end of the table unnerved Erik even though he wasn't the center of their attention, but Matthias simply smiled and waited for a reply.

Finally the thing that resembled a soap bubble in black and green . . . burped out an answer, there was no other description for it. Each word was accompanied by a popping, burbling sound. "We are under attack."

"So . . ." The rest of the sentence was evident even if Matthias did not speak it. *So, why should we care? So, why should we help you? So, isn't this what you deserve?*

The sentiment was echoed around the table. Daya crossed her arms over her chest and Elliot rolled his eyes.

"We have been under attack for centuries by you. Why should we care for your suffering?" Elana's voice was darker than he'd ever heard it, taking on deep echoes that made his stomach shiver.

"Our 'dants are dying as well . . . people like you. A dark comes, it devours them."

Humans, the soap bubble meant. Erik had no hope that the humans were treated well, but that wasn't a reason not to save them. Something sour curdled in Erik's belly and he looked at the Angelics across the table. Didn't they also deserve to be saved? Nothing deserved to be . . . devoured.

"Still I ask, why should we care?"

Daya reached out to put a hand on her girlfriend's shoulder. It sank a millimeter deep, then stayed there.

"You cannot expect to have an alliance with your enemies. Why should we feel badly?" Elliot was frowning as he said it.

Erik wanted to protest, but he'd been involved in this conflict for less than a minute compared to them. Perhaps their anger was justified. Then he thought of Elana's flesh, turned into some horrible garment on the table below the Organization safe house. He hardened his heart and thought about their offer.

"Anyway, if you cannot hurt it, what makes you think we will make any difference?"

"We have powers, do not doubt that." As the two-faced beetle spoke in an oddly harmonious voice, the energy in the room grew so heavy Erik could smell ozone in the air and feel pressure against his skin. Then all at once it receded and his skin felt cold without it. "But our powers are not like yours. They come from the same place perhaps, but we do not express in the same way. None of the 'dants in our world have powers similar to yours. We wondered if you might see if your powers could affect the darkness that attacks us."

"So you want us to what? Cross the veil into enemy territory?" Erik was nervous enough being in this building, let alone following them to some land where he would have even fewer rights than he did in this one. Plus being outnumbered? No, thank you. Tae was already shaking his head and while the Counselors weren't that obvious, it was clear no one would be keen on a trip.

"No, no. We realize that would be asking too much at this point in our . . . relationship. The darkness has made inroads into this world. We felt you could go out with some of our Suits and check it out." It was Byron who spoke and everyone stiffened at the news.

"Where?" Daya growled.

"Not that far from here; we've kept it contained and quiet so far but it won't be long until we can't anymore." Byron grimaced as he said this, as if the words stung the inside of his mouth.

"How exactly are you containing it? You said your powers didn't work on it," Elana questioned.

The pillar of sand answered them. "We said that our powers could not stop it, not that they had no effect. It seems to feed on us, devour our strength. For some reason it is not as aggressive here as it is in our land. It does not tear through your land or people. Here is more a slow, steady taint. We have managed to keep its hunger sated."

Erik did not want to know but also had to ask.

"With who?"

It was the reaction of the other Suit that told Erik he had guessed right. The nervous widening of eyes and quick cover of any emotion was a dead giveaway. Byron and the Angelics betrayed nothing.

Erik didn't know if the others saw it, but then Byron tilted his head to the side, blinked slowly, and said, "No people. We had our allies here channel energy into it."

Erik didn't believe it for a second. He might be new to this but the idea that the Angelics would be willing to give up even an ounce of power to save human lives already seemed ridiculous to him.

"We'll go." Matthias said. "To see. Any talk of an alliance or a deal is tabled until then."

Erik wanted to argue with Matthias, but what could he say? He didn't trust these "allies" at all but if there was a dark invading his world and his city, they could not simply sit back and ignore it. There was no real choice, and the looks of resignation everyone on their side of the table wore clear as day let him know they all knew it and were not happy about it.

"Let us go now then. Why wait?"

Byron rose from the table, as did the other Suit. The other beings stayed seated.

"Our allies will meet us there."

The other Blooded rose and followed them out. Tae stayed close to Erik and managed to whisper, "Well, this isn't suspicious at all."

"I know. Don't trust them," Erik whispered back

"Already there. Also, what do they think we can do exactly? If it's something we can't touch, most of us are already screwed."

Erik nodded as they exited the headquarters into the bright financial district sunshine.

"Hello, my name is Brady," said the Suit, who was tall and pale, with strawberry-blond hair cut into a crew so short it was almost brown. He was wide in the shoulders and the sleeves of his jacket bulged as he moved. He had fallen back next to them without a sound.

Erik said nothing. These people sold off others. They were slavers by another name. None of their fancy suits or office buildings or polite small talk would distract from that.

"Are we not taking a car?" Tae asked.

"No, it is close enough that we should just walk."

"And what exactly do you think we can do, when you have such powerful allies that can do nothing?" Tae asked.

"Well, that's for you to show us, isn't it?"

Erik could feel the anger under his skin. It had been there since this morning at school, but this Suit's smug face flared it higher, warm right below the surface. It made his whole body feel tight, as if it was waiting to burst forth, but it wasn't fighting to do so. Instead it was content to be there, right there, until he needed it. He didn't need it to bash Brady's face in, but oh how he wanted it. He kept calm as they turned the corner and knew where they were going.

The mall barely deserved the name. It was four small, squat, two-story buildings, connected by bridges across all the second stories. Many of the stores were extremely high-end, while others were completely out of business. There seemed to be no in-between. It had been on its last legs for years, with businesses closing and opening rapidly. Blank spaces mocked the customers. Erik only knew of it because of the movie theater, which showed a wide variety of foreign and limited-release indie movies.

Some people wandered about. Most of them were in the dazed fugue state all mall shoppers slipped into as easily as breathing, but a few looked and felt different. Erik moved farther up, leaving Tae and Brady walking in uneasy silence, until he was next to Matthias, who was watching Byron's back with a focus usually reserved for house cats tracking a small rodent. He bumped his shoulder into his Counselor's a couple of times until Matthias finally looked at him, irritated. Erik gestured with his chin to the woman they were passing.

She moved with a determination, her eyes not even taking them in. Matthias looked at her and then gave Erik an even more frustrated look.

He didn't see it.

Erik gestured to another man. Daya was slightly in his way, trying to give space to both her ghostly lover and Elana's twin. He kept his eyes straight ahead but danced around her as if she were no problem.

Matthias frowned.

Erik leaned in. "They're too perfect. Look at how they move, not a hesitation, not a misstep." It wasn't everyone around them by any means, but enough to notice. As they crossed from the first building into the second, the number of them increased. There was silence as they walked, but Matthias and Erik kept their eyes on the strange people, none of whom paid the group the slightest attention. They moved too smoothly and interacted with the world without looking directly at it.

By the time they crossed into the third building, there were more odd humans than normal zombified shoppers, and everyone in the group had noticed. They closed ranks around one another. Byron and Brady kept on the outside, along with, surprisingly, Elana, who floated to and fro, studying the people. They paid her no attention, which, considering they could not see her, made perfect sense.

At least they assumed this, until an older White man covered in brown spots turned the corner and paused after being confronted by her. Then he moved around her and continued on his way.

Elana rushed back to the group, as unsure as the rest of them as to what it meant. Erik met Matthias's eyes and nodded toward Byron ahead of them. He had almost the same movement, the same easy knowledge of what was around him. True, he wasn't as ignorant of his surroundings as the people they were seeing, but Erik could not help but feel the sources were related somehow, if not exactly the same.

As they neared the fourth building, Erik could feel it. No one else reacted, but goosebumps broke out over his skin. There was a chill up ahead, completely unlike any of the other times he felt power build up on his skin. This did not feel like pressure. It felt like a ghost, or a cold wind blowing through his body and sinking into his soul. He felt nauseated as Brady and Byron moved forward into the darkness of the fourth building.

"I do not like this." Elliot said.

There were murmurs of agreement, but no one backed out. There was something ahead of them. Something not of this world. Something cold and dark that sapped the very air around it. It was responsible for the people they had passed. The perfect, empty people.

As Byron and Brady moved deeper into the darkness, Matthias followed. Daya and Elliot attempted to block Erik and enter before him, but he was quicker and didn't have to contend with Tae. At first the inside looked exactly the same as the other three buildings, aside from dimmer lighting and the fact that it was empty of people. As his eyes adjusted, Erik could see that the dimness was not because of the lack of lights or windows. This building was just as open as the other three; it was simply that the light was being devoured.

A tree grew in the center courtyard, glittering in the light that remained. It sucked the illumination from the air in glowing lines that sank into the bark. Fruit hung from a few branches. Some were bright red and ripe but most were brown and shriveled, dead on the branch. The light was not staying with the tree but moving down its trunk like a freeway, feeding the moving dark curled around its base. It shivered and soaked it in and grew and as it moved Erik could see a pair of legs kicking as they stuck out of the darkness at the base of the tree. And he could hear muffled screams.

MATTHIAS

H e had no idea what the Agency, its Suits, or its allies thought that they could do here. Elliot's invisibility and Elana's intangibility would be less than useless against this thing, whatever it was. His own camouflage would not work either.

Thank goodness he had other skills.

Luckily they had come armed for war and not only with their abilities. Elliot was pulling a weapon from his pocket and Matthias did the same. The handguns were loaded with the ammo from the black case. Ammunition invented by the geniuses who worked for the Organization. Those who belonged to the bloodlines of Ogun and Hephaestus, Sophia and Kuebiko. It was a horrible weapon but Matthias was ready to use it.

He felt Erik tremble next to him and then his body's heat increased three times, filling the air with warmth that made the others move closer. Before Matthias could grab his arm, Erik shot forward toward the darkness.

"Daya!"

She was moving before Matthias's yell. Her skin was already hard and gray, and the increased weight was making her slower.

Where were Byron and Brady?

He glanced around as he moved forward until he spotted them, leaning on a pillar and watching the whole fight unfold before them.

Assholes.

Erik reached the base of the tree and darted around a length of shadow that reached for him. He dove for the two feet disappearing into the darkness. Matthias raised the gun and aimed for the other side of the target. As he pulled the trigger he flew back a few steps, despite bracing himself. Primordial forces flew from the nozzle. The things that held the world together, gravity and magnetism and a hundred other forces Matthias didn't understand, twisted and formed to reduce things to their component atoms.

It cut through the darkness, and the thing rose up. A long thin note reverberated in the air, which made even Byron and Brady place their hands over their ears, though neither was near it or doing anything. The invisible energy cut a valley into their target, making it more transparent. Matthias was congratulating himself when the valley healed up as if it had never been there and Erik screamed.

Matthias looked down at his gun and cursed. Some of the forces the gun used must be related to those that Erik was tied to.

Erik's hands were sunk partway into the darkness, refusing to let go of the ankles that it had swallowed. He turned to the side and vomited. When he looked up Matthias could see that the whites of his eyes were completely red. Daya reached his side and clamped her arms around his waist, pulling with him. Elana floated above it, a distraction that dodged tentacles of darkness. Elliot moved about, firing shot after shot into the dark mass of its body.

"Elliot, stop firing!"

Elliot paused at Matthias's yell and turned to look at him.

"Why?"

"Just hold all fire until I tell you!" He didn't want to yell out Erik's problem in front of everyone, but with every shot from Elliot Erik had jerked and screamed a little louder. Everyone would place the blame on his hands sinking into the creature, but Matthias could see the bloody tears running from his eyes and knew the real cause.

Elliot growled and put the gun away. He yelled to the Suits, "Hey assholes! Some help would be appreciated!"

Byron and Brady both looked puzzled at his exclamation, as if they could not understand why he would be asking them for help. Matthias saw that the Angelics had joined them in leaning against the wall and observing. Matthias growled and let his power wrap around him.

Daya and Erik were making progress together and the figure was out of the dark up to its knees. Erik's hands where they had sunken into the thing were not his usual brown but black like burnt meat. As he struggled, Matthias could see the black flaking off, revealing pink, bloody new skin underneath. His healing ability was most likely the only reason that he still had hands at all.

More and more of the dark was separating into tentacles and reaching for Erik and Daya. Elana and Elliot could only distract it so much. Matthias fell flat on the floor to avoid the two tentacles that tried to smash him, evidence his power had no effect on this thing. He let the camouflage drop and rolled to the side as they slammed into the ground where he had been and jumped back to his feet.

"Elana! Over here."

Matthias rose as she rushed to her twin. She sank into him, they were glowing, and suddenly there was one being where there had been two. They were dressed in a loincloth and nothing else, breasts covered by a large multi-strand necklace with bloody bird wings hanging from it. Each of their four arms carried a weapon. The top pair of arms held a kabutowari and a kama, the bottom pair wielded a kusarigama. They flickered between tangible and in- while Matthias and everyone else but Daya gaped.

Then they moved forward and started to hack at pieces of the darkness which fell to the ground and faded. It was exactly the distraction he needed.

Matthias kept moving. While his power might not work on the mass of darkness, it still had other uses. He moved into the corner that Byron and Brady were in, discussing in low murmurs with the Angelics what was happening in front of them.

"Fascinating, they seem to actually be hurting it." This from Furred-Blue-Insect. "Though it is most likely because it does not have a proper hold on this realm yet."

"Yes, but still it is more than we have done." This from Black-Soap-Bubble.

"It will not work on our side but they may be able to come up with something," Flaming-Pillar-of-Sand replied.

Matthias moved away, though he desperately wanted to stay and listen to what they had planned, but he now had a plan himself. Furred-Blue-Insect had said that this dark did not have a proper hold on this world yet, so it had to have some sort of anchor and it was wrapped around the damn tree that was feeding it light.

He moved back toward the fight, watching as Erik and Daya heaved the person out of the darkness. They looked fine with surprisingly no burns that he could see. Erik rushed the person over to the door and laid them on the ground gently. He then returned to the battle, grasping tentacles, screaming as they burned him and yet still ripping them apart with his bare hands. Daya was doing the same, her form providing protection; the shadow ripped through her stone skin but she was able to regrow it in seconds and the dark never reached underneath. Tae was staying back, yelling out helpful hints of where the tentacles would strike next.

ElanaElliot was whirling to and fro, slicing through the darkness. As Matthias watched, a tentacle caught them in the back and they screamed in an odd double voice, then flickered in the light as the tentacle moved through their body. Then ElanaElliot was gone and Elliot was curled on the ground weeping, Elana nowhere to be seen. Erik dived for him and pulled him to safety.

Matthias concentrated, the world in front of him fading from bright color to black and white and then finally to heat signatures. The dark was there in its absence, cold, its edges mapped by the warmth around it. Daya was hard to spot, being nearly the same temperature as the air around her. However, Erik and the tree were lit up in bright white, burning hot. He studied the tree and he could see the place where the darkness was linked to it, the place where it fed.

With a silent apology to Erik, he aimed and fired. Erik screamed and the trunk shattered. Unfortunately, the tree was not nearly as absorbent of damage as the darkness. The shot passed right through it as it dissolved and struck one of the two metal and glass staircases, which then shattered into a million pieces. He watched as those pieces shattered further and further until the whole set of stairs was simply gone, no residue on the floor, as if it had never been.

As soon as the trunk shattered, the invader let out a long shriek. Matthias dropped the weapon to cover his ears with his palms. It did nothing. The dark's scream of pain was not simply sound, but all five senses. His eyes watered, he could taste metal, and his skin was on fire; somewhere he was aware the pain was not his own, but it did not stop him from falling to the ground and crying out as an echo of the dark's pain ripped through his body.

ERIK

He was ripping a tentacle to shreds, ignoring the burning of his hands and the pain as the dark tried to devour him immediately on contact.

Then his whole body lit up with pain and nausea and again all of his skin seemed to be on fire. He would have vomited again had there been anything in his stomach to throw up. Erik managed to remain standing as the tree shattered.

Whatever kind of weapon Elliot and Matthias were using, he wanted every one destroyed. He could feel the way they cut through the world like butter, the way they broke apart the bonds of creation. It was not natural.

Then the screeching began and Erik was the only one not to fall to his knees. He felt the scream inside his own chest as if a part of him were dying, but it paled to what he'd already felt today. He watched the darkness slowly fade from sight, every piece of it gone so quickly that he almost could believe he had imagined it, if it weren't for the destruction everywhere he looked and for the body shallowly breathing near the door.

When the dark was completely gone, the screaming stopped. Everyone began to rise from the floor. Erik felt a wave of relief as he saw Matthias rising to his feet, unsteady, but apparently unharmed. Elliot had stopped weeping but was still shaking as Daya helped him up while questioning him about Elana's whereabouts. He hurried over to the body he'd pulled from the dark. She was young, perhaps midtwenties. Even her clothing—jeans and an iridescent blue-green long sleeve shirt—seemed undamaged.

Her black hijab was slightly askew and Erik wanted to fix it but, unsure of her level of devotion, he called Daya over to check on her instead of doing it himself.

Her eyes began to flutter and they opened like a shot.

She screamed and Erik scrambled back, away from her. She screamed again and Erik realized she was looking over his and Daya's shoulders. When he turned, there was the large white-furred, blue-skinned beetle thing watching them all with both its faces.

"Do you mind?" Erik had not meant to yell so loudly but the adrenaline and fear was still rushing through him, not to mention the throb of pain in his hands and through out his body. It was too late, however, as the woman had fainted again, and who could blame her. Matthias was behind him, already on his b'caster.

"I need a pick-up at Embarcadero Mall, Building Four. A young woman affected by unknown phenomenon, we need to take her in for observation."

"It would be better if we took her. We are closer after all."

Everyone turned to stare at Byron and Brady with anger fairly sparking off their skin.

"I don't fucking think so." Daya's power was still on the surface and her skin looked gray, hard, and able to cut easily, exactly like her tone. "You are some pieces of shit. What in the hell did you think you were doing, just hanging out on the side?"

"We have tried our own strengths against it and have seen how they fared. We wanted to see how you did," Byron said matter-of-factly, as if that would calm their tempers.

"You said you wanted to ally against this. Allies do not keep important secrets that could endanger another ally's life." Matthias voice was quieter than Daya's but no less angry and pointed.

"I don't know what you are talking about." This time it was Brady. None of the Angelics seemed to want to get involved.

"I'm talking about the fact that you knew that thing was not anchored in our world. You knew it didn't have a proper hold on this place, which is pretty vital information."

Erik rose to his feet and nodded behind Matthias. The anger and pain still rode close under his skin and he wanted to take it out on these two, wanted to hear them scream under his hands. They looked at each other and said nothing, which made Erik imagine their throats under his palms.

"Exactly what the hell was that?" Elliot exploded as if he could not keep it inside any longer.

"We do not know. Rest assured that we are working on that question, but we can no longer wait for research; we need action." The thing made of soap bubbles burped.

"More importantly, how did it get a foothold in this world? If it's not here yet, how did it make it through?"

"There are portals from your world to ours, many of them, though they tend to cluster. Our city is the mirror of this one; one of the places it swallowed was our mirror of this place, and so it likely flowed through a crack and made its way here."

Byron stepped forward and tried to put his arms around Erik and Matthias's shoulders. Both ducked out of his grasp, Matthias all but growling. Byron was undeterred and smiled as he said, "But all is well now. We shall join forces and defeat it together."

"We'll have to talk to the Maestres before any such decision is made," Elana spoke up from behind them. She looked paler than usual, but it was her. Daya rushed over.

"Well of course *you* do, but Matthias and Erik don't have to, do they?" He smiled at the two of them. Erik did not like the confidence spread across his face.

"We will still want to discuss things among ourselves."

"Unfortunately there is no time for that. You'll be leaving in the morning."

"Excuse me? I'm sure as hell not going anywhere just because you think I should. It's not going to happen," Erik said. Matthias was livid, his olive-toned skin flushing darker and teeth clenched so tightly you could tell through his cheeks.

Suddenly power began to sing through the air. Winds began to whip around them, and Byron and Brady quickly backed away from them and behind the Angelics. Matthias and Elliot were moving toward the doors while Elana floated above, keeping watch in all directions.

"Incoming!"

Three more Suits rushed into the central plaza as the ground began to shake and buck beneath their feet. Erik and Daya kept their feet longer than the others, but it was as if the earth were deliberately trying to buck them off. The ground under the Suits feet was steady as a rock. Matthias managed to squeeze a shot off, even as he fell. He clipped the thing made of sand and fire and the wind died down immediately, while a scream from a thousand throats rose up from the center of the mass, now missing a crescent chunk from its right side.

Erik groaned and bit his lips bloody, to keep from screaming aloud as the world was ripped apart and reformed all around him. He wiped at the wetness on his face, palm coming away red.

The shaking stopped and the two unharmed Angelics froze. The beetle's fur was rigid and on end and the soap bubble was bubbling frantically, as if boiling. Erik turned to the three Suits. One was floating above the ground, pants legs whipping in a wind only she could feel, the other two looked like twins, both dark haired with chiseled jaws and an S-curl on their forehead.

He dived for the twins, glad to have something to hit, something to relieve this tightness under his skin, this pain that was only slowly fading. Reaching down, he moved the bracelets into place. The twins broke apart and came at him from both sides; he blocked one punch but the other caught him in the temple, turning the world upside down and gray for just a second. He recovered in time to catch a follow-up punch; he broke the fingers with a squeeze and punched him in the jaw, hearing a crack as he connected. The man hit the floor and Erik turned to the other, only to find him gone.

He took in the rest of the fight. Matthias and Elliot simply stood there, weapons trained on the two uninjured Angelics, which stopped them from involving themselves further. As long as they didn't fire, Erik was fine with that. Their companion lay in a pile on the ground, whirling weakly and making little pathetic screams every few seconds.

Elana was feinting with the flying woman, and despite his clumsy moves Tae had the other twin well in hand, always out of the way of a hit and always at the right place to score one of his own.

"Stop!"

Byron's voice echoed through the space and apparently the Suits were accustomed to obeying because they froze midmove. Tae, Elana, and Erik had no such compunctions and used the distraction to knock out their respective opponents, though for Elana it was more scaring the woman into Daya's grasp and letting her take it from there.

"Erik."

The voice stopped him as nothing else had. He turned to find it and there he was on the balcony above them, Daniel, back against Byron's front, Byron's hand wrapped around his throat. His voice was raspy from pressure and fear. He was thinner than when Erik had last seen him, the golden skin of his cheeks sunken. The skin under his eyes was bruised a dark copper.

"We thought you might need some encouragement."

"What in the hell?" This from Tae who had moved up next to him.

"Help." This from Daniel, a tear falling down one side of his face.

"Let him go, Byron." The voice that came from Erik was one he didn't know. An anger he did not call moved through his body. It felt like when his first rages took him, the ones he had faded into. It felt bigger, and larger than his body. "You have one chance. Believe me, if I have to come up there I will rip you limb from limb."

The threat was no idle one, he could see himself doing it, one limb at a time, taking that tall, thin man apart piece by piece.

"Probably, but are you willing to risk his life?" Byron squeezed a little tighter and Erik saw Daniel's eyes bug a little even as his mouth opened to gasp for air. "If I were you I would tell your compatriots to put their weapons down before I tire of this and rip his head off."

The growl he let out next was a promise.

DANIEL

Erik looked different. Even in his terror he could see that. He wasn't a boy any more. It was Daniel's own fault he did not know the man standing below him. He had deleted all of the messages from Erik. He had sent the letters back and refused all the visits. It had been for the good of both of them and he regretted none of it. Daniel had to adjust a wholly different life. One where he was a convicted sex offender, not a cast member in a popular teen show.

A world where his boyfriend was somehow a victim he had done something to. It hadn't mattered to the court how small their difference in ages was.

What had mattered was how he was over eighteen and Erik was under it and they had had sexual contact in North Carolina. That was enough for a conviction. Even then he probably would have gotten a slap on the wrist had it not been for Erik's father's influence. He didn't have the evidence of it yet, but he had people looking for it. The homophobic asshole.

So yeah, when he'd ended up in jail he had taken the advice of his lawyers and parents and everyone else with common sense and cut off all contact with the still-underage Erik. Erik had most likely gotten the same advice. Which he'd of course not listened to. Instead, Erik had walked away from it all and tried to keep in touch. Daniel still deleted all the messages unheard; he had more to worry about for the next while, like surviving. So he tried to push the young man out of his mind the way he had been trying for the past year. Then there had been something else in the cell with him and he had been swept away and now here he was, scared for his life. Now the things in front of him made no sense. Monsters the likes of which he'd never heard or seen, and a young woman translucent and floating. Erik fighting as if he were born to it.

"He's such a pretty boy. I can see why you liked him, Erik."

Suddenly Daniel was flying through the air, dangling over the balcony with his feet kicking in the air. He scrabbled at the hand around his throat, desperate for a breath. Then the voice said, "Shh, just let it happen." And his hands fell to his sides even as his brain was screaming at him to fight back. "Stand down all of you or the innocent dies."

They hesitated, especially the Mediterranean-looking man with the gun in his hand.

"Matthias. Elliot. Put them down." Erik's voice sounded weary but forceful, as if he would make them do so. Even though Daniel didn't really understand what was happening, he did get that this was a major sacrifice. That Erik was putting himself in the path of danger to save Daniel.

They did as he said.

Daniel saw mist suddenly rising from the ground. The thing of floating bubbles in the air was twisting and shifting colors and the mist was doing the same. As soon as Erik and his friends took one whiff, they started to list toward the ground.

Erik was the last to fall, already running for the higher ground, trying to get to Daniel. He felt more tears slip down even as Erik reached the first landing and fell back unconscious, toppling down the stairs. Daniel tried to cry out but was choked off by the hand around his throat. Erik lay still where he'd fallen.

"Well, you served your part well, but I think we've had enough of you."

Then he was flying through the air. He screamed and it came out bloody and scared because he had no way to slow down, no way to stop, and he was flying toward a shimmer in the air, toward the small broken stump that was aimed at his chest like a javelin. It hit and he screamed as he began to die. The blackness came up to take him away and he whispered over and over as he sank into it.

"Erik. Erik. Erik."

ZEBUB

LIL

She argued Chayyliel, and Mayer, out of dressing her in anything more elaborate than what had become her usual pants-and-shirt dinner attire.

"June is an expert in seduction and negotiation. I'm sure they would see through anything we did. Wouldn't they just view it as desperation?" They had eventually agreed, so she was wearing black pants with an odd shimmering green pattern halfway between feathers and scales, along with boots that had the same pattern but more green than black. The shirt was again a simple white thing that buttoned up at the sides with shining black buttons. She kissed Min and Davi good night and nodded to both Arel and Jagi before going outside to wait for her escort. Usually it was one of the Turms. She was unpleasantly surprised to find Haydn walking toward her.

As he got within touching distance, she twitched an arm in his direction and he paused.

"What do you want?"

"Dinner is in Hive Inyades and so I am your escort this evening."

"I'd rather be forced to eat my own entrails." The answer was immediate. A scent was coming off of him, tempting and sweet; she found herself leaning forward to get a stronger whiff. She jerked back almost immediately—it was fragrant on the edge, but when it entered her throat there was rot all over it. She turned her head to the side and hacked until she spit out a sour glob of saliva.

Alchemy.

"What are you up to?"

The smile didn't drop from his face. In fact, it got even more brazen. He took a step closer and laid his hand across her arm. The syllable flew out of her mouth without conscious thought. The word from earlier in the hall, weaker but still primed in the air, snapped closed. Haydn's eyes rolled up in his head and he slumped to the ground.

"Well." She stared at his lump of a form and kicked it hard, once. She didn't have time for more.

He was going to be out for at least the next twelve hours and she could not be late for dinner tonight. She had to see June. She wanted to leave him where he was and go, but she worried it would cause trouble. She did not want him in her rooms, near her sibs. She could ask Arel and Jagi to hide him but she would have to stay here while they did that. Either way she would be late.

She had no other allies but Arel and Jagi. She stopped.

That wasn't strictly true.

But was it possible to call them? She'd never had to before. At Kandake they had always just been there ready to help when she needed it.

Feeling completely foolish, she spoke into the dark hallway.

"Hello? Nif?"

She sighed and it almost turned to a scream when something warm and silky fell across her shoulders. Lil recognized the feeling in time to stifle her voice. They lay across her like her nightly cloak.

Perhaps Lil should thank them but they were a double-edged sword. They helped her but that help also aroused suspicions and turned others further against her. At the moment, however, there was no one about and she felt no qualms asking them for help.

"Can you take him and hide him somewhere? Please."

The stole boiled on her shoulders like hot oil and one corner lifted into the air before spiraling down toward his body, the connection between it and the mass on her shoulders growing thinner and thinner. When the droplet reached his unconscious body, it began to quickly spin and spread out in cocoon around Haydn. Soon he was no longer visible. The connection between the cocoon and her stole snapped and the mass holding Haydn began to slowly hump its way down the hallway. It looked like some monstrous worm had swallowed him. Lil couldn't stop thinking it was exactly what he deserved. She turned and made her own way to dinner.

She nodded to the few Antes she passed as she entered the main hall and then out into courtyard. In the brightness of the three moons she could see one of the Hives was near completion. The other one that had just been starting when they arrived now climbed high in the sky with no signs of ending. Still only the scaffolding was visible now. She moved toward Hive Inyades. It sparkled in the light like a gemstone.

Lil stepped toward it. The closer she got the more translucent and unreal it looked. The door, if she could call it that, was a mass of white light shining from a shifting purple gemstone. Facets broke apart and reformed as she watched. She reached forward slowly and her hand met no resistance. She stepped through the whiteness and found herself on an endless expanse of white sand.

The warmth of the sand radiated through her suddenly bare feet. Tables made of different glowing gemstones punched up through the beach. Dotted among them were pools of water, some so large they should not have been able to fit into the Hive and some so small simply fitting one of her little sibs in it would be tight.

June was easy to spot, with lit-up skin reflecting a hundred different colors that held a group of Antes in thrall to a story. A Turms sat on the chair next to them, which surprised Lil, since their bloodline did not need to eat and rarely attended the dinners as guests. Lil squared her shoulders and approached. The stole of Nif shuddered and flowed down her back into a cape. Mayer and Riana were seated with Razel at a table to her right. They would all be watching her tonight. Krezida was notably absent.

None looked up as she stood by June's table, so she cleared her throat and tried to force her cheeks not to show any embarrassment. As soon as she made the noise June looked up. The snake had known she was there. She smiled too wide at him and nodded a hello.

"I simply came over to say hello but I can see how busy you are. I'll leave you to your little story." She turned to leave without waiting for a reply and faced the table the two Holders and Holder-Apprentice were already seated at with blank faces all around. She could easily read the anger under the surface.

"Wait, lovely lady."

She resisted the urge to grind her teeth at the description. She had a name and June knew it, but she turned back to them with a bright smile.

"Yes?"

"What kind of white snake would I be if I did not offer you my hospitality?"

"A poor one." She only spoke the truth but June laughed all the same.

They turned and nodded to the Turms next to them and the tiny red and white Ante slid onto the ground and headed over to the corner, where a number of its bloodline were gathered. She smirked at June to show she saw exactly what they had done, and they smiled back. Lil draped herself in the chair and admitted only to herself that June was a charmer. Even without the lights turned up full blast, they were beautiful.

She was contemplating her opening gambit when her lips twisted open of their own accord, her tongue started to curl, and she recognized the shape of it. She clamped her jaw down on the word and swallowed. Again her mouth opened of its own accord and again she snapped her lips shut.

This was not like the other times. She was not tired or distracted. She was in control of herself. Why was the Babel trying to slip free?

There was slight burn in her arm. She looked down at the place where Haydn had touched her, only for a second. The skin looked shiny, and now that she was paying attention she noticed an ache spreading from the point.

Damn that piece of shit to the creeping dark! What had he done?

"I was hoping you would attend tonight," June said.

"Have I not been here almost every night?" She struggled to control her mouth.

"Yes, but there is a special performance planned by the delegation from Adlivu tonight. A show of power disguised as entertainment. I thought it might have scared you off." June smiled.

If she was honest, she had forgotten that the Ruling Courts of Zebub were hosting a delegation of Antes from the bay tonight. Now that she looked more closely at the pools of water, she saw tentacles and fins and giant maws of needle-thin teeth rising and falling within the waves.

She forced a smile. She had too much riding on her tonight to worry about the "entertainment"—currently her greatest worry was inadvertently speaking a word of Babel at a Ruling Courts dinner and earning sanctions for Kandake, or much more likely her death.

Was that why Krezida was absent?

"It will be interesting at the very least." She forced out her words and then took a bite of the food on her plate to occupy her mouth and tongue. What had that loathsome toad done to her? Alchemy was about the body's functions. Changing them and charging them. Forcing a body to live forever or turn sick and die. To fall in love or rage and attack and in this case have her speak Babel in front of everyone. She thought as she chewed, biting her tongue a few times when it attempted to force her mouth open. Not just any Babel though; it would have to be something big, something dangerous. Something Krezida did not want to be around for.

The sounds of eating and chatter rose around them as the show began. The pools of water shook, and surfaces began to ripple in violent patterns. Some boiled while others began to frost over. Still others simply dissolved into a veil of mist. She was not the only one to scream when the pools simultaneously exploded, but she was the only 'dant and so the sound carried a bit, especially as it turned to the beginning of a word. She clamped her mouth shut before the word could complete and felt the build up still the air around her.

She looked over to Mayer, who was staring at her with a horrified face. She widened her eyes at him. He had definitely felt that. There was no way to avoid doing what Alchemy wanted of you. It was a temporary power but a strong one and it would not stop until the body did what it had been convinced it needed to do.

The pools were now all fountains shooting water high into the air, not quite high enough to touch the Icarii, Suyucant, and other flying Antes, but she noticed more than a few flying higher just in case. Then the water began to bend over those on the ground. The air had taken on a noticeably damp quality but no actual water dripped from any of the spouts.

June leaned in. "Perhaps you can tell me what exactly you want?"

"What do you mean?" she said through a mouthful of food. She was not surprised June had caught on to her sudden attempt to play nice. It was smart of them to start the conversation now when everyone was too busy watching the performance/threat happening in front of their eyes.

"Come now. It's clear you want something. You did an excellent job. When you're as old as Mayer you might actually become skilled, but I've been doing this since before your grands were born."

Lil merely hummed in response and watched the spouts above them as they bent toward each other and met in the air. It was impressive, the way the water both merged and retained its individual current at the same time. Boiling water and sludged ice water spouts steamed as they touched one another but maintained their temperatures.

"I might be in need of information." She forced out the words. It was getting harder to say what she wanted.

"Really." June's voice became a surprised purr. "Information is my favorite aphrodisiac, but what could an Holder-Apprentice in one of the last great centers of information need of me?"

The pillars of water were now joining into a latticed dome above their heads. She glanced around and saw some of the Antes were moving their eye stalks, sensory appendages, and other basic vision centers all around. They were caged within water. Even if most of it was not steaming or freezing, touching one of them did not seem like a good idea. It reminded Lil of capturing mizzene around the Athenaeum with an upside-down bowl. Of course she'd never had it in her to kill the little things and had simply released them outside. Something told her these bay Antes would not have the same scruples. Still, no one at the center tables, where the most powerful Courts were gathered, seemed worried, so Lil tried to follow their example.

"History."

"History of what exactly?" June sounded wary and Lil could not blame them.

"Anything that could help us find out what this creeping dark is. It cannot have appeared out of nowhere and yet know our weaknesses so intimately. It must have been here before."

June was silent and the Babel came to Lil as she watched the dome above them become solid. Slowly the flying Antes were blocked from view. The words danced through her brain and on the tip of the tongue. A simple thing to bind June in any number of ways with Babel. No need for the blood she had gotten from Arel and Jagi. And so many different bonds with a simple word change, she could bond June to not speak of this, or except in her presence, to forget the conversation ever happened. So many options danced through her brain and she struggled to push them back.

Why not do it? Wouldn't it just make everything easier? She turned to glance at Holder Mayer and he was staring at her, mouth open, standing. She pushed the power away and did not speak the words. It was the hardest thing she had ever done. The need boiled inside her and no matter how she fought, she knew it was only a matter of time before Babel came bursting forth.

"Okay, but I need a favor as well."

NA'AMEN GOBERT TILAHUN

Lil nodded. She had expected no less. She'd rather have this be an exchange than have a favor hanging over her head.

"What?"

"I need you to look for something in the Ossuary."

She froze. Several Antes behind them were discreetly trying to disrupt the wall of water they were seated under. Lil found it better not to look at the water at all. Shapes were swimming through it. Things that should only exist in nightmares. Things that could have no other use than killing.

"Don't look so worried, Holder-in-training. I do not want you to take it from the Ossuary. Merely to confirm that it exists."

Lil thought about it. It did not violate any of the rules she had been given. In fact, she was supposed to be looking for something to help them all. If finding this thing would allow her to get information that could save them, it would be the best use of her time. She nodded.

"Lovely. I will come to your rooms after dinner and we will discuss the details. For now I think I should join my brethren."

Many of the Antes were no longer seated but were up and attacking the barrier with their own powers. The others continued to simply eat and watch. She remembered what June had said about this being entertainment and threat. It was a test. Many of the Antes were having mild success in dissolving the water barrier, but it reestablished itself in seconds.

Lil could still feel the dampness in the air. It was the obvious way for the water to replenish itself.

There was no way to break Alchemy, but she could subvert it. An idea formed in her mind that might allow her to burn the order out of her system. She swallowed the food in her mouth and looked around to make sure no one was watching her. Even Mayer had turned his attention to the wall of water that was slowly shrinking around them.

She let the word start to form and then used all her strength to stop after the first syllable. She studied the curl of her tongue, examined the way her mouth was primed to open. Something that started with that syllable, she thought as her mouth struggled to complete and she held it back. Finally she smiled and allowed a word to slip from her lips. Whatever had intended to form fought against her control but in the end she won.

The word came out cracked and with the wrong emphasis, but the effect was noticeable at once—a dry desert wind began to swirl about in their cage, yanking the dampness from the air and drying it out completely. In minutes the air was so dry she felt her lips cracking as the air around them absorbed moisture from anywhere it could. The Ante's attacks against the water became much more effective and the surrounding barrier looked like Swiss cheese. The shapes that had been floating in the dome quickly fled back into the pools, and finally, when the last remnant of water was scrubbed from the air?

All the Antes began to clap at the show.

Lil joined in, proud of herself until she saw Mayer's face at the next table. It was blank to anyone else, but she could read the banked rage there. Even if he had not seen her use it, he must have felt the echo of Babel in the air and made the obvious assumption. She kept clapping and deliberately turned her face the other way. The yelling and punishment would come soon enough. For now she was proud of herself and would continue to be for the rest of the night.

She picked up a spoon, suddenly ravenous, and started spooning soup into her mouth. It had a distinctly fishy taste and she couldn't help but wonder if she was eating the relative of one of the things in the pools.

NA'AMEN GOBERT TILAHUN

MAYER

He had no chance to talk to Lil as dinner ended; she moved past him much too quickly. As much as it burned him to just let her go, she was on a mission for Chayyliel and they lived at Chayyliel's sufferance right now. But they would discuss her use of Babel in the dining hall. Technically the visitors were included in the vow not to use the language on any Antes, though they could argue it had not been directed at anyone, which was obviously what Lil was counting on. However, what worried him the most was that she had used it so easily, had countered so much power at once.

As he wandered, up to her room to confront Lil, Krezida came out of the dark.

"Holder Mayer."

"Holder Krezida."

She was a thin woman, yet still she seemed to take up the whole of the hallway. She did not move at all, but gave the impression of coming forward and filling his personal space.

"Something I can help you with, Krezida?" His mind whirled to Babel and he painstakingly began to form a word that would push her back.

"Your Holder-Apprentice."

"Yes?"

"She did something to my Holder-Apprentice."

"Did she now? I assume you have evidence of this besides his word."

"I'm sure—"

"No, of course you don't, because if you did you would bring this before both myself and Riana." The word finally came to him and he forced it through his throat, scouring it raw. She was blown back by a force stronger than wind and took refuge against the wall. "Every one of us knows your Holder-Apprentice is the lowest of the low. We all know the crimes he was accused of before he sought sanctuary at Enheduanna. His talent cannot be enough to make up for all of that, can it?"

Krezida rose from her crouch, unsure.

"Do not dare to judge me. You have no idea of my plans. The boy is useful and as long as he remains so he shall remain at my side. At least I am assured of a Holder-Apprentice who will not try to rise above himself and usurp my place. Can you say the same?"

"Lil does what is ordered of her." He would not show any suspicions otherwise to this woman.

"Yes. How convenient her orders allow her to make so many important connections with Antes far above her station. How long until they begin to believe it will be easier to deal with her than with your old crotchety self?" She was again moving toward him, cautiously but steadily. "She may not have to do anything directly. Just get enough of them to like her." She reached for his face and he grabbed her wrist in his hand and turned it over to observe the paste on the underside of her nails.

He repeated the Babel and she was flung back into the wall again.

"Exactly. I am older than you. I remember when you were a simple Holder-Apprentice. I have been here this long because I am smarter than the rest of you. No one shall take my place before I am ready."

He left her there in a frowning crumpled heap and stalked toward Lil's room.

"No one."

LIL

As soon as she arrived at her rooms, Lil went to the bedroom. Min and Davi were sleeping on the bed so she firmly shut the door. Arel and Jagi watched her from their usual spot, entwined on the sofa.

"What's happening?" Arel asked. Lil had started to notice that she could tell them apart by small things. Arel talked more than Jagi, and his voice was less hesitant.

"June is coming by to negotiate."

Both sat up and neither looked particularly happy.

"We'll stay." It was Jagi and Lil saw from the set of his jaw there would be no dissuading him. Not that she had any intention of trying. She wanted Arel and Jagi to stay through the discussion. She did not trust June, no matter that soon they might be allies. There was a loud pounding on the door. Lil jumped up and ran over to answer it before June woke her sibs.

"Why are you pounding—Mayer?" Before she could say anything else, the Holder shoved his way past her and into the room. Arel and Jagi were on their feet but Mayer paid no attention, rounding on her as soon as she closed the door.

"What the hell did you think you were doing?" His voice echoed.

She moved closer and whispered furiously. "First of all, I was saving all of our lives, or at least helping to. Second, keep your voice down. Min and Davi are sleeping and I won't have them disturbed."

Mayer's usually pale face grew a furious red but he said nothing and closed his eyes. Slowly the red faded to a more sedate but still-disturbing pink. When he finally opened his eyes, the fire of anger still burned in them but it was controlled.

"Do you understand the danger you put us in? We could be put to death for what you did tonight!"

Lil tilted her head. He was angry but beneath she could sense his fear.

"No one felt it but you."

"You don't know that."

"Besides, none of my power even touched the Antes—it only touched their magic. I stayed well within the rules."

"And how?"

"Excuse me."

He stepped forward into her space. "Don't pretend. You used to have trouble with small Babel effects and now you are countering a major joint working without strain? Your abilities have grown. What did you find in the Ossuary?"

Lil blinked at him. She knew he was right; simply remembering that terrible night, running from the shadows, body exhausted, barely able to choke out a second word in Babel. It had changed that night, after the creeping dark had almost claimed her, after it had touched her with its burning edge and shattered across her body.

"It has nothing to do with the Ossuary."

"Yes, she bound us before her first visit inside," Jagi said.

Lil cursed under her breath. That was not the defense she currently needed. That was skirting the rules as well, and Mayer didn't need more ammunition. Mayer's eyes widened and he turned to face the two Antes for the first time. Neither reacted to being under his gaze. They stared back, unblinking, their transparent eyelids shut, turning their color to a solid faded gray.

Mayer turned back to Lil and his eyes were wide with fear now.

"You bound them?"

"Voluntarily and with blood, not Babel." Not exactly. The word might have burned in her head but she never said it aloud.

Mayer slowly shut his eyes, accepting the quibbles. "Well, at least you aren't completely stupid."

"I'm not stupid at all. I'm trying. We are hindered at every turn and more and more of Zebub is being devoured."

Mayer sighed and sank down onto the couch. "It's worse than you know. Mitlan, Ufren, and Ennom have had whole districts swallowed by the creeping dark." He paused and Lil opened her mouth to speak when she realized this was not a stopping point—it was that whatever he had to say next was so horrible he needed to pause. She clamped her lips shut and listened with trepidation. "Anoan is gone."

"Gone?" Her voice choked as she said it and Arel and Jagi moved toward her, surprise and horror mirrored on each of their faces.

"Now you understand why I need to know how you became so accomplished with Babel. It may be the only way to fight this thing."

"But the Babel does not harm it or stop it permanently, I thought."

"Not by itself. Tell me."

Lil tilted her head to the side and studied her mentor, the man who had been her supporter and bulwark for years now. When her parents turned against her, afraid of her, this man had offered her a home.

"Haydn came to escort me to dinner tonight. He had some Alchemy on his hands. He touched me before I got away from him."

The look Mayer gave her fairly dripped disbelief, so she hurried on before he asked for more detail and she had to admit she didn't know where Haydn actually was.

"Afterwards, I noticed that as I sat in the hall my tongue tried to twist into Babel. Whatever was done made the Babel build up behind my tongue so when I spoke it came out with much more force than intended."

Some of it was true.

She did not tell him that her ease with the language started before this. She did not reveal the way the tentacle had come for her face as she ran for the Athenaeum. Nor of the way, when she spoke and it broke apart, she had felt something on her tongue like a tiny grain of sand. She did not talk about how, since then, Babel had become more and more natural for her.

Mayer did not seem satisfied by her answer, but he didn't look as hostile as he had when he first appeared either. He opened his mouth but a knock on the door interrupted him.

JUNE

More than Lil were behind the door, June could feel it on all the fine hairs that covered zir body. Four lives were in the room. Two Antes and two 'dants. June could guess which two Antes— Arel and Jagi had been MIA since they were assigned to help the Holder-Apprentice. They returned to their quarters for sleep occasionally but otherwise spent their time with her and her sibs. The other 'dant ze had no idea, but there was only one way to find out. June knocked on the door, making sure zir lights were turned down. It would make zir less noticeable while waiting for the door to open and put the Holder-Apprentice at ease if ze weren't lit up like the Sea of Wisps.

Although if June were seen, most would just assume a tryst of some sort and sneer at zir rather than ask actual questions. The House of the Madame was useful for that.

The door opened and Arel and Jagi stood on either side, staring. June nodded at both of them and strolled in between without waiting for the actual invitation, looking around the small sitting room. The Holder-Apprentice and her Holder were seated next to each other on the couch, with as much room between them as possible.

"Well, shall we get started?"

"Yes. What can you tell us?" The Holder-Apprentice leaned forward while the Holder's mouth snapped shut.

"Nothing until you get my answers for me."

"What exactly is it that you want *my* Holder-Apprentice to do?"

The emphasis was not lost on June, or Lil from the sour twist of her mouth.

"Nothing against the rules. There is something I want her to verify. I am much interested in the history of Zebub and it's not a new obsession. I have been trying to piece together the time line of our history for decades. The written history goes back about twenty thousand years but beyond that it is a blank slate. I have some theories on why and something in the Ossuary would verify them."

"What theories?"

June hesitated but eventually shrugged. Ze had come this far and to quit now would be nothing less than cowardly.

"I do not believe we originated in this world."

Everyone in the room was staring at zir now.

"The Ruling Courts say that our history was lost in a war so devastating that it not only wiped the written record clean but changed the earth itself. However I have . . . allies in other cities who have investigated. Wars leave evidence in the ground, if nowhere else. Dig deep enough inside of Zebub and you will reach a layer of fine white dust. Remnants of the great Athenaeum Wars millennia ago. However, no matter how deep we dig here, the ground remains unchanged. There is no great shift. I do not doubt that something happened twenty thousand years ago. Something that changed everything. I simply doubt that it happened *here*."

They were hypnotized by June's theory. Ze calmly waited for the questions to begin.

"What can I find in the Ossuary that could prove or disprove this?"

"The root."

"A root?"

"No, the root. From a very special tree. In my research I have come across references to the Root, the Tree, and the Fruit. I believe they actually refer to what was used to build this world after the last one. The tree is the ground we walk on, the fruit is the world we live in, and the root is what caused it to grow."

"So it may not be an actual tree root."

"Well, no," June admitted with reluctance. "In fact, I would be very surprised if it were a tree root. It could be anything, but they are seeds of this world. Do you know what that means?"

"No." The Holder was far less impressed by the request than his Apprentice or even Arel and Jagi. June shrugged off his indifference.

"It means that we need not live this way. That the Ante-on-top hierarchy is arbitrary. This is a grown universe. Bigger than the ones that split off from us, but not the true world at all. We made the world this way."

The Holder-Apprentice deflated at his words. "So? Even if this world is an offshoot they built to rule, they still rule because of the power they wield."

"But that power is almost defenseless against the creeping dark, is it not? What if we could get to that other world? What other weapons might we find against my brethren?"

"You say you do not want Lil to break any rules and yet you sit here with treason dripping from your lips. How is it not a crime if she helps you?" Arel spoke up.

June recoiled but recovered zir calm quickly, too well trained to lose it for long.

"I am only asking for information. What I do with that information is my business. Not anyone else's. And I assure you I will not be caught. Do you agree to this? I will give you the answers that might help."

The Holder-Apprentice nodded but it was with clear reluctance. "How exactly would I find this thing? I have no idea what it looks like. The Ossuary is vast."

June smiled and reached into zir pocket to pull out a small bag. It looked like leather but was dahac skin. Long extinct, but the power in their skin hid whatever was wrapped in it. Ze tossed the bag to Lil and she caught it easily. It felt damp and warm in her hands.

"Inside that bag is some of the Fruit. It will react to the Root."

"The Fruit?" Lil opened the bag and upended it into one palm. Seeds fell into her palm. Six of them, blood-red in the electric-plant light. "I thought you said the Fruit was the world that we walked in, not actual fruit seeds."

"The Fruit is many things. These were plucked from the very edge of our world, where the land has not yet grown. Where it still waits to bloom."

June stood to walk out and was stopped by the Holder's voice.

"Wait. How do we know that you even have anything for us? You must give us at least one piece of knowledge. In good faith."

Ze turned back around and smiled. "As you wish. The creeping dark is not of Corpiliu but was brought with us when we came here. We are only an appetizer. After it has devoured us whole? It will move on to the main course."

LIL

L il studied the pouch in her hands. She had replaced the fruit immediately in case it was giving off something that could be sensed. Mayer was pacing back and forth while Arel and Jagi stood behind her with a hand on each shoulder. She was thankful for the comfort and leaned into it.

"We cannot trust June."

"Of course not." Lil did not mean to snap but he had already expressed these points multiple times, yet provided no alternative. If what June said was correct, their world might be gone soon. They would be lucky to see the world end. The Antes would most likely kill them as scapegoats long before. "Who *can* we trust, though?"

It came out sharper than she intended and Mayer stopped to face her. They stared at one another and though some part of Lil wanted to bridge the gap between them, the majority of her held back.

"I am tired. Let's discuss this further tomorrow when we inform Chayyliel."

Mayer frowned. "Who will not like all this talk of treason."

"You are my Holder. I will leave it up to you to decide what you wish to share."

"At least you leave some decisions to me." And if his tone had been more joking and less biting, she could have believed they were in the days before they had come to the Ruling Courts when they could still tease one another. When she had believed she could trust him.

"Yes." It hung in the air between them until he finally nodded and left.

Arel and Jagi were silent as she rose from the couch and began her own pacing. She felt trapped, her decisions not her own. She turned to the Antes.

"What do you think?"

"We are in dangerous times. We must come together if we are going to survive, yet old habits die hard. Everyone jockeys for position and power when it would mean nothing if we all fell. I am surprised they have not announced that Anoan is gone. It might be the thing to shock others into working together."

"Or fear would take over and the streets would rise up and then be put down in an ocean of 'dant blood," Jagi added.

Lil shuddered at the notion. So many roads led to death, hers or others'; it felt as if she stood on one side of a cliff and the only "safe" way to cross was to dive and trust the winds to carry her. She must fly or fall and either way could cause deaths.

"There is also something we must tell you."

Lil watched them warily and nodded slowly. "What is it?"

Jagi and Arel stared at each other.

"There's a prophecy. One that is passed down in our bloodline."

"Okay." She watched them shift from foot to foot and realized it was the first time she'd seen them react with nerves.

"We believe it may be about you."

"And what exactly does it say?" She kept her breath studied. She should be more shocked by this but there was so much already, what was one more pressure? Besides, she had studied prophecies extensively. They were things that might happen, not things that had to or even should happen.

"It says:
She will come
two stars orbiting her.
She will bleed Yanwan,
turn three to four,
the world will shatter
follow her light
and some may be saved." They said it together.

To be honest, she had heard much better; the rhyme scheme was obviously given very little importance and though the topics were pretty large, she had come across plenty of apocalyptic prophecies that had never, ever come to pass.

She could only bring herself to care about things that might actually be about to happen. There was no room in her head for anything else.

"Do you both believe this?"

They frowned and shared another look and then shrugged.

She nodded and thought. "The vow that you both gave to protect Min and Davi."

"We will hold to it, even if the promise was broken. You need not worry about them." Arel stepped forward and took her hand in both of his. Jagi came up and did the same with her other hand. "You need never worry that we will betray you or them."

"We do not simply care for you because of a prophecy."

Even as she saw what was coming, she allowed it. Arel kissed her first, a soft press of closed lips, and as he pulled away Jagi was there, brushing his lips across hers, quiet and shy, so light she was not sure it actually happened. They both turned and left before she said anything and she was grateful because she could think of nothing to say.

MAYER

He called his fellow Holders on his way out of Hive Chayyliel. The courtyard was filled with Antes moving to and fro but none paid him any attention. As he moved toward the Hive of Sorrow and Riches, he called them the old fashioned way, unsure if they were trained in it or would understand the message.

Still, as his feet moved, his mind dived within himself, reached for the place in his thoughts where his connection with Kandake lived. Through long practice he ignored the knowledge that battered at him through the link, unimportant facts, badly written tales, awful poems, controversial opinions—all the rarely read books and rarely shared knowledge tried to force its way into him. To force him to accept it. He batted them aside with the strength of long practice and went deeper into connection until he found it. The knot of power that tied it to the other Athenaeums in Zebub. Smaller, more delicate threads led off into the distance, to other Athenaeums in other cities, but those closest had the strongest connection.

He sent a pulse along the two strongest threads, less words than a feeling paired with a map to the room below the Hive. He knew that they had been doing work for the Courts there as well, though he doubted they knew the same of him or of each other. He was sweating when he was done, but it was the only way he could be sure the message would not be intercepted by anyone.

The Ante guarding the door to the Hive of Sorrow and Riches stood on four hairy bare legs ending in split hooves, half again as tall as the door itself. A monstrous visage of green eyes and dripping fangs barely visible through the tangled brown hair all over its body looked down at Mayer. He paid it no mind and its eyes moved on past him.

He moved into the Hive. The walls were all the healthy pulsing pink he remembered. He went into the core and bypassed the tendril-elevators moving up and down through it. Over in the corner of the central well was a small imperfection in the wall. He dug his finger into it, forcing it into the flesh until it spasmed, once, twice, and then proceeded to suck at his finger.

Instead of resisting he moved into the feeling, slowly letting his entire body be subsumed by the wall. He took a deep breath but kept his eyes open as his face was pulled inside. Traveling through the walls of this Hive was never pleasant, but it was a way to get around without anyone seeing him. His vision filled with pink. The damp of his surroundings ensured that they did not burn from being held open. Unable to move, he was a simple object being passed through the muscled walls of the Hive.

He emerged in the basement, in the room where he did his work. It had been a long time since the Holders had been called in such a way. Long before Krezida and Riana were Holders. Hence his trepidation. He was wondering if he would have to wait long when he heard voices from the room next door.

He opened the door and silently slipped from it into the hall. Riana was already down there hurrying Razel away to the tendril-elevators in the center of the hall. At least he knew for sure the others were working down here as well, and Riana at least was bringing her Apprentice.

"Mayer," she greeted him as she turned to find him watching her.

"Riana."

They were silent.

"So you have been doing work for the Court of Sorrow and Riches as well," Riana questioned, taking a step closer.

"We all do what we must to ensure the survival of our Athenaeums." He watched her proximity. He would be foolish to assume that her jumpsuit didn't hide any number of pockets with mechanical weapons and defenses.

Riana snorted but stayed where she was until they heard the thud of someone falling from the tendril-elevator and cursing themselves. Krezida was brushing her clothing off as she caught sight of them immediately and stiffened. Mayer caught the way her eyes moved to one of the closed doors before returning to them.

"Why did you call us, old man?"

"There are things happening. Things I would share with you." He quickly told them of June's theories and the plans for tomorrow. Both frowned.

"And what does any of that have to do with our current problems?" Trust Riana to stay practical and focused.

"Fool, do you not see the problems this can cause?" Krezida hissed.

Riana took a step toward the other woman and snapped back, "I am no fool, but until we deal with the creeping dark that just might be coming to devour us all, it seems that this June problem is not as pressing."

Mayer could not argue with her logic, but he also could not help but wonder how much of it was swayed by the fact that if Lil's own status were harmed, it would hurt his and Kandake's position.

"She begins to gather allies," Krezida complained.

"Or tools," Mayer interrupted.

Krezida flexed her fingers as if she longed to sink the most-likely-poisoned talons into his flesh. "In either case, we do not need Kandake rising higher than it is already. It is bad enough that Kandake still holds treasures that belong with Enheduanna."

"And Hypatia." Riana stood straighter, ready to dive into the age-old argument again.

Mayer gestured for silence. "Enough. I'll not sit here and listen to the same complaints over and over. It was five thousand years ago, the war that your predecessors started and lost. A price was paid. Also, I am yet to be convinced that Lil is anything to worry about."

"Then why did you call us here?" Krezida asked with a dark smile. "Already she wins favor from Chayyliel and June. Other Antes are impressed with her as well. They are intrigued by her relationship with the Nif and want to see more."

"And you fear her."

Mayer was surprised by Riana's statement, not because it was false but that she had such insight. Riana had never been intuitive about things made of flesh and blood. Then he remembered her Holder-Apprentice and the obvious intelligence in the woman's eyes.

"I fear for her," he answered.

Riana looked stymied before she smiled. "You lie. You worry. As you so recently reminded us, you are older than either of us. In fact, older than our ages combined. You've trained many Holder-Apprentices but none have followed you as Holder. They all challenge you and die. But Liliana could best you, could she not? She could be Holder if she wanted, perhaps even right now."

Mayer frowned at her. He had not thought that Liliana was that powerful yet. Had Riana seen something that he had not?

"There is more to holding an Athenaeum than power. If it were only that, would not Razel be ready to be Holder?"

Riana narrowed her eyes.

"She walks a line, Mayer. You see this. It's a dangerous game and one misstep could cost all of us our lives. Making 'friends' with Antes and spending time with them." Krezida shuddered. "She disrupts the balance we've fought for."

Mayer wasn't convinced, but then he thought of the air in the dining hall suddenly going from water-heavy to dry and choking in a matter of seconds. She had not even been exhausted afterwards.

"What did you have in mind?"

"She must be removed from the equation. Only then can we all focus on what is important."

Mayer stiffened.

"Calm yourself, Holder, we know your power and would not dare kill her, but perhaps we can cause a scandal so that she will be sent from the Ruling Courts."

Mayer wanted Liliana safe. He still cared for the girl but that was no protection from betrayal. Getting her safe and isolated at the Athenaeum was a plan that held infinite appeal.

"How do you think to accomplish this?"

"Simple." Riana smiled. "Her relationship with the white snake Ante. We simply imply the relationship has turned sexual. The Ruling Courts will never tolerate such a thing in their very midst and Chayyliel will have to put a stop to it. He will have to send her away."

Mayer did not smile but he nodded.

"Yes."

In the end, the plan was simple. He would whisper suspicion to Chayyliel himself the next morning. A small seed of doubt. He would let slip the closeness he had noticed between June and Lil. He would imply that he thought their attempt at negotiation becoming a dalliance. Chayyliel would fill the rest in itself. Another Ante having a stronger hold on someone staying in its Hive was one thing, but the hold being so scandalous in nature?

Chayyliel could not allow it.

He felt guilt afterwards but it was an emotion he had much experience with and he knew it would pass.

LIL

O n their next trip into the Ossuary Lil kept her hand in the pocket of her tunic, wrapped tightly around the small bag, afraid that if she did not grasp it, it would disappear somewhere in the odd distortion of travel. Mayer had met with Chayyliel by himself, an attempt to assert his control over her. In any case, the plan had received the go ahead.

Once they appeared in the Ossuary, they all simply dispersed with no speech. They were used to a certain routine.

Lil wandered the aisles, alert, waiting for any little thing that could be a sign. She avoided the others, which was not hard given how large the space was turning out to be. Every time the group thought they might be reaching the edge of the room, they would turn a corner or pass a shelf and discover a whole new extension of shelves. The place seemed endless and Lil wondered if it spread out below the whole of Zebub.

Halfway through their allotted time for the day, Lil had only searched three drawers. She was hampered by the fact that she refused to let go of the bag in her pocket. She was frustrated and angry when she turned a corner and the bag suddenly warmed in her fist. The drawers she stood in front of looked no different from the hundreds others that lined the walls and aisles.

She opened the top one and the contents clattered together as she peered down into a space full of skulls.

At first they all looked like 'dants until she looked more closely. Some of the craniums only had one central hole in the center, others were lined with parallel rows of small bumps on top. Some were missing teeth and instead the mouths housed what looked like calcified bristles. There was nothing that looked like any kind of root she'd ever seen. Plus the bag reacted no differently when the drawer was open. She assumed there would be some additional sign and slammed it shut.

The second drawer was nearly overflowing with gems. Only as she picked one up did she notice the small figures trapped in the center of the stones. Some were insects trapped in yellow, green, blue, and rose. It was the others that worried her, the ones where the trapped figures resembled minuscule 'dants, arms raised as if they banged on their prison. She studied a diamond with a small woman inside. The figure's eyes met her own and the insanity in them was clear and sharp.

Lil dropped it and shivered as she shut the drawer.

When she opened the bottom drawer, the bag in her hand pulsed. The drawer held bags similar to the one curled in her palm. She looked through it, contents clacking and chiming against each other as her hand moved among them. Then her thumb grazed a bag that sent a shock through her, flowing up her arm and across her shoulders. The bag of Fruit sent a shock back in the opposite direction before, she yanked her thumb away. Unclenching the hand in her pocket, she quickly grabbed the bag in the drawer. It was dark, a black fabric threaded through with a raw-looking pink like the damaged flesh under burned skin.

She opened the bag carefully, but no matter how she tilted it Lil could not see the contents, as if they refused to allow the light to touch them. She finally upended the bag and tiny chunks of bone filled her palm. Some were small and thin, thicker on one end—whole finger bones. The other bones were too broken to identify. They vibrated, chasing each other around her cupped palm in odd movements of attraction and repulsion.

Quickly replacing them in the bag, she lowered it back into the drawer. She heard a sound behind her and whirled about to see . . . no one.

HAYDN

The potion he had mixed was not a simple one. Brewing it in such a short time had necessitated certain substitutions, but it was at least the right color and texture. He only hoped it worked properly. He came upon the girl without warning, behind her back as she crouched near a drawer. With his palm in the air, he blew the dust over her face even as she turned. Her body froze and her eyelids drooped but did not completely close. He cursed and worked quickly. She hadn't fallen asleep as she should have. Either the potion was weak or she was more powerful than they had assumed.

He was sad that this was her end. He had seen a different one for her. One he participated in more directly. In any case, he owed her for a night spent in choking darkness, yelling with no one to save him. Yes, it had ended with the coming of the dawn and waking up in a small waste room in Hive Chayyliel, but he'd never been treated in such a way. It would not go unpunished. Even if he could not do the punishing himself.

He pulled the bag from her pocket, the one she'd been handling all morning. Next he reached around her for the bag that she'd just placed back in the drawer. He poured the contents of the first bag on the floor, making a pile. Then he poured the contents of the second bag into the first and placed it in her pocket. Putting the seeds in the second bag, he replaced it in the drawer.

He hesitated, reaching out, but her cheek twitched before he could touch and he quickly backed away. He was an aisle over when he heard her move and softly call out.

"Hello, anyone there?"

"Yes, dear?" Krezida.

"Oh, nothing, I thought someone was behind me. I must have been mistaken."

"Ah, it's these old aisles. There are shadows everywhere and these old metal drawers shift and creak as they settle. It's almost like there's conscious thought behind it." Krezida laughed.

"Yes, that must be it." Lil did not sound convinced.

"What have you found, dear? Anything interesting?"

"Not especially." She shut the drawer. "Only more bones." She sounded tired of it. They all were. There were hundreds of bones in these drawers. Haydn and Krezida knew that none of them were exactly new, but some had been placed in the Ossuary recently, and were still covered with the dirt of their original resting place.

"Well, let us move on then."

Only after he heard their footsteps growing softer did Haydn finally relax and start to breathe normally again. It was done and so was she. Even if she didn't know it yet.

LIL

il left the Ossuary at the end of the day exhausted but triumphant. She'd found the Root. It had just turned out to be more bones, but even if they were disappointed, she still had June's answer. She and Mayer separated from the other Holders and their Apprentices and headed for Hive Chayyliel. She tried to speak of it with Mayer as they walked.

"We are almost there, Holder."

"Yes, almost."

She turned to study him, but he was frowning at the ground as they walked.

"What is it, Holder?"

He turned to look at her. She could feel the drying sweat patches on her shirt, and her disheveled hair, but he looked at her as if he saw none of that.

"Nothing, Lil. You've just grown so much."

She didn't know why that would make him so contemplative, but the positive interaction had her hoping their breach was closing, slowly, on its own. They said nothing more as they separated to go to their rooms but nothing could dampen her mood of accomplishment. She arrived at her room, ready to tell Arel and Jagi the good news, when she opened the sitting room to a crowd of 'dants and Antes.

They were all staring at the her.

All the Holders and the Holder-Apprentices plus a complement of two Ante guards filled her living area. Her first thought was to wonder how everyone had beaten her here, but that was chased from her mind when she saw the two guards holding Davi and Min off the ground. Both of them looked terrified, tears slipping down their faces but neither making a sound.

"What do you think you are doing? Put my sibs down. Now."

Neither of them moved and she turned to Arel and Jagi, who looked terrified. She took a step forward when Chayyliel strode in, face pulled tight in anger, with the points of many feet hitting the ground so hard she expected them to break through. Its golden eyes centered on her and she froze, terror filling her mind with gibberish.

"What have I been but respectful and kind?" Chayyliel's voice was low, the extra mouths echoing the sentiment in lower, threatening tones.

Lil said nothing.

"Why have you chosen to repay me in such a way?" This tone demanded an answer.

"My . . . Queen Chayyliel . . . I don't know what you are talking about."

If anything the feel of anger in the room grew more severe. Two of Chayyliel's back legs curled and rose up behind, scorpion-like, ready to strike.

"Empty your pockets."

Her heart began to race faster but she did as ordered. There was only the bag that June had given her.

"And what is this?"

Chayyliel stared at the bag sitting lonely on the table.

"A gift from June."

"Really?"

Chayyliel nodded to the Turms by its side and they nodded in reply before standing stock still. A few moments later June was escorted in by two more Turms, their head held high and unafraid. It calmed her somewhat that they were so in control.

"It's true. I gave her a bag of fruit seeds. For luck."

It was hardly believable but June was in enough favor to get away with it.

"Only for luck?"

June tilted his head and Chayyliel's head swayed toward Lil again.

"Yes."

"Not as a mark of favor?"

"I—what?" Of all the things Lil had not expected that.

"You dare to mingle in my own Hive, even after I warned you of the consequences for me!"

"I, we haven't!" Lil was stumbling and yelling, losing her cool. June was nodding by her side, mouth opening.

"Silence. Fruit seeds, indeed." Chayyliel said it like it knew it was a lie and the nerves came rushing back. One claw delicately picked up the bag, and she was surprised that it did not rip as Chayyliel unlaced it and brought it close to peer inside. Chayyliel grunted in frustration and a shiver made its way up Lil's back.

The bag was upended onto the table and the bones that fell out were all too familiar. Lil met June's startled gaze. June searched her face, then their own face blazed with anger. They knew now, as she did, that she'd been set up, but there was nothing to do about it. June had taken all the blame they could. There were no options left.

"I thought that I would find some token, something to prove the . . . relations between you two. Instead I find something worse. I do not understand how you brought these out of the Ossuary, but it hardly matters. Do you know what this could do to my standing?" Chayyliel's voice was low and echoed by the shoulder mouths. "What would happen to all the retainers under my protection?" Chayyliel looked at Arel and Jagi at this and another shiver went down her back, the only movement she could accomplish right now.

"Queen, I swear . . ." she tried through a dry throat.

"Did I not say *silence*!"

Lil clamped her mouth closed and knew there was no answer that could save her. Chayyliel did not want the truth. There was too much danger of making this public. Chayyliel wanted the issue gone. Lil was a scapegoat. The sacrifice so that this would pass. The only question was how many of those in the room knew it, and how many had been involved in setting her up.

Perhaps even Queen Chayyliel was nothing but a cat's-paw. A tool right now without knowing it.

It was easier for them to believe this than to dig deeper and uncover too many secrets. She saw now that they were afraid of her. The realization had been growing for days, but she had thought it too absurd. This way they got rid of a problem and a threat all at once. It was why the guards were holding Min and Davi, a warning so that she would behave and simply go to her death.

Did they worry that she'd speak enough Babel to bring the entire Hive down on their heads? Even if the strain of that would kill her, it might be worth it . . . if it would not also kill Min and Davi . . . and Arel and Jagi. She didn't know when the two Antes had become important to her, but it was long before the kisses of last night. There was no time to examine that realization right now and no point, with Chayyliel planning her death before her eyes.

"You must of course be stripped of your position and sent to the punishment rooms." It was only because her knees were locked that Lil remained standing. Chayyliel used one claw to coax the bones back into the bag and placed it on the table. She wanted to look at the faces around the room, see if any of them would give themselves away, except she could not tear her gaze from Chayyliel.

"Only time will see if others must also pay for your indiscretion." Its gaze swept over the people behind her and she could feel them shrink back. Lil nodded. Good, perhaps her betrayers would be paid back.

She had one last chance and she was able to force herself to turn and look at her Holder. He looked away, guilt and anger and sadness and surprise burning in his eyes, but no hope. She remembered his cast-down emotions as they left the Ossuary. Lil's fate was sealed and she felt a sudden calm.

She would die today and that was that.

Everyone waited to see who would make the first move. She turned to Arel and Jagi, who watched her with both fear and banked anger. She could not handle any of their emotions. She had too many of her own.

"Your vow has no time limit. Take care of them," she reminded them.

Arel and Jagi both nodded. They understood what she was saying. She didn't know if the thought has crossed any of their minds yet that her skill with Babel might in fact be genetic.

It was not.

Neither Min nor Davi had ever shown any aptitude for languages at all. It did not matter though. Eventually someone would think it. Perhaps years after this night and then they would come after her sibs. She would die this night, but she would not allow the same fate to befall Min and Davi.

RAZEL

The whole plot was laid bare in front of her. The satisfaction on Krezida's, Riana's, and Haydn's faces, the guilt and surprise that Mayer carried like a cloak—betrayed by his fellow conspirators if she wasn't mistaken. Pure terror changed to settled resignation on Liliana's face and anger on June's. The incandescent rage boiling from Chayyliel was the last clue.

The betrayal had happened and there was nothing to be done. It would be her greatest test to stand stone-faced as a person she would have liked to call friend was dragged away to her death.

She also had to admit the genius of the plan on some level. How does someone fool an Ante searching for theft?

Make sure the victim doesn't know they are stealing.

As Chayyliel approached Liliana to take her away, the older of her two sibs moved.

"No!" she screamed and elbowed the guard holding her and ducked from the hold. She was reaching for her sister when the air turned to ice around her. Before she could call out, her outstretched arm was on the ground, severed cleanly at the shoulder. The stump of the girl's shoulder was not bleeding, flash frozen as it was. The young girl herself collapsed to the ground, eyes wide and mouth gasping. The younger sib was screaming now, struggling in his guard's arms. Arel and Jagi were moving, one toward each guard, but before they could do anything the air changed, as if it had been filled with molten lead.

"You dare!"

Razel had never heard Liliana's voice with such a tone. It was anger and the edge of madness and the next words out of her mouth were in a language no one but Mayer understood, but they all saw the effects.

The guard who'd harmed Lil's sister resembled a small crike wrapped in a sheath of glittering ice—but not for much longer. The temperature in the whole room dropped as suddenly as it had rose, and the Ante screamed.

At least Razel assumed it was a scream. She'd never heard a sound like it before, as if breaking ice could express pain. Its form rose into the air, small cracks beginning to break across its surface. Through the translucent ice Razel could see its bones shattering, bending. It shivered and twisted in the air, crying out as it floated over the maimed girl.

It became smaller, collapsing in on itself.

The young girl screamed and passed out as it joined the stump where her arm had been. The Ante shrieked as it melded with the 'dant's skin there, as it shrank until the girl had a limb of ice. Lil's sib laid out, unconscious, her original right arm on the floor beside her, replaced by all that remained of the Ante who had attacked her.

It took only seconds.

Before anyone thought of anything, Jagi had scooped the young girl up in his arms and darted over to the corner of the room. Razel saw June, who was closest to the door, open it and dive out. She could not blame them.

"You dare to break your vow!" Chayyliel's voice filled the room, made the light bulbs shatter into pulp above them.

Liliana turned to Chayyliel but the madness and anger in her eyes did not abate, it grew. She snarled out something else and the other guard who had been moving around the edge of the room, trying to come up behind her, flew into the Queen's side. They collapsed in a heap of limbs and tentacles.

Krezida and Haydn were trying to head for the door, but Liliana's head snapped around and with a growled word Krezida was thrown to the floor and Haydn was suspended in the air before her.

"You!" The voice was gravelly and bits of blood now flew from her mouth.

Chayyliel had risen from the heap on the floor, as had Krezida. The Holder still moved toward the door, abandoning her Apprentice. Razel was not surprised. Haydn was never going to be Holder. Everyone but he knew that. He was nothing but a placeholder.

Liliana placed Haydn between herself and Chayyliel, as if his life were some sort of barrier. Razel closed her eyes from where she crouched behind a larger pillow with her Holder, because she knew what would happen even before it occurred. She heard the snap of Chayyliel firing upon her.

Most thought the quills that covered the Ante's head were simply Chayyliel's version of hair or an ornamental choice. Chayyliel's bloodline—Asclepti—was one of healing but many chose to forget the flip side of the healer: the torturer, the subtle poison, the silent death.

She could hear the sharp *snikt* of release as Chayyliel allowed the barbs to go flying, the wet sound as they ripped through Haydn's body completely like damp tissue paper, and the scream from Lil as they hit her.

Razel could stand it no longer and looked over the edge of the pillow. Liliana lay on the ground, two barbed shafts sticking out from her side and hip. She still looked angry. She still looked like a threat. Then her eyes started to droop and she barely had time to hiss out a single word before she collapsed to the carpet.

They all froze, waiting to see what her last gambit would do, but nothing happened around them. Chayyliel let out an incoherent growl and moved across the room, reaching down to Liliana's unconscious body. She could not see what the Ante was doing since the tangle of its limbs blocked much of the movement. Finally there was a ripping sound Razel would remember for the rest of her days and Chayyliel stood with a clump of redness held in two pincers.

She realized that Chayyliel held Liliana's tongue. It was only as she turned her face away from the scene that she noticed that the children were gone, along with the two Antes, Arel and Jagi.

Perhaps her attack was not mad at all but a distraction.

Queen Chayyliel turned to face them and noted the absences as well. It turned to the remaining guard, over six feet tall. It resembled a 'dant but was covered head to toe in long golden tentacles. Only when the Ante moved did they part enough to see the disjointed albino-white slug body underneath.

"Find them, bring them all back." Chayyliel paused. "Alive."

The guard left, the tentacles allowing the Ante to quickly rise off the floor and scuttle out the door. Next Chayyliel looked at the Turms, who simply stood there as silent as ever. He gestured to Haydn's fallen body. "Call a guard to take him to the body shapers, see if he can be saved or hopefully turned into something more useful." He looked down at

Liliana. Razel always had trouble reading Ante expressions. Their faces were often so different, but now the satisfaction in Chayyliel's stance was clear. "And another to take her to the rooms. Give her to Oolina and Gluti. Tell them they have no limits."

The gasp that followed this order was loud in the room and it took Razel a minute to realize it came from her own throat. Chayyliel was now looking at them: Mayer, Riana, and herself. The only 'dants left awake in the room.

"No one outside these rooms knows anything of what transpired here. Luckily this shame can be kept in Hive, so no one need know. If someone does find out I will know who is to blame and they will suffer the same fate."

Razel swallowed but nodded along with the other two. The Ruling Courts were the worst gossips of Zebub. It would only be a matter of time. The story would get out and when it did they would be blamed without evidence or cause.

They had to find Krezida before she spoke to anyone. Chayyliel was already turning away and moving out of the door, leaving Haydn's body and Liliana on the floor.

After a minor hesitation and a quick look at Liliana, Mayer followed. Riana did not even glance at the carnage before leaving. As Razel turned to follow, her eyes fell on something under Haydn's splayed leg. She moved his still warm limb and saw the bag of bones. In all the chaos of the attack on Chayyliel and the discovery of Arel and Jagi's running off with the children, everyone had forgotten about the bag that sealed Liliana's fate.

No one had said what they were, but she'd seen the look on June's face. The bag of bones must be important in some way. Razel slipped the bag into her own pocket and hurriedly followed her Holder from the room, not looking at the two broken forms on the ground that made her the sole Holder-Apprentice in Zebub.

NA'AMEN GOBERT TILAHUN

SAN FRANCISCO

DAYA

Her head felt as if it were filled with marbles and cotton wool. It was hard to think and remember. She sat up and saw Elliot, Tae, and the young girl from the mall sprawled out on the hard ground next to her. She rose slowly, looking around. They were surrounded by rough white stone. No doors or windows at all. They were entombed in rock. The walls were sheer and the ceiling was free of any ornament other than a hanging light bulb.

Elana was nowhere to be found, which worried her more than anything, but she refused to panic. Slowly the memory of the fight came back to her.

Elliot groaned and shifted, slowly opening his eyes.

"Ugh, did you get the number of the space shuttle that landed on my head?"

"Nope, but I need you up. Now."

The pained smile dropped from his face and he immediately looked around for a threat. Daya hated herself a little bit. Elliot's crush on her was not the secret he thought it was. It never had been. She tried her best not to take advantage of it or give him false hope, and for his part he never pushed or mentioned it and just acted like a good friend and partner. She knew how rare that was. More rare than it should be.

Still, she knew how he reacted to her using the words "I need," which was why she didn't use them against him often. But right now she did need him. She needed him to be on high alert, she needed him focused on more important things than jokes.

"Where are we?"

"I'm guessing a cell of some kind." Daya was pressing her fingers to the walls, looking for some sort of secret passage. Of course, if there was a secret passage for them to dump prisoners in this place, she sincerely doubted it would open from this side, but you should never discount an enemy's potential stupidity.

"Elana's somewhere above us." He said it quietly.

She let out a relieved breath and some of her panic subsided. "Good."

"At least there are no bodies or bones around?" The forced chipperness was still appreciated.

"bodies? bones?" The voice was a whisper. Daya turned from her examination of one wall to see Tae flipping over to his back, his eyes wide from Elliot's words.

"Relax, I said *no* bodies or bones." Elliot moved over and propped their aspirant on his thighs to steady him. "Which means they are probably coming to find us at some point. This isn't a place they just dump people and forget them. And considering the lack of bathroom facilities, we probably won't have to wait that long."

His chatter was the perfect thing and calmed Tae down until he could sit up and look around. "Where's Erik? Where's Matthias?"

"No idea. A separate cell would be my guess."

Daya was tired of the chatter. She called up her power, relaxing as the cold and numbness crept over her skin. "Everyone to the other side of the cell."

The other two didn't question her, moving as far away from her as the cell would allow, carrying the still-unconscious young woman with them.

Daya's vision had already shifted from color to grayscale and she looked closely at the rock all around them. With her sight like this she saw cracks and fissures more easily, she knew where to hit to break something apart. Except there weren't any such fissures in this cell; it was as if it had been formed out of a piece of solid uniform rock. Still, Daya had been in very few situations where brute force didn't get some sort of result.

She slammed her fist into the wall. The crack of stone meeting stone was loud in the enclosed space but neither her fist nor the wall broke, so she did it again.

And again.

And again.

She only stopped when hands she knew as well as her own wrapped around her body and into her shoulders. She felt the chill of her lover's touch on her underskin.

"Elana." She turned. Others were calling her lover's name as well, but Daya could not look up to see what was happening yet. She was too happy just knowing that she was here and not in some special cell or being experimented on by this group of Angelics.

"Elana, what happened?"

"Some kind of gas. I think that soap-bubble Angelic did it. You all passed out and I went invisible."

Daya sank to the floor. Elana stayed in contact with her body. They faced Tae and Elliot, who was trying to focus on his sister's face rather than the places she and Daya were overlapping.

"Then they gathered you all up—"

"Wait. The gas didn't affect the others?" Tae asked.

"I don't know, we had those three Suits knocked out and no one else was on the first floor with us. And it was gone by the time the reinforcements showed up to take you guys away."

"What about the hostage?"

Her silence answered Tae's question.

"Who was he?" Daya asked quietly.

"The boyfriend who ended up in jail." Elliot answered.

"What?"

Tae looked at Daya and Elana. "How do you not know? Don't you remember the scandal? He played Erik's stepbrother on *With Love*. Then everyone found out they were sleeping together. Since he had just turned eighteen and Erik was only sixteen, Erik's father pressed charges and he got something like two years in jail. Erik quit working after that. It was a good show, though."

"Right?" Elliot turned to him. "They never released it on DVD."

"Oh, I have bootleg copies of all the episodes. I can burn them for you."

"That would be awesome! I can—"

"Boys!" Daya's voice rang through the cell. "Later. More importantly, the boy is dead."

They were all silent at that. Erik was stable in his power, so Daya didn't fear him coming after one of them the way he had Hu, but he had a temper and this was far from likely to improve it.

"Elana, love, can you see if you can find Erik and Matthias?"

She turned in Daya's arms. "I can try, but this place is like a maze. The only reason I was able to find you guys buried under like a whole wall of solid rock was my bond with Elliot."

Daya felt guilty sending her love away, but she couldn't help but think it was better that the one of them who could become incorporeal should be the one to break this news to Erik.

ERIK

Erik woke up cold, alone, and bent into an unnatural position. There was no one light source that he could see, but the white stone all around him was faintly luminescent. There was no space to do anything but stand; the walls around him were so close it was a chore to turn around. He looked up and far above him he made out a grate. His arms were pinned and it took him a deep breath and a hard exhale, plus thinking extra skinny, before he was able to maneuver to raise them both above his head. They were scraped bloody from the rock walls but at least were no longer trapped.

He studied the walls, looking for handholds and footholds. There were small outcroppings of rock but they crumbled under his weight. He was trying to figure out a different way out when he heard the breath and realized he was not alone. As loud as the sound seemed, it did not stir the air around him.

"Elana?"

The breath stopped and started again. It sounded like it was coming from all around him. Erik looked up and there above him, translucent, was a figure in an orange jumpsuit. It was hard to see because the dim light from the walls made features blend and blur, but there was some sort of fringe on the front of the outfit. The bottoms of the feet looked filthy, as if he had been running through mud. His pale golden-brown skin glowed like sunlight. Erik catalogued all these details and more, all in an effort to ignore the truth that had been welling up in him since he first caught sight of that shade of orange. Still so bright and obnoxious. Then the figure glanced down, Erik saw the face, and the ghost was gone.

"Daniel?" The truth choked out of him. It carried the taste of bile and grief and anger.

The orange appeared in front of his face. Daniel kept himself mostly inside the rock wall from a lack of space, but his face and chest gently pushed out a few centimeters. Looking at the gray rock through his skin made him look even more sallow, less human, less like Daniel.

"What—who?" He did not want to ask it, did not want to find out who killed Daniel because then it wasn't a hallucination. It couldn't be an illusion or a shapeshifter. It could not be any of those things if he watched how the figure tilted its head like Daniel, how it pursed its lips like Daniel, when he was tired of some bullshit, or slow-blinked like Daniel when he was being stubborn and would wait forever for Erik to say the first thing.

It was Daniel, now a ghost like Elana. Erik hadn't realized non-Blooded could become ghosts, but the evidence was still waiting for him to speak.

"Byron." It was a cheat, a shortcut to saying the word dead or killed, but Daniel smiled sadly anyway and gave a brisk nod. Erik flicked his eyes up and down over the bits of Daniel he could see and immediately wished he hadn't. His chest was a mess of meat and gristle and bone, cracked and shattered and shredded—that was the fringe he had seen. Little bits of the orange fabric had embedded into the wound and it looked all the more horrible for the way it faded from sight. Its transparency made it seem old and faint even though he knew it had been recent.

"What happened?"

"He threw me. Onto a tree stump."

Erik flinched and tried to back away but there was no space; he simply scratched his back up in the attempt.

"Where is everyone else?"

"I don't exactly know. I was too busy dying to pay attention to the other things happening around me."

Erik flinched at the words scraping a divot in his right cheek.

"I'm sorry." He did not mean just for his callous words but for everything, for Robert and for the pain Daniel endured, for the refusal to leave him alone even as Daniel made it clear he wanted to stop contact, for being the reason the last year of his life had been so hard. He'd tried to say these words a number of times and now his first chance to say it face-to-face was after Daniel's death.

"Being dead isn't really that bad."

Erik wanted to look away and put his hands over his ears. The most painful part was that Daniel wasn't saying this to punish or to grind salt in his wounds. His voice was matter-of-fact. The way it got when he was just musing out loud.

"All the limits of your body are gone. Not the physical limits, though those are gone too, but the emotional ones. The fears we use to limit ourselves and to shrink ourselves down for fear of others' attention or just because the world wants us too. It's all gone."

"I . . ." There wasn't a response that Erik could give to that, at least not one that he understood himself. How do you speak to someone you love who is talking about the pros of being dead?

"You see things differently as well."

"Like what?"

"Like you."

Erik was silent, hoping that would end the conversation.

"You're more than what they tell you."

Erik froze. There was no way for Daniel to know what he'd been told unless he was reading Erik's mind. Did this have something to do with the limits he'd mentioned? He didn't doubt it was Daniel, but a far creepier version, more what he had thought ghosts would be like before he met Elana. He shook his head and closed his eyes. Daniel was always the supportive one, the one who told him he could be more than an ATM for Robert. He thought it was one of the reasons Robert was so harsh on Daniel, which was not really a conversation that he wanted to have . . . ever. He knew Daniel but he also felt a shiver of apprehension as he stared into translucent eyes that saw entirely too much.

"Hello!" His voice echoed up the oubliette but there was no response that he could hear, no returning call, no scuffle of feet, no face blocking the light to peer down at him through the bars up top.

He had to get out of here, now.

He called his power up slowly, let it burn under his skin until the pain of his scrapes was background noise. He braced his back against the wall, then his hands and feet, and began to inch up to the top. Every move strained his muscles and every inch cost him bits of skin and blood left on the rock. A penance.

The back of his shirt was ripped to shreds by the time he was half-way up. Daniel was silent but Erik could feel him, sometimes right above him, sometimes directly below, and sometimes in the very rock he pressed bloody palms to, an unintended benediction.

Daniel was silent, though, only the sound of their twinned breathing filling the narrow shaft. Erik closed his eyes and climbed quickly until his head bumped against the metal bars. Bracing his legs, he raised his hands and took hold of the bars. They creaked as he pushed against them and rock dust showered him as the bolts began to shake loose. With a screech of metal and a shower of shrapnel, the grate came free. He heaved it over and grasped the ragged edge of the hole to drag himself out.

Once free, he lay panting next to the hole with the grate somewhere behind him. He could feel his power still sparking over the surface of his skin.

"Look out."

Erik rolled over onto his back to look up into Daniel's face. In the brighter light, he was even more faint, a whisper of shadow without any fine details. He was not looking down at Erik but across the hole, and as Erik followed his gaze he saw one of the things from before. The Pillar of Sand. Previously the sand that made it up had been all golden, roiling and bubbling over itself in the air. Now the crescent that had been burned out of it was patched with many different colors, black and white and rose sand. There were even some sun-bleached pebbles churning in that space.

It looked like it had been slumped on the ground, but even as he watched the sands began turning faster, the mass becoming a pillar, rising higher in the air and sparking on fire.

Wind blasted him in the face. His skin went tight and dry, and his eyes burned from the lack moisture.

He reached behind himself and his hand closed on the broken grate that had kept him in his prison. Throwing his body forward, almost back into the hole, he used the momentum to fling the grate like a discus. It flew true but the granules of sand blew apart to avoid the projectile. The spinning disc sank into the stone wall behind the Angelic. The sand came back together, a little smaller, a little more wary.

Erik was already on his feet. There was no longer any wind. His skin stung and burned but he could move. He leapt over the hole in the floor and immediately rushed into the body of the creature. Winds began to rip at his face and hands and stripped them raw in seconds. The sands and rocks battered him so that every touch was salt and blood and pain but he did not care. He kept his eyes closed but grasped with his hands, sifting through the scorching sands. The thing was making noises, low whistles and chirps of pain but also high notes of rage and anger. A higher heat rose around him, one that made him gasp for air even as it seared his throat. It made his stomach roil and before he knew it, bile was pushing its way up through his body. He didn't fight it and allowed the vomit to leave his mouth.

Then his hands closed on what he was looking for, something different from the dry touch of sand, something warm and pulsing, damp and sticky, as only the most important things were. Erik grabbed it with both hands as it tried to pull away, tried to yank his arms out of their sockets. He pulled back, sinking his fingers into the tough flesh. He had spotted it when the grate had cut through the main body of the creature, a misshapen bit of red floating in the middle of it. It looked unlike any other part of the Angelic, which he had guessed meant it was important in some way.

With a final pop his fingers pushed through the hard outer shell and sank into something soft and gelatinous. The screams on the wind reached a fever pitch and he could feel his right eardrum burst from the heat, but blood dripped freely from both ears. He pulled his hands apart quickly and the organ ripped apart.

Everything stopped. The wind. The heat. Everything.

Meat slipped through his fingers and coated his palms.

He opened his eyes. It looked like he stood in the middle of a beach. The ground around him was covered in sand. Some of the grains rippled as if they were trying to reform but then simply fell apart. Two halves of something lay at the floor around and on his feet. It looked as if a heart had mated with a brain and then called a bunch of intestines to join the orgy. The inside alternated between empty chambers and twisted roads that looked like brain meat. His hands were raw as if he had started to bleed from his pores, a thousand pinpoints of red.

"Well, that was messy." Erik turned and looked at Daniel, who stared at him from his beginning position across the hole. "And you are covered in . . . gore."

Erik smiled, even though the movement allowed some of the vile white-gray fluid that had exploded from the creature to slip into his mouth. He turned his head to the side and spat.

"Sorry about that." Even though he tried to make it light, it still came out too heavy. Too much like truth.

There was a pause and Erik racked his brain for something else to say, anything to change the atmosphere back from the tense, waiting thing it had become with three little words.

"Me too."

His head snapped back up. Daniel was smiling at him, lightly, the way he used to in Erik's trailer between takes. Right before he would lean forward and kiss him. Right before he would hold Erik close and pretend everything would be all right. How could he fear Daniel, no matter how death had changed him? Who wouldn't be changed?

"There is a lot to talk about, but not here or now. Let's find your friends, right?"

Erik smiled in the near dark. "Yeah." He looked around the room. There was only one door leading out. Before he left, he walked to the wall and pulled the grate from it, an unwieldy weapon compared to his bracelets, which they hadn't removed, but he needed a distance weapon. As he exited the room the cold and distinct *lack* of presence at his back was a sure sign that Daniel was following.

MATTHIAS

"**I**s that all you got?" Blood dripped from his lips but he was not broken, wouldn't allow himself to be. His face and chest were already a mess of bruises.

"Honestly, you are only hurting yourself."

Byron wasn't wrong but Matthias was too angry right now to care. He'd woken up as they were trying to cram him into some hole in the ground and fought his way out of the holds of Byron and Brady. Brady was not especially strong, but Matthias had taken a couple of hits before he realized that the Suit wasn't just lucky but could see him, even with his power burning full-tilt-boogie. The Suit was fast and Matthias was barely able to avoid his fists, let alone land any blows himself, so he was wearing down.

Byron wasn't participating. He watched from the edge of the room, taunting Matthias occasionally.

"We only want to help the world."

Matthias snorted and did not deign to respond. His strength was fading and every minute they continued to circle was another chance for reinforcements to arrive. He maneuvered under a punch and rolled to the side, despite the way it made his ribs scream in pain. Already Brady was coming for him again. He managed to avoid the punch aimed at his face and smiled when he heard a satisfying crunch from where Brady's knuckles slammed into the stone floor.

Brady grunted in pain and Matthias managed to hook his feet behind the Suit's ankles and pull, knocking him off balance and toward the hole. As Brady stumbled to regain his balance, Matthias could tell it wasn't enough. Then there was the sound of running footsteps and the whirl of something flying through the air over his head and a sickening crunch.

Matthias had caused enough death to know the sounds of it, whether it was the quiet last gasp of the final exhale or the crunch of several crushed bones, as this was. He looked at Brady, whose chest was shattered. Some sort of grate stuck out of it and he looked down at it in surprise, as blood dripped from his lips. Matthias craned his neck to see Erik in the doorway.

Erik's face was a mix of rage and devastation that Matthias did not understand. He looked at Brady's wound as if he were seeing something else. The anger was pushed off to the edges of his face by the gray that was filling it. He had blood dripping from dozens of cuts on his hands and face. There was dried brown-red in a thin stream from his ears down to his chin. His skin was flushed and peeling as if he had a sunburn.

Matthias glanced at Byron and saw him staring at Erik in horror.

No, not directly at Erik, at the empty space over Erik's shoulder. The Suit had gone pale, the freckles on his face and arms standing out starkly.

"Erik?" His aspirant glanced at him and Matthias was nervous about the blankness in his eyes. "Erik." He said it again, hard, a tone that was meant to be obeyed.

Erik seemed to shake himself a little. He drew his eyes away from Brady.

"Come over here and help me up."

Erik moved slowly at first, as if remembering how. Color was coming back to his skin, and by the time he crouched down beside Matthias he was moving almost smoothly enough for it to be normal. He kept his eyes averted from Brady's body, but Matthias glanced over as Erik helped him back to his feet. The body had fallen oddly. One leg had slipped into the hole while the rest of his body slumped, stuck outside by a combination of gangly limbs and the grate catching on the rim of the hole.

He glanced at the side of Erik's face and realized with some surprise that blood was still sluggishly leaking from his ears. He already felt a little better simply being close to Erik, within the space of his healing energy. He couldn't imagine why Erik wasn't healed himself.

Looking at the corner where Byron had lurked, he now found it empty, the man taking their distraction to escape. A flash of anger moved through him that whatever thing was wearing his friend's body was still running around. Erik was staring at him, expectation lighting his features. Matthias stared at his aspirant for a second, then looked around the room.

"Are you okay?"

Erik's mouth fell open, shock registering on his face. Finally he shook his head quickly back and forth before calming and answering, "I'm okay. I had to kill one of the Angelics, the one made of sand."

It explained the burns that littered his skin and were very slowly healing "Are you okay with that? And this?" Erik had killed an Angelic before, but that was on the day of his awakening, when instinct was in the driver's seat. He hadn't seemed to care or he'd written it off as something he didn't have much control over. These two, however, had been choices. Someone in control of their powers choosing to kill. He had known stronger people than Erik that had been broken by such a choice.

"Yeah, I'm fine with it."

Something was off in the way Erik stood and spoke. Matthias would have worried, but his next words broke and crackled, each one heavy with unreleased tears.

"They—they killed Daniel."

A tear slipped down his drawn face before it firmed up.

"I'm sorry."

Erik simply nodded and they started for the door. Every step, Matthias felt a little bit better. It became easier to breathe as his ribs went from broken to cracked and the strain on his ankle slowly faded away.

"How do you know?"

Erik simply shook his head again and his lips thinned and almost disappeared as they firmed in annoyance. Then he tilted his head to the side as if listening to something.

"We should go. Byron will have let someone know we've gotten away now. We need to get to the others and get the fuck out of here."

Matthias nodded but continued to worry. Especially because Erik tilted his head every few feet of their journey, as if listening to something Matthias couldn't hear.

ERIK

H
e was confused and worried by the fact that Matthias couldn't see Daniel. He had assumed that Daniel was like Elana and all the other Blooded would be able to see him. That obviously wasn't the case . . . but Byron had been able to see Daniel.

Or rather, whatever was wearing Byron's body had been able to see Daniel. Had that pillar Angelic been able to? Erik tried to think back on the fight. Had he at any point noticed the sand reacting to or attacking Daniel?

He couldn't remember.

"Turn left at this juncture," Erik repeated automatically after Daniel. He saw the way Matthias watched him out of the corner of his eye. He needed to be more circumspect until he figured this out.

They moved through damp stone hallways, some of which carried the scent of sewage. They were underneath the city somewhere. All the passages were narrow, just tall enough for Erik to walk unbent. Matthias, who followed behind since there wasn't room enough for them to walk side by side, was not so lucky and crouch-walked to keep from hitting his head.

The pain was catching up to his body. Erik's right ear throbbed and the cuts on his skin stung in the cold air that blew past them. His skin still burned like a fever, which made him somewhat grateful for the chilled wind. Matthias was slowly walking straighter, his posture growing more stable. The slow drag of a foot that would not cooperate was disappearing.

They came to a dead end. The tunnel simply widened into a stretch of blank wall. Matthias took advantage of the increased space to come up alongside Erik. They both stared at the dead end. Matthias turned his stare to Erik, a question in his gaze. Erik tried to catch a glimpse of Daniel out of the corner of his eyes, but his dead love had nothing more to say.

The smile on Daniel's face dared him to figure this one out on his own.

The wall in front of them was a different material than the other walls they had been passing. Instead of the plain gray stone, this one was slightly illuminated white with veins of sickly green.

"This is like the walls of that hole they put me into."

Matthias's gaze on him sharpened.

"What do you mean?"

"The walls all around me were glowing, they felt weird like something slimy, like they were sticking onto my skin but also wanted me to slip off." He grimaced in embarrassment. "It's hard to explain."

Matthias made an odd humming note in his voice and reached forward to touch the glowing rock. He quickly pulled his hand back and shook it back and forth and then stared down at it. Erik saw the flesh slowly blend and fade. However, unlike the other times Erik had seen Matthias use his power, it still remained there in shadow. It was almost blended, but not quite.

Sweat broke out on Matthias's forehead.

"Did you cut yourself on this rock getting out?"

"Yes."

Matthias hummed again and his hand came back to solid.

"You think there's something in the rock. Something to block our abilities?" Erik asked.

"Maybe so. Or maybe it doesn't block so much as absorb. That must be why you still haven't healed completely. By now you should be fine."

Erik nodded, not worried about himself. "So you think Tae and the others are behind this wall?"

"I don't know about that." Matthias frowned. "You're the one who brought us here, aren't you?"

Erik simply nodded, ignoring the question in Matthias's tone.

"So how would the Suits be around this? They're Blooded too, aren't they?"

"As far as we know, though what one of the Angelics said at the meeting makes me wonder." Matthias seemed lost in thought, but then came back to himself. "In any case, they're enough like us. So it must not be the Suits who maintain this."

"The Angelics have a different power source."

"According to them."

Erik paused and thought about that. They were supposed to be related to these beings. When the Angelics he'd seen had been humanoid, that had been easier to swallow. Now, though, he shuddered. How closely related could they be?

"Our other option is to try and find someone who knows about it and I think that would be a really bad idea," Erik stated.

"As opposed to dragging an actual Angelic back here to do something?" Matthias asked.

"What if all it needs is their presence?"

"Still—"

"What if all it needs is the presence of something that used to be an Angelic?" Erik interrupted.

Matthias looked confused before a dark smile took over his face. A little more discussion and they realized they had nothing to lose from trying it out. In any case, their only other option did seem to be finding someone to explain it to them.

They were turning away when a figure came directly through the wall. Matthias made no move at all but Erik immediately threw a punch that went right through it. He recognized it as Elana right after and took a step back with his hands in the air to show his mistake.

Elana gave him a quick nod of forgiveness but the smile she wore in no way reached her eyes. After a quick glance at Matthias, her gaze stayed on Erik's face, her mouth moving but not opening as if she wanted to say something but was unsure where to begin. He began to get nervous.

She had not acknowledged Daniel at all.

Then she spoke.

"Daniel is dead. Byron killed him."

Hearing it was no less devastating. He could feel his face begin to crumple before he took a deep breath and pulled it together.

"How do you know?"

"I watched it. The gas didn't knock me out, just confused me for a bit." She scrutinized his face further, the sympathy turning to suspicion. "How did you know?"

Erik shrugged and asked a different question. "Is everyone on the other side of that wall?"

She nodded and looked back at it.

"Did you see them get put inside?" Matthias wanted more details.

"No. I followed my bond with Elliot but there's something in the building that muddles it, makes it weak, so it took me a while."

Matthias and Erik both looked at the softly glowing wall.

"What did you see when you got here?"

"Two of those things, the one that looked like soap bubbles and the one made up of all the sand, and the stone was closing up like water."

"Did you see what they did to make it open and close?"

"No, not really. It looked like the soap bubble popped against it a few times. I guess."

"So probably some switch or lever." Matthias moved closer to the wall, not touching it but running his hands right above it, searching for something. Finally with a snort of frustration he laid his hands on the wall, slowly running them up and down.

"Aha." Matthias stopped and ran his hands over the same section again and again until the tip of his finger brushed against a small raised portion of the stone. "There's a small piece of stone here completely invisible to sight. I think it might be the trigger."

Erik saw his arm bulge as he tried to press down or trigger something.

"We should mark it in some way so we don't have to search for it again."

Erik stepped forward and reached up, gathering some of the blood from his ear. He drew a circle around the place Matthias's hand was.

Matthias let his hand fall but kept it away from his body.

"Let's go back and get a piece."

"A piece of what?" Elana asked, but Erik was already walking back to where he left the Angelic. He heard them speaking behind him but didn't pay attention. He had another conversation to conduct quietly, a few feet in front of them.

"What are you? Why can't they see you?"

Daniel had been floating along silently but pretended to not understand what Erik was asking.

"I'm what's left of Daniel after his death."

"So why can't they see you the way they can Elana?"

"If someone comes back from the other side, and it's very rare, usually only those who share close blood ties or a strong emotional connection can see the ghost. Blooded are obviously more powerful than normal humans, that goes for their ghosts too—anyone with the slightest blood relation can see them. Technically all you Blooded and Angelics share a single forebear if you go back far enough. So you can all see Elana. But I'm not Blooded. So they can't see me. You loved me, so you can. Simple enough."

"How do you know all this?" Erik whisper-asked.

"Surely you don't think you come back from the other side without some compensation for the horrible journey?"

Erik blinked at that. It made some sort of sense but he still felt nervous.

"So I should tell them about you?"

Daniel shrugged. "It's up to you. I can't do anything about that, although it seems to me that the time to tell them about me was when you first saw them. It may be too late."

"What do you mean?"

"Look at the way they're looking at you."

Erik glanced behind him quickly. Matthias and Elana were huddled in conversation as they followed him, their eyes darting to him and away many times.

"They worry. Remember what they said about the past berserkers? How they broke?"

"That's what they said about the ones who were used and did not have the same control."

Daniel shrugged as if the difference were negligible. "That's what they think you are. That's the standard they will judge you against. You have gone through much trauma. They will worry."

Daniel was acting like he didn't care one way or the other, but the tone of his words was a subtle threat. Erik had dealt with enough of them to know it. However, it didn't mean he was wrong. Already they were looking at him with an odd tilt to their faces. How much more odd would the look become if they knew he was speaking to the ghost of his ex-boyfriend who died because of him?

That only he could see, other than Byron, and wasn't that great evidence? You guys know that traitor who screwed us over? Well, he can see my brain ghost too! That would not go over well.

They would chalk it up to survivor's guilt and PTSD. The looks did not improve as they passed the room with Brady's broken body suspended above the hole. Erik moved quickly into the room with the remnants of the Angelic. It was hard to tell for sure but its viscera was changing color, slowly turning from a light gray/white to something darker the longer it lay there.

NA'AMEN GOBERT TILAHUN

He reached down and gathered half of the gray-red meat he had ripped apart in one hand, picking up a hand full of sand for good measure.

They headed back in more silence.

At the wall Matthias reached for the effluvia in Erik's hand, but Erik pulled away. His own hand was already soaked in the Angelic blood. He covered it in the sand as well and pressed his palm where Matthias's had been. He felt something shift and yanked his hand back. As the door started to melt open, he threw the remains of the Angelic to the side.

TAE

The young girl from the mall had finally woken up. She said her name was Zaha, with an understandable wariness that could have arisen from a hundred different things. The last thing she remembered was shopping in the mall with her friend.

"Where are we?"

Tae swallowed and tried to answer calmly. He'd heard that trauma victims sometimes mirrored the emotions of the ones talking to them. It was probably bullshit but worth a try.

"In the basement of an office building in San Francisco . . . I think."

Her eyes widened and Tae allowed that this quite probably was not the most calming thing to say.

"Why?"

Tae struggled with an answer. Normally reading a non-Blooded was something that could get you in trouble if the Organization found out, but they were in some extreme circumstances and anyway it wasn't their fault they were in this. He decided to start out smaller than the whole basement thing.

"Because something attacked you at the mall. Do you remember anything about that?"

Zaha rested her head on her knees, eyes closed in confusion.

"I remember being in the mall. I was there with my friend Carlie—" She broke off and her head shot up. "Carlie, did you see her?"

Tae shook his head, not wanting to reveal that her friend was most likely dead or something different, like those others in the mall. The wall in the back of their cell suddenly melted off to the sides like a liquid curtain, flowing and disappearing to reveal Erik, Elana, and Matthias.

Both the live ones looked like they had taken quite a beating. Their clothes were ripped and dried blood adorned them in various places.

Daya and Elliot moved forward, but Tae beat them to Erik. He stopped when he saw the viscous white liquid on his hands, lumpy as if it were milk gone bad.

"I'm glad you're okay."

That was when a scream interrupted them all.

"Who are they? Why are they floating?"

In the rush to greet Erik he'd completely forgotten about Zaha. He turned back to her and she was backed against the opposite wall, her eyes wide and terrified, looking at Elana. Everyone froze, including Elana. This girl could see her. It should have been impossible unless the girl was Blooded in some way. Erik was proof enough they didn't know all of the bloodlines in the Bay Area. Tae hurried over to her.

"It's okay. Elana's, well, she is a ghost but I promise, she's friendly."

Zaha was shaking her head back and forth but she was no longer trembling. Elana was no longer floating in the air above the crowd of people but was hovering very close to the ground, trying to make herself as human-seeming as possible.

"What about the other one?"

Tae immediately looked around, looking for another spirit. Blooded ghosts were rare but not unique. Perhaps the Organization had sent one of the others to look for them. They had to know the meeting had gone rogue by now, but there was no one he could see in the space of air that she was staring at.

"What do you see?" Erik was pale, staring at her as if she were a ghost herself.

"Some guy floating!" She was on the edge of hysteria and it felt like Tae was not that far behind her. He opened himself to the world, opened himself to visions, but still he could see nothing. It had been a long time since he had felt out of his depth in this way.

"Describe him." Erik's voice was now loud and commanding. Tae wondered if he was calling on all his acting training. Wasn't that the sort of thing they taught?

"He—he's younger. His skin is a light, gold brown, his head is shaved, and he's wearing what looks like an orange prison jumpsuit and his chest—oh, lord, above his chest." She screwed her eyes closed and would not look at any of them.

None of them noticed. They were all looking at Erik.

"Erik, who is she talking about?" Matthias's hand hovered over Erik's arm as if he wanted to touch him but didn't know what kind of reaction he would get.

"It's Daniel."

Everyone was silent, looking at each other. A non-Blooded ghost!

"That's how you knew he was dead," Elana accused.

"Yeah, he came to me while I was in the oubliette."

"That's how you've been guiding us? Why didn't you tell me?" Matthias sounded more hurt than angry and still Erik would not even look at him.

"Because you and Elana couldn't see him. I didn't want—"

No one said anything but everyone heard the *you to think I was losing it* on the end of that sentence.

"He says the rest of you can't see him because you weren't emotionally connected to him or blood related. That we can all see Elana because if you go back far enough we're all related to one another."

"That's not wrong," Tae said, still scrutinizing the air Zaha was staring at, straining to see anything. "I should still be able to see him, though."

"How?" Erik asked. "You're not related to him or emotionally connected as far as I know."

"My power is sight, Erik. I and others like me are the reason we know non-Blooded ghosts even exist. I should still be able to see him."

Everyone was quiet. Erik looked at what still looked like a blank space to Tae, no matter how he tried to tune his power.

"He could be part of Byron's plan." Daya sounded like she wanted that to be the case.

"Why would you say that?" Erik asked.

"How many times has one of us lost someone close to us? We've never gotten a ghost back. Why now?"

Erik looked pointedly at Elana. Daya shook her head.

"That's different."

Erik didn't looked convinced. "You told me ghosts were rare, so that explains why it doesn't happen more often." He hesitated. "Anyway, Byron could see Daniel too. He ran when he saw him."

Tae turned to look at Zaha, but she no longer looked terrified. In fact, the argument was having the opposite effect. All the people debating and discussing and accepting it as real had made it more mundane for her. She'd even taken a step forward from the wall. Tae noticed it was toward Elana and away from the other thing she saw.

"So Byron ran from a ghost that only he, yourself, and this girl we just happened to meet can see? That doesn't sound suspicious to you?" Daya asked.

"Of course it does, but what do you suggest? Unless you're hiding something, you know as little as the rest of us," Erik said.

"I know enough to know this is not normal." Daya took a step forward and Tae watched Matthias shake his head and take hold of Erik's arm. Daya should have known better than to challenge Erik in such a direct way, especially after all the things he'd gone through today.

Erik shook off Matthias's hand but didn't step forward or get into Daya's face.

"Well, you know, I think you just want to be special. The only one in love with a ghost around here." No one was looking at Matthias except for Tae, so no one else saw the way the man's face broke at those words before he brought himself back under control.

"And if we're gonna talk about the enemy using our lovers? You need to have a talk with the Organization."

"Erik," Matthias hissed.

"What do you mean?" Daya hesitated to take another step, but she didn't need to. Erik took that final step to bring them nose to nose.

"We found Elana's body, at least what the Angelics left of it. It's been with them this whole time. What have they been doing with her? Using her as a spy somehow?"

Daya looked devastated at the news. Matthias was finally able to pull his aspirant away and got him calmed down in the corner. Elana simply floated with her hand over her mouth before she spoke.

"Matthias, you knew this?"

Matthias turned from Erik and looked at Elana.

"Yeah, sorry, Elana. We found out when we left the safe house. I've been waiting for a time to tell you."

"And you didn't think before now would be best?" Daya exploded.

Erik growled but did not leave the corner.

"Did you think it best to antagonize a traumatized berserker who only awakened two weeks ago?"

Daya looked down but her mouth opened.

Elana chose to interrupt before Daya could reply.

"I hate to break up a lovely go-nowhere fight, but how about we try to get the hell out of here before anyone comes to check on us or the missing Angelic? We'll deal with all of this later, we can figure it out and do some tests when we're safe." She glanced at Erik as she said the last part and then down and away.

No one could argue with that. They filed out with Erik in the lead, head tilted to the side, listening to a ghost none of them could see.

Tae turned back to Zaha and saw what looked like the beginning of shock in her eyes. He was not surprised. She'd had a lot of surprises today, physically and then so many of her beliefs turned on their head.

"Come on, Zaha, let's get out of here."

"Yes please."

She took his hand as they followed the others and he squeezed it in comfort.

ERIK

The trip out of the dungeon-like basement was surprisingly easy, if tedious. Daniel scouted ahead and came back to pass along the floor plan to Erik. Sometimes Elana scouted ahead as well and reported back for the others who did not trust the ghost they could not see.

The others looked at him oddly. Daya wore her suspicion plain as day on her face, but at least the fact that Zaha saw Daniel too made her theory less likely. Why would Byron do anything to her?

"I don't understand why he looks like that." It was Zaha's voice; she was trying to be quiet but it was noticeable to everyone.

"What do you mean?" Tae asked.

"I always though ghosts could control what they looked like, at least that's what the myths say."

"It's true." Elana's voice held quiet assurance.

Daniel simply stared ahead as if he had not heard the conversation at all.

He led them to a set of stone stairs while Erik did his best not to stare at the injury in a way that was obvious. If Elana was telling the truth, and he had no reason to believe the woman would lie, then it could only be one of two things.

Daniel could not change how he looked because he wasn't a ghost but something else. Most likely a dangerous something else.

Or he was choosing to look like that to disturb Erik.

As they climbed, the walls around them and the stairs began to look more modern and less stone-age. They climbed as high as the stairs would allow and found themselves in what looked like a modern basement with a bank of regular square gray corporate elevators in the corner.

"This seems like a pretty shoddy operation," Tae commented. "Not one guard to stop us?"

Matthias stayed silent but he was tense and Erik was as well. It didn't make sense to go through all the trouble of capturing them and betraying the Organization so thoroughly but not protect your investment. Something else was going on.

Tae took the hint and went silent. They rode up to the lobby in silence.

The elevators released them in a small room with one door. As they stepped out the reason they'd met no other Suits in their journey became clear. The mainstream Hollywood heaven decoration had given way to a gross abattoir.

ELANA

Elana had seen and experienced a lot of things in her twenty-three years among the living and her two years among the dead, including of course her own death. She remembered every detail of the Angelic ripping into her body, which made the discovery of her body all the more curious. She remembered the pain, as the Angelic made it last; she remembered when the whiteness of the other side took her. The journey back was vague, a memory it was painful to prod, like a bruise. She did remember waking up floating and looking down at her corpse. A corpse that had no longer looked anything like her.

It had taken her no effort to become visible to other Blooded, but it took a few months to figure out how to become corporeal. It took a lot of concentration and energy and she was barely a wisp of white fog afterward. She usually only became semitangible for her nights with Daya.

None of her experience prepared her for the vision of the main lobby. She was suddenly happy she did not have to touch anything.

The floor was covered in gore. She tried to count the body parts at first, to count the number of Suits that had been ripped into all these tiny pieces, but she had no idea how to add them up, back into something human.

"What in Ophde's name?" Tae had gone pale, leaning back against the door.

Zaha was bent over, vomiting.

Elliot was pale but had stepped out of the room and was looking around for the threat. Daya was doing the same, circling on the outside of their group.

"What did this?" Erik asked. He was looking about, gaze jumping from pile of former human to pile of former human.

"My first guess would be an Angelic. My second would be something they got from the Angelics and then cross-bred," Matthias said, his voice only trembling a bit.

Elana passed over the carnage, taking in everything and searching for some hint of a survivor.

She didn't know why she came back as a ghost when others did not. The Organization said it was some kind of random lottery, but now she wasn't so sure. The new information about her body made her question everything. Was it the Angelics who had made her a ghost somehow? Were they using her even now?

Then there was Daniel, who threw into confusion all the things she'd believed for years. Were these newly dead around them? Invisible to everyone, and unable to be heard? Crying and screaming and staring down at the meat that used to be them?

She was caught up in her own horror, because she did not hear the crying until Erik took off in a sprint. They all took off after him, happy to have something to do rather than simply standing around waiting to see if they would die.

ERIK

Daniel floated ahead of him, staring at the devastation around him, but was as focused on the weeping as Erik was. They followed it through the garden, the grass now matted with blood. Trees were shattered and bodies littered the space. As they exited, Erik froze at the sight of the two Angelics—the bubble one and the two-faced blue beetle hovering over the corpse of something horrible. It looked a cricket grown to the size of a small pony and made of nothing but bone and sinew. Its legs were covered in odd metal boots that ended in wicked points. The double layer of mouth pincers, which he didn't think actual crickets had, were also wearing sharp metal caps.

Standing a few feet away was a young man in a torn suit. He was the one crying while he held a large gun in front of him, aimed at the Angelics. He bled from various wounds, and dark bruises forming on the left side of his face and across pale skin were a testament that he'd been tossed around a bit. His dark hair looked sticky with blood. The gun didn't look standard issue and Erik thought about the guns the Organization had. He had to wonder what the Agency must have, with their access to government funds.

No wonder the Angelics weren't moving or striking him dead on the spot. They probably had no idea what the gun might do. The man was crying big ugly tears that made him squint. His body moved with his gasps and made his aim disturbingly shaky.

"Hey, buddy." The gun swung toward his voice and Erik held his hands up to show that he was no threat.

"What the hell are you doing?" Daniel hissed at him but Erik ignored him and spoke to the Suit.

"What are you doing?"

The gun swung back toward the Angelics. "It's their fault! They killed everyone!"

Erik heard the others come up behind him, stopping as they took in the tableau. The soap bubble spoke but the voice was softer than before, the pops not nearly so loud. "We had nothing to do with this. The one called Byron released one of the creations from the lab."

"That you gave us! It was all a trick, wasn't it?"

"It was not." The beetle thing sounded calm. "Crikes are used for transportation in our land. They are sometimes aggressive but not murderous in such a way. This thing was heavily altered."

Erik looked down at the metal sheaths that the creature was wearing. He believed it. He turned back to the Suit.

"Look, buddy, you're pretty traumatized. You just saw a lot of people you know die."

The crying turned to weeping and his body shook a bit.

"But you're alive and you want to stay that way, don't you?"

The man nodded.

"And here's the thing. You can't take down both of them. No matter how powerful that gun is, or how fast you are. Chances are you're only gonna get to take down one of them before the other one takes you out."

The man was lowering his gun, the glint of recklessness gone from his eyes, the willingness to die gone from his stance. Erik quickly strode forward and took the gun from the man's suddenly nerveless fingers. Once the gun was gone, the man's eyes rolled up in his head and he collapsed into a heap on the floor. Erik hurriedly knelt and checked for the pulse. It was strong and steady.

"We owe you a debt."

Erik rose back to his feet and faced the two Angelics. He held the gun loosely in his hand.

"Well, not exactly. I may have killed your friend."

"We know. We felt Amirand die. We were bound for our trip. If you managed to kill Amirand, then it was weak enough to be killed. The supporters in Zebub will not be happy, but you shall handle it with aplomb, I am sure."

"Why would you think I would go anywhere with you after all this?" Erik gestured to those around him and the dead bodies.

"The kidnapping was not our idea. Byron did this independently."

"But you went along with it. Helped him." Matthias stepped up to Erik's side.

"After the plan was already in action, what would have been the point of denying it, if it proved effective?"

"Still, there's not much you can offer me to come to your world."

"But now we have something to trade. You help with the dark that has invaded our land, and we help you to discover all the perversions done by your government with the things we provided."

Erik hesitated. He looked at the devastation all around him, the pieces of things, and imagined Robert being cornered by one of these things, and almost smiled until Robert changed to his mom and then Matthias. It was too late to save Daniel or any of these Suits, but could he walk away if it would potentially save a bunch of people from suffering the same fate?

He sighed and looked back at Matthias, who nodded. Erik agreed, but Daniel was angrily arguing against.

"You can't go to their world. Look at what they went along with! They have no morals. You don't know what they will do to you once you are on their turf."

Daniel's worry wasn't misplaced, but he was wrong that they didn't have any morals. It was only that their morals were completely outside of the Blooded understanding. Erik had already recognized one aspect of their code, though. They respected strength. He looked at the thing that had ripped its way through this office and had killed so many people, enemies or not. How many facilities did the Agency have? How many of these things were waiting to escape?

"I want your word that myself and any people who accompany me will be allowed to leave at any time. That we will be treated with respect and not harmed by your allies."

"We can agree to those terms. We will meet in seven days in this place so you may accompany us back to Zebub."

They did not wait for Erik's response before they were gone from sight as quick as a thought. He didn't know if giving their word would mean anything, but it was the only protection that he believed he could offer.

"None of you have to come with me," he said as he turned to face them. Daniel had his back turned to him, his stance daring Erik to speak to him.

Matthias and Tae immediately answered him.

"Bullshit."

"We're going."

Elliot and Daya agreed much more reluctantly, and Erik felt they only did so because Tae had.

"Well, let's get out of here before more bullshit happens." They limped out of the building to be greeted by an old and patched Caddy waiting outside with a couple Blooded Elliot and Daya recognized inside. Erik crawled in the back after Matthias.

DAYIDA

She knew her son's new life would be dangerous. She had not wanted children at all, but Robert had and she had liked him so much at the time. She had foolishly hoped that Robert's normal human vitality would swamp whatever gift might come with her blood. It did not work out that way, but still Erik seemed happy, and after finding out his skills she at least didn't worry about him being harmed as much. Still, when Erik came home covered in blood and something that smelled like dead things that had been left in the sewer for weeks, she was understandably worried.

"What the hell, Matthias?" she called to the man behind him.

"He did good, Yida." The way he looked at her son told her there was something else. Something he was worried about.

"I'm going to take a shower and sleep."

"I'll be up to talk to you in a minute." She did not expect Erik to respond, but she would not let him rest without a word or two in his ear.

She turned back to Matthias and said, "Tell me." As she heard the shower start upstairs, he started to tell her everything. He hesitated at points and she wondered if she was getting all the details. She stopped him in the midst of talking about the their battle at the mall when the shower stopped.

"Excuse me for a moment."

She took the stairs two at a time, catching her son's bedroom door closing. She knocked once before she opened the door. Erik was splayed on the bed, his towel covering his backside.

"Erik."

He turned his head toward her so it was no longer buried in the comforter and grunted.

"Are you okay?"

He shook his head, rubbing his eyes against the fabric.

She sat on the bed and he stopped moving. She put her hand on his back and rubbed back and forth.

"I can't talk about it anymore tonight. I just need to sleep."

She waited before rising and heading for the door. "I love you, Erik."

His quiet "Love you too, Mama" nearly broke her heart. She returned downstairs and found Matthias watching her. She sat across from him.

"The time is coming when you won't be able to hide anymore, Yida. Robert has helped you control it all these years, but you're awakened. You can't keep denying it."

"Why not? I don't want to go down that rabbit hole."

"Something dark is coming, Yida. I don't know what, but there have been too many signs for even me to ignore."

Dayida looked away. She had seen some of the signs as well. The surprise meteor shower the other day. The ring around Venus. The rediscovery of certain species thought extinct, like the thylacine. The world was preparing for something.

"I want you to survive what is coming."

"I will, no matter what. But I will think about what you say."

"That's all I can ask." Matthias nodded, reclined on the couch and finished recounting what had happened.

The stab of guilt as he revealed Daniel's fate hit her right in the chest.

"My god. How is Erik dealing?" She looked at the stairs, thinking about going back up and waking Erik up just to hug him again.

Matthias hesitated and she looked back at him.

"What is it, Matthias?"

"He sees Daniel and he's not going mad." He hurried on before she could jump to the obvious conclusion. "Someone else saw and confirmed, but he's not visible to the rest of us."

"You're worried about something." She leaned forward.

"There's just something wrong, Yida. I can't see what it is yet, but I'll keep watching."

She nodded.

"In the meantime." He curled into the couch and looked at her in question. She rolled her eyes and nodded and he was asleep practically before she stood.

The house phone rang. She started, confused because they barely used the house phone any longer. They all had cells.

"Hello?"

"Hello, is Erik available?"

"Who may I ask is calling?"

"This is Patrah Boothe."

"Patrah? It's Yida!"

"Yida, it's so good to hear your voice. How are you doing?"

"I'm fine. Still painting."

"I know. I've been meaning to come to your shows but something keeps coming up. Now that I'm gonna be in the Bay for a while training, though, I hope we can meet up."

"I'd like that." Yida was nervous. The more she let Blooded back into her life, the less likely she felt that she could keep control. But she had been lonely these last few years. First they'd moved down to Los Angeles, then to North Carolina for the filming, and it had just been easier to let all the bonds that weren't family fall by the wayside.

"Quiet, I'll ask," Patrah said, but it was muffled and clearly not intended for her. "Yida, I'm sorry, but my aspirant is freaking out. Everyone else just got back to the safe house and they look pretty worse for the wear. Elliot pulled the idiotic move of saying Erik took the brunt of it and now she won't stop pestering me until she has proof he's fine."

The exasperation in Patrah's voice made Yida chuckle.

"I wish I could help you out, but he's fallen asleep. Who knows when he'll be up. He's been running pretty hot using his powers lately."

"Yeah."

"Here, let me talk to her."

"Erik?" The voice was young and unsure.

"No, this is Erik's mom. I'm sorry, but Erik is asleep right now, he was really tired when he came in."

"He's not answering my texts."

"He probably has the phone on silent so he can sleep. I'll tell him to call you as soon as he wakes up. I promise."

"Okay." There was a lot of hesitation in the voice as if she didn't trust Yida at all.

"Thanks, Yida, she was driving me out of my mind."

"No problem. I'll have him call when he wakes up . . . and let's get together soon."

"Yeah."

They hung up and Dayida looked all around her. She thought about what Matthias had said about the darkness coming. She headed to her studio. As soon as she stepped inside she felt a sense of peace. It was painted in a dark, vibrant maroon, different from the constant blues and greens she grew up around. Her mother had said those colors were calming, conducive to clear thought and healing.

There were a number of stools and easels set up, seven paintings in various states of completion. Her best were always those she started and finished in one go; sometimes it was two days straight of painting but they were always luminous, alive. These would still be amazing, but they just wouldn't have the edge of power her one-session paintings did.

She sat in front of a blank canvas.

She thought again about what Matthias had said and her exhausted child upstairs. If she could make it better in any way, easier for him, shouldn't she try? She wouldn't deny that she wanted to survive whatever was coming, and the more power she had the more likely she was to be a target, sure, but also the more likely she was to survive.

Yida closed her eyes and did something she never had before. She opened herself up to the power that flared in her shoulders. She felt it race up the back of her neck then around in a coronet until it nestled above her eyes. It was a feeling of ice. A terrifying coldness and knowledge that death was inevitable and it was her job to balance lives.

She took a deep breath, took hold of the power, and moved it down into her left arm. She imagined the power guiding her arm and then it was. Her eyes were closed as she worked. She did not want to see the image until it was finished. She froze from the inside out. Her limbs felt stiff and unwieldy, all but the one that moved faster and faster.

Finally her arm hung limp and she opened her eyes. A large battle scene was laid out in front of her. In the center were people on horses, holding lances and swords, fending off a crowd of crazed creatures, all red claws and pale skin. She looked closer at the figures in battle and recognized herself sitting astride a horse, two hammers gripped in her hands, grim look to her face. Floating above the whole thing was the ghostly image of Daniel, the boy she had betrayed.

She rose and moved the painting to the side to dry. She moved another blank canvas in front of her and lifted the brush again, letting the power fill her again and again until she could summon no more, and collapsed to the studio floor with a smile.

ERIK

When he woke up, Erik checked his phone and saw a day had passed, but he felt refreshed. He was slowly getting used to holding the power that was his birthright. He sent a quick reassuring text to Melinda's twenty unread messages. He decided on another shower. The realization that Daniel was gone, all because of him, flooded through him. He heard familiar voices as he made his way to the bathroom but ignored them.

The water could not be turned hot enough, even as he cried into the spray. His skin burned and absorbed the heat. He turned it up higher. The hot water ran out and he finally walked out of the shower, rubbing himself with one of the extra towels, since his was still on the floor of his bedroom. He looked into the mirror.

Daniel was nowhere that he could see and it made him nervous. He reasoned that Daniel would have been bored hanging out while he was sleeping and would be back soon. He hurried to his room and threw on the first pair of jeans and shirt that weren't stiff with dirt and sweat. He headed downstairs toward the voices of his mom and Matthias.

They were sitting at the dining room table and stopped talking as he moved into the doorway.

"Is he here?" was his mom's first question.

"You told her." He aimed it at Matthias.

"Erik, she's your mother. She deserved to know."

His mom stood, drawing his attention back to her and opening her arms. "Sweetie, I'm so sorry."

Erik shook himself and he broke flinging himself into her arms, like he was a child of seven devastated at not getting a part again, not a man of eighteen who had killed and almost been killed already. She stroked his head and murmured soothing sounds in his ears interspersed with exclamations of her love until he stopped shaking and pulled himself back. He savored the closeness. He noticed that she smelled different, though. She carried the scent of metal now, the heat of a forge.

He pulled back to look at her, but Matthias interrupted. "I'm glad I didn't have to wake you up for this."

"For what?"

"A couple of Suits are on their way over, I'm guessing to talk about what happened. The San Francisco building was one of their main facilities. I don't know what the Angelics told them about our deal, but I doubt we come out looking that good in it."

He nodded and moved over to the fridge. In a few minutes he had made a large sandwich stacked with ham, cheese and spinach. He devoured it and made another before the knock on the door. He and Matthias both started for the front hall. His mom stopped them both with a look.

"It's my house. I'll greet the visitors."

A minute later she returned with two women in suits. One was tall, her muscled frame showing off the contours of the suit. Her skin was a gorgeous dark midnight black. Her hair was combed and parted in geometric patterns and gathered into Bantu knots. Her partner was shorter with skin a degree or two darker than Matthias. Her black hair pulled back into a braid that was folded in on itself five times that he could see.

"This is Tassi and Yonas," his mom announced.

The women nodded and without waiting for an invitation pulled out chairs at the table. He saw his mom frown behind them, but her face was composed as she moved around to his side of the table. The two Suits watched her like they expected her to leave them. Her son saw the look and sneered at both of them while she sat in the chair next to them.

"As you know, the San Francisco base was our largest and most active center of operations." Yonas dived right in.

Erik had known nothing of the kind, but he was not about to reveal his ignorance. He nodded.

"As such, the . . . mistakes that happened there are devastating."

THE ROOT

387

"Have you managed to find any evidence of where Byron went?" Matthias interrupted.

Tassi answered, her voice holding a hint of an accent Erik could not place. "No, but many of our people are working on it."

Matthias nodded but it was more in frustration than satisfaction with her answer. Yonas continued, "The Antes—"

"Antes?" his mom questioned.

Yonas paused, cleared her throat. "Yes, well, the Antes are beings from another dimension. They claim some relations to those of us in this universe who—"

"Angelics," Matthias interrupted tersely.

"Ah, got it," his mom replied and Yonas paused before turning back to Erik.

"They have demanded that you be placed in charge of rebuilding the San Francisco office."

The silence in the room was like the pause before a detonation.

"Naturally, our superiors tried to argue, but they said that their treaty was now with you because of trial by combat and favors owed."

"Hu is gonna lose his shit," was Matthias's first comment.

"What—" Erik cleared his throat and started again. "What does this entail exactly?"

"At this time, simply reestablishing our treaty with the Antes. We have been assigned to help you navigate this tricky task."

Erik frowned at their assumption that he would go along with this. And also about the fact that he felt like he would actually have to. He had already made the rash decision to treat with the Angelics in the midst of everything and while he could back out now, what would be the point? He had agreed for reasons that were just as important and valid now as they'd been yesterday.

The government might have a million of those creatures by now. What if they all got free, or worse, what if the darkness crossed over and came for this world?

"Okay."

Tassi and Yonas spent the next few hours filling them all in on the way that they were organized, the things they negotiated for with the Angelics, and the things they traded. It took Erik entirely too long to realize that whenever they said exchange of specimens, they meant people being sold to the Angelics for some of their creatures.

"Stop. How many people do you sell to them in a year?"

They both looked uncomfortable. The euphemism was clearly meant to provide some barrier so they didn't have to acknowledge what they were doing. Erik was determined to get rid of that first.

"Not many."

"I assume someone has the exact number and the names of those you sold off and those who returned. I want it. And it stops. The other offices may trade what they want . . . for now. But we do not sell people. We are not slavers." Yonas and Tassi shared a glance and Yonas nodded nervously. Matthias nodded as well, obviously pleased with this request.

"The last thing on our list is that they want to meet with you today."

Erik suppressed his distaste before it showed on his face. "When and where?"

"Anytime today is fine, and at the HQ downtown."

"Absolutely not. I won't be meeting in that slaughterhouse."

"I assure you it has been cleaned. There is no trace of what happened there."

Except forever in the minds of all of us who saw it, he didn't say. Yonas was trying to sound calm and it made him even more angry. He was not a child. He had seen what was left of the Suits stationed there and it was a perfectly reasonable reaction not to want to return.

"There is a reason why it is our headquarters. The space between their realm and ours is thin there. Ripping a hole in the border costs us almost nothing in terms of energy," Tassi added.

Erik frowned hard but finally nodded. It would be better not to show any weakness. The Suits left, saying they would be in contact and Erik and Matthias decided to head to the meeting then. There was little reason to delay the discomfort.

It was on his way to meet the things—Antes, they liked to be called Antes—that he realized he was still not fully healed. His scrapes were gone, but sound was still muffled in his right ear and the skin of his face and hands still felt sensitive, if not painful. He didn't know why his healing remained so slow. His close presence still helped those around him to heal immediately, but it had slowed when it came to his own injuries. He asked Matthias about it as they entered the building, mostly to distract himself from having the slaughter replay in his mind.

There were a few people wandering about. Most had shell-shocked looks on their faces. Perhaps more of the staff of this place survived than Erik had assumed.

"Anyone affected by the stone has had it wear off by now. Why not me?"

"I don't think it's the stone."

"Well, what else could it be?" Erik was glancing at Matthias's face so he didn't have to look at the floor and remember it slick with others' insides.

"The only other thing I can think is—" Matthias bit his lip and Erik frowned. He had never really seen Matthias hesitate before. "Our powers are affected by our emotional and mental state. They are tied together sometimes—if one suffers, so does the other."

"You know I'm not crazy. Zaha saw Daniel too." Erik stopped walking through the uprooted mess of floor that had once been the garden.

"I'm not saying you're crazy," Matthias answered quickly. "I'm just saying you may not be in the best place emotionally."

They came upon a small table set up in what used to be the center of the garden and Erik was glad for the distraction. The blue beetle and soap bubble were seated at one end, while to Erik's surprise Zaha sat huddled at the table as far away from the two Angelics as possible.

Erik stopped near the girl.

"What is this about?"

"We want the girl." The blue beetle Angelic said out of both of its mouths.

Zaha let out a small sound and shrank back further into her chair.

"Absolutely not." Erik didn't have to think about it. "There will be no more trading of any people."

The Angelics froze as if waiting for him to say more, but he stayed silent. This was no negotiation. This was a warning.

"She was exposed to the darkness. There may be something we can learn from her examination." The soap bubble burped.

The way they said "examination" left little doubt in Erik's mind that she would die during the course of it. It also reminded him that he was allying himself with beings who had been doing this to his people for longer than he'd been alive.

"I. Said. No." In fact, he was within a hairsbreadth of calling everything off when the soap bubble Angelic burp-replied.

"Then what do you have to offer us for this alliance?"

"The chance to not see your entire world devoured?" Matthias spoke from behind him.

"So you will not try to talk sense into your Apprentice?"

"He is no longer that. He is fully-trained, free and independent."

Erik started and leaned over toward Matthias to whisper, "Weren't there supposed to be tests and stuff?"

"Honestly, I think that the last two weeks have been test enough, don't you?"

Erik nodded.

"It seems we have no choice, do we?" The beetle Angelic broke in, bringing them back to the conversation.

"No, you don't," Erik said, his voice firm but distracted. Someone arrived to escort Zaha away and they began to discuss the plans for the trip into Zebub that Erik and his allies would be taking in six days' time. Erik left much of the talking to Matthias. He was distracted by Daniel, who had appeared floating in the corner, shaking his head as if Erik had just made the worst mistake of his life.

MAESTRA LUKA

Things had spiraled out of control much too quickly. The reports from Elliot, Elana, and Daya were on her desk, but she'd already read them a number of times. There was nothing new to glean from them.

The Organization had been contacted by the Agency. It was not happy, but she got the feeling that they were dealing with other crises as well. San Francisco was far from their only base, though it might have been their largest one. And that was only the bases on American soil. The ones they tried to establish overseas were best ignored. The Agency had no intention of dealing with someone they saw as a child any more than they had to and thought he belonged to the Organization. The Maestres had not dissuaded them from thinking this.

They wanted certain protocols put in place. Why they thought the Organization would help them, they had no idea, but then the offers of trade had happened. To some it made sense. Things were obviously changing and perhaps they were entering some state like a cold war. There was a larger threat looming, and perhaps old hostilities had to be laid to bed. Meanwhile the ones who wanted to simply kill Erik were gaining traction and allies in the discussion.

She was starting to lean that way herself, wondering if the young man and Matthias had cost them three of their best West Coast Agents. Elana and Daya had demanded to see Elana's body as soon as they arrived. Well, Daya had demanded. Elana had simply been down there staring at it already when Luka had escorted her girlfriend inside. They said nothing else, simply stared for a long time and then turned and left the facility. Should they choose to leave the Organization over this Elliot would go as well, no doubt.

Disasters upon disasters.

Too late, she had realized that sending that particular group into danger was the worst thing to do. They were volatile, and though she'd hoped the effect would be to break the bonds between them, it seemed to have molded them tighter. For the most part there were tensions, but she could tell there were things they had all left out of their reports. There were gaps. None large enough to be called on, but things that niggled at her as she read them. Even Tae's report had been terse and pointed, with no real details.

She picked up a different sheaf of papers, concessions that the Maestres wanted Erik to agree to as the new liaison to the Angelics and the head of the San Francisco Agency. She had argued against most of them, not because she did not agree, but because she doubted he would agree and thought that presenting them to him would just anger him. She had been trying to talk to Hu about how to approach Erik regarding the rules that both groups wanted him to use in running the San Francisco office. Except Hu had been sulking in his room for the past few hours. She was sure he would call it thinking or brooding, but Luka had a raft of nieces and nephews and she knew a sulk when she saw one.

Finally a spark of light flashed into the room. It bobbed up and down in front of her face to get her attention. She nodded and held out her hand. It landed in her palm and was reabsorbed in her body. She rose from her desk and went to knock on Hu's door.

"What is it?"

"The meeting is about to begin."

There was the slick sound Luka associated with Hu's shape-shifting from behind the door and when it opened he emerged in a fresh suit. He nodded at her and started down the corridor.

Everyone was already there. Erik, with Matthias on one side and his mother, Dayida, whom she recognized from her photos in his file, on the other. Elliot sat next to Matthias, Elana next to him, and finally Daya. Next to Dayida was Patrah, who was leaning over, talking rapidly to the woman and smiling. Melinda sat next to her Counselor and was leaning past her to make faces at Erik, which that he returned. And finally Tae sat on the other side of the girl, grim-faced and silent. There were two empty seats between Daya and Tae.

The distance between Tae and Erik told her something had happened between them. She pulled out a chair and Hu joined her and completed the circle around the table.

Erik nodded at them in greeting.

"We come with a list of demands," Hu began.

Oh, light above, she wanted to break Hu's jaw.

"Demands?" Erik laughed. "By what right do you have to demand things from me?"

Hu sputtered, and though Luka was tempted to allow it to continue simply for entertainment value, she stepped in.

"We have suggestions."

"What sort of requests?"

"We want to help. With the running of the San Francisco office."

"No. There, that was simple, wasn't it." Erik went to rise.

"Wait, we have concessions for you as well."

"What could you possibly have to offer me?"

"The title of Maestro, for one," Hu said.

Erik just frowned. "Why would I care about that?"

"It'll open doors."

"And close others," Matthias interjected. "Most independents won't trust you. If you go outside North America and Europe, most Blooded are independents."

"We have outposts on every continent and people in most major governments," Luka argued.

Matthias snorted. "Yeah, but that means shit all when most people don't trust you."

"Create a new title," Erik said.

"What?" asked Luka.

"Or revive one of the old ones," Dayida suggested. "Something that acknowledges your right to use the Organization resources without the stink of Maestro attached."

Hu frowned but then nodded.

"What would you want in return?" Erik asked.

"Full and unrestricted access to the Agency's notes and records," Luka said immediately.

"Ha! Nope. I don't need a whole bunch of your people tromping through the San Francisco office causing resentment while I'm gone."

"Gone?" Hu questioned.

"Here's what I'll offer in return. You can submit information requests, and if there's nothing wrong with it, myself or my representative will approve it and send it to you."

"Agreed," Luka said immediately. She felt like she was negotiating between two horrible things—Hu's mouth, which got away from him and fucked things up, and a eighteen-year-old who was more cunning than she expected. "What did you mean, gone?"

Erik waved it off.

"Was there anything else?"

"Yes, how did you intend to staff the San Francisco office?" Luka asked.

Matthias smiled, all teeth and no mercy. "I have plenty of Blooded friends who would love to work with the Agency's resources and have access to their records."

Luka swallowed. "We would also like to suggest that you listen to the suggestions of those who've been doing this longer than you."

Erik narrowed his eyes.

"We have experience—"

"You're trading with them, aren't you?" Erik's voice held no emotion, his face went blank as he looked at them. "The Agency. That's the other people you'd want me to listen to. That's why you said 'those who've been doing this longer' and not just 'listen to us.'"

Hu nodded, not seeing or not caring about the angry faces reflected around the circle. "Yes, we've decided on a mutually beneficial exchange."

"So why do you need access to our records at all? Can't your new friends give you that?" Matthias asked.

Dayida was the one who answered. "I'm guessing two reasons. The Maestres may be willing to trade with those they've fought for generations, but they sure as hell don't trust them not to alter the information or delay in delivering it. After all, it's what they'll be doing. I'm also guessing they want access to any new information that may happen soon. Anything to give them an edge."

Hu snapped his mouth closed and nodded.

Erik shook his head. "I would say be careful who you get in bed with, but look where I am right now, so I guess I'm in no place to judge. I'm leaving for Zebub in a few days. My mother shall be placed in charge of the San Francisco office while I am gone."

"Your mother!" Hu exclaimed, standing.

Erik looked at him, calmly raised a hand, and slowly lowered it to the table top. Hu frowned, but his only other option was to stand like a pouting child for the rest of the meeting, so he sat down.

"My grandmother, Hettie Jayl, will be coming to help her. As a concession and sign of alliance between us, I will appoint Blooded Patrah Boothe as official liaison and adviser. All information requests you have can come through her." With that Erik stood, his mother and Matthias rising as well. "Now, if you'll excuse me, I have a lot to take care of before I leave."

They filed out. On his way, Erik ruffled Melinda's hair and after a brief hesitation placed his hand on Tae's shoulder before exiting, leaving only those belonging to the Organization in the room. There was silence before Hu exploded.

"What did you think you all were doing?"

"Don't." Daya rose, leveraging herself up with her fists. "You are not in a place to question anyone else's actions right now. Elana and I will be taking a leave of absence starting immediately. We will be accompanying Erik to Zebub."

"But—"

"We understand." Luka rose herself, speaking over Hu. "We apologize once again for the secrets the Organization kept from you both. We only wanted to know more before we shared with you."

"We understand." Elana had her hands on her girlfriend's shoulders, rubbing back and forth. "We still need time. Elliot will be coming with us, of course."

"Of course." It was just as she had feared, except that luckily they were only calling it a leave of absence for now. They left next, with Tae following behind. He paused by Luka's chair on his way out. He met her eyes.

"I have to trust my gift, and it says I need to stand with him, not with the Organization. I will help my family and friends on my own."

Then he was gone too.

Hu was still standing, just staring off into space.

"Hu, will you sit down? You look ridiculous."

Hu obeyed automatically and Luka turned to Patrah.

"You will, of course, report everything you see and hear."

Patrah nodded and then paused as if waiting for more before grabbing Melinda's hand and guiding her from the room.

Luka looked over at Hu. The man was lost in thought, already trying to figure out how to turn this to his advantage. She would be doing the same soon enough, but for now she simply sat back in the chair. While she still didn't agree with those that had wanted Erik killed right away and still wanted him done away with, she did have to admit they had been right about one point. He had changed the whole board and she needed a new strategy if the Organization was to survive.

ZEBUB

LIL

She woke to pain.

Everywhere.

But especially her face. Her memories were not hazy, she remembered everything, and she'd heard of this room. It would be hard to find a 'dant in the whole of Zebub who had not. The punishment chambers below the Ruling Courts were famous. The names of those that had disappeared below were never spoken aloud again. Even Antes.

Her sight was foggy at first. Everything around her was dim and covered in comforting shadow.

Including the two forms standing over her. Brown-splattered white draped over them from the crown of their heads to as far down as she could see from her position chained to the table. She had no idea how they could see, but perhaps precision was not something that mattered much in their line of work. They had to be Antes. Their proportions were too tall and oddly elongated to be 'dants. The brown splashed across them was blood. That was clear enough.

"Oh, you're finally awake." The voice was light and delightful, musical like Davi's when he'd been granted a treat or some extra attention. She hoped they'd gotten away and that Arel and Jagi had understood her choices. One of the figures leaned over farther. It was slightly taller and wider than its companion. "It's been so boring working you while you sleep. All we got was the occasional whimper. Not nearly as fun as screams."

The pain made itself known again as soon as it was mentioned. Lil's legs and arms were burning with a fire so intense she was sweating, which made the wounds burn even worse. She was bound to the table not just by wrists and ankles but also bands around her neck, forehead, and midsection. She was completely immobilized.

Her mouth was not bound, a foolish mistake on their part. She opened her mouth to speak and felt nothing. Nothing answered her command; there was no muscle.

She tried to scream and what came out was a croaked monstrosity. The two figures above her laughed, the light joyful voice joined by a deeper one with a cracked edge all its own, a cackle that went on just a bit too long.

It was that voice that spoke next.

"Discovered what the Queen did to your pretty weapon, did you? Ripped it right out your head. Quite a sight, I'm told."

Lil thrashed in her bonds. Dimly, a part of her prayed that neither Min nor Davi saw the event, but a larger, more vocal part simply screamed over and over.

"Shh, shh, shh, little one, plenty to scream about. We haven't even gotten to the good part." The one with the soft, mad contralto voice moved out of her line of sight. She strained but could not see where it went and then the pain in the bottom of her foot started.

She cried out as the blade or whatever they were using was twisted. Soon the knife had been so busy she could only pant, cry, and wonder how much of her foot could be left. When would it hit bone? Were they planning to flay her?

Something damp was held against her foot and at first she sighed in relief until the burning came. Her eyes watered, everything lost in a haze of burn/wet/tear. It felt as if her foot was tearing itself apart in an attempt to get away. Her toes curled in the wrong direction trying to escape and fingers took hold and broke them one by one.

Her eyes watered and the darkness of the ceiling swam in her vision. She prayed for the peace of death.

"Do you know why we place you lying down like this?"

Lil was too busy biting through her lips to realize the question was actually expecting an answer until the slap across the face. Her lips burst open further, more blood flooding her throat.

"Pay attention. I'm trying to teach you something. We have you like this because 'dants can take an intense amount of pain while lying down. If you were standing right now, you most likely would have already passed out, and then where would we be?"

The white in her vision, which she now realized had been one of them leaning over her, retreated and she was left with the darkness of the ceiling.

It went on like this for quite some time, little pieces of her broken or cut off and all the time the voices "teaching" her things about her body and its pain threshold as they pushed her past it. Sometimes, in the small breaks they took between sessions, she was able to rise out of the pain.

In those lucid pieces of time she wondered when they would let her die. There was nothing she could do but hope they would grow angry or sloppy enough to end her torment soon. If she did not answer their questions it resulted in being slapped, again and again. Her right eye was swollen shut and blood ran into her mouth like rain from her broken nose.

"We're taking a break, but we'll be back soon. You're the most fun we've had in ages."

This was the first time they had left her completely alone since they started—nights, six-days, moons ago. She tried to crane her neck against the bars and managed to shift enough to catch a glimpse of the door.

Only the upper right corner, but she watched it with a desperate hope. She knew Arel and Jagi were gone, or at least she hoped they were, but surely there was someone else who would come to her.

Lil didn't hope for rescue; that optimism had been cut from her flesh as cleanly as her smallest toes. She only hoped that someone still cared enough to give her a clean death.

She was so busy craning her neck that she only noticed what was happening directly above her when a weight hit her stomach. There was no part of her free of burns and small cuts, so she grunted in pain, then flicked her eyes downward.

A Nif stared back at her, small, star-shaped, bending the top point to look her up and down. It made a sad whistle in its throat. Then another fell onto her shoulder and another onto her hip. She looked up and realized her earlier vision had been correct: the ceiling was shifting and blurring.

With Nif.

More and more of them fell and began to gather around the bars holding her down. She was not hopeful; even if they managed to break her bonds, she would not be able to walk out of here, not with all the damage to her feet.

The bar on her forehead gave first, slowly bending out of the way, then the band holding her neck. She lifted her head slightly, looking down at her body now almost completely covered in an army of the shadow helpers. Something heavier fell onto her chest.

A bag sat there heavily.

The cause of this.

No, that was unfair.

It was Haydn who caused this. She realized the part he had played as soon as she saw his gleeful face and remembered her odd moment in the Ossuary. He had done this, he and whoever conspired with him. Krezida, certainly. Riana, probably.

Razel?

Mayer?

At least Haydn had paid the price. She remembered the look of shock and pain on his face as the projectiles had torn through his lower stomach and crotch. She'd only had a second to enjoy the sight before they had hit her next.

All the bands were gone now, bent and misshapen or torn from the bolts. She was free, but her body protested every futile effort to rise. The Nif chattered and pressed down on her body. Cold enveloped her feet and she looked down to see the individual Nif joining together into a blanket of darkness. She felt a small flare of hope.

They would take her away the same way they had transported Haydn. The where did not matter to her.

Then the door opened. Her head turned quickly despite the pain and the hope rushed out of her. Her torturers were back, both frozen in the doorway. She could feel their shock across the room even if she could not see their faces.

"So it seems you have some tricks left, old girl. Well, so do we." And Lil's whole world became pain, every wound lighting up as if it were being freshly applied to her body. She collapsed panting as the feeling cut off and she became aware of a muffled scream other than hers. She forced herself to focus through the aftershocks that wracked her frame. Both torturers were struggling with black masks covering the whole of their heads.

She realized they were Nif that had fallen on the pair from above. Her body grew colder and colder as her own Nif spread higher, covering her chest. The last thing she saw before becoming fully engulfed was her two tormentors falling to the ground.

AREL & JAGI

The children were quiet. Min had only woken from her shock recently and was staring at her new arm, moving the frosted white limb this way and that. Jagi did not know how much she remembered, but she did not ask how it came to be or what had happened to Lil. Even if she recalled nothing, she took after her sib and was far from dumb. She would understand that the fact that they were running through the dark night—sticking to alleys and mostly unused streets—meant things had not ended in their favor.

They only had a day at most before Court Chayyliel called for a Wild Hunt, and they wanted to get as far from the Ruling Courts as possible tonight.

"Where are we going?" Davi finally asked quietly, his face buried in Arel's chest.

"Somewhere safe."

The answer must have been deemed sufficient because neither Min nor Davi asked another. They paused in an alley, waiting for a small crike to leave the next street over so they could cross without being seen. They shared a look over the children's heads, silently communicating the fact that neither of them had any idea where that safe place might be. Chayyliel was Queen of their Court and Lord of their House, so both would be turned against them now. The safest place would be with those of their bloodline who were at cross-purposes with the House of the Long Arm and/ or Court Chayyliel.

Also, someone who would not simply kill them on sight. Hina would be the only one, but she was high in the Court of Feedings and could not be trusted with this.

Arel's face lit up with an idea. He looked at Jagi and tilted his head southeast. Jagi shook his head vehemently, drawing Min's attention to the argument. She looked up at Jagi and, meeting her gaze, he grimaced and then gave Arel a forced nod.

They crossed the street, turning left on the next one before ducking into another alley. They had a direction now. A place that might give them shelter but also might turn them in, depending on mood and which side June was truly on. Deeper and deeper into 'dant territory they went, avoiding occasional Court patrols and pitched battles between the patrols and small patches of the creeping dark. The dark always disappeared once it had eaten one or two of the patrollers.

They knew they had arrived at their destination when the smell of damp and rot rose around them. The Drowned district had once been completely underwater until the Court of Teardrops decided—centuries ago—to raise it from the ocean floor as a place to put 'dants out of the eyes of Antes. It still flooded on a regular basis, but the residents had their houses on stilts, grew roof gardens, and kept emergency rafts every few blocks in case some 'dants were stuck too far from shelter. They did not care much for most Antes and a few residents on the streets eyed them with ill intentions, but their expressions changed as they caught sight of the children clinging to them.

Though a part of Zebub, the district was a dumping ground that existed with almost no oversight from the Ruling Courts, as long as tributes were paid on time and they caused no trouble. Few if any Antes had reason to come to the district. Arel and Jagi turned down a street and came across the one building in the whole place that looked new and fresh. It squatted, a round ziggurat in the middle of a line of square houses, futilely trying to imitate the decay of the buildings around it with paint and decoration.

The Door greeted them as they approached the gate, clad in a clinging gold sheath from neck to dainty toes. The Door smiled and gestured for them to enter.

"Be welcome in the House of the Madame."

They hurried inside and both of them checked over their shoulders. The Door sensed their urgency and closed the entrance quickly behind them to block any view from the street. The greeting room was opulent without being expensive. There was a feeling of relaxation and hedonism to the plush cushions dotting the floor and the vaguely erotic art lining the walls. The heavy curtains turned the room into a mysterious maze. None of the cloth or materials looked expensive, with the exception of the gold sparkling material covering the Door. It all screamed decadent, but not elitist. A very hard combination to pull off.

"We come to ask for—"

"We know."

Both of them tensed at the plural and the knowledge, wary of another betrayal. The children became still in their arms, picking up on their sudden alertness. The Door smiled and looked to an exit to their left, where a small Turms appeared.

"June had hoped you might come here for sanctuary. We are happy to grant it."

"Why? What do you want in return?" Jagi was agitated and uncertain at the ready acquiescence to their request.

"June feels guilty for their part in Holder Liliana's fall."

Min whimpered against his chest and Jagi gave the Door a dark look, but it was met with a continued smile.

"Perhaps it would help you all to know that no one knows where Liliana is."

This was decidedly not helpful. They knew Chayyliel would dare not expose what had happened. The Holders and their Holder-Apprentices were both feared and revered among the 'dants. To hear that the Ruling Courts had killed one, with the way the city already seethed because of mysterious attacks of the creeping dark?

It would start a riot.

The only way to survive it would be to reveal what had actually happened, in which case Court Chayyliel would lose most of its support from the other Courts and possibly their place.

"We know," Arel said with finality, hoping to stop the Door from going on any further. Min and Davi were back to burying their faces in the their chests.

"You misunderstand me. Queen Chayyliel has lost her."

All their heads came up at this. They stared at the Door in consternation. Arel and Jagi wished this had not been mentioned in front of Davi and Min because they were both smiling and happy through tears, and if this turned out to be a rumor? False hope provided to vulnerable children?

"How do you know this?"

The Door's head tilted to gesture at the quiet Turms standing beside it.

"I regret to tell you that no one knows where she has gotten to. Those assigned to punish her were found passed out on the floor. They say that the Nif helped her. Chayyliel does not believe them, but the Nif of the Ruling Courts are now gone from all the Hives, which leads credence to it. But whether they left or are now under the delicate hands of other punishers no one knows. How would one even torture a Nif?" The Door's head tilted the other way, contemplating the question.

"We will find her," Arel said. Exhaustion pulled at all his limbs, and Davi had already fallen asleep against him despite the good news or perhaps because the news had finally allowed him to relax. He glanced over at Min and saw her fighting heavy eyelids. Now that they had hope that Lil was alive somewhere, things felt less desperate, and their bodies were all succumbing to the events of this evening. "We thank you for the news. May we be shown to a bed?"

"Of course. I regret to say that we are booked tonight, so we only have one room available."

Arel and Jagi nodded. They would not feel comfortable sleeping separately tonight anyway. The Door returned the nod and led them out of the main foyer and up the stairs. There were noises coming from the rooms they passed. Some sounded like weeping and others like lovemaking, but they were too tired to care about anything more than getting their charges to safety and sleeping themselves.

A form appeared in the hall and both of them paused, only unfreezing when the Door greeted the man and turned to introduce him to them.

"Allow me to introduce you to Byron of San Francisco."

They nodded warily to the 'dant in front of them. His curled dark red hair was sticking up at all angles and the skin beneath his eyes was dark and bruised. They did not introduce themselves and the Door seemed to know better as well. Byron did not seem to notice, simply lifting his hand in greeting before he and his two silent companions disappeared behind a door.

Once inside their own room, they laid Min and Davi in the middle of the bed. Jagi moved to the door and opened his mouth. A thin stream of filth came out, forming a tough web over the entrance. Either of them could break the seal easily, but if anyone else tried they would be infected immediately. Arel nodded and they crawled into bed on either side of the children, who had curled into each other. Slowly, they slid their tentacles out. They laced them together above the sleeping children. It gave them comfort to touch each other in this way and to know that any who came for the children would have to go through some part of them.

LIL

Lil woke up. Her first surprise.

The others being that she was warm, had no new hurts that she could discern, no one standing over her with a blade and a laugh she would hear in her nightmares for the rest of her life. It was not that she had forgotten her rescue but that she had lost hope and had thought the whole thing to be some sort of fever dream.

In the times she had been conscious in the Nif cocoon, all she had seen was darkness. She couldn't help but wonder if this was a new torture or if this was death. Was this the return to oneness that she had been promised?

Instead she was on a soft bed, in a room lit by a fire in a center hearth, which kept from getting too hot by the open window that let in sunlight and wind. The smell of burning wood filled the air. Too much for it to be solely the hearth. Without looking outside the window, the smell told her where she was.

She looked around the room and spotted the pool of shadow in the corner. As she stared, it sluggishly formed a hand that waved once before collapsing back into itself. The Nif who had carried her away. Saved her. She had no idea they could even get tired, yet they were exhausted, unable to hold any shape. She had to figure out some way to thank them.

She had a lot of figure out. Where she was. Where her sibs were. What to do next.

First she took a deep breath and yanked the blanket off. So many parts of her body protested the sudden move so violently that all she could do was lie still and try to force air back into her seizing lungs. When she was finally able, she took one shuddering breath and then another. She looked down at her body, nude and a mess. Pink-stained white bandages covered her so completely she looked almost clothed. In some places the bandages were actually concave, where she was missing pieces.

She did not check her tongue until last because she held an insane hope that it was not actually gone. She reached into her mouth and felt the ragged stump that lived there now.

The door opened and Lil yanked her hand from her mouth and recoiled farther into the bed, placing her back against the wall. The woman who entered was ancient for a 'dant, her face a mask of wrinkles. Her hair was bone white and fluttered about her head like fog.

"You're awake? Good."

She was dressed in a white smock with tiny red dots all over it. Lil opened her mouth to reply, then shut it again. The woman noticed, however, and gave her a sad smile. Lil looked away toward the wall.

"Now, none of that." Two things landed on her lap in quick succession and she looked down. A pad of what looked like homemade paper made of cut and woven reeds and a curving stylus formed from pink stone. She looked at the old woman in question.

"Have no worries. Enough of those in this place are literate."

It was a valid concern. Only maybe one in ten 'dants could write their own name; one in twenty could read something more complex than a news pamphlet. Lil nodded and opened the pad. Writing quickly, she held it up for the woman to read.

Why are we in the Out?

"Yes, you would smell that, wouldn't you? Fear hangs over the area. Those who live here are few and far between. They have no love of the Ruling Courts and their secrets and murder. We know when to help one another and when to mind our own business."

Lil nodded slowly. She was unaware that anyone still lived in the Out. Out was short for the Burned Out because at one point it had been a large and sprawling park, filled with a whole community of 'dants that paid no tribute to the Ruling Courts. They lived quietly, on their own, never leaving the protection of the park. Until one of the Courts had burned them out of their leafy home for their trouble.

It had happened almost four hundred years ago. Mayer said that Kandake Athenaeum had taken in many of the survivors and saw them settled in different cities where the Ruling Courts of Zebub could not reach them.

She bent over the pad again.

Who are you?

The woman hesitated. "It's best if someone else tells you. Here, let me help you into a robe and we'll go to the other room."

The woman reached to pull down Lil's blanket, but Lil grasped it tighter to her ravaged body. She met the woman's eyes and looked pointedly at the door. The woman laughed and raised her hands in defeat. She laid the robe on the bed and moved toward the door. Lil waited until it closed completely before throwing the covers off and carefully wiggling into the robe. She did not look at her body as she pulled on the robe. She did not want to see.

It was not vanity but memories. They had done this to her. They had taken something as personal as her body and made it their plaything, had changed it so she did not know it any longer. Her body was new now, and she did not want anyone else to see it yet.

The robe's material was soft and soothing. The chill of it calmed some of the shivers of fever that racked her frame. Rising from the bed was more difficult. She stared at the two smallest toes on her right foot, the only ones left, for a full minute before she could tear her gaze away.

It hurt to stand but whoever she was now the prisoner of, she would not meet them carried or looking weak. Her balance was off and it took her several tries to take the first step. Slowly she limped. Every step brought a pain that shot through her whole body. As she passed the mass of Nif on the floor, the top of it rapidly expanded into a bubble. When the bubble popped the Root lay at her feet, still in its traded bag.

She bent down to gather them in her fist. Rising back up was harder than she imagined at first and she struggled and grunted her way back to her feet. The robe had pockets, so she placed the Root in one. The bag radiated an odd warmth. As it radiated through her hip, it soothed some of her pain. She heard voices through the door as she got closer.

"Where is she?" A younger voice, impatience laced through it.

"She'll come out when she pleases, not a moment before." The older woman she'd already met. "And you will remember that she is an honored guest, and an ally. Not one of your tools to be used and discarded."

She opened the door and they were arrayed before her, five of them, so at least three had kept silent about her. Either smart enough to know she could hear through the door or reserving judgment.

A 'dant stepped forward, barely into her third decade if Lil was correct. She wore a bodysuit of black, faded and painted in places to allow her to blend in with the burnt-out landscape all around them. She smiled as she stepped forward and offered her hand.

"I'm Kima. Welcome to the Resistance."

This is my first published book but I'm going to try and buck the trend and go short:

To my first readers, Christopher Chinn, Charlie Jane Anders, Rachel Swirsky, Justin Goldman, and Elsa Hermens, thank you, this book would not have made it this far without you.
To Borderlands Books & Cafe, Alan, Jude, Cary, John, Jim, Zev, Cole, Devany, & everyone else thank you for believing in me when I did not.
To my family, both born and made, thank you for your support.
To my lovely friends, thank you for listening and caring.
To my editor, Jeremy Lassen, thank you for seeing something in me.

ABOUT THE AUTHOR
ABOUT THE AUTHORR

Na'amen Gobert Tilahun is a bookseller and a freelance writer who split his early years between Los Angeles and San Francisco. He moved to the Bay Area full time to earn his BA in creative writing from San Francisco State University and an MFA in english and fiction from Mills College and never left. His poetry has appeared in *Faggot Dinosaur, StoneTelling, So Speak Up,* and *The Dead Animal Handbook*; his fiction in *Collective Fallout, Full of Crow,* and *The Big Click,* and his essays/reviews in *io9; The Angry Black Woman; The WisCon Chronicles, Vol. 2: Provocative Essays on Feminism, Race, Revolution and the Future; Fantasy Magazine; Queers Dig Time Lords: A Celebration of Doctor Who by the LGBTQ Fans Who Love It;* and *The WisCon Chronicles, Vol. 9: Intersections and Alliances.* He is also cocreator and cohost of the geek podcast *The "NEW" Adventures of Yellow Peril + Magical Negro.*